D0908343

THE SPOILT QUILT AND OTHER FRONTIER STORIES

THE SPOILT QUILT AND OTHER FRONTIER STORIES

PIONEERING WOMEN OF THE WEST

WITH A FOREWORD BY *NEW YORK TIMES* BESTSELLING AUTHOR CHRIS ENSS

EDITED BY HAZEL RUMNEY

FIVE STAR
A part of Gale, a Cengage Company

GALE
A Cengage Company

Farmington Hills, Mich • San Francisco • New York • Waterville, Maine
Meriden, Conn • Mason, Ohio • Chicago

LIBRARY OF CONGRESS CATALOGING-IN-PUBLICATION DATA

Names: Enss, Chris, 1961– writer of foreword. | Rumney, Hazel, editor.
Title: The spoilt quilt and other frontier stories : pioneering women of the West / with a foreword by New York Times bestselling author Chris Enss ; edited by Hazel Rumney.
Description: First edition. | Farmington Hills, Mich. : Five Star, a part of Gale, a Cengage Company, 2019.
Identifiers: LCCN 2019023576 | ISBN 9781432864293 (hardcover)
Subjects: LCSH: Western stories. | Frontier and pioneer life—West (U.S.)—Fiction. | GSAFD: Western fiction.
Classification: LCC PS648.W4 S66 2019 | DDC 813/.087408—dc23
LC record available at https://lccn.loc.gov/2019023576

First Edition. First Printing: November 2019
Find us on Facebook—https://www.facebook.com/FiveStarCengage
Visit our website—http://www.gale.cengage.com/fivestar
Contact Five Star Publishing at FiveStar@cengage.com

Printed in Mexico
Print Number: 03   Print Year: 2019

TABLE OF CONTENTS

5

Table of Contents

FOREWORD

BY NEW YORK TIMES BESTSELLING AUTHOR CHRIS ENSS

For so long she was a footnote. Her story was not included within the main account of westward migration. When she was considered, the western woman was seen primarily as a pioneer mother, a sainted figure immortal in bronze and in the occasional history book. She was prune-faced in a sunbonnet, lingering in the background cooking, sewing, or tending to the children. She was the wife of a farmer, cattleman, or prospector bravely and quietly suffering and enduring in a covered wagon, log cabin, or sod house. She was anonymous—more institution than individual.

To understand the women of the West, it's necessary to look at the circumstances beyond the Mississippi River in the late 1840s. More than 50,000 Americans went west when gold was discovered in California in 1849. Less than ten percent of those who traveled over the plains to take part in the Gold Rush were women. When the first California census was taken in 1850, men outnumbered women approximately twelve to one. The lack of women in mining camps and in the establishing of new towns across the prairie made it difficult for females to be included in the tales of the growth of the region. The perception was there were simply no women around to make mention of their accomplishments or contributions.

The rare presence of a woman in the remote areas of the Sierra Nevada foothills was such a rarity that when it did happen, it was noteworthy. In many instances, she was treated like royalty. Such was the case with the married woman in northern California. "I am afraid I should have a very mistaken impression of my own importance if I had lived long among [these men]," she wrote in her diary. "At every stopping-place they made little fires in their frying pans and set them around me, to keep off the mosquitoes while I took my meal. As the columns of smoke rose about me, I felt like a heathen goddess to whom incense was being offered."

When news of the shortage of females in the West was publicized, enterprising women immediately decided to rectify the situation. Prostitutes arrived in cow towns and mining camps eager to capitalize on the need. Soiled doves set up business in small rooms behind saloons and entertained lonely pioneers, miners, and trappers.

According to the national census records, more than half the working women in the West between 1855 and 1875 were prostitutes. At that time, madams, those women who owned, managed, and maintained brothels, were generally the only women out west who appeared to be in control of their destinies. For that reason alone, the prospect of a career in the "oldest profession," at least at the outset, must have seemed promising.

Those first historians who dared to put down on paper what life was truly like in the early days of such places as Placerville, California; Leadville, Colorado; or Globe, Arizona, may have objected to including sporting girls in their accounts. They were women who went by names such as Silver Dollar Lil', Squirrel Tooth Alice, and Contemporary Mary. Writers, more concerned with morality than accuracy, ignored the influence ladies of easy virtue had on the frontier. The men who chronicled the experience in a new land struggled with admitting the only women many men knew west of the Mississippi were harlots.

The shortage of women created a climate in which prostitutes greatly benefitted, but that same climate enabled others to profit in far more honorable ways. Luzena Stanley Wilson made and lost more than one fortune making biscuits for prospectors who tired of bacon and beans. "I'll give five dollars for one of those biscuits, ma'am," Luzena recalled being told by a miner in her memoirs. "The offer came from a rugged-looking man obviously used to the hardship of living in a gold camp." Luzena parlayed that five-dollar gold piece into a profitable business serving food and then operating a boardinghouse.

Photo artist Eliza Withington earned a decent living photographing miners, ranch hands, and steamship crews from San Francisco to Seattle. Eliza hauled her bulky cameras and tripods from the seaside docks to the snowcapped Sierras shooting pictures of the scenery for newspapers and of pioneers to send to families back home.

As more resourceful and diverse females ventured into western locations, the face of the western woman grew to include more than just the harlots or the long-suffering wives of farmers or prospectors. Ambitious teachers, dedicated to educating and inspiring generations and moving societies forward, arrived on the scene. Women like Mary Gray McLench and Lucia Darling trekked hundreds of miles over treacherous country to bring their gift of teaching to boys and girls in the remote areas of Oregon and Montana. Limited schoolbooks and supplies did not stop teachers like Nevada's Eliza Mott from helping children learn to read. She taught the alphabet to her students using the inscriptions on tombstones at nearby cemeteries.

Concerned women nurses and doctors traveled west as well.

The frontier, with its absence of physicians and high demand for health care, provided women the opportunity to open medical offices. It did not, however, assure them patients. For a while it seemed most trappers, miners, and emigrants would rather suffer and die than consult a woman doctor.

Doctor Eliza Cook had a strong impact on the male-dominated community in Carson Valley, Nevada. Men who felt women were "not blessed with the temperament or disposition to be doctors" changed their minds after years of watching Doctor Cook work. The tall, slender lady from Salt Lake City, Utah, set broken limbs, performed operations, and delivered generations of babies in the small northern Nevada town where she lived. She was a skilled physician and a pharmacist, and she contributed numerous articles to medical journals and magazines on a variety of health issues.

The western pioneer's passion for diversion lured brave actresses, dancers, and singers west. Drawn by the same desire for riches and bringing a variety of talents and programs, many of the most popular women entertainers of the mid and late 1800s performed in the boomtowns that dotted the West. They were mostly well received and sometimes literally showered with gold. Actress Adah Menken, known as the Frenzy of Frisco, ventured beyond the Rockies from New Orleans and captured the hearts of men from Denver, Colorado, to Virginia City, Nevada. As the star of the tragedy *Mazeppa*, Adah preferred to play the part in the nude. Among her most ardent followers were author Mark Twain and prize fighter John "Benicia Boy" Heenan.

Laura Keene was another thespian who amassed a fortune on the western stage. Known for her exceptional comic timing and beautiful costumes, Laura and the play in which she starred, *Our American Cousin*, took the frontier by storm. First Lady Mary Todd Lincoln invited Laura Keene and her troop to perform at Ford's Theatre in April 1865. President Lincoln was shot and killed opening night of the play, and Laura's illustrious career ended shortly thereafter.

Women journalists who believed they had a duty to keep the public thoroughly posted concerning murders and street fights, the railroad, theaters, packtrains, churches, lectures, city and military affairs, highway robberies, Bible societies, and the advantages inherent with westward expansion made their way west, too, and went to work for papers such as the *Hutchinson News* in Kansas, the *Arizona Citizen* in Arizona, and the *Visalia Weekly Delta* in California.

Initially, women were not involved in frontier journalism any more than they were in the front ranks of the Argonauts, the pioneer lumberjacks, or the railroad construction crews. Mrs. Florence Apponyi Loughead was one of the first to serve as a correspondent for the *San Francisco Chronicle*. Florence reported on the events of the day, which occasionally included what women were doing in the community. As more women were hired as correspondents, more stories were written about the contributions women were making on the new frontier.

The western woman, being scarce and highly valued, could do things of which her eastern sister might only dream. The fight for women's rights, particularly the right to vote, was carried on most vigorously in the West, where it was not so easy for men to dismiss, with a flutter of a hand, the female argument that they should be allowed to cast a ballot.

On December 10, 1869, sixty-nine-year-old Louisa Ann Swain became the first woman to vote in the territory of Wyoming. This daring act brought great attention to the suffrage movement and encouraged women across the west to continue pushing for the right to be heard at the polls. One of the leading proponents of the movement was Abigail Scott Duniway, known as the "mother of equal suffrage" in Oregon.

Strong-willed and talented, Mrs. Duniway in May of 1871 established a newspaper called *The New Northwest,* devoted to political, financial, and social equality for women. Besides operating her newspaper, Mrs. Duniway trod the lecture trail, cared for a husband in poor health, raised a family of six, and wrote books.

Ellen Clark Sargent came to the Gold Country from Massachusetts in 1851 with her husband, attorney Aaron Sargent. While Aaron Sargent served as district attorney of Nevada County, California, and later a congressman representing the same area, Ellen founded the first woman's suffrage group in the state. She was the leader of the organization and presided at conventions called to encourage women to fight for the right to vote. In 1871, Ellen, along with their friend Susan B. Anthony, and now Senator Sargent drafted what would eventually become the Nineteenth Amendment.

In 1900, at the age of seventy-four, Ellen went to court in a test case to protest the payment of property tax. She argued in court that since she was not allowed to vote, it was an instance of taxation without representation. Ellen's groundbreaking action was covered in newspapers from San Francisco to Boston.

As more women found their voices through the suffrage movement, the accomplishments of females throughout the west were immortalized in magazines, dime novels, and history books. This anthology about pioneering women in the West bears evidence of the tremendous diversity among those females and the differences in the perceptions and conditions in which they lived, worked, and survived.

The pioneer woman was neither strictly a saint nor sinner, a madam adorned in red velvet surveying her domain from atop a staircase of a saloon, or an overworked schoolmarm struggling to teach an assortment of pupils of various ages on the cold, vast prairie. She was more than the reluctant wife of a stubborn, overland pioneer. She was a physician, a musical star, a business owner, mother, lawmaker, journalist, and an adventurer. She followed a trail often carved out by men, then blazed a new one for herself and all other women to come.

Chris Enss is a *New York Times* bestselling author and Spur Award finalist who has been writing about women of the Old West for more than nineteen years. She has penned more than forty published books on the subject, including the upcoming title *According to Kate: The Life and Times of Big Nose Kate Elder, Doc Holliday's Love*. Visit www.chrisenss.com for more information.

★ ★ ★ ★ ★

THE SPOILT QUILT
BY SANDRA DALLAS

★ ★ ★ ★ ★

The wagon drew up beside the body of the dead man, which lay sprawled in the dirt next to the manure pile. A pitchfork leaned at an angle, although it was still embedded in the man's back.

"Never seen nothing like that," Sheriff Dugan said. He turned to his wife. "No need to look, Puss. I'll take you up to the house so's I can talk to the widow. Heck'll be here pretty quick. Me and him'll load the body and look around." He climbed down from the wagon, shaking his head. "Had to be an awful powerful man to stab a pitchfork like that. Must have smarted some." He glanced at his wife to see if she found the remark humorous. She didn't. In fact, her hand was over her mouth as she stared at the body. Despite her husband's warning, she couldn't help but look.

Puss Dugan slid over on the wagon seat and let her husband help her down. "Awful way to die. Awful," she said. "Awful way for a awful man."

"He was that."

"Who do you think did it, Henry?"

"Take your pick."

"What did Heck tell you?" Heck was the Starks' hired man. He'd shown up at the Dugan house in Mingo at noon that day, right after Puss got home from church. She hadn't even had time to remove her hat. Heck had pounded on the door, yelling for the sheriff, and Dugan had taken him out into the yard

17

because he knew something bad had happened and he didn't want to upset his wife. Then Dugan had come back inside and told Puss, "Keep your hat on. We're going out to Starks'. Wyatt Stark's dead. He's got a pitchfork in his back. Heck found him when he come in from the north field. Body was already cold."

"Oh!" Puss had replied. "How's Maryetta. She all right, is she?"

"Heck says so. He went in the house and told her, said she ought to go with him to get me, but she wouldn't leave. Women grieve in different ways from us. Maybe it couldn't sink in yet he's gone. Heck looked around the place and didn't see nobody, so he figured whoever done it was long gone."

"He shouldn't have left Maryetta by herself. She couldn't fight off a tame cat. What if whoever killed Wyatt came on back?"

"Heck said as much, but she still wouldn't leave. You know how women are. Maybe she hopes she'll die herself now that her man's gone."

"She loved him all right, always did. The Lord knows why, since nobody else did."

Now as she looked down at the body, Puss said, "I wonder who killed him."

Dugan took his time speculating. "I been pondering it all the way here. Heck says there was a man stopped by this morning early. He'd bought a horse off of Stark that come down with the blind staggers. Wanted his money back, but Stark just laughed at him, called him a sucker. Heck didn't catch the name. Then Heck says men was camped over by the river, a mean-looking bunch. And I myself know Mitch Martin had it in for Stark on account of Stark said his wife looked like a sack of flour. Mitch didn't think kindly of that. Them would be fighting words for me." Dugan smiled at his wife for a moment. "But then I expect it could have been a dozen others. Stark wasn't the likenist man in Bondurant County."

"No, he was not." Puss paused and adjusted her hat, wishing now that she'd left it at home. It was as big as a turkey platter, and she knew the wind likely had blown off the egret feather and one or two of the artificial flowers she had artfully attached to it. She wished she'd had time to change out of her Sunday dress and take off her corset, too. She'd have been more comfortable if they'd taken the new Model T, but Dugan had pointed out they needed the wagon to bring Stark's body to the undertaker. You couldn't put a dead body in the rumble seat, he'd told her. "What about Heck? You think he could have killed Wyatt?"

The sheriff cocked his head at his wife and peered over his eyeglasses at her. "Now, Puss, you sure ain't no detective. That's for sure. Heck's got bad arms. Can't raise them above his waist. He couldn't no more throw that pitchfork hard enough to kill a man than you could. 'Sides, Stark's the only man here abouts that'd hire him. With Stark gone, Heck's in a bad place."

"Maybe Maryetta will keep him on."

Dugan chuckled at that. "A woman and a cripple, and a feeble-minded one at that. Now how do you suppose they could run this place?" He patted his wife's arm, then cocked his head. "Say, you think maybe his wife done it, do you?"

Puss snorted. "Maryetta Stark isn't strong enough to *scratch* a body with a pitchfork, let alone throw it in a man's back. Besides, Maryetta thought that man made the moon rise."

Dugan nodded. "I don't understand it, but you spoke the truth. Onliest one that ever had a good word to say about him."

The two walked to the Stark house and went up onto the porch. Puss was glad for the shade, since the sun on Colorado's eastern prairie was hot enough to scorch her arms, and the wind didn't cool but only stirred up dust. Her neck was damp with sweat, and her hands felt gritty.

The door was open, and Dugan called, "Miz Stark. It's Sheriff

Dugan and Miz Dugan. You mind if we come in?"

There was no answer.

"Miz Stark," the sheriff called again. Puss wondered why her husband was being so formal. He'd known Maryetta since the three of them were children. This wasn't a social call, however.

When there was still no answer, Puss called softly, "Maryetta, sweetheart. It's Puss Dugan. Can me and Henry come on inside?"

There was a rustling and a small voice said, "Puss?"

The sheriff started through the door, but his wife edged past him. "Maryetta, are you all right?" Puss asked.

"I'm here."

Puss went to the woman sitting in a rocking chair. She was small and drab and gnarled. "Oh, Maryetta. I am so sorry." Puss sank onto the floor beside the chair, oblivious of her Sunday dress. "You ain't hurt, are you? Whoever done that to Wyatt didn't hurt you none, did he?"

"He's dead," Maryetta said in a monotone.

"Yes, I saw." Puss asked, "Who would do such a awful thing?"

The sheriff cleared his voice and frowned at his wife. Asking questions was his job. He put out his hand to help her up, then nodded at a chair a few feet away. Puss had been inside the house only a few times in the last years, and Maryetta always told her to take the rocker. The big chair was Stark's, and Maryetta wouldn't allow her guests to use it. Puss sat down on the bed.

"You want you a glass of water?" the sheriff asked Maryetta, then glanced at his wife and pointed with his head at the water bucket. The house didn't have a pump in the kitchen, only in the barn. Either Stark or his wife filled buckets there and carried them into the house.

Puss started to get up to fetch the dipper, but Maryetta shook her head, and Puss remained where she was.

"I got to ask you about that man that come here this morning," the sheriff said. "You think he pitchforked Stark?"

Puss cleared her throat at her husband's insensitivity, but she said nothing. Although Dugan didn't understand much about talking to women, he would be displeased if she interfered.

Maryetta shrugged.

"You know him, do you?"

Maryetta shook her head.

"Tell me what happened?"

Maryetta glanced at Puss, then clasped her hands together, the knuckles white. "He called Wyatt to come outside. They talked loud." She put her hands over her ears.

"What did they say?"

"I didn't hear."

"You think he killed your husband?"

Maryetta shrugged.

"Didn't you go to the door or nothing? Wasn't you curious what was going on?" Dugan sounded annoyed.

Puss bit her lip and told herself to keep her mouth shut. She looked around the room. The place was gloomy with only one door and a single window, but that wasn't unusual on a prairie farm in 1908. Men controlled the purse strings, and they spent money on the farm itself, not the house. The Stark barn was well built, and Puss knew it housed the latest equipment. She suspected the house hadn't been upgraded in twenty-five years. There wasn't even a cookstove. Maryetta cooked over an open fire. Puss had never heard her utter a word about it, however. Whenever women at the quilt circle complained about their husbands, Maryetta was silent. When she did speak, it was to praise Stark.

Maryetta had done her best with the house. It was neat, and there was a braided rug on the floor. A jar filled with pretty weeds was on the table. It was knocked over and Puss wondered if Maryetta had been arranging the bouquet when Heck came to tell her Stark was dead. Puss thought to wipe up the water, but she stayed where she was.

Quilts hung on the walls like bright banners covering the faded wallpaper. All the women said that Maryetta Dugan was the best quilter in Bondurant County. Puss was a good hand with a needle, but her quilting couldn't compete with Maryetta's. That woman loved her quilts, loved them almost as if they'd been her children.

What a pity the Starks never had children, Puss thought, as her husband droned on with his questions. He ought to let *her* ask them. She'd be softer, less direct, more sympathetic. She wouldn't hammer Maryetta like a schoolteacher, the way her husband did. Who's been coming around? Who did your husband have trouble with? Who was those men camped on the other side of the creek? What have you seen that I ought to know about? Poor Maryetta had just lost her husband, and here Dugan was hectoring her. Puss would speak to him, but he'd dismiss her suggestions, giving her that sad smile he did when he thought she was being stupid, asking her did she think *she* was the sheriff?

It wasn't that Dugan was a bad husband. Far from it. He was a decent man, the best, in fact—sweet at times, and she'd loved him since grammar school. But he did treat her as if she didn't have a brain.

"You have any trouble with Stark your own self?" Dugan asked. "Maybe there was times you got awful mad at him."

What was that about, Puss wondered. Did Dugan really think Maryetta could have killed her husband? She rolled her eyes. Why would he consider such a thing? She'd never heard Maryetta say a word against Stark. Puss always thought of the marriage as a love match.

There was a noise outside, and Dugan turned to the door,

saying it must be Heck returning. Heck had stayed in town for a moment on account of he had to catch his breath after the rush to the sheriff's office. That meant he'd wanted to visit the saloon for a beer or two. Puss glanced through the open door and saw Heck slide off his mule. She didn't know if he was drunk or his disabilities made him awkward. She hadn't cared much for Wyatt Stark, but at least he'd been good to Heck.

Dugan motioned for Puss to join him outside. She glanced at Maryetta who was staring at her hands. Puss didn't want to leave her alone, but she couldn't deny her husband and went out onto the porch.

"Me and Heck will check out the barn, maybe find something. Then we'll load Stark in the wagon." He lowered his voice. "See if you can get anything out of her. She ain't much for talking, I can tell you. A man, now, you can't shut him up. He'll try to be helpful, give you his opinion. But a woman . . . like as not, she'll disremember." He shook his head.

"I'll try," Puss replied. She squeezed her husband's hand. He was indeed a good man. Dugan squeezed back and might have kissed her cheek if Heck hadn't been around.

Fanning her face with her hand, she watched him stride across the barnyard toward Stark's body, Heck hobbling along behind him. Then she turned back to Maryetta, who was still sitting in the rocker. "Well, sweetheart, I could use a cup of coffee. I bet you could, too." Puss remembered the Sunday dinner she had put into the cookstove before church. She hadn't thought to remove it, and now it would be burned to a crisp. She wondered if Maryetta had eaten anything. "You hungry?"

Maryetta smiled. "I baked bread. It's in the fire," she replied.

Dugan would find it odd that with her husband dead, Maryetta would remember the bread, but Puss understood. Puss went to the fireplace and removed the lid from a Dutch oven to see that the bread was nicely browned. It was as if the dough

23

had raised while Stark was being killed, and Maryetta had put it into the fire after Heck had gone to town for the sheriff. Well, maybe doing something routine helped her deal with the awfulness of what had happened.

Maryetta set the bread on the table, then looked for the butter. She realized then that there was no icebox. The butter must be in the well—but there wasn't a well either. She had noticed on her way to the house that the well was boarded up. How in the world did Maryetta keep things cold? She poked through the shelves of the pie safe until she saw a butter dish with the top broken off. The butter swam inside. "Nothing better than fresh bread and butter," she said, placing it beside the bread.

She'd seen a can of coffee in the pie safe, too, and started for it, but remembered the coffee pot sitting beside the dry sink. She peered inside, and sure enough, there were coffee grounds saved. She hadn't thought the Starks were so poor they had to reuse grounds, but then, Maryetta was frugal. Puss had seen the woman wear the same two dresses for years, and Maryetta didn't seem to own a piece of jewelry, not even a wedding ring. She must have agreed with her husband that money was best spent on the farm. "I'll just heat up the coffee, and we'll have us a nice tea," Puss said, then laughed. "I guess it's not a tea with coffee, is it?"

To Puss's surprise, Maryetta laughed, too. Puss hadn't heard her laugh for a long time, but then, she hadn't seen her in a long time either. As she busied herself, she said, "I'm trying to recall when I seen you last."

Puss didn't expect Maryetta to answer, but the woman said, "It was last year, at the quilting at Mrs. Dorsey's. We had lemon cake."

"Why, that's right. We all commented on how tiny your stitches were. There's not a woman can take stitches as small and even as you."

24

"Oh," Maryetta replied. She looked away, but there was pleasure in her eyes. "I'm not so good," she muttered.

"Oh my, yes, sweet child." As Puss poured boiling water over the coffee grounds and set the pot on a trivet over the fire, she wondered why she had called Maryetta "child." The two were almost the same age. Maryetta had been only a year or two behind her in school.

She remembered that Maryetta was pretty as a child and downright beautiful as she grew older, with hair the color of cottonwood leaves in the fall and skin as smooth and pink as a piglet's. Puss, big herself, had envied Maryetta's small size, which made her friend seem as fragile as a bisque dolly. She still had traces of that beauty, although she was thin rather than petite now, and her once bright blue eyes were clouded from the sun.

Aging young wasn't unusual in that hard land. Maryetta's life hadn't been any more difficult than that of other farm women in eastern Colorado. In fact, Maryetta had had it better than some. Her husband worked hard and made a success of the farm. Maybe that was why Maryetta loved him.

Puss remembered back two decades to when Wyatt Stark had come to Mingo, dressed in black, riding a black horse. Oh, he'd known he was a good looking fellow. The boys all admired him, and the girls, too. Although she was all but pledged to Dugan, Puss herself had sized him up, but she knew that with her drab looks, she wouldn't catch his eye. Besides, there was something about the man that bothered her. There always was—an arrogance maybe, and eyes that were too black.

Stark was handsome as a cowboy in a dime novel. He was smitten with Maryetta right off, although Maryetta didn't seem to care so much about him at first. Maybe she'd been playing hard to get, because she'd had her choice of all the boys. There must have been something about Stark that drew her, however, because the two of them had run off to Denver and got married. When Puss thought about it now, the marriage had made sense. Maryetta's mother and brother had been killed when their buggy overturned, and the father was a lunger. Maryetta couldn't operate the farm by herself. Then there was the baby. It wasn't any time at all before everybody knew Maryetta was in a family way. People whispered, but Puss defended her friend, saying Maryetta showed early because she was so small. Nobody knew for sure when the baby got started, because Maryetta lost it. Folks didn't talk about half-made babies, so Puss never knew what had gone wrong. Maryetta hadn't been pregnant again, or maybe she had and lost those babies before anyone knew about them. Perhaps their childlessness drew the Starks together.

How sad, Puss thought now, Maryetta not having anybody to take care of her—no children, no brothers or sisters. Only Heck, who when you considered it, amounted to about half of a man. What would she do?

"Coffee's ready, nice and hot and thick," Puss said as she poured it into two cracked cups that she'd taken from the pie safe. They didn't match, and one was missing its handle. Puss wondered what had become of the china Maryetta had received from her friends when she went to housekeeping. Maybe the Starks had sold it during the drought. Puss took the cup with the handle to Maryetta. She started to seat herself on the bed, again, but Maryetta pointed at Stark's chair. What did it matter who sat there now? She sat down and placed her cup on the floor so she could remove her hatpin and take off her hat. It was covered with dust, and the veil was torn. She shouldn't have bought the atrocious thing.

"I'll mend the veil," Maryetta said, reaching for the hat.

"No, precious, I'll do it myself when I get to home. It serves me right for buying a hat big enough to eat Sunday dinner off of." She reached over and patted her friend's hand.

"I'll do it," Maryetta insisted and reached into the sewing basket beside her chair and took out a needle. Puss didn't protest again. She knew sewing quieted a woman's nerves.

"I've missed you at quiltings. And church," Puss said.

"Wyatt didn't hold with church."

"Most men don't, but you could have gone your own self."

"Wyatt didn't hold with it."

That was a pity because Maryetta must have been lonely, way out here on the farm, Puss thought. Why hadn't she come out to see her more often? But she knew why. She never felt comfortable around Stark. She thought he didn't like her. He'd sit in that chair and stare at her with those dark eyes whenever she visited.

She had stopped by the year before to insist that Maryetta go to quilting with her.

Puss had looked at her husband for permission. He'd said, "She's got beans to bottle."

"Beans'll wait. Maryetta needs to get out," Puss had told him.

"She don't like to leave the farm."

"Now, Wyatt Stark. A woman's got to get out. You can't keep her to yourself all the time. Besides, we'll be making quilts. How you going to keep warm in the winter if Maryetta doesn't make her quilts."

"A horse blanket'll do." He had laughed at that, but Puss hadn't thought it was funny.

He'd stood and flung out his hand. "Go off if it pleases you," he'd said and went to the barn.

Maryetta had grinned and changed into her second dress and gone with Puss, chattering like a bird. She had had a wonderful time, but in the afternoon, she'd asked Puss to take her home even before the quilt was finished. She hadn't wanted her husband to have to wait for his supper. "He wants me there,

27

and I want to be there." Then she'd added, "I love him, you know."

Now Puss heard footsteps on the porch, and Dugan came into the room carrying a quilt. "Found this on the manure pile. Manure all over it and horse piss, too. I thought we could wrap Stark's body in it."

He opened the quilt and Puss gasped. Maryetta had made the quilt—a story quilt with each square made up of tiny rectangles and triangles and circles that represented something in the quilter's life. It was the finest quilt Puss had ever seen, and now it was stained with excrement. She glanced at Maryetta, who stared at the quilt but didn't seem to understand why it was there.

Maryetta had worked on it for years, maybe since she was a bride. Puss had never seen it completed, although she had seen Maryetta stitching the squares. Each one told a story. The first square Maryetta made was of a man and a woman with a heart behind them and a gold ring above their heads. Other scenes showed the farm, the animals, a picnic, a church. There was even one of a vacant crib with a cross over it. The squares at the top of the quilt—the first ones Maryetta had made—were of happy events with men, women, and children. The later ones were devoid of people, except for here and there a single woman. Puss decided they depicted the loneliness Maryetta felt on the farm without any children to keep her company. No wonder she kept close to Stark.

"It's a work of art—work of art. It ought to be in a museum," Puss told Dugan. "If that was my quilt, I'd kill anybody who ruined it like that."

"That's what I been thinking." Dugan lowered his voice. "Everything I know about killing says it's the person closest that done it. That means a husband or a wife or a father or a mother."

Puss scoffed. The idea was ridiculous. "How about second cousins and great uncles? You really think Maryetta's guilty? She sure set store by that man even if me and you didn't. Besides, how's a bitty woman like that going to heft that pitchfork?"

"You ask her if she did it?"

"I did not!"

"Well you might inquire."

"What reason would she have? I can't think of none."

Dugan considered that, then laughed. "Well, I guess there ain't nobody going to kill nobody over a spoilt quilt. That's for sure."

"No," Puss agreed. "You leave it here. It's too good for a shroud. I'll take it home and see if I can wash it."

Dugan threw the quilt out the door onto the porch. Puss glanced again at Maryetta, who had not moved, then followed her husband outside and picked up the quilt, folding it carefully. In the hot sun, the stench of the manure overwhelmed her, and she dropped the quilt to the floor.

"You get anything out of her about who she thought done it?" Dugan asked.

Puss shook her head. "Not yet."

"Well, try. Heck says she was in the house all day. She must have heard something."

"I think Maryetta's living in shock right now and doesn't half-know what's going on."

"That's why women's no use at trials. Like the fellow says, if they didn't cook breakfast, we'd have to shoot them." He began to laugh, but he stopped when he saw Puss's scorn. "Now, honey, I was just telling a joke. You know I don't really think that, not about you leastways. It's just that some women are foolish, and a man's got to keep his wife in line."

He patted Puss's arm, but she jerked it away.

Dugan dug himself in deeper. "I know Maryetta don't have no reason to turn on her husband. Maybe he wasn't so likable, but he done a good job on his farm."

"*Her* farm," Puss reminded him.

Dugan frowned. "That so?"

Puss nodded. "Remember? It was her father's farm. He homesteaded it. Wyatt did all right when he married her."

"That don't say why *she* married *him*. Maybe it was because he was a big strapping fellow. Ain't that what you women like? Ain't that why you married me?"

He leaned over to kiss his wife's cheek, but she turned and went back into the house, muttering, "What's a man know about love anyway?"

"I'll just take the quilt with me and launder it. Maybe I can get rid of the stains," Puss told Maryetta when she sat down in Stark's chair again.

Maryetta shrugged as if it didn't matter.

Puss picked up her cup by the bowl and sipped the coffee, which was cold and bitter. The room was close, and she felt perspiration run down her back. "Sheriff's going to load the body and take it to the undertaker. You want it buried next to your folks?"

"No."

"I think there's room."

"No," Maryetta said.

Puss didn't ask why, because something occurred to her then, something bad. The idea startled her so much that she spilled the coffee on her dress. "Your pa was still alive when you married Wyatt, wasn't he?"

Maryetta didn't answer but just stared at her friend.

"He died, what, maybe a year later?"

"Almost," Maryetta whispered.

"What was the cause of it? Folks thought his lungs give out.

30

Is that about right?"

Maryetta stared at Puss for a long time. "There was an accident."

Puss tilted her head, inviting Maryetta to go on.

"He fell off the barn roof."

That didn't ring true to Puss. "I heard your pa say once he never climbed up on a roof in his life. He told me he got palpitations when he was high up."

Maryetta didn't respond.

"Then how do you know—?"

"Wyatt told me. I was in town. I came back. Pa was gone."

Puss stared hard at her friend. "So he fell off that roof?"

Maryetta hunched her shoulders and clasped her hands together.

Puss shook her head because confusing thoughts kept crowding into it. Had Stark killed his wife's father? Did Maryetta know that, and if she did, why had she kept it a secret? She could have told Dugan. Or could she? Had she sought to protect Stark, or had she feared him? Puss thought back over the times she had seen the two together. Had it been love that kept Stark by Maryetta's side whenever she visited someone in town? Maryetta could have left her husband, but it was her farm. Besides if Stark had killed her father, she might have feared he'd go after her, too, if she tried to leave him. She was out there in the country all by herself, with only her husband and a hired man who was too simple to understand what was going on. Over the years, Maryetta had stopped entertaining friends. She no longer went to town by herself, and she attended quiltings only when Puss insisted.

"Why did you marry him, Maryetta?" Puss asked suddenly. The question was even more insensitive than the ones Dugan had asked, but Puss now understood more than her husband did.

31

As if she hadn't heard Puss, Maryetta took a length of thread she had wound around a piece of cardboard and licked the end. *The poor woman was so frugal she had to reuse her basting threads,* Puss thought. *Or maybe Wyatt wouldn't let her buy so much as a spool of thread.*

Puss had forgotten about the bread and butter and went to the table, which was covered with oilcloth so old that most of the color had been scrubbed off. The bread was still warm. Puss figured it had baked for an hour. It would have taken another hour, maybe two, to mix and proof the dough. That was three hours. Heck had told her about Stark's body maybe four hours before. Maryetta would have started that bread after her husband was killed. Puss sliced the bread and rubbed the butter on it, then set it on a plate and carried it to Maryetta.

"Why did you marry Wyatt?" Puss asked again. Her voice had been harsh, and she softened it a little. "Was it the hips?" She herself had always liked a man's hips.

Maryetta shook her head, not looking up. She had threaded the needle and made a knot and began stitching, matching the edges of the torn veil so expertly that no one would ever know it had been ripped.

Puss took a deep breath and let it out. Maryetta wasn't going to reply any more than she had when Dugan asked questions.

Then Maryetta set down the sewing and picked up the slice of bread and nibbled on it. "The baby," she said.

"You mean you *had* to get married. Well, you wasn't the first. You was in love. It's nobody's business."

"Not love." Maryetta set down the bread and looked into Puss's eyes. "I hate him. I always did."

Puss didn't understand. "Then why?"

"He made me. I said no. He laughed." Maryetta's eyes were bright, and Puss understood. She knew Maryetta had never told that to anyone before, and the truth must have welled up in her until it spilled over just then. She could say it because Stark was dead. She didn't have to worry how he would react. Maryetta wanted Puss to know that all those years, she hadn't loved Wyatt Stark. She must have feared he'd find out if she told anyone about him. Or maybe she was trying to convince herself she loved her husband. It was as if Puss had primed the pump, and now the water was gushing out. Maryetta didn't have to hold back anymore.

"You poor thing," Puss said. She reached over and took Maryetta in her arms. "You poor precious thing. You mean he . . ."—she couldn't say the word—"he forced you."

"I didn't want to. I didn't even like him. He wanted to marry up with me, but I said no. He held me down and said he had the right. He told me it didn't matter if I said no. It was what he wanted that counted. He said he'd spoil me for anyone else. I couldn't let anybody know what happened, even Pa. He'd have gone after Wyatt, and Wyatt might have killed him—just like he did later on. When I found out I was going to have a baby, I had to beg Wyatt to marry me. Wyatt held that over me, said I tricked him, but I never."

"What happened to the baby?"

"I loved her. I loved her so much I didn't care what Wyatt done to make me marry him."

"Did Wyatt love it, too? Did he blame you when you lost it?"

"He hated her. He said he wasn't going to share me with anybody, and he beat me, beat me till I lost her." Maryetta looked into Puss's eyes, as if begging Puss to believe her. "She was a girl, but she was too tiny. She never lived."

"Precious thing! Has she a grave?"

Maryetta stared silently at Puss as tears began running down her face. Finally, she whispered, "Wyatt said he fed her to the pigs."

Puss closed her eyes, letting the horror of what Maryetta had said wash over her. *How could anyone be that evil?* she wondered. She wanted to ask Maryetta if there had been other babies, but she wouldn't. Stark would have gotten rid of them, too.

For a time, Puss was silent, listening to the sounds of birds outside and the creak of the wagon. Dugan must be loading the body. It wouldn't be long before he came for her. She should tell him about the baby, but she wouldn't, although it might have to do with Stark's death. Maybe something had triggered that pent-up hatred, and Maryetta had finally acted. Had Maryetta confided in her so that Dugan would know? Did she want to be punished? Puss stared at Maryetta, at her arms as thin as broomsticks. One arm stuck out a little, as if it had been broken. And Maryetta's hands. Puss studied them and saw that two of the fingers were twisted. How did the woman manage to sew with her fingers like that, let alone thrust a pitchfork into Stark's back? And why hadn't Puss figured out all that long ago? Perhaps Dugan was right that women were stupid.

Puss stared out the door at what had been Maryetta's flower garden. Maryetta had had a way with flowers. Back in the years when she'd gone to quiltings every month, she had taken bunches of peonies and roses and heart's ease with her. Nobody could get flowers to grow in that dry earth the way Maryetta had. The flowers were gone now. Maryetta didn't plant them anymore. Dried hollyhock stalks leaned against the porch railing, along with the dead canes of rosebushes. Puss wondered if over the years, Wyatt had taken away everything that gave Maryetta pleasure—her baby, her friends, and her garden. "How did you stand it? All these years, how did you stand him?" Puss asked.

"I had my quilts. The days Wyatt hit me or yelled at me or broke my dishes, I had my piecing. I made pictures with the pieces. I pretended I was there, inside the pictures." Maryetta seemed anxious to open her heart now, to let the pain of the past twenty-five years spill out. She was relieving herself of all the secrets. She didn't seem to think of the consequences, or maybe she didn't care.

Puss remembered the scenes in the quilt that her husband had rescued from the manure pile. Maryetta had brought many of those squares to the quiltings, and the women had been astonished at their beauty and delicacy. They were made of tiny scraps no bigger than a fingernail. Maryetta had spent years on them. Puss hadn't known the quilt had been assembled until she saw it in Dugan's hands. The quilt pictures that she thought had shown loneliness, she realized now, actually depicted safety. One was of a house with the door shut and shutters over the windows and another of a woman inside a flower garden with a fence around it.

She wondered what had been unleashed in Maryetta, what had caused her to kill her husband, because surely it was Maryetta who had murdered him. She had lived quietly all those years, pretending she loved Stark, never letting anyone know the heartache she'd endured. She had accepted the loss of her baby and of her father. What had happened that caused her finally to break?

Then suddenly Puss understood. "What was it made you do it?" she asked, although she knew the answer.

Maryetta didn't ask what Puss meant. Puss was a woman. Puss understood. Maryetta smiled a little, then looked out the door at the plot of weeds that had once been her garden. "The quilt," she said softly. "I made a square most every year. My baby was in one and Pa, and me and Wyatt when we were first married, when I thought he would change. The squares, they were what I hoped for. When he hit me, I stood it because I could go inside a picture, and he couldn't hurt me there. Wyatt didn't know how much the piecings meant to me. He said they were silly. I kept them in a flour sack until they were all finished.

Then I put them together. It took a long time because I wanted the stitching to be perfect. I finished the quilt last week, and I hung it over the bed. It was so pretty. Every time I looked at it, I smiled.

"Wyatt, he never paid attention to my sewing. There's other quilts on the wall. He never noticed them. But this morning when he saw how much that quilt pleasured me, he ripped it down. I begged him not to take it. I promised to put it away and never look at it again, but he wouldn't give it back. He said he'd throw it in the fire, but I stood in front of the fireplace and wouldn't let him. He took it outside and went toward the barn. I thought he'd use it for a horse blanket, but instead, he threw it on the manure pile. He stomped on it, then spread manure all over it with the pitchfork. The horse was there, and Wyatt let her . . ." Maryetta stopped and shook her head back and forth. I begged him to stop, but he laughed. He held me off with his hand. He kept on laughing. He killed everything else I cared about. The quilt was all I had. I had to stop him. I picked up the pitchfork and hit him to make him give me back the quilt. I didn't mean to hurt him. I only wanted him to stop. He fell, and he laid there, and I knew he was dead. I put the horse back in the barn, and I came to the house and started my bread."

"You poor darling," Puss said, patting her friend's back. "Anyone would have done the same thing. Anyone." Puss herself began to cry.

Neither of them heard Dugan as he came through the door. He stood awkwardly as he stared at the two women. "Puss?" he said at last.

She looked up, startled. Had Dugan heard Maryetta's confession? Puss gently released her friend and stood.

Dugan motioned with his head for her to join him outside. Puss wondered what she'd tell him. She'd questioned Mayetta just like he'd asked her to. In twenty-five years, Puss had never lied to her husband, but could she betray Maryetta?

"What's going on in there?" Dugan asked his wife.

Puss thought it over. "I think it just hit her that Stark's dead. Some women it takes them time." She rubbed the tears off her cheeks.

"I been pondering that quilt. What was it doing out there? You women are foolish about your quilts. What if Stark throwed it out there on the manure pile, and she went crazy? I been thinking that makes more sense than a horse with the blind staggers. I think maybe Maryetta done it."

Puss was stunned at how close her husband was to the truth. "A bitty thing like Maryetta? How do you think she hefted that pitchfork?"

"Folks that are mad that way, they can get real strong. I heard about a fellow once that got attacked by a bear. He killed it with his own hands. More I think about it, I believe Maryetta saw that quilt out there and went after Stark. Makes sense to me."

Puss thought that over and knew she had to protect her friend. Even if it meant lying to Dugan. Maryetta had suffered enough. She didn't need to be punished for killing a man who had been so cruel to her. She had the right. Suddenly, Puss began to laugh. It was a forced laugh, and Puss hoped her husband couldn't tell she didn't mean it. "Why, Henry, that's the craziest thing I ever heard," she said. "You sure don't understand women, and that's a fact. Maryetta Stark loved that man. Ask anybody. She never said a word against him. She's in there right this minute crying her eyes out for him. Why, she'd be more likely to kill her own self now that he's gone, than she would be to murder her husband."

Dugan looked sheepish as his wife's words seeped in, as he reconsidered his theory.

Puss paused a moment. Then she raised her chin and pushed

back her shoulders. "You said it yourself, Henry. Nobody kills nobody over a spoilt quilt."

Sandra Dallas, former Denver bureau chief of *Business Week* magazine, is the *New York Times* best-selling author of fifteen novels, three mid-grade novels, and ten nonfiction books. She is the recipient of three National Cowboy & Western Heritage Museum Wrangler awards, three Western Writers of America Spur Awards, and four Women Writing the West Willa awards. She lives in Denver and Georgetown, Colorado.

★ ★ ★ ★ ★

NEST
BY DEBORAH MORGAN

★ ★ ★ ★ ★

He kept the peacocks to cover his wife's screams.

Passersby (mercifully as rare as the birds themselves on the vast prairie) admired their beauty—the burnished iridescence of their fans, their imperial air—and when they paused to inquire after spent tailfeathers, he plastered on a smile as thick as the droppings that plastered his yard, then sent them away empty-handed.

He didn't care about their beauty, didn't fawn over their tailfeathers with those painted eyes that seemed to watch his every move. Their distinctive shrieks served his purpose, so he suffered their existence.

With stiff back and creaking joints more fitting a man twice his age, he stooped and gathered a couple of feathers from the ground, then tossed them onto an empty feed sack in a corner of the barn.

The peacocks had begun molting, signaling that summer, too, was near spent. The trains would be gone and the birds' prancing, plume-rattling dance would lie dormant till spring when the feathers would reappear larger than the last.

The morning drill at the barnyard didn't change: The pair of mules waited at the trough, and he scooped oats into it before slopping the hogs and opening gates to release the chickens and peafowl. He fed the cow last, so as to occupy her while he took her milk. She still balked when he grabbed hold, as if she missed the more refined grasp of his wife.

41

On his way back to the house, he hung the bucket of milk in the well to cool it.

He'd wedged hardtack into a mug to soak up coffee and soften. The bitter brew he made reminded him of his wife's talent for making the perfect pot of coffee day after day. He split apart the cracker-like square with a spoon as if splitting logs, and wished it were that easy with the mountain of firewood waiting outside. She usually tended that, too. No more.

Despite the heat, he shivered. Everything about the coming seasons would be different from those before, when his wife had salted meat, churned butter, darned socks, put up their garden vegetables and orchard fruits, and did a hundred other chores he hadn't given thought to previously.

He chewed, thinking how he had sworn after the war that he'd never eat hardtack again. But, he was in another war now, and knowing that all war was about survival, he had started out baking the only thing he knew how.

Even though he found notes she had scribbled during their journey west from other women's accounts of how to prepare food, he couldn't make much sense of them. What good was *knead the dough* if you didn't have particulars? How much leavening went into the mix, and why punch it down only to let it rise again? Still, he tried. More than one batch had been thrown to the hogs, and when spring planting kicked off his busy seasons, he abandoned it altogether.

He looked in on her, assured himself the drug had taken hold. He started to remove the pistol from the nightstand drawer, but decided against it. Although she didn't have the strength to retrieve it, she had always felt safer knowing it was there. He grabbed the .12-gauge shotgun from above the fireplace mantel on his way out.

At the barn, he hitched the mules to a wagon loaded with baskets of tomatoes, peaches, and green beans alongside gunny sacks of potatoes and ears of corn.

Smokehouse and root cellar preserved foods to a degree, but now that his wife was unable to put up jars of their harvest for the coming winter, he relied upon trade with the mercantile to expand their larder beyond the usual staples of coffee and flour.

The two-hour journey into town was once a respite from the hard but rewarding work of his place. Time passed quickly then while he plotted and turned fields in his mind, planned their future, envisioned a family working together on the prime piece of land.

Lately, the idleness of travel allowed his mind to dwell, twist his dreams into worries, turn his plans to mirages.

His work used to be cut and dried: he tilled and plowed, furrowed and planted, hoed and prayed for rain. And when it came, it came and came, and he prayed for it to stop.

But, his wife's chores? He never seemed to find a cutoff point. He hadn't seen that coming—the extra workload, the sheer number of tasks both large and small that she completed every day. Night, too.

He hadn't noticed before what was never left undone. Instead, he had blindly rested in the comfort of the surroundings she had created. He had taken it all for granted.

He looked up from the mules, surveyed the cloudless sky, then his surroundings. Another hour or so before he would arrive at the mercantile.

While he had labored in the fields, she had watched for day's end. When sun and supper were set, she had clanged the dinner bell and declared his day done.

Not anymore. No ringing for supper, no meal on the table when he dragged into the house after a full day. No rest.

Now, the future was hidden by a fog that he struggled to push away while he clung to the slim chance of emerging on the other side in one piece.

Weary of these thoughts, he tried to distract himself by studying the distant mountains.

After a few miles, a memory from his childhood surfaced. Memories of his upbringing never seemed to end well, and try as he might to tamp this new one down, he failed.

An aunt, his pa's older sister and a spinster who visited (invited or not) with the change of every season, upon entering their home skimmed past polished furniture and tidy tabletops to point out a fly speck on a windowpane or a hair on the washbasin. Once, his ma called her an old biddy or busybody or something that started with a "b"—the boy wasn't sure at the time—and his pa had seized Ma's upper arm and dragged her to the back of the house. The boy bolted out the door.

A few months later, that aunt moved in with them and wormed her way into the running of the place. His ma faded deeper and deeper into the background until finally she disappeared entirely.

He vaguely recalled her burial, but he remembered plotting his escape and he remembered being afraid.

You remember fear the most. You remember good times, too, but the good times are like paintings: smudged strokes of color, images that shift if studied too closely. Fear is razor-sharp. Fear is precise, like a watchmaker's hand. It's jagged nerves edged on whetstone, nerves that spark and singe your skin.

Next to him a woman dodged, pushed a brood of children along the crowded boardwalk.

Dazed, he looked around. He was standing in front of the mercantile. He remembered nothing of the journey's last mile.

The mules were accustomed to the habits of their bimonthly trips, though, and he was certain they were at the loading dock around back.

The mercantile proprietor and his missus greeted the man and he replied in kind, then handed his list to the missus on his way toward the back dock where he set about unloading his wagon.

He was finishing the tally in the storeroom's ledger and begrudging the need to add cash to cover his order when the proprietor joined him and glanced over the sums.

With hushed voice, the proprietor inquired after peacock feathers for the brothel operating near the new train depot. He said that a healthy profit was to be made, although the missus frowned upon it for two reasons: She feigned ignorance regarding the existence of soiled doves, believing this kept her right with God while she traded their ill-earned bills for common goods—and peacock feathers were *not* common goods. Further, she held to the belief that bringing them indoors was a bad omen, and discouraged her husband's stocking them.

Therefore, any special requests were furtively seen to by the proprietor, who began rattling off names of items and practices the man had never heard of before.

The man's gaze dropped to the floor. He waved away the words, afraid some dark corner of his mind might grab hold of them.

As savvy businessmen do, the proprietor next spoke as if an agreement had been reached, instructing the man to deliver a wrapped bundle at the back door next trip into town. Easy as pie, the proprietor added, and a hefty credit to your account. He tapped the ledger twice for emphasis.

The man pondered this as they returned to the front of the store.

The missus announced his order wrapped and ready, adding that she had included a small treat for his wife. Her expression indicated curiosity, with an ear open to elaboration on his part, then changed to irritation when he offered none.

He nodded his thanks, fished coins from his pocket, and flung up a hand without looking back as the proprietor said they looked forward to seeing him again soon.

The words *easy as pie* carried no weight with the man, since he had tried and failed to make one. But, *hefty credit?* He could choose what they needed, when they needed it. And they would need plenty if his wife continued her descent.

He stopped at the old doc's office before the trudge home.

A fly buzzed overhead, drawing his attention from the cold supper to the hovering quilt frame he had constructed of oak and with a pulley system the wife had easily managed. Long empty of her handiwork, the skeletal frame was tethered near the ceiling with rope wound over hooks behind the back door, all coated with the grime of neglect.

A thin, high-pitched scream pierced the air of the small house. The peacocks echoed from their coop in the barnyard. The man sighed, groaned as he lifted his weary body from the chair, and picked up a bowl on his way to the bedroom.

He coaxed laudanum down her throat, then propped her with pillows and rolled quilts, and spooned warm soup into her before the drug carried her away.

Hands clenching bedsheets soaked with sweat, she ate greedily. He mopped her chin, her mouth. He wanted that mouth. He missed her kisses, her smile, the laughter, their talks of the future. He studied her glassy eyes, searched for a glimmer of sanity, of recognition while the drug relaxed her. Early on, it was there, and at times he still believed he saw it.

During the worse times, when she flailed arms with a strength he couldn't believe she had in her, she begged him to end her misery, to send her ahead with their babies. Tonight, he had gotten the drug into her fast enough to avoid her pleas, and for that he was grateful.

He turned the sheets, grateful she was unaware of it. The thought of stripping them day after day, though, and of heating water, scrubbing them on the washboard, and wringing gallons from them before hanging them to dry utterly exhausted him.

There was a period when he had been able to calm her, assure her there would be more babies. And there had been. And every one of them had died.

After the first loss, she visited the grave under the maple tree on the hill morning and evening for three months. Only when she was certain another baby was on the way did she curtail the visits and concentrate her energies on preparing for the new arrival.

When she lost the second one, she dragged her weak body to the pair of tiny graves, slumped onto the ground, and leaned against the tree cooing and singing to her little ones.

When three crosses were lined up in a row as in the crucifixion, she dragged the rocking chair from the front porch to her personal Golgotha and sat for hours on end.

She stopped smiling, stopped taking care of herself like she had before. No combs in her hair each morning, no brush-strokes before bed. She lost weight, grew increasingly frail. Still, she attempted to keep up with her chores. She cooked, but her heart wasn't in it; the extra touches were gone. Looking back and with the weight of everything now on his shoulders, he wondered how she had managed at all.

And yet, she didn't give up the desire, the near-manic obsession, to have a child. When she told him of the fourth seed, he feigned happiness. By that point she wasn't much more than skin and bones, and he doubted her body could nourish the thing growing inside of her. He held onto hope, though, that this one would survive and that his wife would snap out of it.

Instead, the child was stillborn and the last thread upon which his wife clung snapped with a near-audible *plink* and she fell—no, plummeted—to a sort of alter-world into which he had no access.

She never saw the fourth grave, or the last cross he had carved. She hadn't stood beside him when he placed the tiny bundle in the pine box. He tried not to think about all the little boxes he had built.

The old doc had been fetched each time. His advice after the first two losses was to try for another child, but after the fourth had nearly killed the woman, he explained to the man that it was no longer an option.

The vibrant beauty who had worked tirelessly alongside him crumbled into a fetal-shaped lump onto what had been their wedding bed.

When they had first arrived, they were so completely entwined in each other that they didn't bother with neighbors who might exist beyond the world they were creating. Idealistic in their need only for one another and the offspring they would eventually have, they worked hard and they loved hard.

These days, he saw the folly of it and cursed the lack of an extra pair of hands while replacing a corral board, harvesting the fields, or repairing a busted wagon wheel. His wife had always run to his aid, no matter what chore of hers he now realized he had interrupted. He missed those hands, the help. He missed her touch.

At times, it crossed his mind to hire help for the household chores. Then again, he knew his wife would've been mortified for another woman to see the unkempt house—to say nothing of her own unhinged state—and he reached deep inside himself for more strength.

She had always taken the Good Book literally, and had kept things clean and tidy, had feathered their nest, had done everything she believed was expected of a good and godly woman.

The notion of pioneering had excited her—so much so, in

fact, that he had feared she would tire quickly of it when met with its realities.

While outfitting to join the wagon train, he had heard other men speak of discord, fear, and even outrage among their women. But, even in the weeks confined to their covered wagon while awaiting the departure date, his wife hadn't uttered a single concern. His chest had swelled with pride. There was something to be said for a wife who trusted you like that.

Maybe that was it. Maybe pride had prompted God to take him down a peg or two. He buried his face in his hands. *I'm all out of pegs, God. Now what?*

That evening, cutting up potatoes and throwing them in a pot, he wondered how much laudanum it would take to end it for both of them.

A commotion in the chicken coop yanked him away. He grabbed the .12 gauge on his way out, shot at and missed a coyote holding a hen in its mouth and loping toward a patch of woods. He had forgotten to latch the gate.

Peacock feathers shimmered in the dim light of dusk. He gathered them and tossed them onto the growing pile in the corner of the barn.

The harsh odor of scorched food hit him as he approached the porch. He bolted to the kitchen, grabbed the smoking stockpot with a rag, and flung it out the back door.

How could he have forgotten to add water? He was constantly hauling water, heating water—water for drinking, for coffee, for cooking; water for bathing, for laundry. Water was everything.

As he poked around for another stewpot, he cursed himself for wasting food.

The smokehouse, once full of cured pork hanging from hooks, now showed gaping holes like a boxer's grin. In the root cellar, burlap hammocks his wife had rigged to cradle potatoes and protect them from rot were fast emptying. In the past, shelves groaned with food preserved in jars she arranged in rows of color like the quilts she made. Now, the empty jars he returned to the shelves outnumbered full ones.

Finally, he achieved something akin to soup. It was late, and he breathed a sigh of relief that she hadn't started screeching. He filled a bowl, and grabbed a lantern on his way to the bedroom.

He walked in on his wife chopping away locks of her waist-long amber hair with her big sewing scissors.

He thrust the lantern and bowl onto the nightstand and grabbed for the scissors. She lunged at him, swung wide, and knocked over the lantern. The globe shattered, exploded as the embroidered scarf covering the stand burst into flames. She screamed, recoiled. He seized the pitcher of water from the washstand and doused the fire, leaving them in blackness.

He groped his way to the front room, lit another lantern, and hung it on a ceiling hook in the bedroom. She coughed as he scooped the soggy remains into the basin.

Their lives weren't much more than moments like this: fragments of silence and terror strung by turns along the tightrope that had become their existence.

And in this moment, there was nothing for him to do but finish the shearing.

The ends looked like the jagged teeth of a sawblade, but at least it brushed her shoulders. Much shorter, and she would've looked like a boy. He moved her sewing basket with its shears and long needles to her empty chair by the hearth, then dished up another bowl of soup.

As he fed her, he searched her face, searched for the woman who used to skillfully trim his hair on their front porch.

She worsened as the weeks passed. The old doc increased the

dosage of laudanum, which worked till it didn't. She waffled between a lifeless shell and a tornado-like frenzy when its effects wore off. The man struggled to stay ahead of the storm.

She begged him again to end her suffering, begged till her voice failed her, and her tormented eyes took up the plea.

While working the fields, he pushed himself in order to gain slivers of time, and during those slivers he ran to the house to administer more of the drug.

He considered tying her wrists to the bedposts for her own safety in case her fits came before his return, but panic gripped him and dark thoughts filled him with shock and despair.

A shiver ran down the back of his neck. What if he died before she did? What if he were kicked in the head by one of his mules, or a tree limb fell and struck him dead? How long before he and his wife would be found? His death might be quick from an accident, but hers while constrained? His stomach lurched at the thought.

Dosing laudanum was a game of chance, the stakes high, the house forever changing the rules. Despite his attempts to sedate her for the night, he was awakened often by her fits. After one battle that left his face looking as if he'd tangled with a badger, he held her down and forced laudanum into her, then cut her nails near the quick. This cut him to the quick, too, for she had always been mindful of her hands.

He was infuriated with himself. He stormed from the house, slamming the door. Glass shattered as something inside crashed to the floor. A part of him knew he should investigate, but he was too near done-in to heed it. Over the next week, he would feel a difference in the door, would execute an extra step to secure the latch, but his packed days would allow no time for a proper repair.

He leaned against the corral fence and stared into the darkness. He questioned himself, worried whether he, too, was about to snap. Did that mean the time had come to end it?

At length, he reckoned that if he could question whether he was finished, he had enough left in him to hold on—for now, anyway. He was aware of one thing, though: his timing must be precise—not too soon for her, not too late for him.

He returned to the bedroom and made a pallet on the floor—nearby if she needed tending, but far enough away from her assaults while he slept. What used to be a partnership of both friendship and passion had become a daily sentence of caregiving and loneliness.

Her pleas filled the cracks between comatose and hysteria. The more he heard them, the more commonplace they became, until he grew numb to them.

The old doc nodded when the man confided these things. Condolence filled his gaze, and he sent the man away with three bottles of laudanum. *Use as much as it takes,* he prescribed.

The meaning was not lost on the man.

He struggled, though, with how much to dispense. One bottle should do it for a small thing like his wife, but for a man of his size? Two, maybe more. The uncertainty of it bothered him, threatened to spoil his belief that they should die together.

He held her hands in one of his, and the pistol in his other, when she smiled at him.

Lettie? Are you come back?

She laughed. *I never left. Was only a wicked fever, though not as wicked as the one that took our junior boy.*

A tear slipped down her face toward her ear. Knowing she hated the sensation, he let go of her hand and brushed away the wet trail with a kerchief.

The gun went off. He jumped with the report, fumbled

through bedding and pawed the floor searching for the firearm. It had been a dream. Still, he bolted to the nightstand, jerked opened the drawer. The gun was where he'd left it. In the bed, his wife whimpered, then settled back into silence.

He returned to his pallet, willed his heart to stop pounding. If he mustered the courage to grant her plea, he would not send her ahead alone. If he dispatched her to the next world, he would be in the seat beside her for the journey—and by whatever means she had been sent away. If he couldn't face the method, he certainly couldn't use it on her. Speculation and rumors by meddlers were to be expected. He didn't care what they said about him, but he would make sure they had no grounds for sullying her good name. One thing was certain: he shouldn't be accused of cowardice by sparing himself.

If he were forced to choose the worst task in the long list of tasks added to his own as a result of his wife's undoing, it would be that of bathing her. He put it off for as long as possible.

Washing her breasts always prompted her to mumble *baby* and he knew deep inside her there still burned the spark of motherhood.

Although her dignity seemed intact when he cleaned her weak body after setting her on the chamber pot, she took his touching her while she was in their bed as a violation. She screamed for help till her voice grew hoarse. Her screams set off the peacocks and they echoed her until he thought that he, too, might crack under the shrill chaos and strain.

He chased flying arms through the air, attempted to pin them down. She bit. He wrestled her down, confined her, cleaned her most private areas as best he could. She clawed, leaving streaks like fence lines across his neck and reminding him that he had waited too long between clippings. She kicked, sending the washbasin across the bed, its water forming a spray that arced like a wave before dropping and soaking the sheets as the enamel pan banged and rattled across the floorboards.

When he had finished, and both had fallen limp and panting in an entangled heap of limbs and wet sheets, he felt as if he'd done the very thing she accused him of doing. Anger, bitterness surged through him. He clenched his teeth. His eyes stung as he fought back tears. He cursed, blew air, then dispensed an extra dose of laudanum.

He moved her naked body to the rocking chair where she bobbed forward and back, setting it into motion as she muttered *baby* repeatedly. He placed a fresh nightgown over her head and pulled her arms through the sleeves, then stripped the bedsheets and flung them toward the basin that had come to rest in a corner. An extra set was still flapping on the line outside, so he sandwiched her between quilts and waited.

When she was out, he went to the spare room to rummage the trunk for more bed linens. A pieced quilt top was folded to fit the opening. He removed it, studied the squares and rectangles of cloth that made up a repeating pattern. He recognized many of the patches—salvaged from dresses, aprons, and shirts she had sewn for their journey west. They triggered memories, emotions, and he wondered when he had become so sentimental. He blamed it on weariness. Maybe women were tired much of the time, which would explain their moods, their sensitive natures, even their need to gather and visit. He wondered if his wife missed fellowship with other women.

Next, he lifted stack after stack of baby clothes—layettes, she had called them—from the trunk and built towers on the floor around him, creating a fortress.

With calloused hands, he cradled the tiny gowns, caressed the delicate embroidered flowers on bonnet brims and crocheted scallops that edged soft flannel blankets. For the first time, he felt the extent of her investment. He felt the loss as she must have felt it. And for the first time in his adult life, he cried, and the crying seemed to him the end of his own sanity. But, when at last he stopped, he felt as if a pressure valve had been released. He would try to hold on for a while longer.

When he could no longer put off making a trip into town, he loaded the wagon, cutting the usual amount of vegetables by a third. He worried over the empty places in the larder, the dwindling supply. After a moment of deliberation, he gathered the tailfeathers, folding the burlap so the fixed eyes couldn't stare at him, and placed the bundle in the wagon bed with the rest of the harvest.

He hesitated, regarded the house.

What if her body quit her while he was gone? What good would the promise of supplies traded for the feathers be if he and his wife weren't around to use them? What if the house caught fire? The horror of fire haunted him constantly while he was away.

He secured the leads, jumped from the wagon.

For the second time that morning, he checked to see that nothing was left on the stove, that no dish towel was near enough to catch fire. He placed a palm on the cast-iron surface. Relieved that it had cooled considerably, he walked quietly to the bedroom door.

She looked peaceful, angelic.

He wasn't sure if he could follow through with his plan, or when. How could he when she was like this, when white faith reached out its hand? Yet, if he did it during one of her explosive fits, those crucial seconds between ending her life and taking his own would be torture. He questioned whether his soul would rise with hers, or plunge into damnation.

The proprietor stepped onto the loading dock as the man reined in the mules, nodded before going back inside. The man took it as a signal and grabbed the burlap bundle.

The painted woman startled him.

Rouged lips and kohled eyes emphasized lines on her face, and jewels about a creased neck glinted like broken glass. Her gown shimmered and its train rustled when she moved. A row of small, spiked plumes perched atop her hat like pins poked into a cushion for sewing. She looked like a peacock that had seen better days.

She asked after his wife. This startled him more than her appearance.

He murmured that she was still poorly. A weak little word that didn't scratch the surface, but one that reaped nods of sympathy and halted further questions.

The proprietor relieved him of the bundle and uncomfortable company by asking him to unload the other goods.

A few moments later, he averted his gaze as the painted woman slipped away down the alley, the bundle cradled in her arms.

Back home, he was unharnessing the mules when his wife screamed, that faint high pitch. The cocks echoed, instantly followed by a gunshot.

It had come from inside. He grabbed the .12 gauge and ran to the house, his heart slamming against his chest. Was there an intruder, or had she somehow retrieved the pistol and spared him the unspeakable job of ending her life?

The front door was open. He knew he had pulled it to, but with the latch thrown off, the wind might have jarred it loose. He snugged the stock into his shoulder and hooked a finger over the trigger as he crept to the bedroom.

She was staring at the floor where a peacock lay still, save for the twitching of a foot. Its claw scraped faintly against a floorboard before slowing, until at last it came to rest.

The pistol rested in her lap. He wondered how she had managed to retrieve it, let alone aim with such accuracy.

Slowly, he propped the rifle in a corner, approached her as he held her gaze. Did he detect a hint of recognition, or had the explosion jolted her into a sort of composed state? He took the gun from her and, just in case she understood, he nodded his approval. He scooped up the dead bird and carried it outside.

Had the screaming of the peacocks been setting off his wife's screaming, agitating her on a level he hadn't realized? They weren't her sole undoing, he knew that. But, what if the birds' shrill cries were suspending her over the edge, pinning her just beyond reach of sanity?

In the barnyard, the remaining two peacocks fought over a wormy ear of corn. Peahens emerged from the coop, likely expecting food from the man.

Upon seeing the harem, the cocks abandoned the tussle and set about wooing the hens. The males screamed and danced. The fixed eyes of their plumed tailfeathers stared at the man, taunted him, dared him. The hens strolled and studied, as if window shopping, until which time one would grant permission to the dominant male.

The man cut a wide berth, deposited the carcass in the barn, then stood inside the door and waited.

When the mating ritual was complete, he emerged and fired two shots. One by one, he lifted the carcasses and placed them in the barn with the first.

To kill a thing of beauty is not an easy thing.

Clenching the gun, he walked toward the house.

The loss of their children had caused his wife's initial undoing, and he wondered whether God himself struggled with taking His own children from the earth. He wondered whether God mourned the loss of the woman's devotion, steadfastness, faith—and whether He was a gracious God who might restore it.

She shivered, bed linens clutched to her breast, and looked questioningly at him.

His feather trade that day was enough to cover winter supplies, as well as seeds for planting come spring. The final harvest from the three carcasses would buy double again that credit. And, buying credit meant buying time.

He returned the gun to the drawer, picked up his wife's brush, and gently worried away the tangles of her hair.

Deborah Morgan's short story, "Tinsel Town," was a finalist for the Western Writers of America Spur Award in 2016. In 2013, she won WWA's Stirrup Award for her *Roundup* magazine article. Also an award-winning author in the mystery genre, Morgan grew up on a ranch in Oklahoma, and currently resides in Michigan.

★ ★ ★ ★ ★

The Well-Witcher's Daughter
by Charlotte Hinger

★ ★ ★ ★ ★

She had killed her mother. Her father told her so. That was the first thing she knew about herself. As soon as she learned what a mother was, she was overwhelmed with shame, the sheer terror of what she had done. Better she had been the one who had died during the birth, her father told her. She ushered in the hard times.

She lived in silence because her father didn't like it when she tried making sounds. She was born to bone-piercing cold because their home was an old wagon. When she was three years old, she learned for some people life was a lot better and they were warm too. Her father drove up to a soddy on a chilly evening at the start of spring thaw. She peeped out through the raggedy, ratty hole in the canvas and saw a light that was not the stars, not the sun, and remembered a few months earlier when she had been to just such a place and a woman there cried out when she saw her.

Maggie Cochran had scolded her father, snatched her from the wagon, wrapped her in a blanket and held her on her lap.

"Here, sweetheart, open wide. It's warm soup. Precious little wren. Would you like some milk too?"

Her father's face darkened.

"Cherry Ann's a dummy, Miz Cochran," he said. "Can't talk."

Surprised, Cherry Ann choked back a yelp, then clamped her lips tightly together, knowing he was right. She couldn't talk. Not really. Warbling like a lark, cooing like a dove or yelping like a coyote didn't count. So, she knew then she wasn't supposed to try. She was very good at figuring out what she was supposed to do.

"Teched in her head, she is. She's slow in other ways too."

"But she can walk," Maggie said. "She walks just fine."

"Not slow in every way. Just slow in some ways."

"But the wee wren has such a hard life, just traveling with you. No real home. No mother, or kith or kin. Seems like she's never really had a chance. Isn't there someone you could leave her with?"

Cherry Ann's heart fluttered. Her cheek was pressed against the woman's breast and she wanted this kind warm lady to say "I'll keep her. She can come live with me."

"No, ma'am, there's not. Besides, I love the little wild thing. Her mother died birthing her, and it would be like tearing my own heart out to give her up too. Besides, she can barely stand to be apart from me. She's a clinger."

Again, Cherry Ann knew what she was supposed to do. She wiggled down from the woman's lap, ran to her father, and clung to his leg. He reached down, scooped her up, and kissed the top of her head.

"Well, I'll swan," Maggie Cochran said.

Cherry Ann got to eat all she wanted that evening while her father talked with Eldon Cochran about the well he would be witching. She knew her father was special. 'Twas said he had the gift.

Traveling the plains of Western Kansas, he went from soddy to soddy, bringing water. Blessed water. When they drove up to a place in their old wagon, people ran out to greet them. They fed their mules. Fed them too, and apologized for not being able to offer fancier. They fussed over her, pinched her cheeks.

Cherry Ann knew that during the two weeks it took them to dig a well, she would be warm and have enough to eat, even if there were only men around. Usually she would get to sleep inside a soddy because she'd noticed that people just living in little sheds or wagons like theirs didn't ask her father to find water.

There would be a stove and fire. She checked for hay cats or buffalo chips the moment she stepped inside a place. Only a quick flush on her cheeks betrayed her gleeful relief when she spied an abundant pile of fuel.

Too little to dig and too young to cook, she was free. She could sit inside the soddy or in the sun and make cloud pictures. She'd learned that folks didn't mind if she grabbed a blanket and wrapped it around her. Even her father didn't mind that.

Great huge blankets made from buffalo hides were best. There were more likely to be these gigantic coverings in the houses where there were just men around. She learned to snuggle deep with the woolly skin next to her body. The great weight kept her safe and warm. Then she slept. She could not sleep well in the wagon because she was always so miserably cold.

Often in houses where there was a woman, the blankets would be thin and they would not be enough to keep her warm. But they were beautiful. There were colors and shapes and she'd noticed that some of them were the same colors as the flowers she saw when they crossed the plains.

Other times the colors were as blue as the sky or as yellow as the sun and in her head, she began to change these shapes and colors on her own and whisk them in and out and back and forth. She could see them, bright and perfect. She could not kill a buffalo. She could not get the biggest and best prize for herself, but she could see herself making these little blocks.

Sometimes when she had her sleep out and had eaten enough food so she wasn't distracted by the constant sharp pain in her belly, she would wander about in the houses. She picked up things, turned over dishes to see the marks there, gazed at the pictures on the walls, ran her fingers over book covers. She loved staying in houses, even when there were only men hooting and braying like donkeys at night.

"Don't act like some dog looking to be kicked," her father said. "When we're at folks' homes show some affection for the father that loves you and kept you—murdering little half-wit that you are—when you should be living in the hills with the wolves."

So even when he pulled out his cards and she could see his crafty eyes sizing up the game ahead, she would sidle up to him and lift her arms as though she couldn't bear to sleep without the evening ritual. He would put down his bottle and press his whiskey lips to her cheek and always, always, the men grew quiet and would delicately look away from the loving father burdened with the damaged daughter.

Curses, sudden hard silences, bottles thrown across the room, chairs crashing to the floor, jangling sounds kept her from sleeping well. When she awoke in the night, she'd learned when there was a pile of coins in front of her father, he would be in a very good mood the next day and when there was not, it would go hard with her. There was no way for her to change that.

It was all in the cards.

Every time they passed close to the Cochrans, a feeling for which she had no name made Cherry Ann's body tremble with anticipation at seeing Maggie, eating her good bread, basking in her warmth.

The next time they were back at the Cochrans, her father was angry. She knew this by the tone of his voice and was surprised that others didn't. Other men's voices grew loud and clapped like thunder, but her father's became dangerously soft. She understood what that would mean for her. She began to sway back and forth and pressed her hands over her ears to block out their words.

"Stop that, both of you," Maggie snapped. "You're scaring the little wren half to death. Look at her now. She can't stop crying. She doesn't understand a thing that's going on here. The poor child."

"Stay out of this, Maggie," Eldon said. "He promised a good well and it's dry as a bone just a scant month later. He swore he had the gift. Said there was no need for me to fetch Injun Tom. Said he could do it just as good. Well, he can't."

"Didn't swear to no las'ing results," her father said. "Said I had the gift, and I do. Said I'd find water and I did. Didn't promise it would las' forever."

"Paid you plenty. Should have lasted longer than a month."

"Ah, mister, now that's where you're wrong, dead wrong. You scarcely paid me enough to spit twenty yards, let alone secure las'ing moisture."

Eldon Cochran flushed, and Cherry Ann knew her father had him. He would move in for the kill.

"Times have been hard," Cochran said, looking away, his eyes glazed with shame. "I was going to pay you the balance, come spring."

"I've heard words like this before. Too many times," said her father, with great dignity. "Far too many times."

"It's true. You know I pay my debts."

"Back where you came from, maybe, but money comes hard out here, mister. Damn hard. And the land has a way of changing what people think is right and true."

Maggie Cochran gave a little cry, and picked up Cherry Ann. "You're upsetting the wee one. I'll not have her hear another word." She rushed outside.

But Cherry Ann knew who was the most upset of all and her tears blended with those of Maggie Cochran as she paced back and forth in the wild wind.

"Used to be he would walk a mile to pay a man a penny," Maggie said. "It's killing him not to be able to pay his debts. Shh, now. Don't cry, little wren. Don't cry. Everything's going to be all right."

Easing Cherry Ann to the ground, Maggie sat slump-shouldered on a washtub and stared at the grass dipping and waving in the wind.

Knowing Maggie's love of quilts and patterns, her sense of order, Cherry Ann knelt down in the dust and picked up a stick and quickly drew out squares. She would have snatched the sun and the flowers and poked in a bit of blue sky if she could have, but the design would have to do. She could not bring color, but she could make order.

The woman, looked, saw, then gasped. "Child, that's the Ohio Star you've drawn. God in heaven. A little daft thing, and you knew to draw the star. Ohio. We're going back to Ohio. It's a sign from God. A sign. Maybe we'll be going home soon."

Awed, she looked at Cherry Ann. "Or maybe it means I'll have a child of my own someday, or maybe just learn to live with the wind and my husband so changed that I hardly know he's the same man. But it's a sign." Then she wiped her eyes and stared hard at the star Cherry Ann had drawn. "Or, child, maybe you're not as daft as your father would have us believe."

Her father stomped out, shaking his fist at Eldon Cochran, and shoved her into the wagon, while Maggie watched in anguished silence. After the soddy faded from sight, Cherry Ann crawled out to join her father on the seat.

She tugged on his sleeve, tearfully making human sounds like Maggie Cochran. She had been practicing. He had always just laughed at her little bird chirps as they rode along, so she was stunned when she made her new sounds—words like Maggie used—and her father hit her so hard she nearly fell off the seat. But she worked it out that he didn't want to lose folks' pity for an old man trying to do right by his addled daughter.

When she was nine years old, her father stopped their wagon on a creek bank and led the horses down into the water. She picked up a broken willow branch that looked just like the one he carried in the wagon. She had watched him walk back and forth across a homesteader's acreage tightly clutching the prongs in his hands with the stem pointed skyward.

As she walked along the bank, the stem suddenly twisted in her hand and pointed toward the ground. She could not stop it. Amazed she tried it again and once again the branch twisted.

There was a soft breeze. Cottonwood leaves sparkled silver and green and the grass was sweet and moist. She didn't hear her father come up behind her. When he spoke, she jumped like a rabbit and dropped the stick.

"Pick it up."

She bent and quickly grabbed the stick and offered it to her father.

"No, I want to see something." His voice trembled. "Now hold these two prongs hard and point the tail of the Y toward the sky."

She did, and as before, the branch twisted violently in her hands. She could not stop it.

"God in heaven," said her father. "You have the gift. The gift. No faking, no putting on like you do, you actually have the gift." Then he picked her up and swung her around. "We're going to be rich, Cherry Ann. Rich. You have the gift for real. Give me that stick."

"No."

Stunned, he studied her hard.

"No," she said again, with the voice of her beloved Maggie.

The muscles in his jaw worked. She froze. Stood helplessly as his hand drew back.

She woke later still clutching the willow twig. She wobbled to the bank, knelt over the muddy water, and vomited.

But her father let her keep the stick.

She had a lot more food after that. For the first time in her life, she felt people look at her with respect. With awe, even. Her father had been quick to spread the word.

"She takes after her old man, she does. She has the gift, she does." And those who knew of his devotion to his little daughter all agreed the Lord moved in mysterious ways and it was a fair and right ending to the tragic loss of his wife and the burden he had carried afterward.

Cherry Ann was so accurate that they were no more summoned to one place, than they would be called to the next. She no longer had the luxury of sleeping long days in piles of scented quilts while they waited to be sure the well was going to come in. Everyone simply took it for granted it would, and her father did not have to stay to dig.

She saw Maggie Cochran from time to time because the Cochran homestead lay in the center of the territory they covered. Her father loved lording it over the luckless, childless couple when Cherry Ann witched their neighbors a new well in exchange for occasional room and board. Even wells witched by Injun Tom on the Cochran's land had gone dry in a year or so and there were now three dry boarded-up holes in the tall grass around their soddy.

As she bounced along on the wagon seat, Cherry Ann said Maggie's cooing words in her mind and heart and when her father left her to play his wicked cards, she said them with her tongue too.

Once, after she had turned ten and they stopped at the Cochrans for the night, she reached for the quilt block Maggie was piecing. Her hands trembled, but she reached for the needle also. Cherry Ann felt the tension in the air, her father's fury holding her back. Silently, Maggie looked hard at her father, and blood rushed to her hot face as she handed the threaded needle to Cherry Ann.

"This is the nine-patch child. It's a simple pattern and I think you can do this."

She ignored the scowling man watching darkly from the corner of the room.

"Let me show you, darling. Hold the needle like so and take tiny little stitches. Yes, like so, exactly like that."

A black dark feeling coursed through Cherry Ann, robbing her of the pleasure of finally getting to hold the little blocks. For the past year now, she had begun to realize how much money they got when she witched a well. A wealth of coins passed through her father's hands. She knew now what money was for and what it would buy, and she realized they should be rich. She should have all the fabrics she wanted. It was she who witched the wells. Brought them honor.

Now her father no longer looked for a small game at a soddy. The minute a homesteader paid them, he would head for town and a saloon.

There were women there too.

"There's old Cletus," they trilled. "We've missed you, honey." And one after another, "Come see me, honey."

He always pulled Cherry Ann inside and the women would set her on a bar and sometimes give her a bath. She hated the heavy cloying smell of their rooms. They would wash her black hair and comb it and put a little rouge on her cheeks and smudge a little color on her lids and then drape her with soft pretty red cloth.

She knew better than to spit at them or bite them, but her shame ran so deep she would rather lie in the smelly wagon than feel their hands petting her, holding cloth up against her skin.

"She'll be a raving beauty someday."

"Those cheeks, those eyes. A touch of Injun you think?"

"More like Spanish. A little French, maybe."

"She'll be worth a mint. Too bad she can't talk."

"To most men's thinking, she be worth more mute."

She felt like a mule being checked for value. She hated the tinkling jangling music and felt like vomiting or running away. She hated having her face turned in their hands, their hot soft hands examining her like she was merchandise setting on a shelf.

But the saloons were warm, blessedly warm, and when night came and the men came into the saloon, the women would leave her alone and put on their red and black shiny dresses. Then Cherry Ann would creep into a corner with her needle and thread and her little blocks and try to make sense of the world.

"Come see me, honey. Come see me, honey," she murmured, her voice trembling with agitation, her hands flighty and unsure, as she took the squares apart, then put them back together, over and over, until she settled down and the hawk stopped swooping down to take her little wren heart.

Spring was especially lovely when she turned thirteen. Rain brought a reprieve. Giddy with pleasure, she felt the sun on her face as she sat on the seat beside her father and watched the prairie green up day after day.

He was pleased with her. She had witched a fine well for a Swedish family and he knew they would tell their neighbors. Swedes were prosperous and only trusted words from their own kind. She liked the Swedish women with their clean fine-smelling homes and their good bread.

They stopped at the Lundstroms. Invited to spend the night, she wistfully fingered the quilts stacked against the wall. She helped with the dishes, smiled at the womenfolk, then settled into her corner and listened.

The next day after she had witched the well, when they collected their money, her father headed to town.

"Cletus, come see us, honey. We've missed you. We were beginning to think you'd forgotten us."

Cherry Ann followed him into the saloon, because he would not allow her to stay by herself in the wagon.

"Your daughter, how she's grown. A little beauty now, isn't she?"

The very air in the room changed that night. She could feel her father's fury as he lost game after game.

"*No*," she mourned silently, "*no, no, no*," as she realized he had gambled away the fine mules that pulled their wagon. "*We won't have a way to get from farm to farm. It's all we have, all we have.*" She pulled the blanket tighter around her and huddled in the corner.

"It's all I have," her father said. "All."

Cherry Ann had watched, listened, surprised that she, a dummy, had seen what her father could not. They had waited for him. This was planned. She had felt a current there. Earlier, she had heard the women talking, whispering.

"It's not all you have," said the dealer. "Not all."

Her father looked at him stupidly. "The shirt off my back, maybe. A few pots and pans."

"You have a girl child. A virgin."

Her father gasped, then his eyes narrowed. "What kind of man do you think I am?"

"We know what kind of man you are."

"You think I would sell my own daughter?"

"Oh, we think you would sell your own mother. Selling your daughter will come plenty easy enough to the likes of you."

Daddy, daddy, daddy, she thought, her little heart nearly leaping out her body. *Don't, don't, don't let these evil people come near me. Don't let them touch me.*

"How much?"

"One thousand dollars."

"For her? You must be daft. She has the gift. She would be worth ten times that price even if she was a broken-down old hag."

"Five thousand."

"It's my daughter," he said haughtily, "My own flesh and blood."

"Then it's jail for you. You owe money all up and down the line."

Her father stood abruptly and with a bellow crossed to her corner and yanked her to her feet.

"Take her then, you lying hordes of whores and thieves."

Terrified, Cherry Ann wriggled free and raced out the door.

She ran behind the buildings toward the open prairie, toward the Cochrans, toward the only warmth she had ever known.

She ran gasping up to their soddy, then realized she could not go inside. She had no words for what was going to happen to her. This family would accept any explanation her father offered for his child's wild flight.

With a groan, Cherry Ann ran to the far side of the useless well her father had witched and fell sobbing onto the grass, knowing he would guess she would turn to Maggie. For what her father lacked in a true gift for well-witching, he made up for in knowing persons' hearts.

Clutching her stick, she laid there, numb with shame.

"Come see me, honey," she murmured. "Come see me, honey."

She sensed her father slipping through the tall grass, and knew he was moving quietly because he was worried about explaining to the Cochrans why his daughter would be hiding in the dead of night.

Paralyzed with terror, she clutched her stick, knowing her life was ending, seeing herself in black and red silk. But perhaps this was a fitting end after all for a dummy who had killed her own mother.

"Come see me, honey," she said in Maggie Cochran's voice, the only loving voice she knew, and words that had always quieted her little wren heart. "Come see me, honey."

Her father stopped. He held his breath. Then edged forward.

"Maggie? Maggie Cochran?" His voice trembled with bewildered anticipation, then bellowed with surprise as he fell in the deep useless dry well he had witched.

There was no sound from the well. Clutching the willow stick, Cherry Ann peered over the edge. She backed away in horror and then ran for the soddy.

"Come. See," she stammered when Maggie opened the door. She pulled on the woman and led her to the dry hole.

"Oh my God." Maggie quickly pressed Cherry Ann's face against her body. "Don't look, honey. Don't look."

"And the Lord loosed her tongue that very night," Maggie told the astonished members of her quilting circle. "It was a miracle. The child spoke the words herself trying to get help for her poor father that had nourished her and cared for her all these years. Tears in her eyes, I tell you, and she said 'come see.' It's the Lord's truth. The child spoke."

"What's to become of her now?" asked old Mrs. Tompkins. She was one of many who had quickly volunteered to keep Cherry Ann and her witching rod. She still needed looking after, they all reasoned. And gifts were gifts. They were meant to be shared. Plenty of scripture backed them up on that.

"She'll stay with us," Maggie said quietly.

After the funeral, Maggie started teaching Cherry Ann to quilt. But coaxing her to give up the willow stick was like weaning a baby. The child kept looking for it like it could keep her safe. Finally, the day came when Maggie could whisk the stick away and put it in the toolshed. Worried that witching was the devil's doing, she wanted to burn the damned thing. But the forked willow stub was the child's only possession that had belonged to her father.

Then a miracle helped Cherry Ann lose her broodiness. There were finally babies. Three in all. She was too busy helping with all the chores to miss her willow stick.

When Cherry Ann was seventeen a young man came courting. A gentle loving man who played the fiddle. There was a rightness between them. Even though this daughter would be moving away, Maggie now had three little towheads to keep her company.

It was hard times. The second year of a drought. But happily, the young man owned a mercantile store in another county. The giddy young couple wouldn't be trying to scrabble a living out of the unyielding earth. There was dryness all around. Just one good well could save a homestead. Keep the bankers from circling like buzzards. Keep a man going until the rains started again. And the Cochrans were in peril again after four years of blessed relief.

Maggie pushed her troubles aside and presented the bride with one of her perfect quilts. "For you, my darling. For all the blessings you brought to us."

Cherry Ann could not hold back her tears. She threw her arms around Maggie. "You're the one who gave everything to me. Everything. And I have one last gift for you. I found this in the shed when I was packing. My old willow stick. You've never liked it. But before I let you throw it away, let's see if it still works. Just one last time."

She watched Maggie carefully for some trace of hope, but belief didn't matter none. Belief had nothing to do with it. Before Maggie could stop her, Cherry Ann began to pace. The stick trembled. The fork vibrated, and the prong darted down to living water.

Faith didn't matter. Digging did.

"Here. Here. You'll see."

She smiled at Maggie's puzzlement and handed the stick back knowing Maggie would bury it deep somewhere. It didn't matter. Any old willow stick would do. The power was in her blood. Besides, bad memories were attached to that stick. She shuddered. She was shut of that business now. "Like I said, Maggie, this was the last time. Just funning around. Never again."

The two women clasped hands and laughed at the silly ritual. But Cherry Ann knew the Cochrans would drill now even if they thought it was hopeless. "Doesn't make sense to put more dry holes in our dirt," they'd say.

But she knew they would try again. They couldn't help themselves when a well-witcher said it was the right spot. Even if the witcher had been as beloved as a daughter.

"Wouldn't hurt none to try," they'd tell themselves.

Cherry Ann smiled. There would be water.

Charlotte Hinger is a multi-award-winning novelist and Kansas historian. Five Star published her novel, *The Healer's Daughter*, in March 2019. The book is set in Nicodemus, Kansas, the legendary first black settlement on the Great Plains. *Kirkus Reviews* selected *Hidden Heritage* (Poisoned Pen Press), the third book in her Lottie Albright mystery series, as one of the best mysteries and one of the best fiction books of 2013.

★ ★ ★ ★ ★

THE HARROWS
BY LARRY D. SWEAZY

★ ★ ★ ★ ★

1.
ELIZA'S RETURN

May 1865

There is a heartening that I can hardly put into words as the land transforms itself from mystery to familiar. My body secretly relaxes and falls into a comfortable rhythm with the rise and fall of a known hill or a recognizable oak tree; arms wide open, reaching out with a welcoming sigh. Wind off the mountain is an old friend, too. The moment of recognition is framed in perfection all the way down to the ray of light piercing the untested forest canopy. I imagined and hoped for this sight under the darkness of a thousand uncertain nights; in the throes of rage and weakness, at my best moment and at my worst, covered in blood, surrounded by death, fighting for life, searching for a sign of any kind of lightness and joy at all. I am tempted to pinch myself to see if I am awake. *If I am truly home.*

The air, too, is tainted with memories of all of the seasons. With it being late spring, the season of hope and renewal is my most favorite. I can almost conjure an ounce of faith, truly believe that bodies and spirits can actually be restored, wounds healed, and the past laid to rest. The springs of my youth were idyllic, perfect in every way, until the shadow of man's hate turned to darkness, and the greed of war blew everything I loved and cherished to the four corners of this broken nation. My father and brothers marched off long before I did; they took up arms while I was left to mend the wounds of their battles. I've had the healing touch since I was but a girl. I knew how to

79

set a broken goldfinch's wing before I could explain why it needed done. Seeds I planted sprouted in dirt where nothing else would grow. Stitches in skin I sewed barely left a mark. All of which seemed as natural as breathing to me and my family. I come from a long line of healers; the women in my history have always wrapped the men in their lives with linen and love, set their bones just as easy as we've captured their hearts. Those skills served my days and fortified my nights. We all longed for the end of the war, for the blood to stop flowing. When it came, I was as surprised as anyone else that any of us were left standing.

The spring beauties are past their prime since they are one of the first flowers to rise up from the ground after a long winter's sleep, but Solomon's seal, fragrant as any perfume I have had the pleasure to smell, hovers along the hillside in clumps that remind me of small villages; white flags surrendering over every house. I have never considered abundant beauty in defeat until now. There are other flowers to be noticed by my beleaguered eyes as I travel forth; three different kinds of trillium, yellow violets, and a striped trout lily here and there if I look close enough. They all litter the floor of the thick woods along the road, reaching for the sun, aching for warmth and the touch of a bee's wing. And this is where the twain meets, my return home and my fear of it; anxiousness and dread roiled together just under my thinned and burgeoning skin. The land before me looks unscarred, but I know the closer to my destination that I travel, it will not be. I have heard tell in my three years of duty of more than one bloody battle fought on the soil of my family's legacy. I fear there is nothing left of my former life.

I cannot force myself to relax on the buckboard seat. Instead I pull forward to the edge, dressed in my tattered scarlet travel clothes, carpetbag at my feet, pressed against the back of my calves, pining to see around the next bend. Thankfully, my driver, a Mister Paxton Byles, from Greeneville, has remained quiet in our travels. He is as uninterested in my company as I am his. I hold no fervent desire to discuss my departure from Charleston, my previous experiences, or my views held of the occupation that I have so recently departed. He is aware of my destination, of my good name, and the assurance that I can pay a decent fare for my transport. There is no other requirement of our venture. I have never been much for small talk, especially with strangers. The less I know of Mister Byles, the better, and the less he knows about me and the future of my endeavors, the better off he is. His eyes and ears do not appear to be able to bear one more tale of sadness and defeat.

The bed of the lorry holds a load of empty gunny sacks, bundled and stacked waist high. It is a light load, a slight demand on the efforts of the two mules that pull us toward our mutual destinations. His, I was told in Charleston, was the mill at Fortner's Creek, though I had to wonder why with it being planting season, instead of the harvest. I do have to restrain the question, but I find the purpose of the load odd and unknowable. The gunny sacks are made of old burlap, the stenciling faded so deep that I cannot make out any of the words. None of the bags are the same, which seems more of a curiosity, but only because I occupy myself with the thought, fearing what I will encounter up the road.

The sight of the spring beauties and the trillium pain my heart in a way in which I am not prepared. They are too fragile, too untouched; I envy their short life more than my own. I know their season is brief, their days under the sun numbered and in decline. The blooms signal their death, their return to the dirt. In all of their glory, I grieve for the tiny flowers, too, as much as everything else. It is impossible to look away from melancholy and death. My blood is tainted with a gray affliction just as my touch is gifted to heal.

"I'll be getting off right around the bend, Mister Byles," I say.

He doesn't respond right away. His eyes are fixed forward, burned into the space that separates the mules. "I suppose you will." He glances over to me then, looks me in the eye, then to the bump in my belly that I've tried so hard to conceal. "You best prepare yourself. There's not much left."

"I've heard, but thank you just the same."

Mister Byles looks away then, focuses his attention back on the mules, starts to rein them in and slow their pace. "Don't expect you need any surprises in your condition."

The words pierce my ears like the sting of a hornet. *In your condition.* I am embarrassed, ashamed. There is no hiding the coming of another life no matter how hard I try to deny that it is true.

2.
HARROW HOUSE

I stand on the side of the road and bid Mister Byles adieu. My carpetbag sits at my feet, and my pride and worth is lost to the wind. He offered no explanation of his load and had barely said goodbye. I suppose I should get accustomed to such treatment, even though he knows nothing of why I travel alone, or of the origin of my presupposed condition.

There is no one to greet me. I have not sent word of my impending arrival. The lane that leads up to Harrow House looks just as I remember it: Lined with ancient oak trees, their vibrant and healthy arms reaching upward, adorned with moss that looks like dyed sheets, shredded green by wind and time. The ground is carpeted with spring beauties, and the moisture of the new season smells fresh and clean; fragrant with possibility instead of the reality of dread from the past winter. Once upon a time, I wove a crown of flowers and pretended that I was a fairy princess among giants in the very place that I stand. Oak trees acted as ogres and I was adorned with special powers because I was the only girl in my family. I was just a child then, before William Thrombo tried to kiss me under the shelter of deep leaves in a pouring rainstorm, before the reality of my age caught up with me, and I was forced to watch my three brothers walk up this very lane for a waiting company of soldiers. I can still hear them marching off, each foot in unison with the other, each sole falling to the ground echoing the solemn drumbeat of war.

I have to gird myself for more sad news as I walk forward, toward home, toward Harrow House. I do my best to blink away tears that are seeded by the pain of the past and the presence of the future. I cannot see the house. It sits at the crest of a hill, just past a slight lean in the road, overlooking the creek that has run aside our house and lives since the beginning of time. The sound of running water is a comfort that I have longed for on the loneliest nights of my absence.

I square my shoulders, breathe deep, and force my feet to carry me the rest of the way up the lane. The truth is, I have nowhere else to go. I can only hope that there is someone waiting for me in the place of my birth, that a roof still stands to cover us from the inclement weather and the storms that are sure to come.

No one is truly relieved that the war is over. There is a painful healing to come. Scars to bind and toughen up. It will take years to rebuild what has been destroyed. Anger and rage still salt the wounds of the victors, who will surely gloat with nothing more than their mere presence. We are now a union of one nation once again, though I do not believe that for a minute, and no one else that I know, especially those who served in some capacity of the cause, believes it either. We are shattered and lost, and no amount of peace-talking rhetoric can force all of the broken pieces back together. Only time can do that, and I am not certain that such a thing is possible. I have seen broken things mended with great attempt, and they are never the same again.

I quicken my pace, certain of the knowledge of the house that waits just at the bend. I pray it into existence, have cherished the memory of it since my departure. It is all I can do not to collapse when at last I lay my eyes upon the very place that kept me safe and warm for most all of my life. There is hardly anything I recognize that still stands.

I stop, close my eyes, and do my best to will every nail, every joist, rafter, and shingle back to its original place. When I open my eyes, I see nothing but a ruin: three red brick chimneys jutting into the air, marred by soot and ash, all blurred by the touch of tears. Blackened beams have crashed through the floor, then burned away, leaving piles of dust. Posts that once held up the veranda are weak and coated by the remains of fire. There is no second floor, no roof, no windows. Only the ghost in my mind of what once was. The entire house has been destroyed. There can be no repair. Reconstruction is beyond consideration. That would take more money than I can ever consider stumbling across. I only have a few coins in my purse. I'm not even sure how I am going to eat dinner, much less provide a roof over my head now that I see the truth of what I have been told. My heart sinks into a deep, irretrievable pit. I shiver even though it is a luscious, warm spring day.

I can hardly begin to consider the loss of the contents inside the house, of all of the possessions accumulated over a lifetime by my family. All that came before me and after is lost to the touch of a flame. And for what? How much blood and treasury was spent to destroy the dreams of those who wanted nothing to do with a war in the first place? Even the victors must face their own ounce of destruction upon returning from the battlefield. Sadness falls over my entire body like it has been attacked by an incurable sickness.

I can hardly see forward as my vision is blurred so severely by salty tears. The world is warped, foggy, fragile, water-filled, and to be honest, what hope I had stashed away is forsaken; gone in the moment of one long breath. I have lost my home, my center, the place that begged me to return in my dreams and waking moments. *What is there in this world for me now?*

Even filtered through my tears, I see movement, the image of a man coming toward me. He limps, looks familiar, but distant, like the memory of someone I once knew. I wipe my eyes clear, and before me, walking toward me with a look of great surprise, is my middle brother, Titus. Titus Milan Harrow. Two years older than I, and a survivor of war. I cannot believe he is here, before me, alive, crying at the sight of me just as I am him.

But he is not whole, not untouched by the ravages of conflict any more than I am. I can see that right away. The limp is not a limp. It is the walk of a man who only has one leg. He stands with the aid of a crutch carved from a hickory tree. He stops thirty feet from me and clears his eyes, just as I do my own. He can't believe I am alive. He must wonder if I am real in my godforsaken state. He must see in me what everyone else sees: a wisp of what I once was, changed like a dead tree facing north, spindly and gray, no longer reaching for the burn of the sun. Icarus lies at my feet, dead in a heap; the cautionary tale reverberates in my mind with warning and gladness.

3.
TITUS'S GARDEN

We have never been a family who greets each other with physical contact, with a warm embrace, but the aftermath of war changes a person's restrictions just as it changes the face of a nation. Titus and I collapse into each other and hold on for fear of falling off the earth. He smells of woodsmoke and sweat. I wonder if he is able to toil at will, or if the joy of work has been taken from him, too. Titus always worked harder than the rest of us. He had to prove himself being the middle son. It was easy to get lost between Clendon's beauty and Emerson's God-given talents. Emerson could mend anything that was broken, including the hearts of half of the girls in the county. Clendon glowed even when he slept, especially when he slept. My brothers have always been like Greek gods to me.

Titus pulls back and looks at me. I can see the wear of pain and loss on his face; his skin is tight over his jaw, and black whiskers struggle to grow. He reminds me of a fallow field in the winter, the stubbles touched lightly by an unexpected snow.

"I feared you were dead, sister," Titus whispers. He holds both of my shoulders with his hands—hands that still bear heavy calluses—but remain tender in their touch.

"And I you."

"You heard of Clendon's brave death at Chancellorsville?"

"Regrettably so," I say. My gaze falls to the ground as Titus allows both of his hands to fall to his side. One, the right, automatically steadies the crutch as he shifts his weight. I think he feared I would collapse if I did not already know of Clendon's fate. "A letter of Mother's found me in Atlanta, three months past the news. It nearly took my feet from under me."

"You two were very close," he says.

"I love all of my brothers."

Titus stares at me, forces a smile, then looks grimly to the remains of the house. "There's not much left. Mother tried to put the fire out. But that was her undoing. She should have let it burn."

It is my turn to whisper. "She is dead?"

Titus shakes his head. "She only wishes so. She suffers from the burns on her hands and on the skin of half her body. Infections come and go doing their best to force her under the ground, but she resists. She is waiting for Father to walk up the lane. And, you, of course. She missed you the most."

I can hardly stand the thought of being my mother's favorite, but I know what Titus says is true. My mother, Cleda Dawnitide Farrell Harrow, is a headstrong woman, thick with opinions that live on the tip of her quick tongue. It has been said that she and I are just alike. And I suppose we are, which has always presented itself as the friction between us that has lit a thousand flares, as well as provided the grease that complements us in our unified efforts. I smile at the thought of our battles. They would shoo the boys from the kitchen, causing them to return on tepid feet, as if all the carpets in the house were made of brittle and combustible fibers. Mother and I, of course, would be long past the eruption, and most likely be in the middle of consideration for the design of my latest dress or bonnet.

"I am happy that she survives," I say.

Titus looks at me, takes me in just as I took him in. I did not know that he had lost a leg, and he, of course, knows nothing of my condition.

"You surprise me, Eliza," he says.

"And why is that?"

"I thought your heart only belonged to William Thrombo."

It takes all I have not to pepper him with daggers from both eyes. Titus is the last person I wish to discuss my loves and losses with. But he has always been bold that way, saying what no one else would to me—out of earshot of Mother, of course. Along with his work ethic, his boldness was how he competed against his brothers for my attention, even when it brought a rage upon him.

"We will have a lot to talk about once I get settled," I finally say.

"Yes, I suppose we will." Titus turns away from me, and starts to make his way up the lane, one hop and one crutch at a time. "I was about to pick some radishes from the garden when I saw you. Are you coming with me?" he asks, over his shoulder.

It would be just like Titus not to offer to throw my bag over his back. I would have insisted on carrying it myself anyway. But the offer would have been nice. The warmth of our embrace has faded quickly, and it is the first realization that I have arrived, at last, to my one and only home.

4.
ALL MY FALLEN LEAVES

Only one shanty stands beyond the remains of Harrow House. The rest of them have burned to the ground. As I look out over the rise, over what once was a wide vista of cotton fields covering everything in sight—flowering, then offering an abundance of fabric to the world; spun, woven, mended, all burned now as fuel for a former rage—I am saddened all over again by the loss of what once was. All that remains is my broken memory. Now, the perennial plants of cotton rise to maturity, offering praise and hope. The fields have grown amuck, unattended for a matter of years. Experienced hands have fled to the north. The shot at Sumter was an alarm bell, awakening the living and dead, offering them the chance to run if they so chose. Father was early in his recognition that the cause would fail. Keeping human labor always troubled his converted Methodist heart, but he had inherited the land, the house, and the sins of his father. War offered him the opportunity to break the chain. The separation from the past cost him his life and the future fortune his heirs may have received. Perhaps there is luck in that. It is too early to tell. My heart breaks at just the thought of it.

"Mother will not leave the shack," Titus says. "She fears the light, and the gaze of judgmental eyes upon her discolored skin."

"It is all she has," I say.

Titus holds a bunch of radishes and bib lettuce. It is our dinner. That, and what remains of an unfortunate rabbit who wandered into Titus's bead before my arrival. Sustenance is no longer an immediate concern, and for that I am glad.

My words cause a look of confusion to cross Titus's weathered face. His nose has always been hooked and his eyes are a little closer together than they should be. Daguerreotypes suggest he favors the Farrells, Mother's side of the family. The resemblance and severity of his permanent expression has always made it easy for Titus to be misunderstood. He looks perpetually angry, enraged at the world for all that has occurred in his short lifetime. It is no wonder that he favors rage, but I wish he would turn that gaze to those who deserve it.

"You know how people are," he says.

My body reacts. My chin drops toward the ground in acknowledgment. But I say nothing. Titus's gaze falls again to pry at the unusual growth in my belly. I offer him no explanation, even though one must come eventually. I cannot keep the condition a secret much longer, but the ground under my feet is soft and unsure. I am yet to fully acknowledge the life that grows under my skin as my own; lest I say it was not of my doing. My body was another landscape in the war to be plundered and pillaged.

"You should tell her I am here," I say. "I don't want to startle her."

"You should prepare yourself."

"One must always be prepared."

"Her words."

"They follow me wherever I go."

"It is your choice, then." Titus lowers his head, walks to the shack, and deposits the vegetables in a stained wicker basket that stands next to the door. He hesitates before walking inside, allowing me time to pick up my carpetbag and join him.

Mother does not gasp with surprise when she first lays eyes on me. She wavers a bit before looking at me wholly, then says, "Of all my children, I knew it would be you that would return home fully intact. I knew it would be Eliza who would make the venture home to find me burned, withered, and unrecognizable. But you, too, have been touched by the mood of demolition. I see no ring on your finger," she says, wearing the same question as Titus on her wrinkled face. "Is this a joy or a tragedy, dear daughter?"

"Tragedy," I say, offering no more. I do not need to. Mother understands what has happened to me. I pray that I will be saved of sharing the details, but I know I will not be.

"Ah, then all of my leaves have fallen. A cold season lays on us even though the earth celebrates with warmth and birdsong. How sad."

5.

A MIDNIGHT SCAR

There are just the three of us in this life now. The last of the Harrows. Clendon and Emerson are lost to us, their earthly remains buried near Chancellorsville and Shiloh, while Father's body is scattered in the soil of Gettysburg. Each of us bear external and internal injuries from the war. Mother and her burns. Titus with the loss of his leg. And me, with the burden of a child that will soon venture into the world, innocent for only a moment. The world and all of its voices will have their say about the child's prospects, about its heritage, and the place of certainty or uncertainty in the line of Harrows. The poor infant survives on tainted blood and a loveless beginning. What lie must I tell so I may be looked upon as a decent mother? I worry that I will not be able to offer any kind of love to the progeny of the enemy, of a war-mad stranger. Where is the comfort in the results of a nightmare, perpetuated in heat of battle? Can I heal myself? This baby? These thoughts are my own. Titus and Mother have their own difficulties to face.

One day passes to the next and for the most part our lives are isolated and remote. Society has suffered an eclipse; a transition from dark to light, but no one has the money to host balls or cotillions, and I, above all, hold no desire to attend Sunday services or venture into town for provisions and small talk. The desire for normal life to return exists only in the distant gaze of survivors. Titus wears the face of the Farrells and Harrows. Though there is rumor in town of my return, I cannot find it in myself to show my face to familiar eyes. I cannot answer questions that I do not have answers to. Instead, I stay and work the land, planting, weeding, clearing, ensuring that we all will have enough food for the coming winter. Titus has secured a small flock of bantam hens, allowing for a sudden bounty of eggs and the occasional pot of meat on our table. The recollection of low battle rations is never far from my mind. Not only did I witness physical effects of the lack of food, but of the spirit and mind, as well. A man with rickets and no hope is a horrible sight, one that can never be expunged from any decent human being's memory.

The days have settled into a comfortable rhythm with mornings left to my touch on Mother's skin with the attempt to heal what has burned away. I have nothing but the medicines found in the woods and in my memory. Mud protects open wounds. Stinging nettle nourishes Mother's muscles and digestion. The flower called self-heal aides in the mending of her skin, though it will always be rippled by the flames. Mother glints in the sunlight when she dares to venture out into it; her glow is one of pain, unlike Clendon's. Along with the bantams, Titus has also been able to secure codeine from town to ease Mother's pain. Beyond these medicines, keeping Mother's dressings clean and changed is all that I can offer her. Attending to her spirits is more of a challenge. She grieves deeply for her husband and sons. As do we all.

There is plenty of fieldwork to attend to as the cotton grows toward the summer harvest. Between his errands to town and tending the chickens and garden, Titus stays busy. He rarely complains, but navigating with one leg frustrates him. He wants to do more. I do what healing I can for him, too, attending to his stump as it continues to heal. He does not talk about his dark day, and has, to my great relief, relinquished expectations of me to talk of mine. Once I offered no explanation and did not moon over some unknown beau, Titus arrived at a silent conclusion about the cause of my condition on his own. He knows the abominable acts men commit in war. He has killed more men than he ever dreamed he would. Sins regardless, but somehow forgiven, at least in the light of day, for those who take up arms for the state. A government's permission to kill overrides God's command not to, but there is punishment nonetheless. Titus is restless at night. Sometimes he whimpers like a suckling pig in search of its mother.

As the days roll on, the life in me continues to grow. I have yet to decide whether the baby is a boy or a girl. Mother cringes when I call the child an *it*, but I know of nothing else to call it. She fears for the baby's safety now and after it arrives, but doesn't say so aloud. It has never occurred to me to inflict pain or distress to the child inside me. I have spent my life healing wounds, first at home, then at war as a nurse in the surgeon's tent, and now, back home again. Harming the unborn seems unconscionable to me, though deep in my own difficult nights, I worry if it is a boy, if it will grow into the same kind of man who conquered my flesh and left a deep wound on my soul. Can I prevent that? I shall try. But I worry of it just the same. I worry, too, if the child is a girl. What do I know of this man who left me with a child to raise on my own? He knows nothing of the result of his loathsome deed. He does not care what happens to the seed he has sown. Has the government forgiven him this act of war, too? Is that what I am to tell this child of mine? That the father is forgiven? I know they will call her a bastard. Will they berate a dear daughter even though she had nothing to do with how she came into this world? I suppose they will. I will do what I must to prevent that, too.

I hide among the poppies when the post arrives, and do my best, like Mother, to keep myself unseen, but it is impossible, especially once Titus employs the services of Mira Smoot, the local midwife. I objected, of course, certain that I could attend to the birth on my own, but Titus insisted on telling Mira Smoot of my predicament. She arrives once weekly astride a swayback mare the color of a midnight scar. Mira has a mixed history herself, with one foot in the Negro world and the other foot in the land of a cotton field master who took his pleasure at Mira's mother's expense. If anyone would understand my plight, it is Mira. She is a rare breed, blessed with the will made of iron, and the ability to deflect hate like no other woman I have ever met. She has been beaten, threatened, and raped herself, and yet, there is never a moment when she does not wear a smile. Especially when there is a new life to bring into the world. She says it is her calling from the Lord to see to it that babies arrive on this earth as safely as possible. Mira does carry a fault, though, and that is her lack of ability to be discreet. She is a talker, a storyteller of great renown. She has that wonderful voice that warms a soul like a stew warms a stomach on a cold night. It is from her tongue that most all of Markleburg County has learned of my return, and of my condition.

As my time grows near, so does the fullness of the moon. July days are long, hot, and miserable. The nights are no different. Harvest time demands that Titus and I work the field, picking cotton and placing the heads in a drag-bag that grows to an unbearable weight. This task is difficult for both of us. My belly is swollen to a girth that I could hardly imagine. It looks like I have swallowed two watermelons.

Titus steadies himself on one knee and his stump. Our progress is slow, but each day, we work from sunup to sundown. We cannot afford to hire labor, and we both fear that the profit of our efforts will not see us through the coming winter. If it weren't for the perennial plant, we would have no hope at all. Sadly, midway through the month, Titus is left to work the harvest on his own. As I pull myself through the field, my water breaks and floods under me. Titus tears out after Mira Smoot, and in the coming of night, I am racked with such pain as I have ever felt. I scream into the night, cursing every man who has walked the earth, but especially one. I will always curse him. Mira knows of my fate; my worst living moment. I confess to her under the duress of pain and fear that a renegade group of soldiers overwhelmed the surgeon's tent. They killed every man, and left the three of us who were nurses to live and take their pleasures with. Minutes seemed like hours. The catastrophe of childbirth brought forth a torrent of liquid memories. Mira cradled me, rocked me, told me that she understood my pain. She has suffered the same disgrace. After it is all said and done, a bloody, hollering, healthy boy is placed in my arms, and for the first time in my life, I don't know how to stop the cries of another human being.

6.
THE FALL

I named the boy, Charles Emerson Clendon Harrow. Titus didn't seem to mind the omission of his name. He still lives while our father and brothers have perished under the call of duty. I hope that the legacy is fitting, will somehow find its way to encourage the child to aspire to honor. It is the only good start I have to offer him.

"My only objection is the surname. He is not a Harrow," Titus says.

We have arranged our meager furniture in the shack so that a bassinet stands next to my bed. Charles sleeps peacefully nearby. He is not a fussy baby, which is a great relief for us all. "And what else would you have me call this child? He is as much a Harrow as you and I."

Titus's face flushes red. "People will know."

"How can I prevent that?"

"I worry for him, for you."

"And yourself?"

"For us all, living and dead."

"So I should not have returned home?"

Titus exhales deeply with the knowledge that he cannot win the argument that he has provoked, then heads to the door, and stops. "I will not speak of this again."

"He will need his uncle," I say.

Titus looks to the sleeping baby, then to me; the anger melts from his face. For a moment, I see his sensitivities. I am relieved that not everything good has been amputated.

"And I will need him," Titus says, then exits the shack, the fall of the crutch as solid and determined as his footstep.

Mother, to her credit, has remained tight-lipped during the exchange with my brother, but she cannot restrain herself any longer. "He is right, you know."

"What else am I to do?"

Mother looks away from me because she has no answer to my question. Silence invades the shack, and I am suddenly hot to the toes. When I look down to Charles, he is staring up at me with his droopy deep brown eyes. The Harrows are all blue-eyed, and this is yet another way that the boy will be different from us all. If there was any woodland herb I could eat and change the flavor of my milk so the color of his eyes would change to blue, I would, but there is no such magic in this world that I know of. I want him to be like us more than anything.

I am still in search of recognition of his face. Sadly, there is none. Maybe the fact that he has the face of a stranger is another blessing. What if I see the aggressor every time I look at my son's face? Would I hate him? Fear him? Loathe him? I am safe from that for now. I hope the memory of that face has been permanently erased from my mind, replaced with the subtlety of love and the connection of blood. I am sure of the connection. The being erupted from my body; I felt it, saw it, whether I could believe it or not. I fear the love, though I feel it, know it exists. My heart aches when I am gone from Charles for any length of time. I worry for his welfare, for his every breath. It is a different kind of love as I've ever known.

I am back in the field now, still offering my contribution to the harvest. My body recovers slowly, and my strength is only half of its normal gauge, but Titus cannot do all of the picking on his own. We both fear a loss of the crop. Weevils have been reported in a nearby county. Destruction is at hand if we don't hurry. I have no choice but to leave the baby in Mother's care and spend as many hours in the field as I am physically able. I have no choice but to leave Charles's side, no matter how much it pains us both. He cries out in separation, and that binds us even tighter.

7.
THE RISING STORM

I have resisted going into town for as long as I could, but Titus is ill, and we need grain. Milk must be bartered with the Fergusons outside of Allwhich. I will ride past the farm on my return. I have no choice but to take Charles with me. He needs to suckle, and there is always chance of delay. If we are going to face the world, it will be together.

I drive into town on our buckboard, pulled by a gray workhorse named Jimbo. The gelding is the progeny of horses that have served the lands of Harrow House since my grandfather took the mortgage. I trust Jimbo implicitly. He is a fine horse with an amenable personality. It is a smooth ride into the realm of the populated, and Charles sleeps most of the way.

I do not dillydally. I head straight to Maxwell's feed store, park the wagon, and ignore any looks my arrival has provoked. It is with great relief that Vern Maxwell has other business to attend to, and his wife, Marletta, tends to my needs. The owner of the general store is a dyed-in-the-wool believer of the cause. Vern was too old to take up arms and stayed behind to serve those, like my mother, who were forced to wait out the war. Men like him found power in the operation of the town that they did not hold before the war. His store is my only option; otherwise, I would have found a different outlet from which to purchase my grain.

Marletta Maxwell is a mouse of a woman, and I can hardly remember the sound of her voice. I cannot hide my pleasure from seeing her, and she seems so of me, when I enter the store. She barely says a word during our transaction, outside of the requirements of business, until I prepare to leave.

"I heard you was back," Marletta says. "But I didn't believe everything that I heard." She had obviously found a power in the war she did not possess before, too.

I had turned to leave after depositing my money in her palm, but her words stop me. "And what was it you heard?" I ask as I spin around to face her.

Marletta's face blushes red, and she looks away from me. "I cannot speak of such things."

"But you just did." I pull Charles tighter to me, and force his face to my shoulder by cupping the back of his head with my hand. "What did you hear?" I want to protect Charles, put my fingers in his ears, but I cannot.

Marletta looks past me as if she is in hopes that a customer will enter the store. Outside, I hear the bags of grain being loaded onto my wagon. I could walk away, but I can't. Not now.

The storekeeper's wife exhales and says. "I don't believe it. I don't believe any of it."

"Tell me."

"They say you gave yourself to the soldiers in exchange for your life. That the boy is willfully Union blood."

"They say worse than that." I knew it was Mira Smoot who had told the tale of Charles's origin, but I was also smart enough to know that a tale takes on a life of its own, just as that of a lie. Mira would not attach that embellishment to my story, I am sure of it. People add and subtract what pleases them for their own benefit, for their own purpose. Charles has been anointed with the hate against the victors. He would always be a blue-coat, a betrayer of the cause. Men would blame him for the loss of their legs and pass down the rage to their sons and daughters. Life in school would be a misery. No matter the talents that Charles inherits from the Farrells and Harrows, beauty, mechanics, a healing touch, it will be overruled by the unknown blood that runs through his veins.

"They do say worse than that," Marletta says. "I thought you should know."

Footsteps on the boardwalk and the ring of the bell save me from saying something that I would regret for the rest of my life. I want to scream at Marletta and her husband, in his absence, for helping to spread such falsehoods, even though I know I will only make things worse for myself and for my son.

I spin, and hurry past Caroline Renny as she enters the store. Caroline, who lost two sons in the war, doesn't say a word to me. Disapproval and hate anchor her chin upon seeing me holding Charles tight against my chest. I worry that she is building a ball of spit to throw my way. If not now, it will come soon. I am sure of it. She has already heard the tale of my duty, of my time away. It matters not how much relief of suffering I have provided to the boys on our side. All that matters is that I was overrun, did not fight back hard enough, that I brought back that shame with me—which is hardly the truth. But people like Marletta and Caroline are not interested in the truth. They are only interested in distractions from their own pain, from their own shame—and my son is the repository that they have chosen for such a thing. Over my dead body.

I see judgment and ugliness everywhere I look as I leave town. In every eye, in every face, in every soul, I see a story that is not true, but cannot be controlled or changed. I am grateful that Charles is only a baby.

I refuse to allow tears or rage to drive me home. Even though my worst fears have come true, I am relieved. Relieved to know what I must do, how I must proceed. The only trouble will be convincing Mother and Titus that our time on this land is past. Charles is not safe here, and neither are we.

8.

THE WIND AT OUR BACKS

Mother sits inside the shack watching as I pack the last of our belongings into the wagon. She has been the most difficult to persuade to leave. In the end, I challenged her to a ride into town to see for herself what lives we face, but she declined. Mother knows how she would be looked upon, scarred, burned from trying to save her home, her beauty taken by the flames— she is a monster who cannot look at her own reflection in the mirror. But it is not her appearance that kept her from the trip. It is her love of Charles that prevents her from experiencing the hate that she knows exists, no matter our good name or the former standing in society. She cannot stomach seeing the last of the Harrows spit on, sworn at, begrudged for a crime that he did not commit.

I hoist Charles's bassinet onto the back of the wagon, tie it down, then face Mother and Titus. Charles is cradled in Mother's arms, sleeping amid the racket of packing. He is too young to remember this day, and for that I find another feather of gladness to add to the wings that will carry us away.

"That's it, then," I say.

Mother nods. "No tears." She looks up to the clear autumn sky, blue as the China her father bought in Williamsburg and gave her for a wedding present, then to me. "We won't get far."

"We have a good month," I say. "If we have to hole up in St. Louis, then so be it."

Titus exhales. He is glad to leave Harrow House behind more than any of us, I think. He knows, like we all do, even if the house could be rebuilt, that we will be haunted by the past, by the war, by the aftermath. He was the first to say that we all need a fresh start, a place to remake ourselves, to build another life. "And then to California," he says.

"Yes, as long as it takes," I answer. We have sold our property to Mister Biles for pennies on the dollar, and scrounged up every cent we could find for the journey, selling what survived the fire and our sad bank account. Mother wouldn't sell her gold wedding band that Father had placed on her finger, and I couldn't blame her. Its value wouldn't have got us much farther as it was. It will take everything we have to finish the trek, and there will be times when we may well have to stop and work, or hunt the land for a season, but we are determined to finish what we start. We are determined to start over in California.

Titus nods. Mother nods. We're all ready to go. Then she covers her head with a light hood, walks out into the sun, hands Charles to me, and climbs, with the aid of Titus, to her spot in the rear of the wagon. We follow suit with Titus in the driver's seat, and me next to him, holding my son.

Titus nickers Jimbo, and we start our journey in silence. I take the direction of my mother, offering no tears to the wool. But inside, I am in a panic, knowing that I will never see this beloved land again. I know I will never smell the air whipping through the oaks on a stormy spring day, or embrace the hickory burning in the hearth. The voices of my family have been silenced on this land as we roll along; our war with it is lost. I can hardly bear to say goodbye, but I am glad for the leaving as much as Titus and Mother. Maybe more.

We will have a chance to become ourselves again in California—if we get there—have a life far away from the war, the memory of it, the pain of it, the sight of it. And in doing so, in going west, Charles will grow up as my son, a Harrow through and through, without judgment and hate, until that fateful day when he is old enough to ask of his father. When he can understand my words, digest the tale, I will tell him the truth. I hope I can heal his pain. I hope my own pain is healed by then.

Perhaps, if luck smiles on us all, our journey west will be the best thing that has ever happened to us.

Larry D. Sweazy (www.larrydsweazy.com) is a multiple award-winning author of fourteen novels. He lives in Indiana with his wife, Rose, two dogs, and a cat, and is hard at work on his next novel.

★ ★ ★ ★ ★

CAST FROM HEAVEN
BY SHARON FRAME GAY

★ ★ ★ ★ ★

Sedona, Arizona, 1939

Clara cradled the ragged journal found in the abandoned hut. She wiped it off, cracked it open. The writing was elegant, educated, ink fading into sepia tones. Blowing away the dust, she turned to the man standing beside her.

"Shall I read this to you, Father?"

He nodded, running his fingers over tattered canvas that once served as a door to the empty dwelling. Inside were frayed blankets, a hunting knife, and an arrowhead. The wind blew through the chinked walls, a soft whistling sound. Several feet away was a gravesite with a cross.

Clara sat on a rock next to an empty firepit. The old man lowered himself to the ground beside her. She turned to the first page and read:

Journal of George Booker, 1878

On days like this, I think I was cast from heaven, tumbling to earth and landing in the dirt that slapped my face, coated my tongue. If one believes in past lives, I must have been a mean son of a bitch to carry this one, a heavy lift to be sure.

I cannot move in either direction without standing alone. Like a compass, my soul comes back to isolation time and again. Now I spend my days at the bottom of this great canyon, with an old mule, Packy, and a few hawks for company.

Life wasn't always like this. Educated in Boston, I terminated studies at Harvard Law School and joined the U.S. Cavalry after the Civil War. There was a great surge westward, and requests for soldiers to help conquer the territories. The romantic idea of leaving the hallowed halls of learning for an adventure in unknown territory proved too tempting. Against my family's fervent wishes, I signed up and caught a train to Kansas, heart thrumming with the excitement and glamour of the West.

Basic training was at Fort Riley. When the Army thought I was fit enough to be called a Horse Soldier, I was transferred deeper into Indian territory to Fort Bowie, Arizona, where the whole idea of soldiering lost its glamour. Instead of lush plains, we rode out each day in searing heat, our uniforms scratchy and hot in the June afternoons. Horses were flecked with sweat, dust catching on wet flanks, turning into streaks of warm mud that ran down their legs. Boots were crusted in dirt, and our hats did little to keep us from nearly swooning every day. Some men did. Fell right off their horses and onto the desert floor. They were the lucky ones, I thought, because the captain splashed cool water on them from an extra canteen. I wanted to wipe their faces with my fingers, sip the droplets. Most of the soldiers believed they were stationed in Hell, including me.

It started with the Indians. We were here to keep them in line, and the Apaches were not about to be domesticated. They fled the reservations and wandered all over the territory. Our job was rounding them up and settling them back on the reservation, which was a thankless, stupid task. The Apaches glared at us, then did what they wanted to do. They got even by stealing our horses or setting fire to a few settlers' huts, robbing a stagecoach or two. Some of them went further, declaring war with outright killing and scalping.

I had no opinion of them, just like I felt about slaves. To my great shame, I didn't give much thought to what it meant to be a slave or an Indian. I never knew a real slave. They seemed to be an apparition that rose from the South and drew anger and derision that divided our country. It was through ignorance that I blamed those slaves sometimes even though they were caught up in the War Between the States and white men's ideals. They were pawns in the middle of a conflict that pitted us against ourselves. I know now that the Indians were pawns, too, as white folks settled the new territories.

Once the war was over, the United States government aimed West, taking over the land in greedy gulps, forcing the Natives on to reservations. The Apaches rebelled, so we were dispatched to put out the fires. The more we pushed, the angrier they became. Before long we were right in the middle of the Indian Wars.

When the Apaches heard the Cavalry coming, they disappeared like smoke, hightailed it up into the red rocks, picking us off with arrows and rifles if we came too close. These were the lone wolves, bachelors, young men who flaunted their freedom and laughed at our own imprisonment serving in the Army.

I rode towards the back of the line on our missions and seldom shot my firearm, or saw many of the elusive Apache. Once, an arrow flew past my shoulder and scared the hell out of me. It landed in the dirt like a spear, quivering in the dust. On the way back to the fort, I saw it again, leaned down, and pulled it up. Still have it here with me. Sometimes I run my fingers over the flint, and wonder who honed it into a fine head, wound it into the arrow, who the hell shot at me on a sweltering summer day.

The whole idea of forcing people onto reservations didn't sit well with me. Realizing it was a mistake joining the Cavalry, I was putting in my time until my stint was up. Then I had plans to move to San Francisco, find myself a proper woman, start a life, a family, get this bad choice behind me. Maybe even continue my schooling, become a lawyer.

It was a windy day in November, cooler than usual, a godsend. A scout rode in that night, said he found an Apache village about twenty miles away, tucked into some rocks and high chaparral. The next morning, we set out to disperse them, run them back to the reservation. We rode easy for two days, then melted into a quiet canyon and waited for the scouts to return, let us know what was what.

To be honest before God, I thought we might shoot a brave or two and shake up the rest of the folks, then march them back to the reservation.

Coming up at dawn on the quiet village, I figured we'd wait for a command to roll forward, and reined in my mount.

My horse snorted, shifted restlessly beneath me. Far in the distance, a dog barked. Without warning, soldiers surged forward, firing with fury into the sleeping village. Startled, I galloped right into the thick of it with the rest of them, as our superior urged us on, screaming into the face of Hell like demons. The soldiers shot at anything that moved. They killed women, children, and old men. We burned homes, gut-shot their horses, trampled and beat them. I shot my rifle into the air, refusing to aim at anyone. But in the end, it didn't matter. It was a massacre. And I was part of it.

An officer dispatched me to the back of the settlement to tighten the perimeter. I kicked my mare in the side and set off at a gallop.

Behind a smoldering wickiup was a young kid, maybe seven years old, with a rifle pointed straight at my chest. Without thinking I pulled my trigger and watched him fall over like a sapling. Then, before I could slow down, a tiny girl ran right under my horse. There was a sickening crunch. When I wheeled around, she was on her back, staring at the sky. I leaned over and threw up.

A woman burst out of a wickiup, running for the little girl. In the smoke and dust, she raced to the child, picked her up, then headed into the brush. I let her go.

I stopped my horse and stared back at the whole scene from Hades.

Then deserted the U.S. Cavalry.

I kept running until the horse couldn't go any further. Fell off right where we stood and didn't come to until the next morning when the sun was bright overhead and the mare was nudging me.

Removing the Army saddle, I stripped down to my union suit and pants, got rid of everything else except the rifle, a pistol, and canteen, and rode bareback through the desert. Didn't stop until I reached New Mexico, then tried to find work near Gallup. A ranch gave me a job shuffling cattle around. Although the boys in the bunkhouse didn't like me much, they left me alone.

I hunkered down at the ranch for weeks, until I figured the Army had lost track of me, then moved on. After what happened back in the Apache village, I didn't feel like I deserved to live among civilized society, so thoughts of going home to Boston were banished. Besides, I would likely be found and court-martialed. Hanged. And even that would be too good for me. I deserved much worse.

Trading the Army horse for an Indian pony and a few woven blankets, I quit the ranch, turned back into Arizona territory, heading north. Alone again, I took my time riding through the brush and desert, trying to figure out what to do next.

Up near a big red rock canyon was a deer path that seemed to go straight to the center of the earth. The pony was willing, so I gave him his head and we trekked down through dizzying switchbacks and over rocks, into the heart of the canyon.

It was cooler below, a lush river meandering through huge boulders. I dismounted and looked up. All I could see was a bowl of sky, stark against the rim, and heard nothing but rushing water. I made camp that night and thought to stay awhile. It was as good a place as any for a lone wolf like me. I could catch a few fish, even snare a rabbit or two, but if I stayed here, I needed a few provisions. There was still coin in my pocket, so after a couple of weeks, I headed back up the gorge.

I made my way to an outpost several miles away, run by a white man and an Indian. The Indian looked at me with expressionless eyes, but I knew right away he had me figured as a soldier. He turned away, spit into the dust. My hand twitched along my hip towards a pistol, rested there.

I traded with the white man, a grizzled old guy named Lou. He sold me food, ammo, and a pack mule. Blankets and a skillet were added to the pile on the counter as I reached into my pocket for money.

"You settling down anywhere around here?" Lou asked.

"Yeah, I'm thinking the canyon."

He handed me a twist of tobacco. "Good life around the canyon if you can stand to be lonely."

I paid for my gear, stepped out into the glare of day.

The Indian was standing there, holding the reins to the pack mule. He handed them over, our fingers brushing. I said, "Much obliged."

He looked me in the eye and said quietly, "Don't come back this way, you hear?"

I nodded, throat tight, and swung up on to the pony, dragging the lead behind me. The mule fell in step, his ears waving back and forth as though bidding goodbye.

The sun beat down like fiery fists. In the distance were watery mirages here and there, scattered across the landscape. Little pools of water shimmered, then disappeared as we got closer.

Far ahead was something on the ground. Thinking it might be a deer, I kicked the pony in the sides, reached for the rifle in its sheath. If it was fresh dead, or injured, I might have food for quite a while. I searched the sky for predators, hawks, or vultures, but nothing wheeled overhead so it probably hadn't been dead for long.

Drawing closer, I saw it was a person. I approached, keeping the rifle up along my thigh, ready to shoot.

It was an Indian woman. She was curled up on the ground, her hair glinting in the sun like a raven's wing.

"Hey, are you okay?" I asked, a foolish thing to say out here in the middle of nowhere. She raised her head, then dropped it back down, eyes dull. I peered around, wondering if this was an ambush. If it was, it seemed to be a fitting way to die, so I dismounted and grabbed the canteen, walked over to her.

I squatted down and offered a sip of water. She turned her head away. Her body was shaking with heat and weakness, but she wouldn't accept my help.

"Do you talk English?" I asked.

No answer.

She struggled to get up and fell back down, legs scabbed and dusty. Her moccasins were frayed and useless. There were multiple small cuts all over her body. Black hair was chopped off in uneven patches.

I didn't know what to do. If I left her to die, that would be just one more sin for me to talk to God about one day, but she wasn't asking for help. I figured that this was what she wanted, to just rot away out here in the middle of nowhere.

She tried to get to her feet one more time and fainted dead away. I checked for weapons, found a hunting knife in a belt, took it off her, then lifted the woman up and over Packy's back, trussed her up with a rope from the outpost.

We traveled slowly down into the canyon. If she was dying, I could at least make a decent burial along the river. Once in a while it seemed like she came to, but then closed her eyes again.

We reached camp. I set her on a few blankets in the shade, rubbed water against her dry, cracked lips. Then I walked down to the river and fished a bit, came back with a few brookies, scaled and cooked them. Pressed a little meat against her mouth. She swallowed, looked up at me for the first time since I found her.

"My name is George Booker," I said.

She shook her head, turned away.

"Who cut you up all over?" I asked, looking at her arms, her legs, crusty with blood, oozing a bit. There was no response.

By the next morning, the woman seemed to have revived. She was leaning up against a tree on the blankets, gazing out at the river with such yearning that I wanted to cry, just looking at her. I brought fresh water from the river and made up a hoecake in the pan. She took a few bites, then quit.

"George Booker," I said again to her, pointing to my chest.

Silence, then in a raspy voice she said, "Onawa."

I nodded. Patted the canteen. "Water," I said. Handed it over. She took a long drink.

"Water," she pointed to the river.

I nodded. "Yep, that's water."

This was how it was for several days. She sat under a tree and looked out at the canyon. About a week later she walked around the campsite, wandered down to the bank, over to the fire, back and forth.

I came up from the river one evening with a few fish I'd gutted and scaled. Onawa reached out, took them from me. Without a word, she skewered them on a stick, then set them above the fire, turning them slowly until they were crisp.

So began our friendship down here in the canyon. Together we built a lean-to with rocks, tree limbs, and an old piece of canvas I found. I offered it to Onawa and gestured that I would sleep outside, but she shook her head, and slept on the ground by the fire outside every night.

It was early fall now. The canyon was beautiful. Birds flew in and out of the river in a vast migration. Once in a while I shot one. Onawa plucked them and saved the feathers in a small hole in the ground, I figured to make a mattress if we got cloth at an outpost. I rejoiced when I shot a deer and Onawa smiled. We feasted on the meat, worked the hide off the carcass, dried it in the sun.

One warm day as I was heading over the rocky shore to the river, her voice rang out. "George Booker, a snake! Don't move!"

I froze. Right in front of me was one of the biggest diamondbacks I'd ever seen, stretched out like a rope right across the path. My heart thumped as it coiled and rattled, looking straight at me. Onawa looped around us with a long branch, then lightly prodded the snake until it slithered off into some brush. I leaned over, weak in the knees.

"Thank you," I whispered. Then I froze again.

"You talk English?"

"Yes. Some," she grunted.

Shocked, I nodded, then headed down to the water.

I spoke to her more than usual that night, hoping she'd say something back, but she only said a few halting words before adding wood to the fire, then walked away.

My silent companion, I thought. I felt a sweetness overtake me as I watched her get ready for the night. The slant of the waning sun splayed along her cheekbone, her hair shining like a raven's wing, growing longer. The cuts on her body were healing over, tiny fissures that pinked up in the sun against her dark brown skin. I longed to take Onawa's hand, comfort her, make her feel safe.

The days grew shorter, and the canyon was much cooler than it was up on top. I talked to Onawa about winter.

"Should we break camp, go up top for a while?" I asked.

She shook her head. "Colder up there soon."

I nodded. "Guess we should tighten things up down here, then."

A storm formed on top of the canyon. Clouds were dark and roiling, and the air smelled of snow. The river looked gray and deep as it brushed by, the ground growing colder each day.

The first flakes fell to the canyon floor. We added more wood to the fire outside the shelter. By evening, the snow had stopped, the stars had come out high above the ridge.

That night, I heard a rustling near me and sat up in the lean-to, reaching for the pistol by my side. It was Onawa. She dropped to her knees, then settled in alongside me, sharing our warmth. I put my arm around her, held her close. Onawa did not turn away but let me hold her all night long. I longed to kiss the back of her neck, rub her breasts, put my hands upon her hips and lift them up on top of me but dared not move. She relaxed against my chest, then deepened into sleep. Folding myself around her, I drifted off. When I woke the next morning, she was gone. I heard her moving about outside and joined her.

She said not a word about the night but went back to her quiet ways and I went down to the river for a while, thinking about what happened.

Onawa joined me every night. We held each other, kept each other warm as the winter winds whistled down the canyon and sent chills through the air like ghosts. Sometimes she said a few words here and there and I answered them, a quiet companionship during our long nights.

Finally one night, Onawa turned to me. She had been silent

all day, her eyes drifting to the rim of the canyon as though she were a bird and wanted to fly right up to the top and away. We crawled into the hut together and I took off my shoes, my shirt, slid under the blanket. She knelt beside me. Hands reached for me and my belly tightened. Without a word, I helped her out of her dress, then holding her hair in my hands, I drew her into me and covered her body with kisses. She opened like a thunderstorm in the desert, blooming beneath me until I could not take even a moment more, and poured myself into her.

Afterwards, she was even quieter for several days. It was as though she were making her mind up about something.

One afternoon as I came back from fishing, she looked up and smiled.

"George Booker," she said. "I am happy to see you."

My heart leapt. I knew we were going to be okay together now. I kissed the top of her head and she laughed. That evening we sat in front of our fire, hands clasped, the both of us at the bottom of this canyon like two birds on a twig.

We decided to build a bigger hut. Onawa and I spent days cutting down lodgepole pine, skinning them, building a crude cabin. Onawa made a paste of dried grasses mixed with river water and clay, packed them between the poles. There was room to move around in our new home. I could stand up completely, and there was a small space for a fire to keep us warm. We harvested and skinned fish, then hung them in strips near the heat drying them. Onawa made baskets from reed and pine bark, storing the fish in corners of our cabin. Life was simple and so good that I never dreamed it would end the way it did.

It was a morning in early spring. The sun was so bright it hurt my eyes, splayed against the red rock of the canyon. The few clouds scudding by were interlopers, painting their part of the sky and letting the wind carry them across the rim.

I turned to Onawa as we sat on the ground, working a deer hide.

"I've been thinking about what happened the day I found you. You were so sick and cut up. I praise God I found you, but I don't know why you were there. Never wanted to put pressure on you to tell me the story, but I can't help but wonder . . ." My voice drifted off and I ran my hand across my mouth, as though apologizing for the words.

Onawa nodded, then moved closer, her leg pressing against mine.

"George Booker, you made me live. I was there to die. The cuts were my own. My knife bit me over and over, and still my sorrow was thirsty."

I touched her hand. "Go on."

She closed her eyes a moment, then sighed. Her fingers tightened around mine. I felt her trembling.

"I lived in a village with my husband and children," she began, trying to find the right words in English. "He went with others to look for food, leaving us behind. They were gone a long time."

She drew her knees up to her chest, laid her cheek against them, and spoke.

"One day there was noise and gunfire. I was in the back of the village, but heard screaming and shots fired. White men were attacking the village. Army men. They were shooting all my people and burning our homes to the ground." She clenched her hands together, set the deerskin down, bent her head. Tears trickled out of the corners of her eyes.

"My son, Kuruk, ran from our wickiup with a rifle my husband left behind. Kuruk wanted to protect me. He was shot dead by a soldier."

She struggled, then sighed, her breath a sad song. "My little girl, Liluye, ran after Kuruk. The white man who shot my son trampled her with his horse. I picked her up and ran to the trees. I tripped and fell in the brush, and hid from the soldiers. Liluye died in my arms.

"The men rounded up those who lived. I hid while they laughed and joked, burned more of our homes, killed our goats and roasted them. By the next morning, they left, taking the stragglers with them.

"I was afraid to go back to the burning village to bury Kuruk. I dug a hole for Liluye among the rocks and waited nearby for my husband and the others to return. But they did not come back. After a few days I began to walk. I walked alone for a long time, eating berries and bugs, until my soul was ready to leave my body, then I cut it everywhere, letting my spirit out, the blood out, so I could die quicker. That is when you found me, George Booker."

I could not breathe. Could not think. I could not grasp a God so cruel as to set us up in this canyon like a hellish game of chess.

I staggered to my feet, walked into the hut, took my shirt off, picked up the rifle. Walked over to Onawa and placed it in her hand. Stood before her, hands at my side, chest bared to her. My heart was pounding so hard, I could no longer hear the river. My voice came out in a whisper.

"It was me. I'm the one who killed your children." As she stared at me in bewilderment, huge sobs wracked my body and shook me to my knees.

"Onawa," I said, her name a thousand shards of sorrow in my mouth. "I never meant to kill your children, or anybody. I ran away from the Army that day after what happened." My voice broke. I pointed at the muzzle of the rifle. "Shoot me now. Kill me! Take the horse and mule, get up out of this canyon. Please." I stopped, looked at her in agony. "I am begging you."

Trembling, Onawa rose and came forward with the rifle,

aimed at my heart. She staggered, fell to her knees, dropped the rifle in the dirt, pulled on her hair, moaning, rocking back and forth. I reached out for her, and we clung together, crying.

It was a damnation so cruel, I swear angels were shaking their fists at Heaven.

"I know you can't forgive me," I said, clasping her head to my chest. "I don't want you to forgive me. I want you to hate me and hurt me and cast me away. Kill me. I beg you." In anguish, I scratched at my arms and legs, long red trails welting up on my skin in angry lines. I pounded my head with fists until my vision swam, bursts of light inside my skull.

Still, Onawa said nothing. She rocked back and forth, her hands at her heart as though she might pluck it out of her chest and toss it into the river.

I stood up, left the rifle with her, walked down to the banks of the river. Turned away from her so she could shoot me, waited for the explosion in my back. Scooped up water and stared at the pure drops as they sifted through my fingers. I waited for them to turn to blood, leave copper traces swirling in the water. I raised the droplets to my lips. They tasted like betrayal, heartbreak, and tears.

Turning back towards camp, I saw Onawa on the ground, her eyes closed, breath shallow. She looked like she did the day I found her. Along her legs were fresh cuts, seeping into the dust. I choked back sobs and fell to my knees again, begging forgiveness. Onawa did not open her eyes, but flinched when I touched her hand. I held it long after dusk as she lay there in silence, her face turned away from me.

In the darkness, I rose and headed for the hut. Onawa did not follow. I didn't think she would. I placed my loaded pistol right outside the door, a silent invitation. I would have put it in my mouth, pulled the trigger myself, but I could not take that from her. I sat in the darkness, praying for redemption, asking for forgiveness again and again to God, to Onawa, to the canyon that let me live among its red rocks, despite being the worst kind of sinner there was. During the long night I lost track of time and drifted into a grieving sleep.

When I woke the next morning, Onawa was gone, along with the pony. Her clothing lay in a heap, knife placed on top, as though her soul had stepped out of her body and disappeared. I took the mule, looked for tracks, headed upstream, deeper into the canyon, calling her name. A cold wind blew against my bare chest, whistled through the gorge. My voice rang against the rocks, met only with silence.

We hadn't gone far when Packy snorted, balked, hooves ringing out on the rocks. The pony stood a few feet away, reins dragging on the ground. He lifted his head and nickered.

Onawa was hanging from a Joshua tree. Her body swayed in the morning breeze like a flag of surrender. I rushed over, cut her down, but I knew she was already somewhere I could never be. Her sightless eyes looked upwards as though searching for her children. The canyon was silent except for my cries, long waves of sorrow that echoed over and over.

I thought of taking the rope, climbing into that tree, and jumping off straight into Hell and be done with it. But I knew it was too easy. A quick moment of pain and fright, then freedom from this earthly bind was not fitting for a sinner such as me. No, Hell can wait a while longer, while I spend my days living it on earth.

I buried her near camp. Made a little cross with her name carved on it. Kept her frayed dress and knife. At night I sleep with the dress by my side, stroking the soft deer hide. Every morning when the sun comes up, I cut out a piece of my flesh, letting my blood mingle with hers on the blade.

Dying is too good for me, release is the soft way out. The years have gone by in a harvest of pain and guilt, no solace will

I take. I write in this damned journal, and I figure when I get to the last page, I'll stand up and walk right into that river and let it carry me away.

Until then, I wear this sorrow every day, let it carve into my soul until I turn to stone, just like this canyon, so deep below the sun that the devil catches up to me. George Booker, Arizona Territory.

Clara closed the journal with a sigh, gazed at her father. "So, it was true. She was here. With him." She ran her hands through her hair, stood up.

Her father turned and stared out at the river. Clara placed her hand on his shoulder.

"I'm sorry, Father," she said. "If only there had been a way to find her back then."

He nodded, reached for her hand, his fingers gnarled and dry.

"Tell me your story again, Father," Clara said. She gestured towards the old grave. "Tell it to Onawa."

The old man blew out through his cheeks, wiped at his eyes, then began to talk.

"When I woke up, I was spread-eagled in the dirt. My shoulder was broken from the backfire of the rifle when I shot at the soldier, throwing me backwards, knocking me out. There was smoke everywhere, rifles firing and the sound of people screaming. I dragged myself back to our wickiup, but my mother and sister were gone. Our home was smoldering. I put it out with a blanket, then huddled beneath it for what seemed like hours, days, before the soldiers left. Then, there was silence. Only the sound of the wind. The smell of smoke. Birds wheeling in circles overhead."

He lifted his head, gazed up at the sky, remembering.

"After many days, Father came home and found me near

death in the wickiup. He searched the area for Mother and Liluye. There were so many bodies, so many dead children." He paused for a moment, shook his head sadly.

"He looked for days, then Father put me on the back of his pony and we rode away, trying to track Mother, or anybody from our village. They all seemed to vanish. We traveled throughout the territory, stopping and asking if anybody had seen Onawa and Liluye.

"After many weeks, Father gave up, and we journeyed to the reservation, where he turned himself in. Father died a broken man, but I never gave up the idea that Mother and Liluye might be alive.

"Over time, there were stories. Tales about a white man and an Apache woman living at the bottom of a canyon.

"When I grew into a man, I left the reservation, worked throughout Arizona as a ranch hand. Over the years, I explored many canyons. But I always came back up empty."

He cupped Clara's head in his hand and whispered, "I never gave up. Never. Over time I met your mother and we had you. The years came and went.

"Then one day I heard about a canyon deep in the rocks up north, near Sedona. I asked Apaches in the area if they had known my mother and sister. Somebody told me he heard of a man who lived alone in the canyon for many years, and a beautiful Apache woman once lived there, too."

The old man leaned on Clara, nodded at the grave. "So now it is done," Kuruk said. "I have found my mother."

Clara knelt, wrapped her arms around her father, held him tight. "Onawa would have been proud of you," she said. "You never gave up."

The rim of the canyon darkened as though a ghost shadowed it. The sky was no longer blue, thunderheads had gathered, a few raindrops touched Kuruk's cheek like tears. Clara reached for the journal, tucked it in her backpack, gathered the two mules that would carry them back up the canyon. She helped Kuruk mount, then put her foot in the stirrup and settled into the saddle, leading the way.

As they passed an old Joshua tree, ravens flew up from the limbs, soaring towards the sky straight into the rain clouds. Clara shivered and turned the mule towards home.

Sharon Frame Gay is an award-winning author who lives in the Pacific Northwest. She has been internationally published in many anthologies and literary journals. You can find her on Amazon as well as on Facebook as Sharon Frame Gay–Writer.

★ ★ ★ ★ ★

Peaches
by Matthew P. Mayo

★ ★ ★ ★ ★

A stream courses low and dark beneath its crusted surface. Withered leaves rattle as a breeze worries a scrag of streamside brush. A young man leans over a thick length of branch propped beneath his arm and grunts with each hopping step.

The sight of the shack across the iced flowage surprises him. Little more than a low line of roof wedged into the hill behind, a mound of snow atop might be a chimney, he thinks. Vertical logs beneath, man height, frame a crude plank door in the center.

He doubts it has seen use in recent years. No matter. It is the most welcome thing he has seen in two days, and he indulges in hope. Thoughts of meat, a fire, blankets fill his head as he chooses his slow path across the half-frozen creek. But food first. He must eat. He cannot recall ever having such a feeling, a hunger clawing him from within like a spiny creature seeking a way out.

The young woman steps into a patch of downing sun on the crusted slope above the shelter. The rising breeze has been troublesome and is now a wind that follows her, smacking her bloodied skirts against her legs and carrying with it no sign of her pursuer. But that means little.

In a lull, a faint smell stills her . . . smoke, surprising this high up when she expects to be alone.

She tops the last rise, and below sees a thin gray wisp rising from the snow, then dissipating in a gust. She grunts and approaches the shelter with interest, for she had intended to hole up there herself.

The door spasms inward and the young man, crouching before the fireplace, shouts, "Oh, no!" He falls to his backside, struggles upright, one leg bent outward.

"You are trespassing," says a young woman, perhaps a girl, aiming at him a pistol that looks as long as her arm.

"No, no! I—"

She looks around the room and sniffs, her nostrils flexing. "It still stinks of mice and smoke and sweat."

The young man stares at her. He is reminded of a dime novel he'd been taken with some months before, *Bathsheba of the Plains*. One line in particular comes to him: "She was a young, deadly thing, all freckles and pistols."

But that feels a long time ago, back in the spring of the year when he'd set off for the West, when he'd been certain of his place in the world. Now he is about to die by the hand of a flinty young woman, the future little more than a lark.

The light in the shelter is meager, but enough to glow the length of the gun, her cheek, and nose and chin. Shadowed hair sticks, wet, against her forehead and drips melt on her brow. More snow bunches on her thin shoulders. She wears a light pattern dress, what colors he cannot tell. The skirts are stained up high. He looks aside.

"How do you do?" He extends a shaking hand as he rises.

She looks at his hand, at his face, then cocks the gun and holds it steady on him. "I'd as soon kill you and be done with it."

"Kill me? Why?" He touches his throat. "I am defenseless. If it's your shanty you are worried about, I will leave once the storm passes. I'd rather not right now."

126

"It is not a shanty. It is a dugout."

"Fine, then. A dugout."

She turns, still holding the gun on him, and fumbles at the door.

"There is no lock," he says.

Still she jerks the handle, somehow wedges it tight.

"The fire," she says, nodding at his small, flickering effort.

"Yes, it was lucky for me there were matches in a tin on the mantel. Though there is little wood left to burn." With his boot toe, he nudges an empty can on the hearth. "I found that as well. I didn't know what it might be—it had no label. I pried it open. Peaches . . ."

She stares at the wall and holds a finger to her lips. "The wind has changed."

"I expect it will do that all night," he says. "I can't make heads nor tails of the weather out here. It's not like home when a breeze off the bay washes ashore, same as the waves. Wind here will do most anything it wants, it seems."

"Stop talking." Her eyes narrow and she turns her head. "He will have smelled the smoke."

"Who?"

She looks at the young man again, not seeing him. "It would not matter. He will follow my tracks. Even a dullard can track in the snow."

"Who is he?"

She looks at the door. After some time, she whispers, "Davidson."

"Davidson?"

She regards him as if she caught him eating a handful of dirt. "I expect you were an annoying child."

She looks back to the door. "I doubted him from the first.

127

My father, on the other hand, suspected him of some merit. Papa is kindly but prone to fits of unwarranted charity. Such was the case in his assessment of Mr. Davidson, who came to us from nowhere, seeking work."

"What has he done then, this Davidson?"

"Hush!" The girl growls the word, not looking at him. "Do you hear that?" She eyes along the front wall, the door, as if watching a speck on the horizon. She stands, the pistol held across her chest.

Through gaps in the door's planking, lines of quick-shifting yellow light leak in, disappear, move left and right, then back again.

"You are in there, girl! I seen your tracks and I smelled your smoke!" The voice from outside the door is loud and thick, as if shouted through a quilt.

The girl says nothing, but licks her lips. The young man watches her breath, silver clouds in the near-dark of the cold room.

A long moment passes.

"This is no way to treat your beloved!"

The young man expects the girl to shout a reply, but she says nothing.

He pulls in a deep breath. "You had better leave me alone, mister." His voice does not sound as menacing as he had intended. "I am armed . . . and angry!"

The girl stares with wide eyes at the young man, then turns back to the door. Still, she says nothing.

A small flame licks at the last of the wood, pinches out.

"I thought I seen two sets of tracks! So, you are with another already!"

"I am armed!" the young man shouts. "Go away!" He lays a hand atop the end of the snapped branch he uses as a crutch.

"I'll go nowhere but in!" The door bucks inward once more,

revealing a large man holding a lantern's bail in a wind-reddened hand. In the other, a rifle, aimed at the room. He dips his big, shaggy head to look in, and smiles. "We are not through, girl."

He shoves forward, and once inside stands full height. "Who are you?" he says to the young man. "The one who shouts that he is armed? Two arms is all I see!" The big man laughs. Wind blows snow at his back and he hunches, then closes the door.

Davidson wears an unbuttoned, untucked wool shirt of black and white checks, red long johns beneath, and below, dark trousers bunching atop black boots.

"Back!" he shouts.

The girl steps away from him.

His bottom lip sits wet and quivery. His veined eyes, too, are moist with anticipations that hang like bad smells in the close room. "You are of breeding age, and I am not yet through with you, girl."

"That is enough of your filthy talk, sir!" The young man points at Davidson. The big man pays him no attention.

The young woman aims the pistol at the big man. "I am of an age and of a mind to kill you," she says. Her voice is small and it shakes.

"That's the bold girl I like. But that old relic of a pistol is not loaded." He hefts his rifle and shakes it. "This is."

He sets the lantern on the mantel. "Now, you are of an age to do as I say, nothing more. I may choose to bend you over my knee . . ." He tugs a nearly empty bottle of rye from a trouser pocket, swigs and sighs, drizzling liquor down his haired chin. He tosses the bottle to the floor and drags a cuff across his wet mouth.

"No matter." His eyes close as he speaks. "I will get what I want, just not as often as I want. But I will have your ranch, and though I would prefer to also have you with it, the ranch will win the day. As for you, little girl, once we are through, you will rest with your beloved papa."

He spits on the floor and his red eyes rove the dark room, then settle once more on the young man. "What are you? Worth my time or that of a bullet?"

Davidson looks down the young man's thin body. "What's this?" He steps forward, a leer forming on his wide, haired face. "I see you are a gimp." He glances at the girl, then back at the man's swollen, bent ankle wrapped in rags that had once been a shirt. "Where is your boot?"

"I lost it."

"I should say!" Davidson laughs and, with a grunt, kicks the young man's afflicted foot once, twice, his teeth gritted behind a stretched smile.

The young man screams. Even through the hot wash of pain flowering up his leg, the sound shocks him. It is a shriek no man should give voice to, yet he cannot stop.

"Shut up that yowling!" Davidson claws the young man's collar and shoves him to the floor. His head bounces on the packed dirt and his breath snags, stuttering in his throat.

"Stay put!" The big man wags the rifle at the young man. "You will be the last thing I attend to."

Davidson steps poorly toward the girl, steadies himself, and stares at her while slipping the braces from his shoulders. His trousers drop to his knees and he shuffles forward, backing the girl to a wall. With his free hand he yanks the pistol from her and drops it to the dirt.

The young man watches, shaking, fixed by the surprise of what he sees. As the heavy-breathing man bends low and pushes himself against her, the girl looks down at the young man, her eyes wide.

The moment is enough. The young man grabs the bed frame and shoves himself up, sucking in breath through tight teeth.

He hefts his crude crutch, hops forward, and swings it hard at the side of the man's wide head. A quick, dark spray blooms outward.

Davidson stiffens and groans, the sound reminding the young man of a bullock he heard many years before as a child visiting his uncle's farm. He cannot see the girl and thinks he hit her as well, but she pushes past the groaning man before he drops to his knees, facing the wall.

She yanks the rifle from the man's weak left hand, steps back, and swings it as the young man had the crutch, smacking the barrel's end hard against the other side of the big man's head. A breath rushes from him and he flops forward. His forehead scuffs the log wall as he slides facedown to the floor.

"What should we do?"

"Kill him," she says, cocking the rifle.

Davidson moans and lifts his head. It wobbles and thunks once more to the floor.

"No, no!" The young man holds out trembling hands as if to push away the idea. "Don't do that. Surely there's a better way."

"Shut up," she says. "You know nothing."

"I am a baker. I don't want such trouble on my conscience."

"Then hobble on out of here, Mr. Baker, and I will deal with it myself." Her voice is low and steady and she does not look up as she sights along the barrel at Davidson's head. "I will sleep like a kitten tonight knowing this foul bastard is sucking mud and I am the one who felled him."

"Oh, Lord, young lady, this is not the way."

"Lord? You use his name as if we are at a church supper. The Lord has nothing to do with it. This beast killed my papa and worked me over so bad I can hardly stand, and you want me to let him live? Hell no, I say. The Lord himself has a whole lot of

131

explaining to do as it is."

Her finger flexes on the trigger for a long moment, then her shoulders sag, but she does not lower the rifle. "Pull off his boots, his socks, and his trousers. That shirt as well."

"What?"

"Do it now."

The young man regards her a moment, then, wincing, lowers himself to his good knee and commences the task. The second boot is troublesome and the man's socks are wet. What wool not worn through on the soles has stuck to the feet as if grown into them.

"Is this necessary?"

"Yes."

"I refuse to do any more."

"Then I will shoot you both."

The young man sighs and bends once more to his distasteful chore. When he finishes, the girl motions him back to the bed.

Eerie shadows stretch in the lantern's warm, low light. Despite the pulsing ache in his ankle, the young man fights drowsing, his eyes close and his head drops forward, only to jerk upright again. The girl does not move. She stands above the prone man, the rifle pointed at his head.

Eventually Davidson groans and groans, and when it seems to the young man as if the brute has expended all effort in groaning, the big man pushes himself to his knees. He touches his head and grunts.

"Stand up now."

"Huh?"

"On your feet."

It takes more groans and much effort, but Davidson gains his feet, swaying and creating new, leering shadows on the wall and ceiling.

A sudden slam of wind pushes at the door, forcing fine snow

through gaps between planks.

The girl smiles. "You will take your leave now, Davidson."

"Huh?"

She points the rifle at the door. "Out. Now."

The man seems to awaken then, becomes aware of what the girl means. He shakes his head. "No," he says. The word becomes a plea, then sounds that are not words fill the air. Soon he is snotting himself and trying to drop to his knees to beg.

"Shut your foul mouth or I will shoot you deader than dead. Now leave."

"But where? I ain't got my boots!"

"Make for the ranch."

The young man knows he can never forget the sight of Davidson outside the door, staring in, standing stark against a swirl of white. His red long underwear, unbuttoned in the middle, sags open, as black and haired there as is his shaggy head, save for its two wide, white eyes. He howls as the girl slams the door and pushes against it, jamming the latch once more.

"Drag that bed here."

The door rattles.

The young man stays seated atop the sag-rope frame.

She eyes him, then picks up his crutch and wedges an end beneath a crosspiece in the center of the wooden door. She stomps the other end into the packed dirt floor.

For long minutes Davidson pounds the door, begging with desperate sounds, words lost on the wind. The girl faces the door with the rifle drawn and does not move.

The whimpering from without diminishes, reappears, pinches out, further off each time.

"This is no way to solve the matter," whispers the young man.

Some time later she replies. "I disagree. A solution solves a problem."

He looks at her. "But he is still alive."

The wind pushes a spray of snow down the cold chimney.

She smiles. "I will be surprised if he finds his way back to the ranch."

"You said he could go back there."

She shakes her head. "I suggested he might make for it. I myself might end up living in a castle in England, but it is not likely."

"What do you mean?"

"I trusted Papa. I knew his faulty judgments, yet I trusted him. He said Davidson was a solid sort, perhaps not a scholar, but steadfast and true. Those were his words." She shakes her head hard, as if in disagreement with an unseen presence. "How wrong we both were."

She opens her eyes wide and stares at the young man. "Davidson stuffed his grimy kerchief in my mouth."

She turns away, wipes at her eyes with a thin wrist.

"He was finished by the time Papa returned from chores in the stable. Then he clubbed Papa to death in the kitchen with a split of stovewood. I ran for the door, saw Papa's cap-and-ball service pistol hanging in the holster and I pulled it free. But I did not dare turn around. I felt him behind me, knew he was behind me. All the way here."

Outside, in whipping gusts, they hear the man's shouts once more, distant and thin.

"He'll be turned around by now," she says quietly.

The young man stares at the wall.

She sits before the cold fireplace, the rifle leaning against her thigh, the cap-and-ball pistol in her lap.

Some time later, the young man drapes a tatter of wool

blanket on her shoulders. She does not move. He watches her breath.

The lantern gives out hours before dawn, the wind tires to an occasional whisper. Still she stares at the black ashes.

The young man does not sleep, but watches her and shivers and thinks of it all, over and over, hearing shouts that are not there.

"He was of dumber stock than I took him to be." She turns to the young man. "And that is saying something."

They stare down at Davidson, hunched in the snow as if trying to curl up into a coil so tight he might warm himself somehow from within. His skin, where it shows, has purpled, and his eyes are crusted with blown snow. A thin drift has formed along the curve of his back, but the worn red of his underwear is bare along his pooched belly and thighs and knees.

"We should bury him," says the young man. "Or at least drag him back to the dugout."

She closes her eyes, her nostrils flaring. "He was dumb and filled with ill intent. Because of that, he is dead."

"But . . ."

"Do as you wish. I will mourn one man today and it is not this bastard. I am going home."

He watches her slight figure walk away, her steps punching holes in the crust. Her arms, each laden with a gun, sway with the effort.

After a few moments, he shouts, "Do you have need of a baker at your ranch?"

This stops her. She turns and looks at him, the hand gripping her father's pistol held above her eyes. "I expect very few people in the world, if they are honest, have need of a baker." She regards him a moment longer, then turns away and resumes walking.

He watches her, then looks back at the snow-crusted hump of the dead man, and beyond, the low, wind-gnawed drift atop the dugout.

When he turns back, only the girl's dark hair is visible. Then that, too, disappears, hidden by a slope in the land. I am alone once more, he thinks. He also thinks she did not actually say she had no need of a baker.

The young man squints across the brittle, rolling sweep before him and breathes deep of the cold morning air. Hobbling forward, one step at a time, he follows her tracks.

Matthew P. Mayo is an award-winning author of novels and short stories. His novel, *Stranded: A Story of Frontier Survival* (Five Star), won the Western Heritage Wrangler Award, the Spur Award, and the Willa Award, among others. He and his wife, videographer Jennifer Smith-Mayo, along with their trusty pup/trail scout, Miss Tess, rove the byways of North America in search of hot coffee, tasty whiskey, and high adventure. For more information, drop by Matthew's website at Matthew Mayo.com.

* * * * *

The Devil's Rope
by Randi Samuelson-Brown

* * * * *

1889

It took a desperate kind of stubborn to live on the range, especially as cattle prices plummeted. The vast, wide-open empty of the Wyoming Territory unfurled in all directions. Endless silver sage expanses beckoned beneath the searing blue. Hillocks, scattered rock outcroppings, and chalk cliff promontories stood sentinel as tall stands of cottonwood trees interrupted the false flats, signaling the possibility of water. There was a rhythm to the windblown land as the seasons turned and life went on. In dry summer, the palette was a sunbaked expanse of tough prairie grasses and sage that slipped into golden autumn. Desolation drifted along with the gusting snow in winter: frozen scrub and barren, reaching trees. But the jewel of the region was the Medicine Bow River itself, a sinuous thread snaking through the rugged land and bringing life. Fringed with ice in the winter, swollen and pregnant during the spring runoff, the river danced through every season. But for now, it was full-on summer; the heat searing the greenish-ocher scrub into a pale, dry tinder as hawks hunted in pairs overhead.

Lenora took solace in the movement and gentle song of the flowing river; unsure if she measured up to the demands of life in that isolated corner. Standing atop the ridge behind their squat lean-to, the vistas unfurled beneath rolling thunderheads that bloomed tall in the sky. Leaning into the ever-present

Wyoming wind, she didn't trap the strands of hair dancing about her face: tangled brown tendrils sprung free. At twenty-five years of age she might not be considered young, but she didn't set much store in numbers.

And there she stood, a married woman with one hundred and sixty acres of land to prove. That was a number she had to reckon with.

Long bones hung together with sinew, Lenora had once appeared poised for spinsterhood if the Cheyenne gossips were right. True, she married late in life, but that was no crime. Had anyone asked her straight out, she would have defended her status as a deliberate choice on her part. Rashness, in such matters, often led to tragic lives that lasted far too long in misery. Being left on the shelf never held the fear her mother tried to instill; she was capable of work, so Lenora simply waited and trusted in fate.

And fate, in this instance, didn't let her down.

She was wiping tables at a restaurant when a range-weathered man of few words ordered a cup of coffee. Their courtship was brief and to the point; her name exchanged for his without qualm. And that man now climbed up the hill to stand at her side, breathing sage-scented air and admiring the river demarcating the southern edge of their plat from the vast beyond. Hayden held out his calloused hand without saying a word. Lenora smiled and placed her long-fingered hand in his. Together they stood, shoulder to shoulder and exchanged knowing smiles.

The new bride moved into the rough lean-to—suitable for a man batching, but not exactly cut out for a woman. Still, Lenora figured it would be fine enough for a while. Neither of them had much in the way of possessions, but she set out to do what she could. There was never any shortage of chores, and she was a willing worker. It was a Wednesday. Taking advantage of the hot dry weather, Lenora set the washtub in front of the door while Hayden worked on a horse shelter to the far side of the corral, hammer blows ringing clear. Humming a tune of her own making, she drew water from the well and set up her laundry operations in the shade. Humming as she scrubbed their worn shirts and linens against the washboard, she found a tempo in her invented tune.

A low, insistent rumble swelled in the distance, small at first, but growing. Lost in her own world, the crack of a bullwhip slicing through her song changed that right quick.

Hayden came running, and she dropped whatever her hands held back into the soapy water.

Yips and high-pitched whistles. Rough yee-hawing. Cattle bawling and thundering, coming close. The din of hundreds of hooves. No easy approach, this was cattle rushing and almost stampeding through.

"They've caught the scent of water," Hayden said, but they both knew there was more to it than that.

Bullwhips cracking over the herd, goading the cattle on and on.

"They aren't turning!" Hayden grabbed her arm, pulling her to the lean-to's wall. Sure enough, the cowboys aimed the herd right by the building, making straight for the river. One rider even had the effrontery to wink at Lenora with a cold blue eye—a bandana pulled over his face. Four masked cowboys wheeling, laughing, and hooting. Features obscured and indistinguishable; all except for the man with the cold-water stare.

A vein in Hayden's neck throbbed.

"Get in the house." He pushed her through the door, then darted back outside, taking the rifle left loaded on the rack.

"This here is private property," Hayden shouted, walking

toward the men slow and steady. Determined. Rifle balanced in his hand, fingers flexing, ready.

One of the riders pulled down his bandana, jaw square and mean. "You sure about that?"

"Your kind ain't wanted here!" A sweat-stained man jeered, wheeling his horse around and ready to charge the mound where Hayden stood.

Cold-Eye didn't say a damn thing, just leaned on his saddle horn and waited. Waited, like the outcome was all but expected.

Standing his ground—Hayden's shoulders were wide and taut, arms held a few inches from his hips. "You're on my land."

Cold-Eye nudged his horse straight at Hayden, hand poised to pull his rifle from the saddle scabbard.

Four armed men to one.

Mouth gone dry, she couldn't stand by and do nothing. Edging from the house, white-knuckled grip on a broom, she advanced toward the men.

Cold-Eye burst into cruel laughter when he marked her.

Her knees almost buckled.

"Leave them be!" The commanding voice belonged to one of the other riders. "No one said anything about bringing a woman into this."

"Shoot." The sweat-stained cowboy spat a glob of tobacco juice onto the ground. "What's she going to do, hit us with her broom?"

"I'd like to see her try," Cold-Eye drawled.

Hayden lifted the rifle to his shoulder. The hammer click meant business.

The dissenting rider rode up behind Cold-Eye and the stained shirt. "Let's go! I *said*, ride on out!"

The men both took their time about turning their horses. "We're leaving," Cold-Eye said but it didn't sound like a permanent arrangement.

Hayden didn't move, but kept his rifle trained as the men rounded up the strung-out cattle and thundered out into the free range beyond.

"They might have killed you," she stammered, releasing her death grip on the handle.

"But they didn't," her husband replied, defiant. "We're putting up some wire to mark our land."

And she knew that would only make the strife worse. But Hayden's mind was set on the matter, and she simply held her tongue.

That forced stampede changed how she felt about the range and their claim. For the first time, Lenora understood, deep in her bones, what it meant to be unwelcome in the middle of the Great American Desert. Worries about the harsh weather and isolation fell away, replaced by the worries of the other inhabitants and what they might do. Whether the cattlemen liked it or not, the drive to break and corral the range was on, and change bred consequences. Homesteaders like themselves trickled into the high plains and labored toward improvement. Improvement of the land, improvement of themselves, improvement of their situation. All that improvement placed them at odds with the big cattle outfits, precarious and balanced on a sharp knife's edge. The Wyoming Stock Growers Association had different views of ownership. They aimed to control the range with a tight fist of money, organization, and political influence. Everyone was locked in a fight to control the wide-open expanses, one way or another. It all just came down to the perspective a body held.

"The law's on our side, Len," Hayden told her more than once, but his confidence was unraveling along the edges.

Times turned hard in more ways than one as cattle prices

continued to fall.

Hayden never spoke much, but what few words he had dried up like shallow watering holes in the summer heat. They tended to the fifteen head in their herd; none of those fifteen head would fetch hardly anything at market. He went about his chores with a grim determination, the windmill creaking and protesting in the ceaseless wind. She tried to bolster his flagging spirits, and her own. Not long after the trespassers had run roughshod over them, he sat down at noontime, head resting in his hands for a good, long moment. With a short, angry sigh he looked at her straight.

"We're going into town for supplies. How much money's left in the box?"

The battered tin on the solitary shelf held all the money they had in the world. Reluctant, she pulled off the lid: a few silver dollars, a wad of bills, and a whole bunch of small coins.

She counted them out. "Thirty-seven dollars and eighty-two cents . . ."

Rubbing the back of his head, hair sticking up in ruffled tufts, he offered a slim, threadbare explanation. "It's time. And if it's not, it will be shortly."

He was, of course, talking about the wire.

"That's all the money we have." Her voice came out unnaturally small and tight.

"We can sell a beef or two if we have to. The old ones." He stabbed the meat on his plate, and shoved a bite into his mouth, matter decided once and for all.

But she knew, and he did as well, no one would buy old beeves. "Don't suppose there's enough for cloth, do you? Your shirts are threadbare, and my skirts aren't much better."

His eyes softened a bit as he looked up at her. "There's nothing I'd rather see than you in a pretty new dress. You know that. But we'll have to wait for the market to turn."

She patted him on the shoulder before taking her place at the table. "I know." She offered a confident smile that she didn't feel. The last thing she wanted was for him to get the notion he wasn't providing good enough.

But it was hard, and Lenora wasn't accustomed to keeping important comments to herself. "I can't help thinking a fence will just provoke them. Next time events might not turn out so well."

His eyes turned to flint. "Next time I'll shoot them. Damned if I won't."

"Leaving me a widow."

"It won't come to that," he muttered down into his plate and then resumed eating. "There are laws."

Hayden's saddle horse and old Gus hitched, together they drove the wagon to the far-flung crossroads of River Rock. If their trouble wasn't forgotten, it receded as the road improved and houses started springing up in windblown clusters.

Inside the mercantile, Hayden leaned up alongside the counter. "How much barbed wire and posts will twenty-five dollars buy?"

The storekeep in a white apron totted up the lengths and made his calculations. "That looks like two coils of wire and twenty-two posts. Whatcha aiming to do?"

"Put up a fence."

"One hundred and sixty acres? That's not enough to get that all in. Your homestead shaped square?"

"Not down by the river, but the rest is."

"I can extend the remainder on credit if you like." The store-keep eyed him.

A shrug and a pause. "Don't like to be beholden to nobody. You heard of anyone on the lookout for extra help?"

That caught her short. He'd never mentioned a thing about

hiring himself out to her.

All the while, Hayden kept his eyes trained on the clerk. Deliberately.

If the man noticed the strain, he didn't show it. "I heard just the other day that the Swan Ranch is hiring on. Over Chugwater way."

Hayden nodded, taking the news under consideration. Time took on a strange slant as he pulled out his wallet and handed the money over. The man rang up the sale on the till, the bell singing clear and bright at the tally.

On the way back, Lenora gave him the long-eyed stare of a displeased woman. "Just how do you expect me to manage everything on my own?"

"I don't doubt you for a second," he replied. "Besides, you know we need the money."

But he didn't understand that she doubted herself. And the rest of the return trip with their load of shiny new wire and fence posts passed in an uncharacteristic, uncomfortable silence.

"Some call this the Devil's rope," Hayden grunted.

Potholing and stringing wire proved blistering, slow work. Each length of Brotherton's Flat Barbed Wire needed to be turned taut around each and every line post before going on to the next.

Lenora pulled on the tail end with her full body weight. "That supposed to make me feel any better?"

To her surprise, he grinned. "I don't see why not."

All wasn't forgiven, but she dropped the grudge at his smile. Nothing would change, anyhow. He would still leave once the two segments of fencing were done.

She grumbled, although a smile tugged as she stopped pulling. "I don't see why we couldn't have strung this on the western side toward town. Since this is what all our money is wrapped up in, I'd sure like people to take notice."

"The ones that matter will see it alright. Trouble won't be coming from town." Hayden's eyes didn't quite meet hers, his mouth falling into a tight thin line. "You know that."

"They haven't come back."

His gray eyes didn't waver but met hers straight on. "No, and maybe they won't. They wouldn't bother a woman on her own, but I'm leaving you with the rifle all the same."

She arched her eyebrows and he had the good grace to color. There was no guarantee where the night riders were concerned.

He shoved the brim of his hat back and looked at her. "This job will afford cloth for that nice new dress you wanted."

"Not to mention more barbed wire."

"Not to mention."

She stuck the postholer into the ground and stomped on the shoulder with her boot. "Given the choice between a new dress and having you home, I'd pick having you home."

"It's just for a short time. No one thought prices would go so low. That's the only way to get money that I can think of that's honest."

Honest. "What if those men were Swan's riders?"

"We'll never know. But if they were Swan's, I'm sure as hell not going to let them turn up here again."

"So, you all would just go to some other place and scare those people, is that it?"

His voice grew tight. "You know it isn't. What happened wasn't right, and I'd take no part in such dealings."

But everyone knew people were forced to take sides. Cattle bosses didn't have a reputation for taking kindly to being told "no" to anything.

"Sure hope you don't have to make that choice." In some hidden place along her vertebra, she kept her suspicions, which were better left unsaid.

The next four days of postholing and stretching wire were hard, and the outcome uncertain. Maybe the segments would turn cattle, maybe they wouldn't. Herds being run roughshod would either go around or the fence would get knocked down. So much depended on the cowboys and their intent at the time. Intentions were a hell of a thing, as they both had learned firsthand. But while Lenora took the message to heart, it only seemed to get Hayden's back up.

Lenora was fearful, and Hayden was angry. Either way didn't help matters at all.

But one thing was for certain. Getting left out on her own scared the hell out of her.

"I don't exactly feel right about any of this," he told her, tying his bedroll onto the back of the saddle's cantle.

Other women had managed before, but those other women hadn't been her.

Tears welled, and she swatted them away with an angry hand. She only nodded as he stuck his foot in the stirrup, swung up, and legged over.

"I'll be back in two weeks' time, Lennie. The foreman understands I need to come home to check on things and do some of the heavy work. It's just fourteen days."

Separation, heartache, and the unknown. All for thirty dollars a month.

As he loped off down the wagon tracks, his horse's hooves kicked up a cloud of lingering dust. As long as she could manage, she marked the repaired left shoulder of his shirt. Maybe it would hold together until he got back home, maybe it wouldn't. He looked over his shoulder at her once or twice and she lifted her hand in a limp farewell, standing abandoned in the ruts.

But she didn't move, didn't turn back to the house or the endless awaiting chores.

Instead, she lied to herself. Pretending that she wasn't watching him disappear but was waiting for the building storm in the direction he traveled. True, the sky filled with rolling dark gunmetal underpinnings.

Perhaps it would bring rain, or perhaps just more wind. Enough blasted wind to set her nerves on edge.

Later in the deep blue of the night, the plaintive low song of a solitary coyote carried through the dark.

Responding howls rang crystal clear from different directions, several voices in full-throated chorus. Lying in bed, Lenora could just about see the moon through the window, her husband's side empty. Bone-weary and unable to sleep—she wasn't alone and that had her spooked. If trouble came, there would be no answering response from the distance. In that, the high-yipping coyotes had the advantage. Chugwater was a good, long ride away.

And it was the two-legged animals that worried her, and they could ride horses well. Far better than her.

Beyond the coyotes' calling songs, she strained to hear a different sound. A sound apart from the moonlit howls—something beneath the surface. Striving to make out a warning of trouble of a more dangerous sort. At some point her efforts yielded nothing and she drifted off.

When the morning light streaked low against the horizon and heavy from lack of decent sleep, Hayden's empty pillow lay next to hers. Hugging it to her chest, another day was set up and starting out, whether she was ready or not. Throwing aside the covers, she set her feet down on the rough plank floor.

Her first full day on her own.

A full week passed, uneventful and quietly isolated.

A time of few distractions, a hawk's cry overhead caused her

to smile. Circling for prey and gliding in the sky with an as-
suredness that made her feel small. Sharp-eyed and deadly, with
one plummeting swoop it rose triumphant, winging straight up
into the sky, a limp rodent hanging in its talons. That's just the
way life was. The strong preyed upon the weak, and she could
only hope the mouse was all the way dead. The hawk would
have meat to eat, which was more than she could say for the
time being.

Everyone lived as best they could.

She had choices, unlike that poor mouse. She could either
ride the perimeters of their homestead or resume digging on the
irrigation ditch. But dang it, she was tired of wielding a hoe and
a pickaxe.

Pulling the saddle off the rack, she approached old Gus, a
horse who hadn't enough gumption to go tearing across the
land without a rider, much less with anyone on his back. She
nudged him out toward the fence posts in the distance, standing sentinel over their land. Too late for second thoughts, the
meadowlarks fluted, and the cattle weren't too far scattered.
Grazing and staring at her sloe-eyed, they preferred the bounty
of the good grass along the river's edge to the dry scrub further
out.

Fourteen head of cattle and the one new calf. Everything as
it should be.

That is, until she noticed a cow trailing a calf coming over
one of the small sand hills. She watched, waiting until they
came closer. Sure enough, the number 66—a mark belonging to
one of the larger outfits. Teschemacher and De Billier, she
reckoned, but one was as good as another.

More interestingly, the calf looked about big enough to be
weaned.

Returning livestock was no simple matter, especially when it
was down to just her. The two strays joined the others bankside

just as natural as apple pie. They blended in with the rest of the herd, watering. Going up against the Teschemacher and De Billier Cattle Company was no small prospect, but two head would never be missed from an operation that size.

Preoccupied and turning the issue about the cow and calf over in her mind, she still had a job to do. Reaching the corner outpost, she tucked her skirt under her thighs wary of the sharp barbs and the gusting wind. Gus's mane rippled, and grit sprayed into her face. Riding along, they hadn't gotten far when the wire seemed a bit limp. A few steps further along, the Brotherton's Flat Barbed Wire was indeed slack and sagging. Coming unfurled.

She took the risk of dismounting.

A few more steps in, she had her answer. The wire snaked along the ground, severed and helpless. Four segments down, the wire lay uncoiled from the posts, sprawled out. Cut. Three posts yanked out and flung aside.

Stomach tightening, she'd be damned if she was going to just leave everything lying aground, letting them win—thinking she and Hayden would cower.

That segment of fence meant everything to her husband, and by extension, to her.

Heart thudding, she hefted up the posts and stuck them back into their holes. Without pliers, there was nothing she could do about the wire. It was a two-person job to rejoin the ends. Forced to leave it and still heartsick at the damage, a strange chill brushed her neck. Maybe the vandal was still nearby, hiding. The land held plenty of places for hiding if a person took the notion.

Uneasy and suddenly vulnerable, she hefted herself back up on the saddle, and aimed homeward at as fast a clip as she dared. That night she latched the door and kept retuning to inspect it again and again. Checking to make certain, just one more time, that it was secure. Deep down, she felt ashamed. And her shame was tied up in that damned, ruined wire.

The next morning rose pale, the dawn blushing, and no strangers had come banging on the door in the dead of the pitch-black night. Over a cup of reheated coffee, the problem of the wire plagued her. The value of that wandering cow and calf had the potential to tip the balance in their favor. If they were still with the others, she would have a distinct choice to make.

She ought to just drive them off. That would be the end of any dilemma as far as she was concerned. But that wire cost money. Sure, the ends could somehow be twisted together, but intentional damage had been caused. Intentional damage deserved recompense.

That calf was old enough to brand.

If she took up the notion to steal, that was. When she went outside to see about the horse, the branding iron issued an unspoken challenge, hanging on the stall's wall in plain sight.

Crossing the yard and casting a passing glance at the irrigation ditch that needed working, the De Billier's cow and calf stood with the others. They hadn't returned home as they ought.

Of course, there was a right way and a wrong way to handle such situations, but common sense was another matter. Mavericks were once divvied up come roundup time, but the large operations had ended all that cooperation. Instead they forced all mavericks to be auctioned off to the highest bidder. It stood to reason the small holders couldn't pay what the wealthy holders bid. Just another way of forcing the homesteaders to kowtow to larger demands.

But damn it, they had a right to a livelihood, too.

"We don't just have to do what they want," Lenora remarked to her husband during the course of such conversations.

He would grin. "That's right. There's no law that says we

have to do their bidding."

Little did they know, they were stepping out into a strange and dangerous territory.

Hayden set his mouth into a thin line as he stared at the damage and her attempted repairs.

"We'll bind up the wire where it's cut, stronger than before. And if the bastards cut it again, we'll mend it again. Probably no sense in bothering to report it."

"Too far," she replied.

Not to mention the law might even be in the cattle barons' pockets. A sheriff's pay didn't stretch far, and he had miles of district to cover.

Lenora stood behind her husband as he whacked the top of the post, driving it further into the parched land. When he finished, she patted in the loose dirt to fill the gaps, cheeks stinging. Perhaps he thought she couldn't manage after all, and that rubbed her the wrong way.

Problems were coming from all directions, that much was for certain. Slow movements, she turned to face him. "A cow and her big calf wandered into our herd. We could brand the calf, and no one would be the wiser. The cow'd cause more of a problem, but we could butcher her or turn her out on the range. It don't make much difference to me, although some meat wouldn't go amiss."

Hayden stopped working. "Never took you for an . . . enterprising type."

She felt her cheeks flush. "Never had to be, before."

Lenora grabbed the pick and headed down toward the river. Hacking out an irrigation ditch was hot, dirty work. A man's job, but she could manage. Hefting the pick high, she struck down into the hard-baked land, yanking upwards to turn the earth inside out. Fifty yards or so of baked dirt to whack through before a ribbon of water slipped from the Medicine Bow into the newly created trough.

An obligation in proving up the land, the work had to be done.

Another heave of the pick and an arc back down into the earth with a dull thud. A far better sound than the ringing scrape of rock, she consoled herself as she wrenched it free. Pulling back up with dirt clods upturning, her attention was caught by a telltale dust cloud signaling an unexpected rider. Her stomach went cold, but she didn't go running. Instead she stood deer-still waiting; shielding her eyes from the sun.

Picking his way down the rutted tracks, the rider had approximately the same cut as Hayden. She had to look twice before deciding it was, in fact, him. Not expected for another five days, he approached at a fast-enough clip for matters to be serious.

She dropped the pick, then halfway ran to meet him.

Mouth drawn and countenance gray, anyone could see for themselves it was no social call. "Everything alright here?"

Pleased to see him, all the same, something was wrong for him to be standing before her. "Yes." She gestured around her at the homestead. "Nothing of note. Why?"

"There's been trouble. A man and a *woman* got lynched over in Natrona. There's plenty of talk going 'round. The newspapers claim it's for rustling, but I don't like the sound of it. I told the foreman I wanted to check on things here, and he let me go." Hayden pulled out a newspaper from his saddlebag. "Here."

Pulling off her work gloves, Lenora wiped the sweat on her skirt before handling the folded paper.

THE RANGE QUEEN

July 24.-James Averell and the notorious "Cattle" Kate Maxwell were lynched by night riders. The bodies of the "rustler" and "range queen" dangled from the same limb of a big Cotton-wood this morning. The scene of this justifiable deed is on the Sweetwater River near Independence Rock. Averell was Postmaster at Sweetwater. Kate Maxwell is the heroine of a shameful story which appeared throughout the country three months ago. A known woman of ill-fame, she traded her favors for mavericks. The stockmen of the Sweetwater region have long been victims of cattle thieves. Due to the prejudice against large outfits, it has been impossible to convict on this charge, and the "rustlers" have become bold and shameless. Averell and his so-called wife were in possession of fifty freshly branded yearling steers last Sunday morning. A stock detective, whose suspicions were aroused, was driven from the place when he was noticed viewing the stolen property. Averell and the woman have several times been ordered to cease appropriating "mavericks" but had disregarded all warning. Word was passed along the river, and fifteen to twenty men gathered at a designated place. They galloped to the cabin of Averell and Cattle Kate surprising the "rustlers" at home. The pair of thieves were dealt with, and their bodies cut down as of this morning.

Lenora swallowed, stopped reading, and searched her husband's face. "They lynched a couple for mavericking. Not horse stealing or cattle rustling, but *mavericking.*" Met with gray-eyed confusion mirroring her own, she stammered, "That can't be right."

A slow exhale and a bitter, choking response. "Of course, it ain't right. They say that Averell wasn't hesitant about sharing his opinions, so the papers are dragging their names through the mud. Averell and his wife also had two combined claims. Good claims along a river and a meadow full of grass for haying."

Lenora froze, the similarity plain. "That's why you've come."

He nodded in that slow way of his. "There's also been talk

about pulling wire down. Ours still standing?"

She nodded, worrying a rock with the toe of her boot. The calf's brand had scabbed over but wasn't all the way healed. "Don't suppose there's any talk of who took part in this, is there?"

Hayden spat. "There's talk, but it's all hearsay. No one's going to want to go admitting to a thing like that, especially hanging a woman. But large outfits are hiring stock detectives."

Everyone had a few mavericks in their herds, but neither of them said as much.

"I'm taking the cow over to Swan's for the time being. Don't want her here. Nothing good'll come of it."

Nothing good, other than beef to eat. But too much meat for her to eat on her own. And, for the time being, too dangerous to try.

Hayden stayed home that night, just long enough to look things over. In the morning, he roped the cow who had other thoughts on the matter. Lassoed around the neck and the rope tied off on the saddle horn, it was going to be a long ride the way the cow kept fighting. He was right of course, it was foolish to try to keep the cow.

He brushed her cheek with the back of his hand before he left and said nothing.

The rest of the day passed long and lonely.

Late in that same afternoon, another rider came unannounced. He surprised her out by the well. "You Mrs. Thayer?"

The cold-water blue eyes she had seen before. "Yes."

Silence. He stared at her and she stared at him, heart choking.

He broke first. "Your husband around?"

The rifle was too far away. "What do you want?"

That same crooked smile. He found the fear she tried to hide laughable. "I want to look at the brands on your cattle."

"Just who are you, exactly?"

"One of Bothwell's stock detectives, not that I owe you an explanation."

"You do, if you're standing on our land. I'm now asking you to leave." The tough words bolstered her up.

"Like I said. Is your husband around?"

She didn't let on like she recognized him. "I'll go in the house and get him. He's feeling poorly. You wait right here."

She hurried to the house, knees quaking. Of course, she emerged with the rifle, poised and ready to shoot. "He said to tell you to get off our land."

"And he sends a woman to do his fighting for him, is that it?"

She didn't answer.

He stared at her, made his words slow. "Tell him we'll be back. We're going to make him an offer on this land that he might want to seriously consider. For both of your best interests."

He rode off at a clip, and never bothered once to look back.

She stood beneath the windmill shaking. The land was good, they had chosen well. Perhaps too well.

And the vigilantes, stock detectives, or whatever they were, would, without doubt, return.

The low hills provided cover for those who wanted to be hid. She saw nothing out of the ordinary, but that didn't mean the man wasn't hiding. Cold-Eye didn't believe that Hayden was home at all. Maybe the hills were concealing others in league with him. It stood to reason that they would test the situation before striking. She headed into the lean-to where Gus stood waiting for his feed. Any offer couldn't be accepted without Hayden there to hear it, and he wouldn't sell out. Never, not in a hundred years.

Then again, the man hadn't exactly said anything about money.

The Putnam's homestead was seven miles distant. She could saddle up Gus and try to make it, but she'd never been the strongest of riders. Numbers offered safety but guaranteed nothing in the end. Not against professional fighters, and maybe that's exactly what she was up against. Being caught alone, out in the open would be the worst of all outcomes. That man could easily be out there, watching and lying in wait.

Making quick work of her chores, she shut herself up inside the house.

Half expecting to hear a man's step on the rough porch, measured and deadly, the evening drew out into nightfall, yet nothing happened. Nerves a-snapping, she waited. Decided how they needed a dog the very next chance they got. Trying to listen through the wind, eventually she gave up and went to bed, glad that Hayden had taken that mother cow away. If the man really was a stock detective there was nothing for him to find that he could prove. She didn't think he was a real stock detective, and that was part of the problem.

He could easily be one of those night riders that hung the postmaster and his wife. She'd even seen the woman once, or so she thought. Didn't look like a harlot at all. In fact, she looked just the same as the other homesteading wives, wind-burned and determinedly capable.

Shoulders tight, Lenora couldn't shake the image of two bodies hanging from a tree. None of it should have happened. Even more, it meant that none of them were safe.

A horse's smart trotting gait interrupted the morning.

Lenora grabbed the rifle just to make sure, but in the pit of her stomach she already had her answer. The man with the cold-water stare was aimed square toward her. Retreating back inside, shaking fingers fumbled with the door latch, knowing it wouldn't take all that much to kick it in.

A few planks of wood was all that stood between her and violence.

The horse clipped into the yard, blowing as it came to a full stop. No sound beyond the slow creaking of shifting weight in the saddle, until he chose to start. "I know you're in there, and I know your man's not around!"

Throbbing heart and breaths drawn jagged, none of what was about to kick off would end well.

Intent upon the sound of a man dismounting, she clenched the rifle barrel hard and pressed her forehead against the cold steel. She offered up a swift prayer.

"Not one step further!"

"Well, now. I just wanna talk, but if you don't come out, it won't be pretty."

She braced herself and pulled back the rifle's hammer. Standing half-crouched beside the door and out of the line of sight, she bumped up the latch with the tip of the rifle. The door opened a crack.

"Stay right there," she called. "I mean it!"

A low laugh. "Now, is that any way to be?"

His spurs jangled, closer. Hesitating on the porch, he laid his hand flat against the door and pushed it open wider. Already halfway through and surveying the interior, he half-stopped when he marked her, crouched against the wall.

She never hesitated. She pulled the trigger.

Blood and brains sprayed as his body crumpled in a foul heap, half in and half out of the door.

A dark red lake of pooling blood widened and spread along the floor.

The body wasn't going to move itself.

Time was draining away, and she didn't have forever. Yet she stood looking down at the shattered skull, half-stunned at the damage. Emerging into the open, rifle in hand, and searching the nearby hills and swells for riders or the telltale glint of steel, nothing stood out in the vastness.

A vastness that could swallow a man whole.

Grabbing a tarp and rope from the horse shelter, her blood cooled. Crossing the dirt expanse, it was a strange site seeing a man's legs protruding from the door. Whatever the case, the soles of his boots looked good.

Tempted, she knew she shouldn't. No matter that they looked Hayden's size.

Unfurling the tarp against the lip of the porch, she yanked on those boots, struggling against the deadweight. The corpse budged, but not enough. Again, she tried and strained, and got even less purchase. Kneeling in the dirt and breathing hard, she sized up the prospect knowing she wasn't strong enough.

But a horse was. And Cold-Eye's bay horse stood waiting.

Approaching the beast with caution, she spoke in a low, gentle voice and laid a comforting hand aside his neck, before leading him to his master. She roped the body and leveraged the rope around the saddle horn and backed his horse up. The body landed with a dull thud on the tarp, facedown.

His employer would send people looking. It was only a matter of time.

Drawing water from the well, with black lye soap and brush, she attacked the gore. Scrubbing hard, traces remained and discolored the floor. Flinging the old rag rug over the stain, she doubted it would be enough, but fretting wouldn't fix it any better.

Back outside, she undid the rope, covered the body with the tarp, and looped the rope as best she could for dragging.

Saddling up old Gus, she set out in the direction of the open range, leading Cold-Eye's horse and dragging his body along in an odd, stretched-out funeral procession. The body caught on brush now and again, their progress a slow walking pace. Yet they ventured out into the wide-open, which wasn't always as empty as one might suppose.

Story ready if needed; she'd say he'd been by the one time but had never returned. Other homesteaders must have been targeted as well, and most men wouldn't believe a woman would have the guts to shoot a man down.

But they'd be wrong.

Over an hour away, she found what she was looking for, a rock outcropping well away from their homestead. Deep enough to hide the body, she hobbled Gus and led Cold-Eye's horse as close to the overhang as she could. Remembering to rifle through the dead man's pockets, she found a ten-dollar gold piece and a battered watch, but nothing else that could establish his identity. She sat on the ground and used her legs to push him out of sight and wedged him away from view.

After checking the saddlebags and coming up with nothing more than jerky and hardtack, she slapped the horse's rump, and away he ran with a riderless saddle, mane fluttering free in the breeze.

The searing blue sky was vast and unyielding overhead, witness to the wide-open empty that hid secrets well. The watch fell from her fingers in the sage; she returned home and never once looked back.

The Wyoming wind picked up, obscured any traces of the dragged body, and she was grateful.

That day marked the change when she knew, in her heart, she was strong enough to survive in that harsh dry land.

The Devil's rope was their right.

Randi Samuelson-Brown is the author of *The Beaten Territory*, a finalist in multiple awards. She comes from Colorado and is interested in telling stories of the Old West from diverse female perspectives.

★ ★ ★ ★ ★

CALL ME MERCY
BY C.K. CRIGGER

★ ★ ★ ★ ★

Mercy Seabrook ain't . . . I mean, *isn't* . . . my real name. It isn't the name I had before or after I took up with Dougan, either. I'm not going to tell you what them names was. I picked Seabrook because I like water. *Sea,* 'cause I always wanted to get to the ocean, and *brook,* 'cause there ain't no sweeter music in the whole world than water gurgling over a rocky streambed. And I liked the sound of Mercy. The good Lord only knows I could've used some of it.

That's all beside the point now. I don't expect it matters much in regards to what happened, although it'll ease my heart to write those events down. Maybe it'll be important to some other woman, someday, to help show her what she has to do. What she *can do.* But when you come down to it, every woman has to find her own courage.

I've been told I should take note of every detail as I write. That you never know what might be the most *significant*—which is a fancy word I've just learned—detail. So here goes.

In the fall of 1895, I rode the train west to Washington State. At my own expense, too, although the advertisement I'd read in the *Chillicothe Morning Constitution*—that's Chillicothe, Missouri, not Chillicothe, Ohio—said I'd be reimbursed at the completion of my journey, when both parties signed the marriage contract. The advertisement was an old one, having reached Linneus about a month after publication, and I was a *credulous* fool. Desperation can strike you in unwholesome ways, for sure. But of course, I didn't know that then, and like a fourteen-year-old instead of a grown woman, I signed up to become a mail-order bride.

So there I was, six days later, stepping down those steep iron steps from the train, and landing knee-deep in mud. Seemed like it, anyhow. Rain flooded down in a steady stream, and it being almost seven o'clock in the evening, it was darker than the back end of a cave. My knees shook from hunger and cold, and I'd gotten sick from eating some bad food I bought on the cheap from a vendor in Missoula. Sad to say, I not only wasn't over the sickness yet, I smelled real bad.

Four men stood on the depot platform, hats tilted against the rain. Nearby, a fifth man astride a scrawny horse didn't bother to dismount. He simply sat there as if he didn't even notice the downpour, watching under the flickering light from the lanterns the four men on the platform held.

Three other women who'd also signed up to be brides had beat me off the train. They huddled together, trying to act confident and happy. They'd taken time to straighten their hats, brush cinders and soot from their dresses and coats, and layer on gloves. Ladies, or that's how they presented themselves. I wasn't so sure what kind of ladies they was.

Me? I felt too unwell to bother with gloves, cinders, or hats. Mainly because I didn't own a hat. Or gloves. I took a breath and stood behind them, one of the group, and yet not, our only similarity being that we'd each signed on for one of them marriage contracts.

A stout man, his paunch hanging over his belt line, spoke up, his voice hesitant. "Which of you is Miss Jones?" The lantern in his hand vibrated as the train puffed smoke and shook the platform with its rumble.

The three women looked at each other and after a moment,

the short, squatty gal raised her hand. "I am."

"Miss Smith?" Another man questioned.

"That's me." This woman wore purple gloves with a red coat, and a hat with three or four pheasant feathers sticking out of a pink band. The feathers were quickly becoming frazzled due to the rain.

Her man smiled as though relieved at his choice.

The next man, tall and cavernous, sort of like a drawing of Abraham Lincoln I'd seen in the paper, held out his hand to the last woman. Last besides me, that is. "Are you Miss Cleveland, by any chance?" His tone indicated he really hoped so.

"Why, yes," she said, bouncing on her toes like a gleeful child. "I am Miss Cleveland. Frances is my first name."

I snorted. Maybe a little louder than I should've because it earned me more than one critical look. The three women whispered behind their hands to one another. Miss Jones glared a little at Miss Cleveland, but shot daggers at me.

Smith, Jones, Cleveland—Frances Cleveland, no less—like the president's wife. Hah! I'd be willing to bet none of those were the names they'd been born with.

At the last, although one man and one woman remained unclaimed on the platform, he didn't speak my name. Then six pairs of eyes swiveled my way.

Miss Jones's man cocked an eyebrow at the last man. "Howard?"

Howard was the name on the contract I held, but he couldn't shake his head fast enough. "She'll have to go back. I won't pay. The contract says healthy, but she doesn't appear healthy to me. And look at her. She's no lady. Why, she isn't even dressed proper. And she's taller than I am!"

My hands clenched into fists. Maybe I should've told them about the railroad conductor who'd tossed my bag onto the platform in Kellogg. When I jumped him about it, he said he thought the valise belonged to a raggedy old man that'd gotten off there. Doubt the excuse woulda done me any good with these people, though.

Anyway, all I owned in this world was what I stood up in. They were my everyday clothes as I, like the other three women, had been saving my better set for this meeting. As it was, the coat I wore, which once belonged to my brother and got left behind when he ran off to Texas, had holes in the elbows and a pocket about torn off. My skirt had puke on the hem where a bout of sickness had struck too quickly for me to get it out of the way. And I was wearing my barn boots, although I'd had a fairly decent pair of shoes in the valise. Not something most women would want to steal since my stature put me several sizes above the average female. Yes, and even above some of the men, as "Howard" had pointed out. See, I'm coming up on six feet tall.

Coughing, I tried to clear the thickening from my throat. "You're unkind, sir. What ails me is eating some poisoned food. I'll soon be over it. And I ain't climbing back on this train. For one thing, they won't have me."

Miss Smith giggled behind a purple glove. "Why not? 'Cause they think you're a cow? A big, ugly cow?"

Miss Cleveland wasn't to be left out. "Maybe she's the cow-catcher."

The three women tittered like mama mice.

The Abraham Lincoln man gave a little frown, although he said nothing.

I refused to answer. Why should I tell the world my last nickel had gone for that poisoned food? And so, I clamped my mouth shut and tried to pretend all the water running down my cheeks came from rain.

The three couples took their lanterns and, followed by Mr.

Howard, slogged off into the night without a backward glance. They left me alone on the cold, dark, and rain-swept train platform with no place to go and nowhere to turn.

And I was cold—so cold.

"You. Woman."

A man speaking up out of the blue like that came near to scaring all Billy hell outta me. I jumped like I'd been jabbed with a red-hot poker. I, like those other people, had forgotten him sitting there aboard his horse.

"I'll take you," he said. "You can be my wife."

"You'd marry me? Why?"

"You can work, can't you? Soon as you get over that bad food you et."

"Yes," I said. I always could work rings around any other womenfolk I knew—and men, too.

I'd quit my bawling already, since I ain't much of one to sit around bemoaning my fate. Never noticed it did anyone any good, unless maybe a pretty little lady with gold hair and blue eyes, which don't describe me.

"Welp, fine. I need somebody to help me around the farm. Somebody who ain't gonna keel over at the first touch of the sun, or turn blue when it gets cold."

I stiffened. "I ain't the fainting kind."

"Didn't figure. Then follow me over to the livery. I got a pack pony over there. You can fit yourself in amongst my grub and ride him to the ranch."

I looked out into the rain and the dark and saw nothing. Nothing ahead and nothing behind.

So, I did what he said. I walked along behind his horse, its hooves throwing even more mud onto my skirt and even into my face, the whole three blocks to the aforementioned livery. Once there, I mounted the swaybacked old nag he used for a pack pony, and rode off into the night with him.

What else could I do?

If you're noticing a thing or two here that don't make sense or seem logical—well, you're right. After two years, I can tick off a few of them myself. For instance, he said I'd be his wife, but we didn't stop at any churches on our way out of town. I didn't see hide nor hair of a preacher until the next summer when a travelin' feller set up a tent in the big meadow down by the river and held himself a revival. Most folks would say not insisting we be married right away was my first mistake, although to my way of thinking, it might've already been the third or fourth. The first had been thinking I'd do better coming out west. The second error was in agreeing to a contract, which, in my simple mind, meant I had to abide by it. Yes. Even if nobody else did. A contract that didn't, in the end, mean a damn thing.

But on this night, the other thing I did wrong? The stupidest thing? I put my trust in a stranger. I didn't even ask his name, which worked both ways, you notice. Never thought of it. So much for logic.

The journey out to his ranch, which he just as often called a farm, took us up a mountain, through deep woods, and at long last came out in a meadow of no more than a couple or three acres. Later, I found the whole place consisted of a one-room shack, a lean-to barn, and an outhouse built of boards so warped you could see through the gaps. There were no fields and no livestock aside from the two horses, although he told me he ran cattle in amongst the trees.

Not that I noticed when we first arrived what with the dark and a heavy rain slowly turning to snow.

He left me standing outside the shed while he unsaddled his horse and removed the packs from the animal I'd rode. Tossing some moldy-smelling, badly cured hay onto the ground for the critters, he handed me one of the packs and told me to take it on up to the house.

I ought to have ran right back down the trail into town. I knew it even then, but I didn't. Couldn't. Too sick, too cold, too weary. He'd said he'd marry me, and I held the thought in my mind. It'd be all right, so I told myself. Tomorrow would be better. Tomorrow I'd be better.

Sometimes during that first night, I wondered if tomorrow would ever come. Or if I wanted it to.

"Bed's over in the corner." He'd come into the cabin right behind me and closed the door real quick.

Relief came gushing in. Remember? Sick, cold, tired—weak? I figured he'd build a fire seeing it was colder inside than out, but the only match he struck lit a kerosene lamp with a sooted-up glass chimney. By its weak glimmer I saw a filthy, ramshackle . . . Lordy, I can't even tell you. Suffice it to say I've seen tidier bears' dens. I stood frozen, trying to catch my breath in the dirt and the stench, and maybe he saw me shiver 'cause he said again, "Get in the bed, woman. I'll get you warmed up real quick."

Peering in the direction he indicated, I took one look and said, "Why, I'd sooner sleep with the horses than in this pigsty."

I meant it too, and turned toward the door, which is when he lashed out. He caught me by surprise, a smashing blow into my already sore belly. I wouldn't have gone down even as sick as I was otherwise. He hooked thick fingers into my hair and dragged me up onto my feet. I cried out with the pain, and finally saw what I should've seen in the first place.

I'm a big woman, but he was a bigger man. Tall as I am, he topped me by another half foot. Heavy-boned and broad along with it, in this light I saw he was scary ugly, had bad teeth, and had probably gone unbathed since the heat of summer.

"No," he said. "Yer my wife now and yer going to sleep with

me. Only . . ." and here he grinned, showing a set of crusty, yellowed teeth, "we ain't going to be sleeping much."

He didn't lie. I didn't sleep at all, and him only in spurts in between the attacks he made on my body. He liked hurting me. Pain, *my pain,* made him get all swelled up with joy.

Well, as you can see, I lived through the night, though even yet I'm surprised I did. And I lived through a good many more nights, too. Over 365 of them and I counted every one.

Why didn't I run off? I don't reckon I have a good answer, but the best I can do is to say I was too ashamed.

See, poor folks are always ashamed of being poor, and women of being big and plain. There was the indignity of getting stinking sick just when I should've been at my best, and then by being robbed of my already scant possessions. Most of all, I hated that I'd been so stupid and believing in the first place, which made me too mortified to let anyone know I got duped.

Though it's not, thinking about the situation these many months later, as if I had anyone who gave a rat's ass.

Turns out it took me longer to get over the food poisoning than I figured. Maybe because of the godawful stuff, except for the premium Chase & Sanborn coffee, the man had stocked up on to eat. He wanted meat and bread at every meal. No vegetables, not even taters. No fruit, unless maybe apple pie, which, when you think about it, is as much bread stuff as fruit. And the only reason there was apple pie is because he sent me out chasing runaway horses one day and I found two trees at an old campsite. Some wormy fruit hung on even into November, but hell, a worm or two never bothered anybody.

That isn't true, by the way. I cut out the wormy parts. Not that he would've cared, but I did.

Never once did I spot any of the cattle the man said he owned, so there was no accounting for the hindquarter of a beef he toted back to the shack one day, if my calculations weren't off, before Christmas.

He aimed to hang the beef in the barn where, in theory, nothing could get at it. Personally, I wondered about the rats and mice, but those critters never appeared to bother him. I just hoped the bears, of which we often saw sign, stayed away or didn't get a taste for horse meat.

I made the mistake of asking where he got the beef.

Standing on the stump he used for a block to chop firewood, he tossed a rope over the barn rafters and raised the hindquarter overhead. From there, he loomed over me and glared.

"What's it matter, woman? It eats the same whether bought, found, or stole. I ain't noticed you being too picky with your food."

Well, no, provided I didn't want to starve. And I didn't. I planned on leaving in the spring no matter what, when it warmed up and the trail became passable to a woman on foot.

But his answer, though he didn't come right out and say so, told me enough. He stole it, all right, is what he did. Kind of scared me, to tell the truth. Folks don't much cotton to other folks who rustle their beeves, then add to the insult by wasting most of the meat by leaving it to be et by coyotes, birds, and bugs. And here I was. The cooking and eating of that beef made me just as guilty as him.

"Aren't you afraid of getting caught?" I asked.

He sliced off a couple steaks and jumped down from the chopping block. Clouting me in the shoulder before he thrust the bloody steaks into my bare hands, he said, "Why should I be scared. There ain't anything to show where that hindquarter came from." He grabbed my chin and pinched it—hard. Tears spurted of their own accord, and later, when I looked in his shaving mirror, I seen fingermark bruises amongst all the other damage he inflicted on me that day. "And if anybody asks, you just close your trap. Anyways, I'll have it et before Rogers knows it's missing." He pinched harder. "You hear me?"

Oh, I heard him, all right. I was standing there trying to figure out if he'd broke my jaw when three men rode outta the trees into the meadow. All three carried rifles. Across their saddlebows, I mean, not in their scabbards. They were determined-looking men, angry for sure, and out for revenge.

Couldn't help it. I snickered. "Is that Rogers? Better get to eating. I'd say he knows his beef is missing."

He growled like a big, angry dog and, with those men looking on, slapped my face.

Seeing as how the barn had a whole open end, those riders couldn't help but spot the fresh hindquarter hanging from the rafter and the two of us froze there as if glued to the spot. I figure we looked guilty as original sin.

The oldest feller, who sat tall and straight in his saddle, was the spokesman. Rogers, I guessed, correctly, as it happened. "You looking to get strung up, Dougan? Won't nobody blame a man who hangs a cattle thief." He glanced around the barn and spoke to his men. "Boys, go find a good, stout tree. This is a poor excuse of a barn and I'd hate to bungle a hanging by having it fall down when he takes the drop. Him being a big man and all."

I hoped they would. Hang him, I mean to say, not bungle it. Then a thought struck me. The feller called him Dougan. After two months he'd never told me his name, nor asked for mine. He still just called me "woman."

Dougan didn't roll over, though. He blustered. "Now wait a minute, Rogers. The hell. Dunno what you're talking about. I bought this here meat off an Indian that came around peddlin' it. Ain't no law against me buying butchered meat. How am I to know where he got it?"

One of the men spat a brown glob of tobacco juice off to the side and said, "He's a lyin' sonofabitch. I tracked him here. Followed those same boot prints straight from the kill to this barn. There's no mistake. This is your rustler."

"Am not." Dougan made himself sound plumb insulted.

"Talk to his woman," the youngest man, third in line, said. "Look at her. Maybe she did it. God knows she's big enough to have wrestled that old cow into the ground by herself."

A wave of hot blood ran through me. It's not like I can shrink myself, you know. But one thing for sure. I didn't plan on taking the blame for the man's guilt. No, nor hanging in his place or alongside him, neither. So I spoke up, God help me, in his defense.

"There was an Indian," I stated. "He brought the meat."

Beside me, Dougan tensed.

Rogers looked over at me and raised an eyebrow. "You see this Indian?"

There's only so much lying I can do without figuring to burn for all eternity. "No, but he"—I cocked my thumb at Dougan—"he told me. Dunno why he'd say it if it ain't true."

Dougan shot me a lowering look.

"And it's just raw meat," I added. "No brand to say where it's from." I know. Pretty much the same as Dougan had said.

After some cussing and fuming, and allowing as how they were apt to be in trouble for hanging a man without trial and jury, the three men turned their horses to go.

Panic touched me, then. These were the first folks I'd seen in all the time I'd been here. Maybe there was a chance . . .

"Take me with you?" I blurted. "I need a ride to town. Please, help me?"

Well, they didn't have time to say aye, yes, or no before Dougan's hand slammed into my face. Blood squirted from my cut lip and I reeled backward, landing on my butt in the dirt. Pain robbed all the breath from my lungs, so I couldn't say more.

My bleary eyes watched Dougan's heavy boot come up as if to kick me in the ribs.

Then came the snick as a shell was levered into a rifle. Rogers's rifle, which he pointed at Dougan.

"Ah ah," he said, sharp, like he was talking to a dog. "None of that. Guess I can see why she wants to leave but," he motioned with the rifle, "I won't be getting in the middle of a family feud. Unless I'm forced."

Dougan lowered his foot as Rogers held steady aim and spoke again. "I hear this woman is dead, mister, you'd better be watching the underbrush. Could be a sniper waiting there. One that don't care for a woman killer nor a rustler. Hear me?" And louder, when Dougan only glared. "You hear me?"

Dougan jerked his head.

Well, I figure you can guess he beat the holy livin' outta me soon as they disappeared from sight. Stopped short of killing me, though he knocked out two teeth and broke a couple ribs.

I washed off the teeth and stuck them back in the holes. Strange to say, they took root and grew in strong. And so him and me coasted along until spring when I finally figured out he'd dropped a baby into me.

I wanted to die.

Turns out I spent several months of the new year sick as a poisoned coyote, morning, noon, and night. Took more than sickness to put Dougan off, though. He kept at me and kept at me. I think a lesser woman would've been dead. Truth to tell, most times I wished I was one of those lesser women.

Thing is, I'm not the kind to give up.

Dougan made it kind of chancy keeping the shack even halfway clean. I had to start in slow and work up to it gradual, although he didn't let on like he noticed. But then I'd see his eyes narrow and next time I went out to chop wood or attend some other chore, when I came back there'd be a nasty mess layin' around. A few times he went so far as to piss in the corner where we slept. He did love to bedevil me.

In all things, not just the filth.

For instance, I cooked some early greens I found growing down by the crick, along with a mess of fiddlehead ferns and wild onions. He told me if I liked them so much, I should just live on them and leave the meat for him. Had to sneak bites of bread and meat when he had his head turned after that.

The garden I started came to life in a roundabout way. An old duffer from a couple miles farther up the mountain, when he somehow heard a woman lived nearby, braved Dougan's wrath and asked me to bake him some yeast-raised bread. I'd've done it for free but Dougan demanded money for my time. Seeing the straits I was in, as a bonus, the feller brought me a half-dozen wrinkledy sprouted taters, a handful each of bean and pea seeds, and, oddly enough, carrots.

"For a garden," he said. "I do admire carrots in a stew."

It seemed a powerful long time before I got the benefit of his generosity, I can tell you, but I surely did appreciate it when my crops ripened.

Thinking back, it's strange Dougan didn't tear the garden out. Maybe it smacked too much of work. He never lifted a finger in his own behalf the whole time except to pump some water for his horses. Guess he couldn't get to town on his monthly drunk unless he kept them alive.

Some might of said I was making a home. I'd've said, "fighting for survival." I don't think a day went by that he didn't hurt me in some way. The days he spent away from the shack were blessings, although drink made him meaner than ever when he returned.

Summer came. My belly swelled, but my bones prodded at

the skin with angles and knobs, until I looked like a starving cow.

Whether I managed to shield my belly or he avoided hitting me there—preferring a mess of bruises to color my face—the baby got borned on a hot August night close to the time I calculated.

She might've been some early, as she was a tiny little thing to have sprouted from people as big as Dougan and me. Didn't have, and didn't need, any help with the birthing, as I'd seen plenty of critters born on the farm back in Missouri. I named her Callie, after my grandma. I'd liked my grandma, see, although she passed when I was but five years old.

Dougan, soon as he saw I'd dropped a girl, not only lost any interest, but was put out something fierce, and said he wished he'd pummeled my belly, after all. "A girl. Only one thing they're good for and until they're ready to be of use, it's a waste to keep 'em fed."

Dear God, how I hated that man.

Baby Callie cried a lot. Hunger, I expect. I didn't have much in the way of milk, seeing as I didn't have enough food to supply my own body. There wasn't anything else for her unless she could eat some watered-down mashed taters. I tried it once, but she couldn't figure out how to swallow. Damn near choked her to death, poor mite.

I haven't said how I felt or what I thought. See, I was trying hard not to feel or to think. Wanting to escape, I couldn't think of how to do it before the baby, and her presence stymied me after.

Sad to say, I didn't love her. Why would I? But she was my responsibility and I did my best.

There came a time when I had either to fight, or to lay down and die. My self-respect, lacking in the first place and I reckon you can see why, my cowardly weakness of character, my shame of being me . . . Everything kind of gathered into a wad and came together on the day Dougan killed the baby.

To this day I don't quite remember what happened. Unconnected pictures jump into my mind. A few red and gold leaves hanging onto the trees as the temperature went down to freezing. Night drawing in early as the daylight hours grew fewer. The shack cold and drafty. A fierce wind howling outside. The wood box empty and Dougan seated at the rickety excuse for a table, a full glass of some cheap rotgut whiskey in front of him. His pistol, a Colt .45, encased in a good leather holster, hung from the post on his chair, handy because a coyote had been sniffing around the shed.

And Callie, crying, crying, crying.

Dougan was complaining because his supper wasn't ready and he aimed a steady string of cuss words at me. Finally, he said, "Lay that worthless brat down and bring in some wood. I'm cold and I'm hungry."

"She's cold, too," I snapped back, grasping her icy little fingers in mine and trying to warm them. I held her close. "And hungry. So am I. Why don't you bring in some wood? It ain't like you're too busy."

"I brought home the meat." He slammed his palm onto the table, the smack sounding like a shot from his rifle. "Get your lazy ass moving and get to cooking. Unless you want a fist in your gut."

His noise made Callie scream all the louder.

"My God, shut her up." Dougan put his hands over his ears, shouting over the baby's cries.

He'd brought home another hindquarter of beef that afternoon, and I had my suspicions where it came from. Could be, I remember thinking, I'd better get it both cooked and eaten. Best to cover up the evidence in case Rogers came by again. I didn't want him to see me, so thin and ugly and wearing the same old rags I'd been wearing a year ago. They hung on me now like cloth draped over a clothesline.

Patting Callie on the back trying to soothe her, I went to lay her in the orange crate the neighbor who'd paid me with garden seeds had brought over to use for a crib.

As I went past him, Dougan kicked out, collapsing my leg beneath me. Callie and I went sprawling, with me barely sheltering her head from knocking against the floor. Of course, she hollered all the more. Of course, she did.

"Jesus!" Dougan yelled. "Get a move on, woman."

His fury worried me. I didn't want to leave her, yet I couldn't take her outside with me. So, I left her there. With him.

A few minutes later, when I hurried inside with an armload of freshly split red fir, the shack was oddly quiet. Dougan didn't appear to have moved, except a fresh jar of whiskey sat in front of him. A smirk lifted the corner of his upper lip. He'd taken out his pistol and was spinning the cylinder in a lazy fashion.

In her crib, Callie was silent. Something, I don't know what, although from the sudden chill I suspect a passing ghost, forced the wood to drop from my arms. The clatter onto the floor made no difference. Callie didn't stir. My heart thumping, I trod over to the orange crate and saw she was dead.

He'd killed her. Snapped her neck like some folks would do to an unwanted kitten. Her poor little head lay kinked all the way to her shoulder. Tears still glistened on her cheeks but her blue eyes were dim with a look of aged misery.

I stood for a time staring down at her, unable to breathe. Eventually, I drew in a long shuddering gasp and let it out in a shriek.

"*Aiaiaiai.*" Sorrow, horror, a blossoming of courage—unless when I stood up to Dougan at last it only meant I was done. I didn't care what happened now. "You kilt her. You kilt that baby." I hollered loud enough to fill the room with my rage.

His chair, which rocked on the back legs as he'd watched me, hit the floor hard enough that one splintered. "Hush that cater-waulin', woman. It was bound to die anyhow, squallin' and mewlin' and pukin'."

I called him the worst words I knew. "Murderer. Baby killer. Half-brained worthless lush."

Well, he objected to that, I can tell you. I'd known he would, but I kept it up, anyway. I just wanted to hit him, to smash his ugly mouth, to make him hurt as he'd hurt poor Callie. To make him pay for his torment, of her and of me. I wanted him to bleed.

For a while it looked like I'd be the one to do the bleeding. He picked up the pistol and pointed it at me.

And there we were, practically toe-to-toe.

"Stop, in the name of God!"

The words dropped between us and we froze. Dougan broke first.

"Who the hell are you?" Pushing me to the side, his gun waved toward the quartet of men crowding through the open doorway.

"I am Joshua Lincoln, pastor for this area." The man, maybe forty years of age, looked like a bundled-up grizzly, but he stood firm and acted unafraid as Dougan aimed the pistol at him.

Dougan's pistol wavered and moved on as he took a bead on the next man in line.

This man's rifle pointed at Dougan. "I'm the sheriff. We've met before. I'm sure you haven't forgot."

From the look on Dougan's face, the sheriff was right.

A third man stood behind them. I knew this one. Rogers, come, no doubt, to claim his due. But ignoring him and one of his riders, I had eyes only for the sheriff.

"He killed that baby," I said, making a motion toward the

orange crate. "Snapped her neck. Murdered her."

"Lying bitch. She did it herself. She's crazy."

As from a distance, I heard muttering. Rogers, saying they should get a rope. The sheriff saying he'd take Dougan and me both into custody, soon as somebody disarmed Dougan. And the preacher still blathering something about "In the name of God."

Me? I agreed with Rogers.

Dougan's Colt came around toward me again, but I ignored the threat. Right then I felt that if he killed me, it would be a relief. Maybe even my only way out of this horror of a life. So I lunged for the gun.

He sure as hell wasn't expecting me to defend myself, seeing I never had before, but the baby's death snapped something in me. I may not have loved her like a mother should, but she'd been born of my body and it fell to me to take care of her. Yes, I'd failed, but then and there I made up my mind Dougan had to pay.

My grip seemed made of iron as my fingers closed around the gun barrel and forced it down. The pistol went off, the bullet tearing into the floor.

As from faraway, I heard those men yelling, the preacher's voice swearing right along with the others.

"Grab Dougan," somebody said, but nobody did. Just me. We wrestled like two of them gladiators you read about. He was bigger, stronger. Drunk. For once my size gave me an advantage. My fury gave me strength.

And so, as he pushed and I pulled, that old Colt got shoved down between us. His finger was still on the trigger, and I kept on squeezing.

The shot, muffled by both our bodies, wasn't loud at all. Blood, hot and coppery, flooded down between us. The Colt fell to the floor.

It was Dougan who sank to his knees like a collapsing sack. Stepping back, I allowed him to fall on his ugly face and turned to face the men with the front of my dress drenched in his blood.

"Holy mother of God," Rogers's rider said. He must've been a Catholic.

The others, apparently speechless, gaped, a silence that held for what seemed an eternity. Then Rogers said, "Well now, saved me from ruining a good rope."

"Killed himself," the sheriff said.

The preacher added his bit. "Lord have mercy on his soul, amen."

Mercy.

Maybe that's what put the word I chose for my name into my mind. Didn't I deserve some, too?

I went before a judge and a panel of men, like a jury, but they called it something else. Scared me something fierce, I can tell you. But those good men, the sheriff, the preacher, and even Rogers and his rider, testified they'd heard Dougan admit to murdering Callie, then attempted to kill me right in front of them. That he brought his death down on his own head and I only defended myself.

I buried the baby. And Dougan, may he burn in hell. I'll finish this tale by saying it took a year to recover my self-respect. To gather my courage and escape those chains Dougan wrapped me in.

I'm free now. Unafraid, and I don't care what people say about me, about my size or the way I look. This is my true story and I pray it may have opened the way for other women to defend themselves against men like Dougan. That someday there'll be laws that admit women are not the chattel of men.

I sure do hope so.

C.K. Crigger writes fiction set in the northwest, which she thinks is underrepresented in western writing. Her latest China Bohannon story is *Five Days, Five Dead,* and a traditional western, *Yester's Ride,* her latest release. A 2019 Spur Award winner for *The Woman Who Built a Bridge,* as well as a two-time Spur Award finalist, she also reviews books and writes occasional articles for *Roundup* magazine.

★ ★ ★ ★ ★

The Storekeeper's
Daughter
by W. Michael Farmer

★ ★ ★ ★ ★

Maggie Godwin slid on heavy, leather gloves, lifted a few choice lumps of coal sparkling with frost jewels, and dropped them in the scuttle to carry back to the fire she had just started in the big, potbellied stove that warmed the first floor of her store and that the farmers liked to sit around as they talked crops, hogs, cattle, and politics while they smoked or chewed.

Inside the store, she thought it actually felt colder than it did outside as she flipped open the stove door and tossed in several pieces from the scuttle on to the crackling kindling. As the anthracite caught fire, the stove took the chill off the room air and her blue speckled, enameled coffee pot began to bubble while she looked through her customer charge books, making a mental tally of how much she should expect from her farmer friends and customers after crops were all in.

She let the coffee perk a little while, then poured a cup and stood holding it between her big, strong hands and, taking quick sips, watched the tops of the morning mists off the Missouri River rise and disappear in the far distance across big, flat fields. She heard children laughing and running as they charged down the road to await the school bus at the store and swap eggs stolen from their mother's hens for something sweet. Her right cheek made a half smile as she thought, *Another day, another dollar.*

As the school bus chugged off down the road with her first customers, she saw John Lee Eaton park his T-Model Ford truck out front, out of the way of passing traffic and just past her red gravity pumps with their tall clear cylinders. Approaching the store's big double doors, he paused, but Maggie, watching him through the vertical bars in front of the big display windows, smiled and waved him on inside.

"John Lee, I haven't seen you since spring. Come on in. What can I get you?"

"Mornin', Maggie. Just out gettin' some air and wound up here at your store. That coffee sure smells good."

"Well, sit down! Keep me company, and I'll pour you a cup."

"How much you askin' for it?"

She smiled. John Lee always had to pay his way. "Why, nothing at all. Just sharing coffee with an old friend on a nice, cool fall mornin'." She nodded toward a table holding a checkerboard. "Go on, sit down there by the window, and I'll bring it to you, and we can get caught up."

"That's mighty nice of you, Maggie. Believe I'll accept your hospitality."

Maggie had known John Lee since they were in the first grade at Mrs. Gillman's one-room school. He had worked on his family's farm from the time he was a small boy barely tall and strong enough to drive his daddy's tractor with the big spiked steel wheels. They swapped stories on the latest news and local gossip. Mrs. Hildebrand claimed Nellie Lynn Jones left town because she was pregnant and the Johnson boy wouldn't marry her; there was talk of adding another room to the schoolhouse and getting a new schoolteacher; prices on corn were better than expected; Maggie's brothers had actually shown a profit on their farm after going shares with Charlie Studebaker; John Lee's cousins were talking about selling their place in the next county and trying to make their fortune with an almond orchard in California.

As they talked, Maggie sensed rather than saw John Lee

Eaton was not quite right. He seemed sad and withdrawn, his soft brown eyes had a ten-thousand-mile stare, and he never used his left arm. She was tempted to ask him about it but decided he'd tell her when he was ready.

She tried to cheer him up by recalling sweet memories of the days when they raced each other on workhorses in old man Magee's orchard, played hide-and-seek in the woods, skipped rocks down the creek, or had tomato fights, throwing nearly rotten tomatoes at each other. She had a good arm and had clocked him once with one that was still a little hard. He laughed, and his spirits seemed to lift over the memory of the old hound, Beau, that had caught a skunk when they were playing in a barn, though they all wished he hadn't.

Mrs. Beal came in for her groceries and waved at them. John Lee raised his cup to her, swallowed down the last bitter dregs, and said, "Thanks for the coffee, Maggie. It's been the best time I've had in a long while. I'll be seeing you."

Maggie smiled. "Come back anytime, John Lee. The door is always open."

She thought of John Lee often the rest of the day. They had grown up together but somehow never made a close connection in their teens or early adulthood. Now she owned and ran her father's store, and he was a bachelor farmer working six hundred forty acres of corn. They just didn't have much time to socialize, which made her wonder why John Lee was wandering up and down the road in the first place. Normally, he spent fall days making equipment repairs and doing other chores to get ready for spring planting.

A slow, steady rain fell the next morning. Maggie was carrying her scuttle of coal to the stove when she saw John Lee's truck creeping down the muddy road. She was surprised to see him again so soon, but glad for the company he offered.

He shook the rain off his yellow slicker and laid it across tall RC Cola bottle crates stacked by the door. Wiping his feet on the big fiber mat, he grinned and said, "Thought I'd come have some more of that fine coffee you brew, and this time I'll pay."

"No, you won't. It's nice to have some adult company here early in the mornin'. Usually the only folks that give me any conversation this time o' day are just kids waitin' to get on that old school bus. Come on and sit down."

They sipped their coffee, not talking, content listening to the gentle rain pattering in the puddles out by the gas pumps. She got up to pour them another cup.

After a night to think about John Lee, her curiosity overruled her manners. Looking over her shoulder as she poured the coffee, she said, "John Lee, are you all right? I've been wondering what happened to your left arm. You didn't use it at all yesterday, just seemed to kind of hang there. What's the matter with it?"

He studied her a moment and then grimaced and sighed.

"Back last spring I was on the tractor and started seeing things like I was havin' a bad migraine. You know, jagged, black streaks shimmering in a mirage across the middle of your vision. I had to use my side vision to keep that old John Deere tractor pulling the cultivator straight 'til I could get back to the house and not veer off the row and tear others up, which would've ruined a piece of the comin' crop. That was when my arm went numb, and it's stayed that-a-way."

Maggie squinted at him over the top her glasses. "Did you see Doc?"

"Yep, I did." There was a long silence as he stared at the floor.

"Well, what did he say? Was it a stroke?"

John Lee shrugged his shoulders. "He thought so at first, but with the high blood pressure and me passing out every once in a while, now he says it's a brain tumor, says I have a year, maybe two."

Sorrow filled her heart as she covered John Lee's rough, stubby-fingered hand with her own. Her heart sank, falling like a stone tossed in a deep well. It couldn't be. She'd known John Lee since they were children. He had always been strong as a horse, didn't drink, smoke, or chase women, and was honest to a fault. It just couldn't be.

Every morning that winter when the road was passable, John Lee drove to the store for coffee and continued their long, intermittent conversations about their lives, the other lives lived on the section roads, church saints and hypocrites, and politics.

Maggie told him how her pa, a tight-fisted curmudgeon, first built the store, and then through cold-blooded calculation and collection on debts owed him by poor farmers—most of the community spat on the ground when they mentioned his name—got the farms next to John Lee's for far below their fair values and combined them into one of the biggest farms in the county. While rich in land, her father refused to spend the money to fix up any of the houses left on the farms he had tied together, raising his family of five, instead, on the second floor of the store. When Maggie was sixteen, her mother had died from flu, and her pa, needing a partner to help with myriad tasks of running a store, had taught her the business. In the process, he ran off any suitors, cowboys or farmers, who tried to court her. When the old man passed away, he gave her brothers the farm and left her the store.

Maggie knew that when John Lee was twenty, his parents, returning from a Saturday night square dance, raced to beat a freight train at a crossing, but the truck was too slow, and six hundred forty acres suddenly became his. He cared for the land and loved it like it was his child, but he had never married.

Maggie asked why.

He shrugged and said, "I've been engaged twice. Guess I run my fiancées off 'cause I don't ever speak easy words, just the truth, and sometimes that hurts. One of 'em waited 'til two days before the wedding to give me back my ring." Maggie grimaced and touched his hand. He gave her half a smile and said, "Aw, I probably wasn't meant to marry, and given the short time I have left, it's providential I didn't."

She shook her head. "John Lee, you'd have been a fine husband for any woman. Don't you go blamin' God for those women not takin' the opportunity he gave them."

Winter faded, and the spring days filled with honeysuckle perfume and flashes of purple wisteria growing by the roadside. John Lee decided that he'd go shares on crops with Charlie Studebaker rather than try to do the work himself. The morning after he closed the deal, he was looking especially glum, and Maggie asked him why. He shook his head and said, "I gave Charlie Studebaker most of the profits if he'd do all the work. I just ain't up to it. I'm feeling weaker every day. But, Maggie, I have to tell you I despise not being able to work my own land. It puts me in the same company with your brothers. They always share out the land your pa left 'em and drink up every cent the shares pay, and then they try to sponge off you. Their houses are falling apart, and they leave valuable machinery rusting in the weather. Pardon me for sayin' so, but they ain't worth a damn when it comes to farming, and they give goin' shares a bad name."

Maggie shook her head and half smiled. "No need to apologize for tellin' the truth, John Lee. If I had that land, I wouldn't want 'em on it either."

One morning, in the middle of June, John Lee didn't come to

the store. Maggie waited until nearly eight o'clock, hung the *Closed* sign on the door window, cranked her T-Model, and roared off to John Lee's farm.

Knocking on the screen door, she called out to him. "John Lee?"

She thought she heard him. The doorknob turned easily. She pushed her way in and, calling out for him, found him in bed.

His left cheek gave her a half smile. "Just didn't have the steam to get up this mornin'. You got a store to run. I'm glad you came, but I'll be okay. Go on back; you can't neglect your business for me."

She put her fists on her waist and shook her head. "Why didn't you call me? We both got telephones. You scared ten years of life right out of me. Are you hurtin'? What do you need me to do?"

"Sorry I scared you. Naw, I ain't hurtin'. Just don't seem to have any strength. Can you help me up so I can get to the bathroom? Ain't been since I woke up and my eyeballs are about to float clean out of my head. I got on my drawers, so I don't think I'll embarrass you."

"You won't embarrass me. I was born naked, grew up with two brothers, and nursed my daddy when he was sick. Now, I'm gonna look after you. I'll get my cousin to look after the store when I'm here." She helped him up and supported him as they tottered down the hall.

As the summer days drifted into fall, Maggie went from stopping by an hour or so morning, noon, and evening to living full-time in John Lee's house. She cooked his meals, washed, cleaned, read the paper to him, and gave him his medicines.

One day Reverend Tulip stopped by for his weekly visit. Maggie was giving John Lee his lunch and asked the reverend to join them. He didn't waste any time taking off his coat and pulling a chair up to the table while she made his sandwich and poured him a glass of iced tea. He asked John Lee how he was feeling and wanted to know if there was anything he could do for him. John Lee shook his head and said, "That's mighty kind of you, Reverend, but Maggie and I have things under control."

Maggie gave the reverend his sandwich and tea and sat back down to finish hers. He thanked her and took a couple of bites before he sheepishly mentioned the gossip flying up and down the road. He said, "Mrs. Hildebrand told me every time she drives by your place, she sees Maggie's T-Model parked here. She called me and said, and this is a direct quote, 'I never dreamed Maggie would stoop to shacking up with John Lee Eaton. She must be mighty desperate. Well, I ain't gonna buy my groceries from no woman like that. Don't you think she oughta be kicked out of the church, Reverend?' Course I told her telling stories on people is the devil's work, and she hadn't said anything to me since, but you know Mrs. Hildebrand. She's still running her mouth. John Lee, Maggie, gossip is an awful thing. I know Maggie's just looking after you, and Mrs. Hildebrand doesn't have any business running her mouth like that, but you need to stop that nasty talk before it gets out of hand."

Maggie raised her brows and John Lee glared at him.

"Reverend, in the first place, it ain't none of your damned business. In the second, Maggie here is a saint, and there ain't anything immoral or illegal goin' on in this house. Now git outta here, and don't come back."

Tulip, ignoring John Lee's anger and Maggie's frown, stumbled like a Saturday night drunk through a short sermon to convince them that they needed to marry and do the right thing until he finally mumbled, "John Lee, I hope you get to feelin' better. We'll be prayin' for you. See you in church, Maggie."

That evening, Maggie sat by the bedside lamp and read the

paper to him. He lay on top of the sheet with his eyes closed, the window fan keeping them cool. She read for a few minutes before he held up his hand, fingers wide, as a sign to stop.

"What did you think about what Tulip said today?" he asked, and he opened his eyes and looked at her.

She shook her head. "Mrs. Hildebrand is always poking her nose in other people's business. Tulip is in a hard spot. Let it be."

"You heard what he said about how we needed to get married to save your reputation and to keep us from goin' to hell."

She nodded, not sure where the conversation was headed.

"Listen here, Maggie. Maybe you need to leave. I'n afford a nurse and a housekeeper. You got a life besides just lookin' after me. I ain't about to get you thrown out of church cause the gossips think we're livin' in sin. If I did the right thing, I'd reward all your kind attention by marrying you—that way you'd get everything I own after I'm gone."

Shaking her head, she said, "I'm here 'cause I want to look after you. I have my store and my own money. I'm not here for any reward."

"I know that, and I thank you from the depths of my soul. I want you to know I'd ask you to marry me in a minute except for one thing."

Maggie slowly crossed her arms. *Now, after all these years, I'll finally learn why you never came courting and I've had to live in that store alone.* She said, "Not that I'd necessarily accept your proposal, but what keeps you from askin' me?"

He sighed and clenched his teeth. "It's your brothers. They're lazy, no-good bums. I can't stand the thought of them ownin' this land. They would get it, too, if you owned it and passed away. They ain't never gonna get anything I own. I'm sorry, Maggie, I just can't risk them gettin' it."

She sat rocking, saying nothing, her arms crossed, an elbow

in each hand, and thinking, *That's about the dumbest thing I ever heard anybody say, John Lee. Your nose is too close to the bark to see the tree. You're just too blind to see what your pride has cost you and me. We'll never be able to share anything now except your last days. They're all we have.*

John Lee stared at her. At last, she said, "I'm stayin' with you. Church or no church, gossip or no gossip, reward or none, I'm stayin'. You do what you have to do. I came to stay with you because you need me and I have feelin's for you. Those are the only reasons. Now get some sleep."

He squeezed her hand and sighed as she turned off the lamp. She sat out on the porch gazing out over the long, straight corn rows rustling in the cool, white moonlight and listened to the tree peepers and cicadas. *Ah me,* Maggie thought, *those were happy times before Ma got sick when I didn't know anything about keeping a store. If she could have just lived a few years longer, I wouldn't be an old maid selling groceries and pumping gas and hearing nasty stories coming out of old lady Hildebrand because I'm trying to do the right thing.*

She sighed, shrugged her shoulders, and mumbled to herself, *Life's not like Daddy told me it was when he said, "It don't matter the hand dealt you, it's how you play it is all that matters." This place should have been my home.*

The hot summer days brought more gossip, worse than before. One of Maggie's friends told her she had heard Mrs. Hildebrand holding forth with three or four other ladies at a church dinner, ". . . John Lee Eaton is so sick he's gonna die pretty soon. Maggie's just lookin' after him so he'll marry her. She don't care nothin' about John Lee. She's after his land. It borders her brothers' land, don't it? She watched her daddy steal land for debts in his store. She's just takin' advantage of John Lee when he's weak. He marries her, it'll all be nice and legal, just like when her daddy stole them other places."

Even though she was carrying more than fifty charge accounts until harvest, her store's business was half what it had been before she started living at John Lee's house. Maggie thought she might have to close by Thanksgiving. She loved the independence the store gave her and hated to lose it, but she wasn't about to leave John Lee when he needed her.

Maggie sat with John Lee one afternoon in early September. He had been drifting in and out of reality since sunrise. He opened his eyes, feebly grasped her hand, and whispered, "Goodbye, Maggie. You've been mighty kind."

She cried softly as he breathed his last and was gone. She sat by him late into the evening studying his hands and simple face, committing every feature to memory before calling the reverend.

John Lee was buried next to his parents in the family cemetery not more than a hundred yards from his house in a casket from Maggie's store. She gave it to his only surviving family, the two cousins who lived in the next county. They had never visited him the entire time he was sick, but John Lee had left them the farm. Everyone living on the section roads and quite a few from town attended John Lee's funeral. Maggie knew John Lee would have been embarrassed over what the reverend said about him being a rare man who kept his word, that he was kind and good to anyone in need, and that he deserved every good memory the crowd had of him, but she thought it was a good service.

Maggie spent her days in the store again. For a while, hardly anyone used her store except John Lee's cousins. She encouraged them to work the farm and gave them all the credit they needed against next year's harvest to get through the winter and plant again.

Shortly after John Lee's passing, the reverend preached a sermon about the Good Samaritan and said people like Maggie were perfect models of good neighbors because she cared for

John Lee with no thought of reward. Her customers started using the store again. The crops were good ones that fall and every account was paid in full. The store actually made a good profit for the year.

Maggie thought John Lee's cousins were a perfect pair—one tall, thin, and dumb, the other short, heavy, and nasty tempered. She thought of them as Fats and Skinny. Their first planting season, summer drought followed by weeks of unrelenting rain had left most of their meager crops rotting in the fields. When their credit came due, they appeared at the store. The short heavy one didn't waste any time sliding a check across her counter.

"Miss Maggie, that check is only about a third of what we owe you. We'll pay you the rest soon as we can. The drought and rain just about wiped us out. We was wonderin' if maybe you'd advance us some credit for next year so we can plant again and then pay off everything we owe you with that crop. Can you help us out?"

She glanced at the check and then looked Fats in the eye. "How do you boys like that new Buick roadster?"

Skinny grinned. "Oh, we like it just fine! It's a lot easier to get into town now than it was with John Lee's old truck." Fats glared at him but said nothing.

Maggie nodded. "Boys, I'm operating right on the thin edge myself. I'll have to have more collateral than just the promise of next year's harvest. What can you put up besides a share of the harvest?"

Fats rubbed his chin thinking. "How 'bout half the harvest and the Buick?"

She crossed her arms and shook her head. "No, I don't think so. Sorry."

Fats frowned. "How about the farm?"

Her brow wrinkled. She remembered and then repeated her daddy's words to his debtors. "The farm? It's worth a lot more than any credit I can give you. You sure you want to do it? It'd have to be all or nothing."

Fats nodded. "Yes, ma'am, that'll work." He grinned, "We're gonna bet the farm. Yes, we are. They ain't gonna be two years back-to-back like this last one. We'll be outta your debt by this time next year."

Feeling like a gambler holding four aces, she bit the inside of her lip to keep from smiling. "All right, I'll have a lawyer draw up an agreement."

The following summer was a mirror image of the one before. When Maggie's claim came due, Fats and Skinny were already gone. The courts didn't hesitate to give her John Lee's farm. Besides Maggie having a valid claim, the cousins owed two years in back taxes that she had to pay to claim the deed.

Fats and Skinny left John Lee's place a disaster. Equipment was stuck rusting in the fields. The tractor didn't run. Weeds were knee-high in the yard, paint was peeling off the clapboard, and shingles were missing off the roof.

John Lee's house still needed more work inside when Maggie moved there from the store's second floor, but she didn't care. Standing on the porch and gazing over the long, straight ridge rows where corn had been, she smiled and thought, *Maybe Pa was right after all when he said, "It don't matter the hand dealt you, it's how you play it is all that matters."* John Lee, I'm home.

W. Michael Farmer has published short stories in anthologies, and award-winning essays. His historical fiction novels have won Will Rogers Medallion Awards and New Mexico–Arizona

W. Michael Farmer

Book Awards for Adventure–Drama, Historical Fiction, and History.

★ ★ ★ ★ ★

BERSERKER ON THE PRAIRIE
BY CANDACE SIMAR

★ ★ ★ ★ ★

Olava Wick straggled into Nickelbo astride her ancient pony as the sun peeked over the eastern Dakota sky. The streets stood empty of buggies or wagons. The smoky smells from morning fires filled the air. The only person in sight was Old Man Larson sitting on his daughter's front stoop. He tipped his hat as Olava rode past.

She urged her pony down the deserted street, shivering in the cold. Her little house stood across town. Maybe a few coals in her stove had lasted through the night. If Ronald were still alive, he would have coffee brewing on the stove and a brisk fire going. A widow's lot.

She had been up all night. Bertina Swenson had survived, thank God, but the baby came blue and silent. The wails of the grieving mother had given Olava a headache and stirred the ancient storm within her.

Someday she would ask God why babies died.

Mr. Rorvig stepped from the General Store waving his arms. "Doctor Gamla!" He flapped like a wounded pelican, almost comical had it not been so early and she so tired.

Olava Wick was not a doctor, but the Norwegian settlers of Nickelbo called her Doctor Gamla, the old doctor woman. She was as close to a real doctor as they would likely know. Olava birthed babies, tended wounds, set bones, and had been known to cut off a frozen toe or two after a blizzard.

"What's the trouble?" Olava said around a yawn.

"It's Julius Peterson out on the Mad Dog River," Rorvig said. He was wild-haired and wore a sweater that hung below the crotch of his trousers. "Ax slipped while he was cutting firewood."

"Bad?" Maybe it could wait until after she slept.

"Wife fears mortification," Rorvig said. "She sent word with Dickie Anderson. Happened day before yesterday."

Mad Dog River was a long ride, and she was past the age when she should be out gallivanting over the prairie. Some days the rocking chair called her name.

"Ask Stubby," Olava said, referring to the local barber. He had been an orderly in the War Between the States, and had worked alongside a field surgeon. Stubby sawed on Rebs when the surgeon was up to his eyeballs in Union amputations. "He's the one to deal with a leg."

"*Nei,*" Rorvig said with a shake of his head. "Stubby is under the weather. Has been for more than a week."

"Bottle fever." She snorted in disgust. The storm rose in her chest until she felt as if she might explode. "That no good son-of-a-gun can get off his hind end and pull his weight, for a change."

"That horse left the barn long ago," Rorvig said with a sad smile. "Wouldn't trust him to pull a calf in his condition."

It was always the same. Men expected women to clean up their messes. They took their pleasure and hid in the barn when their wives' pains came upon them. Left their families high and dry when it suited them. Drank up the harvest and left the woman to make do. Olava could tell stories.

Someday she would ask God why men were so worthless.

She grasped the saddle horn and took deep breaths to calm herself. She reached inside her apron pocket for a dried bit of lemon rind. She bit into it. Chewed hard. The acrid taste and bitter fragrance cleared her thoughts and calmed the storm.

"Come in for coffee." Rorvig helped her down from the pony, her joints creaking and popping like corn.

She stumbled after him into the dark store that reeked of kerosene and rotting fruit. He lit a lamp. The warmth of the room caused her nose to run. She sniffed into a handkerchief as she looked around the crowded shelves. Yard goods, farm supplies, canned meat, and men's overalls stacked in the shadows. Black licorice whips curled from nails like strange vines. Jars of peppermints and horehound candies huddled on the counter. A barrel of pickles and another of crackers tucked under the eaves. A bushel of apples and a box of roasted peanuts rested on a tabletop beside a tattered checkerboard and a dog-eared deck of playing cards.

He pulled a chair closer to the checkerboard and motioned for her to sit down. "I'll fetch Tillie to bring you some breakfast." He went into the back room. Muffled voices.

"You're up early," Tillie said as she poured coffee from a blue enameled pot. Tillie Rorvig was a plain woman, close-mouthed and mostly silent. She fetched a plate of doughnuts dusted with white sugar.

"Not early, but to bed late," Olava answered. The coffee was weak but hot. She wrapped both hands around the cup, letting the warmth thaw her gnarled fingers. Her shivering stopped. "Up with the Swensons. Bertina made it through, but the baby did not. Promised I would let the preacher know."

"Oh my," Tillie said. "I'll carry the message to the parsonage myself." She wrapped a shawl around her shoulders and scurried out the door.

Olava liked her. Not given to gossip, Tillie was one to do a good deed and keep her mouth shut about it. It took a woman to get things done.

Olava ate one doughnut and then another. The doughnuts

weren't fresh. A pinch of nutmeg would have improved their flavor.

Tillie never asked how people were doing or how they were holding up. Olava had no response for stupidity. Olava refused to add a single detail to the Nickelbo rumor mill. The suffering ones deserved at least a shred of privacy. Let people think what they would. She wanted no part of it.

Behind her back, townspeople named Olava a witch. Not that it discouraged anyone from calling for her help when they took sick. Olava carried a knowledge of herbal medicines from her Norwegian homeland. No witchery involved. If she were a witch, she would cast such a spell on Stubby the bottle-fever barber that he could never drink again. She would curse him with elbows that would not bend. She would lock his jaws when he tried to imbibe. She would turn his liquor to cow piss.

The storm stirred again, and she willed herself to calmness. If she were a man, she would give Stubby a *chiliwink* he would not soon forget, a slap on the side of his head that would leave his ears ringing for a month. Bottle fever indeed.

Olava did her best in spite of her age. At least she didn't hide behind a bottle. She would not hang her head on judgment day when she gave account of how she had helped her neighbors. Not once had she required payment for her services. Not once had she turned anyone away. Not even today when she was dog tired. She would finish her coffee and tend to Julius Peterson. It was her penance for greater sins.

Rorvig must have noticed her lack of enthusiasm.

"There's a mess of downed trees from last spring's tornado on Mad Dog River. Free for the taking," Rorvig said. "I'll take the wagon and fetch a load of firewood this morning. You can ride along to the Peterson place. Catch a little rest on the way. Save us both time."

Olava let out a grateful sigh. She needed sleep.

Rorvig called his son to care for Olava's mount, then left to hitch the wagon. Johnny fetched the sack of supplies from Olava's saddlebag at her bidding. The boy looked to be about twelve, but Olava knew he was only nine. She had delivered him herself between blizzards that stormy winter of 1879. Olava had counted herself lucky to be in town rather than out in a claim shack in the middle of the prairie.

Someday she would ask God why babies came during blizzards.

"Poor Bruno has earned a measure of oats," she told Johnny with a wink. "Careful. He's a biter."

She finished her coffee and poured herself another cup. Rorvig returned, rubbed his hands together, and reached for the coffee pot.

"I'll take a spool of silk thread and a paper of needles." Olava fished a coin from her apron pocket and slid it across the counter. "The large, curved ones used for leather work."

"Your money's no good here," Rorvig said. He slid the coin back across the counter. "At least not this early in the morning."

He was a kindly person who carried more than his share of unpaid notes from struggling settlers. Not much of a businessman, she suspected. Might as well stir up a little commerce for him in return for his favor.

"You might bring a few boards and nails," Olava said.

Rorvig looked at her with a blank stare.

"Widow will need coffin-making supplies if things go sour."

Rorvig nodded and lugged boards and a sack of ten-penny nails out to the wagon. Tillie returned and wrapped the rest of the doughnuts into a clean rag. She handed the bundle to Olava.

"You might get hungry," she said. "Folks in trouble forget about cooking."

Rorvig kissed his wife goodbye and urged Olava out to the

wagon. He helped her onto the seat just as the sun broke free from the horizon. Frost sparkled on the grass. Roosters crowed from behind the tavern. A dog barked by the livery stable. Olava wrapped tighter in her shawl and wished for a pillow.

It was early October, and the wheat was tucked securely in sacks and sheds across Nickelbo Township. Not a banner year, but enough to get them through. Everyone in Nickelbo was scrambling to put up wood for the winter—not an easy thing on the prairie. Trees grew only along riverbanks where cotton-woods, box elders, elm, and ash clung to the shoreline. That and the never-ending cow chips the settlers gathered on the prairie.

Rorvig jabbered about the high price of coal, the trapper who predicted a long winter, and the invasion of mice and rats. He asked if she knew of any cats for sale, whether she had tried the newfangled mousetraps, and a million other topics of no interest to Olava. Men never knew when to keep still.

Olava knew how to quiet him, but she hoped it wouldn't be necessary. She'd rather not put Rorvig in his place since he was nice enough to give her a ride and the needles and thread. She drifted to sleep with the racket of his voice rattling in her ears and her chin resting on her chest.

"It died," Olava said when a bump in the trail jolted her awake and he was still talking. Enough was enough. Childbed talk always closed men's mouths and stilled their tongues. "She lost her baby, Bertina Swenson did. There was a lot of blood."

That shut him up. Worked every time.

Olava napped until the wagon pulled to a stop. They were not yet at Mad Dog River. A young girl crawled in a patch of Indian paintbrushes along the trail, her blond hair bright among the scarlet blooms.

"It's his missus," Rorvig said. "She's been to the store a time or two."

The girl crawled from flower to flower, pulling one up by the roots and then another, holding them up to the light as if identifying them—like a mad woman.

"Where is it?" she said, her voice shrill. "I dreamed it grew here." Her hair had fallen out of its pins and dipped down her back in messy tangles. A bloody apron covered a dirty, white nightgown. She was barefooted, and in this weather. "Mama used yarrow for wounds. It's got to be here somewhere."

"Rest yourself, child," Olava said. Such a young thing had no business homesteading. Prairie life was hard on women. She could tell stories. "I've yarrow aplenty in my sack. Warm your poor feet with my shawl."

The young woman hesitated, looking at the flowers and then to Rorvig.

"Don't worry," Rorvig said. "I've brought Doctor Gamla. She'll take care of Julius."

"A doctor!" The young woman clambered up onto the wagon box and sat beside Olava. She smelled of blood and cooked meat. "He's in a bad way, my Julius." She wiped tears with the back of her arm and blew her nose into the bloody apron. "He's bad. What will I do if he dies?"

"Now, now," Olava said. Young people were all the same, worrying about the funeral before the medicine had a chance to get down the gullet. "We'll see what can be done for your man. He'll be fine." She pulled a lemon rind from her pocket. "Suck on this, Mrs. Peterson. It will clear your head."

"Call me Magda," she said.

Olava had spoken more confidently than she felt. Wounds were a tricky lot. A suppurating wound terrified her. Give her a fever or a childbed any day of the week. But a gash from an ax. Heaven help her. Olava had never cut off a limb. A few toes, yes, but never a limb. She felt a shudder go through her.

The storm roiled in her chest. Olava wanted to turn the

wagon around, fetch that barber by his balls and drag him out to Mad Dog River. Useless as teats on a boar, men were. Stubby was a poor specimen of a man in the best of situations and a piss-poor barber to boot. He could barely pull a tooth. But he did know how to amputate limbs. And he had a sturdy meat saw.

She took a deep breath and tried to calm herself with another bit of lemon rind. She committed it all into the hands of God. If He saw fit to drop a suppuration into her lap, He would help her find a way to deal with it. Made sense that God couldn't depend on Stubby to do the job. Her salve had worked wonders before. Maybe she was meant to save Julius's leg.

"I need yarrow!" the woman strained to leave the wagon, though Rorvig's horse was in full motion.

"Hush now," Olava said with a restraining hand on the woman's shoulder. How thin she felt beneath the clothing. Her bones like that of a small bird. "I have a special salve. Some swear it draws ten-penny nails out of a barn door, it has such drawing power."

A few questions and the story of her husband's accident gushed out of Magda like an unclogged spring. Her man had shot a rabbit in the cornfield behind the house and she had baked a rabbit pie for dinner on Tuesday, or was it Wednesday, but her man didn't come in as he always did. She went outside to check the time. The sun indicated noon, but no sign of his coming. Earlier that morning she heard the echoing blows of the ax from where she hung the clean linens on the clothesline. Or maybe it was a batch of rags she hung out to dry. She wanted her fall cleaning finished before the weather set in and it became harder to haul water for washing.

She looked at Olava with round eyes. "Mama always waited until November, but I thought it would not matter if I started early." She paused. "Was I wrong?"

Olava shook her head and murmured that it didn't matter as long as it was done before Christmas. She wanted to urge the poor woman to jump ahead to the wound itself, but she knew better than to interrupt. People in an agitated state invariably started over from the beginning if interrupted, and Olava had heard enough about laundry and fall cleaning.

"When I didn't hear the ax, I figured he was on his way home. He only went around the bend where the cyclone downed those trees."

They arrived at the homestead as she finished her story. He had crawled home. She found him fainted by the riverbank.

The house made of sod stood near Mad Dog River. Unwise to build so close to the water. The Mad Dog snaked through the cattails most of the year, but turned into a roaring monster during spring flooding. No doubt Julius thought to make it easier to fetch water by building closer to the river. Like a man to lack common sense to go along with generous intentions.

"I'll let you ladies off and return early afternoon," Rorvig said. "Need to be home well before dark." He scanned the skies. "Looks like the weather will cooperate. Be back before you know it."

He didn't offer to come in. It would have been a comfort to have someone else in case the man had already died. Olava shook her head. Rorvig couldn't help that he was a man. Men talked big but skulked away at the least sign of blood. Even her own man could not face the harsh reality of life. She reached for another lemon rind. The storm roiled within her and she breathed deeply until the dark spots cleared from before her eyes.

Ronald had blamed her rages on her berserker blood. Born in Vik, where the Vikings wintered back during the Middle Ages, Olava was of their lineage. The berserkers, so fierce in battle, so easily enraged, could not be killed with iron weapons. A berserker she was. There was no denying it. She would have been a warrior maiden fighting alongside the men. She could have done it.

She followed Magda into the dark sod house. It felt like stepping into a grave. Everything smelled of damp earth and boiled cabbage. Magda lit a candle. Julius wasn't in the unmade bed. He wasn't by the table. His wife called his name, searching under the table and behind the black cookstove. Foolish girl to leave him alone.

"Maybe he went to the back house," Olava said. Lord Almighty, the man might have died crawling to the river for a drink of water or gone to the barn to do chores. Fever did that to people. Made them do stupid things that hurried their deaths.

Julius wasn't in the outhouse. Nor was he by the woodshed. Olava scanned the riverbanks, but didn't see him. Then Magda screamed from behind the haystack.

Julius lay sprawled facedown in a muddy patch. He wore only a nightshirt with a sloppy rag loose around his upper thigh. He was passed out cold, and chickens pecked around him and perched on his back. Magda screeched at the hens, punching them with her fists and kicking at the flapping wings. Such a commotion of arms and feathers.

"Stop," Olava said. She was too old for this. The man looked dead. Olava knelt in the dirty straw and rested her ear on his back. He burned with fever. His heart pounded. "He lives."

Magda burst into loud wails. "It's my fault. I've killed him."

"Enough!" Olava said. "Get a hold of yourself." She spoke roughly, not knowing how else to shake sense into the girl. "You're doing no good by carrying on like this. Run to the house and fetch a blanket and a cup of water. Be useful."

Rorvig should have stayed. Once she could have toted a man over her shoulder, but not in her old age. The simplest way, of course, would be for Julius to wake up and carry himself to the house under his own power. Such a good-looking young man. Tall and strong. A real Viking boy with blond hair and blue eyes.

Olava rolled him over and grasped his nose tightly between her thumb and forefinger. She had done this once before at a desperate time. She grabbed as tightly as she could. He squirmed and kicked. Olava held on. Finally, he pushed her arm away and sat up, gasping for breath.

"Stop! You're killing me." He looked around and shook himself awake. "What are you doing?"

"Don't!" Magda ran toward them, spilling water all the way. "You're hurting him."

"Can you stand?" Olava said as she wrapped the blanket around his shoulders and pressed the cup to his lips. "Take a drink. Then you must get into bed."

He nodded, and they pulled him to his feet.

The sun inched upward. A flock of geese made a vee toward the south in a sky of clearest blue, honking goodbye to this north country as they winged somewhere warmer. Smarter than people.

Julius shivered with fever, though his skin felt burning hot through his nightshirt. He slumped on their shoulders.

"The ax slipped," Julius muttered. "I couldn't find my way."

They half dragged him into the house, and settled him on the bed. He smelled of urine and sweat. Magda stood white as milk. Her eyes puffed almost closed. She dropped to her knees by the bed, sobbing.

"Hush now." Julius stretched out a hand toward Magda. "I'll be all right," he assured her. "You'll see."

"I've killed you," Magda shrieked. "It's my fault if you die."

Her keening wails brought back the sharp pain to Olava's forehead. Her work lay ahead and she needed all her strength. She had no time for hysterics.

"Don't leave me. Don't die. I'll not make it without you," Magda wailed and gripped Julius until she almost pulled him out of the bed.

Enough was enough. "Quit crying or I'll give you something to cry about," Olava barked. The girl was hopeless. "Stoke the fire and heat lots of water." A list of necessary steps to meet the situation slipped into Olava's brain. Ronald had always said she was at her best during emergencies. Olava didn't know if this were true or not, but she usually knew what had to be done. "Be quick about it. I've no time for foolishness."

Magda swiped across her face with her sleeve, glared at Olava, yanked the empty bucket by the dry sink, and stormed out of the house. Olava lit a second lamp, but the soddy was still too dark to examine the wound. She dug in her sack and pulled out a candle. So precarious was life. A moment of carelessness and worlds collided. She took a breath and yanked away the bandage.

"Stop," Julius said with a moan.

Olava held the candle close and examined the gash. She laid the flesh back with a bit of towel and viewed the exposed sheen of bone, a layer of yellow fat and red muscle.

It had missed the artery. It had missed the bone. Thank God.

She bent low and sniffed. One area about two inches long flamed angry red. She bent and sniffed again. The sickening smell of rotting flesh, the sweet smell that always brought the storm in her chest to its fullest measure.

Tears slid down her nose. It took both shaking hands to replace the candle on the table. She was too late. Stubby should take the leg. Perhaps if Magda had sent for help sooner. If they didn't live so far from town. The storm blazed red hot in her chest. "What were you thinking to be so careless?"

"Cutting wood," Julius said. "Doing what I always do."

"It's your fault," Olava said. The words bitter on her tongue.

"A mind wanders and something goes wrong. Happens all the time."

She pulled a clean towel from a shelf, ripping a corner with her teeth to tear a bandage. She had to try. A dull ax. A glancing blow at a stubborn knot of wood. A crazy wife crawling around the prairie in her nightgown. A house built too close to the river.

They would never survive on the prairie if they didn't get smarter faster. Words stuck in her throat. She grabbed the whiskey bottle pulled from her sack of supplies and made Julius guzzle right from the bottle. Then she took a swig herself. She reached for the brown turpentine bottle always kept in her sack. She took a deep breath, and poured turpentine into the cavern of wound, sopping the overflow with the towel.

"Stop!" Julius screamed. "You're killing me."

Magda pushed into the house, splashing water over the floor. "What are you doing to him?"

"I'm doing what you should have done," Olava said. She poured another flood of turpentine into the wound. Julius groaned in agony. "Cleansing his wound."

Magda demanded that she stop at once. Olava ignored her and poured another stream of liquid fire into the wound cavity. Magda pulled the hunting rifle from its place over the door and turned it on Olava. The rifle barrel shaking in her hands. The black circle like a hideous eye looking at her.

Olava snorted. "You think I'm afraid of death?" she chuckled. "I could use some rest. The good people of Nickelbo allow me none in this life."

"Get out of my house." Her eyes wild. "We don't want you here."

Olava faced Magda with hands on her hips. "I'm saving his life," she said. She would not lose a man without a fight. "Go ahead and shoot me if you want. Right now, I'm the only chance he has to live."

"Magda, put the gun down," Julius said with gasping breath. "Let Doctor Gamla do her work." Tears poured down his cheeks. "The cow is bawling to be milked."

Magda glared at Olava and stomped out of the house, putting the gun back in its place as she went.

Turpentine was used in lumber camps for ax wounds. It wouldn't be enough, not now. Olava saw the path ahead. A desperate act. A painful, last chance at life. If she succeeded, he would suffer, but live. If she failed, at least she had tried.

She dug for her butcher knife wrapped in a bit of leather. She opened the grate of the stove and poked in another cow chip. When the flames burned hot, Olava shoved the knife blade into the flames. She must act quickly before Magda came inside again. She handed Julius the whiskey bottle.

"This will hurt like hell, but it's your only chance to save your leg," she said. "I'm going to burn the worst part of your wound with the blade of my knife. Then I'm going to stitch up the gash and apply my salve. You'll keep your leg if you can take it."

She hoped she hadn't lied to the man. She threaded the curved needle, holding it up to the lamplight to see the eye. She pushed it into the front of her apron for safekeeping. Then she pulled the knife out of the flames.

The steel blade glowed red hot. Julius's eyes bulged, and what little color he had dropped out of his face. He scooted backwards in the bed, away from her.

"No," he pleaded. "Not that."

"Viking blood flows in your veins," Olava said. "Act like it," her voice as cold as the blade was hot. She always grew mean with worrying. No one could blame her for worrying about this one. She had every reason to be sharp.

"This is nothing. I've pulled babies out of dead mothers. I've seen whole families die of the pox." Oh, Olava could tell stories. Sometimes she thought she had seen everything that could be seen. "You'd rather go through this, by God, than watch Magda gored by a bull or have one of your children burned to death in a prairie fire. Believe me. This is a small thing. A little pain and it's over." The storm roiled until she fetched another bit of lemon rind. She bit down hard. She needed a level head for what was ahead. "Don't waste your chance to live. Think of your wife. Do it for her."

Julius reached for the whiskey bottle and took a choking swallow. "Hurry, then, before Magda comes back."

She handed him a wooden spoon. "Bite on this."

She lay the knife blade flat across the mortified spot. He screamed and swooned.

The smell of seared flesh made Olava a little woozy, too, but she had no time for weakness. That would come later. She pushed the needle through his flesh and tugged the edges together where the flesh blistered and blackened. She tugged the ends together and tied a knot with shaking fingers. He would need about a dozen more stitches to hold it secure.

She stabbed again and Julius groaned into the wooden spoon. She had hoped he would be swooned until she finished. No such luck. Great drops of sweat dripped down his pasty face. He gripped the sides of the straw tick until his fingers pierced through the cloth ticking and bits of straw floated in the air.

"I once cured a man with a frozen foot," she said. Love slipped inter her voice again, as she hoped to distract him with her story. "They were sending him by railcar to Saint Paul to have his leg amputated at a big hospital there."

Julius writhed with pain. She continued with the stitches. "He knew about my salve, the man did. It's that famous, you know." She stretched the thread across to the opposite side of the gash and stabbed into the tender edges, careful to go through all the layers of skin. Julius squirmed but did not cry out.

"I took one look at his foot and saw a chance to save his leg. Not his toes, mind you, but at least the leg." She pulled the thread through and tied another knot. Two down and ten to go. She straightened up and reached for more thread.

Olava stabbed the next stitch. Julius swooned again, and his head tipped to one side. She fingered a throbbing pulse. Good. She hurried to finish before he woke again. All in all, she put in fourteen stitches. Two extra over the middle.

Olava stood back and surveyed her handiwork. Like railroad tracks over the prairie, tracks laid by a drunken Chinaman. She laughed then, a shaky laugh that turned into hooting shrieks. She was the drunken Chinamen who had laid the track. She could braid her long gray hair into a single braid and let it hang down her back like the Chinese did. She could trade her black widow's weeds for a coolie jacket and trousers. She laughed until she gasped for breath.

"What's wrong?" Magda said as she pushed into the soddy. "Does he live?"

"Nothing wrong," Olava said, wiping her eyes and blowing her nose. "It's done."

Magda looked at the stitches on his flesh and glared at Olava as if she were the cruelest person in the world. She would think differently if he survived. Olava had seen it before. Laboring women blaming her for the pain. Injured men cursing her for setting their broken bones.

Someday she would ask God why sick people blamed the healers trying to help them.

Magda put porridge on the stove to cook and filled a kettle. She stirred the fire, her face so white and drawn. Poor girl needed rest as much as Olava did.

Julius might live. If he suppurated, the leg must yet come off.

That would be a job for Stubby. By God, she'd make that little weasel come out and take the limb if she had to drag him by the short hairs all the way from Nickelbo. She smeared salve across the stitches.

She had learned about the salve from an old doctor in Norway. If she were a greedy person, she might sell it and become a millionaire. But Olava was not greedy, and she figured a life of service to others might offset her great sin of not loving her husband enough.

The sins of youth grew heavier with the years. Surely God, in His wisdom, allowed her extra years for penance.

She wrapped Julius's stiches neatly in strips of toweling, then propped a pillow under his leg. Yarrow might have spared him the burning blade, but maybe not. She must assure Magda that yarrow would not have helped. Olava would not lay blame on another person, not after what she had been through herself. A merciful act to sometimes spare the whole truth.

Julius woke then. His face ashen, sweat dripping across his pale forehead. Magda brought a cup of tea.

"Lie still," Olava said. "You don't want to bust those stitches open."

Julius was of good Viking stock and blood always showed. He had shown mettle, and by God, that was rarified behavior in men. A woman could suffer childbed with barely a scream. But men? Worthless as teats on a boar.

"How long will it take?" Julius said.

"Depends," Olava said. A curtain of fatigue pressed down upon her. She pulled her quilt from her bag of supplies and laid it on the earthen floor beside the bed. "Weeks maybe, if all goes well."

"*Nei*," Julius groaned, "My fall work to do."

His voice sounded like Ronald's voice when he learned they were losing their farm in Norway. Nothing more to be done.

Backs up against the wall. Crops failed. Taxes due. Creditors at the door. No money. Olava had worried then. She said hateful things to Ronald, though she loved him more than life itself. Still she hurled words at him—mean, hurtful words that stayed with her all these years. She had blamed Ronald for the farm's failing. She had blamed him, accused him of not working hard enough to make a go of it. She had said that she should have married Bjorn, the older neighbor who had courted her for years. She had lashed out in anger, saying wicked, horrible things. Her berserker rage. Her very blood.

He had not been to blame for bad weather, failed crops, and a scourge of grasshoppers.

Not until she found Ronald swinging in the grove of maple trees behind the barn did she understand her sin. His body limp against a backdrop of golden leaves, hanging like a bat from a branch. Seeing him swinging had cleared her vision, but, by then, it was too late.

She should have been kinder, more understanding. They had their health and could have started over together. She should have assured him, comforted him, and promised him that she would stand with him. He gave up because of her sin. Her berserker blood had robbed poor Ronald of his manhood as surely as if she had done the work with a castrating knife.

"Rest now," Olava said. The air had gone out of her lungs and the words came out in a whisper. Julius drank the tea and slumped back against the pillow with a groan.

"Are you having pain?" Magda said. Her face creased with concern, her hands fluttering around his face, pulling up the blankets, and straightening the pillow.

He shook his head and reached for Magda's hand. Liar. Olava knew the pain must be fierce, burning fire along the wound, enough to weaken the bones of the strongest man. He was a real Viking.

Magda fetched a bowl of porridge, but Julius waved it away. Olava nodded and motioned Magda to crawl into bed beside him. They closed their eyes to merciful sleep.

Olava gathered her needles and thread into her sack. If Julius lived, he would survive somehow. People usually found a way to endure hard times. The young couple owned a flock of laying hens and a milk cow. They wouldn't starve. The neighbors would help as they could. She would send word with Rorvig about the fall work. The young couple would tighten their belts and get through whatever happened.

Still, Olava pitied them. The worst part of growing older was knowing the grim truth. They wouldn't have it easy. No one had it easy in this life. She gathered her knife and soaked the bloody rags in one of the water buckets. She blew out the lamp.

Rorvig rapped on the door. Olava tiptoed past the sleeping couple and stepped outside.

"I daren't leave yet," Olava said.

Rorvig scratched his head. Olava could almost hear his brain grinding out possible ways to get the old doctor woman back to Nickelbo.

"Don't you worry about that," Olava said with a laugh. He would surely believe the rumors that she was a witch when he realized she answered his unspoken thoughts. "Someone will bust a leg or take a fever. Tell them where I'm at and they'll come fetch me."

"I'll care for your mount while you're gone," Rorvig said.

"This poor man won't get his wood in or finish his fall work. Old Man Larson might be persuaded to come and spend a few days to help out." If she had said such a thing to Tillie, Olava would now be looking at the back of Tillie's head as she left to line up a work crew.

"Too bad," Rorvig said, shaking his head sadly. "Hard to be laid up."

Someday she would ask God why men lacked all common sense.

"Find Stubby and sober him up. The leg might still need to come off," Olava said. "Send him out in a couple of days with his meat saw and barber bag." She looked over her shoulder hoping the young couple hadn't heard. A discouraging word could undo all the good she had done this day. Her voice dropped to a fierce whisper. "Tell Stubby he'll answer to me if he doesn't show up."

Olava Wick watched Rorvig head back toward Nickelbo. Stubby better come out. God help him if his bottle fever caused the death of young Julius. Olava would see him tarred and feathered, run out of town on a rail. By God, he'd better not mess with her or he'd see a berserker in action.

The sun showed it was past dinnertime. Too tired to eat. A gentle breeze rolled over the prairie grass, wave after wave of dipping and bowing grasses. A flock of ducks landed on the waters of Mad Dog River.

"Doctor Gamla," Magda whispered when Olava finally stretched out on her quilt.

"Rest yourself," Olava said. "We've done what we can." Sleep weighed down her eyelids and took over her body. "Now we enter into the healing silence."

They were in the hands of God.

Candace Simar is a Minnesota writer with a passion for her Scandinavian heritage and the way things might have been. She has received awards from the Western Writers of America, Women Writing the West, the Midwest Book Awards, *Writer's Digest,* and the League of Minnesota Poets. See more at www.candacesimar.com

★ ★ ★ ★ ★

ABANDONED PLACES
BY PATRICIA GRADY COX

★ ★ ★ ★ ★

As soon as she arrives at the old house, emotions long buried—diluted, softened versions—wash over her. She tests each step up to the porch until she reaches the top where she sits, placing her bag one stair below. Wild mint struggles across the rotted risers and releases its fragrance when the fabric brushes against it.

She sits on the edge of the porch and looks out across what used to be a pasture. Decaying wooden posts and railings lay helter-skelter, and a section of rusty barbed wire, looped upon itself, pokes up from dry, yellow grass. Tall weeds sway in the breeze. Beyond the meadow, grown wild over the years, a line of trees snugs up to the foothills. Beyond that, mountains loom.

How much time had slipped away since the day she'd moved into the room upstairs? She'd lived in that one room, accessible by a stairway at the far end of the porch, and sees every detail in her mind's eye; no need to climb those stairs now. She shifts position, resting her tired back against the balusters, and watches the distant buttes and mesas turn rose-colored, then purple, then red, silhouetted against the darkening red sky. The blood slowly seeps away, replaced by pale gray. She twists a sprig of mint, crushes the leaves in her hand, and raises it to her nose.

Shadow creeps from the hills, across the pasture, right up to the steps, and envelops her. She imagines horses gently cropping the grassy field, imagines she hears their gentle grumbling noises, huffing breaths, a quiet hoof step, a soft nicker. In the moonlight they raise their ethereal heads and stare at her, eyes shining like moons.

Theodosius Wheeler arrived in the Arizona Territory hoping to wed. After her father died, she'd answered an advertisement in the Boston Globe. A western rancher sought a wife, and she was well aware her advanced age of thirty diminished her chances of finding a husband in New Hampshire. Left in poverty, a situation embarrassing and desperate, she gratefully accepted this man's offer of marriage and a paid passage via locomotive.

She arrived in Maricopa, sooty and exhausted, to the news that an irritable cow had trampled her intended to death a week prior. The town marshal met her at the train station and broke the news.

Learning she had no funds, he offered her the temporary accommodations of the jail until she could find a suitable position. "I reckon the rooms above the saloon would not be fittin' for a lady of your caliber, ma'am." He held the desk chair out and motioned her to take a seat.

"Perhaps we could inquire into a position with a family. There are well-heeled folks in Tombstone. Perhaps looking for a maid? Or a cook?"

Perspiration and dirt stained her embroidered handkerchief as she wiped the crevices of her face. A position as a maid or cook struck her as reasonable. Had she married, she would be both and have to provide other unsavory wifely services as well. "Either would be acceptable."

That evening Marshal Daigle's wife brought her a hot supper on a tray. A man stood outside the cell, folded bedding in his arms.

"This is Mr. Abraham Spaid." Mrs. Daigle handed over the

tray. "My husband, the marshal, told me you are in need of employment." She took the sheets, pillow, and blanket from the tall, dark-haired man. "Mr. Spaid's folks is elderly and live outside of town. They are in need of help. You know, cooking and cleaning. Mr. Spaid's wife was helpin' out but . . ." Her voice trailed off and she shrugged, keeping her eyes downcast.

"There's a room on the second floor, ma'am," Mr. Spaid said. "You'd be most welcome to use it. Of course, you'd take your meals with my folks. Wouldn't cost you nothing to live there and I'll pay you as well."

It seemed a fortuitous offer. She had no money to buy passage back east, and what would she do anyway if she managed to get there? This offer was likely as good as any would be.

"I did care for my father until his death. It sounds like a suitable arrangement."

Mrs. Daigle had busied herself, taking extra care to tuck in the corners of the blanket, then tucking them in again. At Theodosius's expression of interest in the position, she thought she saw the woman close her eyes and exhale.

"I'll do my best to make your parents comfortable, Mr. Spaid."

"I'm obliged, ma'am. My wife and I will come in the morning to carry you out to the old homestead. And please call me Abe. Mr. Spaid is my father." His shy smile assured her she'd made a good decision.

"All right, Abe."

A two-story farmhouse a couple of miles from town, the old homestead lived up to its name. Old. Peeling paint, windows a checkerboard of glass and wooden squares nailed over broken panes, a shutter on a slant, hanging from one hinge.

"Always pains me to see the place," Abe said. "Wish I could keep it up like it used to be."

227

Mrs. Spaid sat next to her husband. Theodosius, relegated to the bed of the buckboard along with a dog that growled every time she looked at it, saw no indication of warmth or kindness in the stiff back and tightly restrained bun of brown hair streaked with gray. Mrs. Spaid whipped her head so she could look at Theodosius from the corner of her eye. "My husband has more than enough to do on our own place. He's spent far too much time out here as it is. And so have I."

Theodosius held her carpetbag in her lap and leaned against her small trunk as the wagon jerked and rolled up to the front porch. "Yes, ma'am. I'm glad I'll be able to help."

Mrs. Spaid huffed and looked straight ahead again. Theodosius could almost hear her thoughts: *Not doing it out of kindness, doing it out of a need for a roof and food, doing it out of desperation.* Or were those her own thoughts? Abe climbed down and walked around to pull her trunk into his arms. "Follow me, ma'am." She lugged her carpetbag up the stairs that arose from the far end of the porch to a landing and doorway on the second floor. "I hope you'll find these accommodations fit enough."

One room, about the size of her parlor back east, with slanted ceilings and a window at each tall end. A cot. A table beside it held a lamp, and nearby stood a washstand with pitcher and bowl and rungs for towels. A mirror hung above a four-drawer dresser, and she looked away from her reflection. One of the slanted walls held cupboards and a woodstove for cooking, placed so she would not hit her head as long as she was careful. Two cast-iron fry pans hung from the wall and a kettle sat on the stovetop. She imagined dishes and flatware might be inside the cupboards, although she was to take her meals with Abe's parents downstairs. A layer of dust covered everything and puffed when she dropped her carpetbag on the tick mattress. "I'm sure it will be quite comfortable."

"I'll go down and get some sheets and such. Anything else

you might need?"

She looked around the sparse room. Unless she ransacked the cupboards in front of him, she had no idea what else she needed. She shrugged.

"I reckon you need to get settled first. I come by every day to take care of the animals and check on the folks. You can just let me know whatever you need, and I'll get it for you. Bring it the next day."

"Thank you, Mr. Spaid. I mean Abe."

"Come down and meet the folks when you're ready."

After he left, she found water in a pitcher, splashed some on her face, and checked her hair in the mirror. Presentable enough. She descended the rickety stairs, and flakes of paint flew off from beneath her hand as it slid along the railing. When she reached the porch, Mrs. Spaid turned to look at her and quickly turned away again. She still sat in the buckboard, still with that ramrod-straight back.

Theodosius knocked on the door. Abe held it open and motioned her inside. Her eyes, used to the bright sunlight, could barely discern two shapes in wooden rocking chairs, silhouetted by the flames in the fireplace. Abe, speaking loudly, introduced her. She moved closer as she became used to the dim light, and held out a hand to the old man.

"I'm very pleased to meet you, Mr. Spaid." She had never seen a man who looked so old. Tufts of white hair sprouted from an otherwise bald head spotted with raised, brown spots. The wrinkled skin hanging from eyebrow to eyelid appeared to reduce his vision to slits. And how strange that old people retained the size of their noses and ears no matter how diminished the rest of their bodies became. He looked like a troll from a child's picture book. The old man slammed shut the Bible in his lap, laid it on the stained and threadbare plaid blanket covering his legs. He looked her up and down.

"And who are you?"

She let her hand drop to her side. "My name is Theodosius Wheeler. Your son hired me to take care of you and your wife." She smiled at the elder Mrs. Spaid, who rocked briskly, her hands on the chair's arms, and never looked up. Skin and bones. Wiry white hair hung wildly past her shoulders. Her son watched her with a sad expression.

"She don't really know where she is anymore."

"I understand."

"Well," Abe said with a forced cheerfulness. "Let's show you around." He led her to where the cleaning supplies were stored, the copper tub for laundry, broom, rags. Showed her the pantry of canned goods, made sure she was familiar with how to use the woodstove, and pointed through the window to the chicken coop and root cellar. "Well, I think me and the missus will head back to town. You can go ahead and fix their noon meal. I'm sure everybody must be hungry by now!"

Her life fell into a routine differing little from what she had left behind. After years caring for her ailing father, she now cared for two ailing old people. If her plans had worked out, she would be married. She would still have to haul water and wood, cook meals, dust, sweep, take care of laundry and bread baking and making soap. Except she would also have to perform other wifely duties, duties that seemed mysterious and just a little distasteful, a feeling she'd garnered from the older women who called on occasion with cakes or casseroles during her father's illness.

The elderly Mrs. Spaid was easy enough to care for. While she seemed to live in a fog of unawareness, she was able to take care of her own personal needs. She could never walk out back to the privy on her own, but a chamber pot was within her ability to manage, and she could dress, if one considered a clean nightgown dressing, and feed herself. She never spoke. She seemed wraithlike, with her thick white hair falling down her back. Theodosius tried several times to comb and braid it, but the old woman lost patience and struck at the brush, so it remained a mass of tangles.

Theodosius never laid eyes on Abe's wife, the younger Mrs. Spaid, after that first day. The elder Mr. Spaid often rambled on with curses and growls of disgust whenever her name came up. He was a Baptist. She was a Lutheran. She may as well have been a Satan worshipper as far as Old Mr. Spaid was concerned. Theodosius learned quickly to not bring up the woman's name, and proclaimed herself to be a Baptist for the sake of household tranquility.

One day, not long after she arrived, Mr. Spaid said he had something for her. "This used to belong to her." He nodded his head toward his wife. "It ain't no use to her no more. You bein' a good Baptist woman might like to have it." He held out a battered leather-bound Bible, smiling widely enough to show his toothless gums.

"Why, thank you, Mr. Spaid. It's very thoughtful of you." She took the book and put it on the table near the door. "I'll take it upstairs tonight."

She turned back to the room and almost bumped into him. He'd followed her and now stood not six inches way. She could smell his musty breath and rank body odors. He reached out with freckled and wrinkled fingers to touch her arm. She stepped back and his expression became blank.

"I didn't mean no offense. Surely you know you are an appealing woman." He reached out again.

She gently pushed his hand away, trying not to show revulsion. "Mr. Spaid, you are a married man. What does that Bible say about that?" She pointed to the book. "And I'm an employee of your son."

He hung his head and shuffled back to his chair. As he

lowered himself down, he muttered, "Yes, a married man." He looked at his wife who rocked mindlessly, staring into the fireplace. "How could I forget."

In the evenings, after dinner and chores, she'd get the old folks ready for bed, then walk to the fence that enclosed the pasture. At that time, early evening, the world fell quiet. She stood near the horses as they ripped grass and chewed, pawing the dirt, shaking a head, swishing a tail. They sometimes came to her, let her touch their silky noses, gently bobbed their heads up and down or shook, grass flying from their manes. Their hooves, soft on the soil, their quiet nickers and huffing breaths, soothed her.

After a while, by the time the sky burst into sunset colors, Abe would show up to check on the stock, feed the chickens, look in on his parents. He always touched the edge of his wide-brimmed slouch hat and nodded when he saw her by the fence. He'd tie his horse to the porch railing and go into the barn, then the house. Often she stayed out by the horses until darkness fell, until Abe called goodnight to his parents. The door would bang shut, his boots would clomp down the porch steps, he'd mount his horse, and ride past her. No acknowledgment of her standing there; she was invisible in the darkness. His saddle creaked, the horse's hooves on the dusty trail made soft thuds that faded as he rode away. When they became faint, she'd look to see the long, black shadow he cast across the pasture on moonlit nights before he disappeared into the wagon road.

She would say goodnight to the horses before climbing the stairs to what she had come to consider her private sanctuary. Abe had brought her a rocking chair and she would sit in it every night, reading novels by the bedside table until sleepiness drove her to blow out the lamp and climb into bed.

The weather cooled. The grass turned yellow in the pasture.

Sunset came too early for her to greet it outside with the horses. Abe arrived after dark in the wagon. He filled the barn with hay bales and prepared to bring the stock in for the winter.

After a fitful night, Theodosius awoke exhausted. Bad dreams and a chill in the air kept restful sleep at bay. She'd gotten up for an extra blanket but still awakened frequently throughout the rest of the night. When the sky turned a predawn gray, she threw on her clothes and a shawl and went downstairs to fix breakfast for the old man and woman, scraping frost off the railing as her hand slid along it. When she reached the porch and opened the door, a sharp, sour stench assaulted her. Had they knocked over the chamber pot?

"About time you got here," the old man said as soon as she stepped inside, before she had removed her shawl. "Look at her!"

Upon first glance, the old lady looked the same as always, slumped in her rocking chair, dressed in her nightgown, hair askew. But the chair did not rock. The old lady stared straight ahead, her jaw slack, her head a bit off-kilter. Theodosius ran to her and knelt. The old woman was not dead. Perhaps she'd had a stroke. She'd relieved herself in the chair. "Here, Mrs. Spaid, let me get you cleaned up."

The old woman stood quietly as Theodosius helped her up and removed the soiled nightgown. "I'll have to heat water for a bath." She was about to go for a blanket to wrap the woman in when she saw the marks. Angry red marks on both her arms, from elbow to shoulder, some fading into bruises. She turned to the old man in time to see him quickly look away. "What happened here?"

The old man rocked his chair, his head lowered to his Bible.

"Mr. Spaid! What happened to your wife? She has marks all over her arms. Look!"

But the old man kept his head lowered. He glanced out of

the corner of his eye. "How would I know? Must've done it to herself."

Theodosius managed to bathe the old woman who was mostly just skin draped over bone and weighed no more than a small child. After drying her, Theodosius put her in a clean nightgown, and lowered her into the rocking chair. The old lady tipped to one side or the other until Theodosius helped her up and led her to the bed. Images of her father's last days came to her as she propped the frail woman on pillows. How long would she now be cleaning her daily? Spoon-feeding her.

"You gonna make breakfast?" the old man yelled. "That stove needs wood. It's cold in here."

"Mr. Spaid, please. I'll take care of all that once I've made your wife comfortable."

Grumbling, he bent his head again to the Bible in his lap. Theodosius pulled the blanket up to the woman's chest. Mrs. Spaid's claw-like hand grabbed her forearm with surprising strength, and Theodosius looked down into pale blue eyes opened wide, round, and very much aware. And filled with fear. Theodosius's heart ached with compassion. To be so old and to know death is coming. "There, there, Mrs. Spaid." She patted the dry skin of the woman's hand, felt the brittle bones beneath. "You're going to be fine. I'm going to take care of you." She gently pulled the woman's hand away and lay it on top of the blankets. The vacant stare returned.

That night she stayed downstairs with the old ones until Abe arrived.

"Your mother has some red marks on her skin. I don't know what they are." She pushed the nightgown sleeve up to show him. "And she's been like this since I arrived this morning. She seems unable to get up or walk, and I feared she would fall out of the chair. She can't use the chamber pot."

Abe leaned over his mother. "Mother? Can you hear me? Do

234

you know who I am?"

The old lady stared into space, her mouth hanging open, a bit of spittle gathered in the crease by her lip.

"Well, I reckon she won't be with us too much longer. I hope it's not too much extra work for you."

She almost laughed. What else did she have to do? "It is more work, but I can manage. What do you make of those marks?"

He lifted his mother's arm and looked again, then shook his head. "Don't know." He touched them, pressed lightly, watching his mother. "Don't seem to bother her none."

But each day Theodosius found more of the red marks on the old lady. Each day old Mr. Spaid looked away, grumbling into his lap, lifting his head only to yell out complaints about being hungry or cold. The frigid weather required her to bring in more wood, haul more water, cook more hot food, and wash more laundry due to the old lady's incontinence. Sunset came earlier each day, shortening the daylight time in which to work.

One evening was so cold she almost skipped visiting with the horses but felt a strong need to be near them. Their quiet presence comforted her so. The old lady had been going downhill more each day. Today she was nonresponsive. Theodosius would have thought her dead except her bodily fluids still managed to be pushed out onto the clean sheets. She felt ashamed of her impatience, yet still thought *die, please, and sooner rather than later.* She removed her gloves to pet the horses' soft noses. Abe rode past her. These days darkness came so early he didn't see her when he arrived, and she seldom stayed outside long enough to watch him ride away. Exhausted, she climbed the stairway to her room as slow as an old lady herself.

Her room felt cozy as she read in the lamplight. The woodstove was stoked and throwing out plenty of heat. The harder the wind blew outside, the safer she felt in her sanctuary. It didn't matter how strenuous, physically and mentally, the days had become, as long as she had her room and her quiet evenings. Tonight she read poetry. Wordsworth. The Bible the old man had insisted she take sat untouched on the dresser. As far as she was concerned, it was as much fiction as the novels she sometimes read.

Something tapped at the windows, a steady rapping. She pulled her shawl closer and walked to the north-facing window. No moonlight or starlight lit the yard. All was total blackness. She pushed up the sash and the icy air took her breath. Snowflakes, frozen hard as pebbles, gusted into the room. Her shawl fell to the floor in her mad rush to pull the window closed. She picked it up, hung it on the back of the rocking chair, and went to bed.

She awoke during the night. Remembering the storm, she wasn't sure of the time. Still night? Dawn hidden by clouds and falling snow? She gasped when the lamp by the bed suddenly brightened the room.

Flailing out of the covers, she turned to see the old lady standing over her, naked, wild white hair streaming out as if windblown. The eyes! Again that look of awareness and fear, even though the face was slack, the mouth hung open, the head tilted at an odd angle. Slowly the old woman's arm rose from her side, skin like crepe paper hanging translucent. Paralyzed with horror, Theodosius stared as the old woman pointed one finger toward the door and made crackling moaning noises. The raised red marks covered her entire body. The noises became long undulating shrieks.

Theodosius awoke in the morning with sunshine streaming in the windows. Had she blacked out from terror? The thought of the sight and sounds of the old lady again made her heart race. Twisting to see where the old woman had gone, she realized she was alone. She lay in bed a long time, relieved that the horrible vision of last night was just that. A nightmare.

She dressed and carefully descended the snow-covered stairs. When she opened the door, a sickening, sharp odor caused her to instinctively raise her hand to cover her mouth and nose.

After the brightness of the morning and the sun glinting on the fresh snow, her eyes could not adjust to the dim light indoors. She went inside, searching her apron pocket for matches, but her vision cleared. The rocking chairs were both empty. The old man was kneeling by the bed, muttering as he read from his open Bible. He barely turned his head when she came in.

"She's dead," he said.

Theodosius hurried over. The old lady looked the same as she ever did, except her chest did not rise and fall. Except the smell was much worse than usual. Except she was naked. Except she was covered with red marks. Some on her neck.

She pulled a sheet up to cover the old lady's face with shaking hands. When she felt she could speak, she asked, "What happened? How did she get like this?"

The old man pushed on the bed, springs creaking and the old lady bouncing slightly, enough to give Theodosius a start. The old man arose, picked up his Bible, and shuffled over to his chair. He threw the plaid blanket over his legs. "It's past breakfast, you know. I'm hungry."

The snows came in earnest and Abe moved the stock into the barn. He came every night after he'd finished his own chores in town, no matter how cold, no matter the weather. He'd check on his father and then tend to the animals. Theodosius pulled her chair to the window and no longer read at night. She watched the lantern light streaming from the barn, watched the shadows move as he worked, back and forth. It seemed he stayed later and later. Often she fell asleep in the chair. When she awoke, her candle burned down and extinguished, she'd go to the window and look out at the darkened barn . . .

Each day, she spent more time upstairs, was up and down the stairs more often than before. She didn't feel comfortable alone in the house with just the old man, didn't like the way he watched her. Now and then he would try to make conversation, but it was always more like an inquisition into her beliefs.

"You been reading the Bible I give ye?"

"I read it every night before I go to bed."

"What book you in?"

"Here, your food is ready. Come to the table."

And she would take her own food upstairs. She didn't clean the house thoroughly or often. Laundry piled up until she absolutely had to take care of it.

Often while she worked, she felt his eyes boring into her. Today he complained more loudly than usual.

"You spend too much time upstairs. You're paid to take care of me, you know."

"I know. I do take care of you."

How had he managed to sneak up behind her? She was stirring a pot of stew at the stove and suddenly arms went around her waist.

"There's more ways than food and laundry to care for a man."

"Mr. Spaid!" She twisted away.

"People be talking, the two of us living out here like this. Together."

"We don't live together. I live upstairs. This is my job."

His troll face contorted into a toothless smile. His hand darted out and pinched her breast. "Ye like that, don't ye?" He cackled as she slapped at his fingers.

She thought of the red marks on the old lady. Did he think she had liked that? Had he taken pleasure in torturing her in her final days? She looked at the demented old troll and contemplated throwing the pot of stew at him. "And do you like the idea of living out here by yourself? With nobody to cook your meals or wash your clothes? Because if you touch me again, that's what will happen. I promise."

The smile faded. He shot her a glaring look before shuffling to the table. "You keep reading that Bible. You'll come to your senses." He picked up the tin plate and banged it on the table. "Now serve me my supper."

She waited for the lantern to light up the barn, then quietly slipped down the stairs and across the yard. She pulled the door open just enough to squeeze inside, then leaned against it until he looked up from the stall. He dumped a shovelful of manure into the wheelbarrow.

"Hey," he said. A slight smile creased the lines around gentle eyes. "Was you in need of something? Something from town?"

"I hear your father coughing during the night. More so of late."

He leaned on the shovel for a moment, his head down. "Thanks. I know. He's got the consumption." The smile had disappeared but the gentle eyes seemed even more so. "Surprised he's lasted this long."

"I'm so very sorry. I didn't know." She'd known the old man was frail but not that he suffered from the white death.

"He don't like people feeling sorry for him."

He returned to shoveling out the stall. She stayed leaning against the door, breathing in the smell of hay and horses and manure, the moist warmth of the barn pressing against her face, listening to the sounds of the clucking chickens, animals knocking their feed buckets, slurping water. The steady sound of the shovel scraping across the barn floor mesmerized her.

When Abe rolled the wheelbarrow toward another stall, she slid the door open for him. "I know what it's like to lose a parent. If you'd like to talk, I can make some hot cocoa. Mrs. Daigle was kind enough to bring me some powder when she made her condolence call. Back when your mother passed."

"Well, I guess I could do that. My wife's at a meeting at the church tonight." He let the wheelbarrow's legs rest and straightened, pushed his hat back on his forehead. "And I ain't my father. I don't mind a pretty lady feeling sorry for me."

Heat rose up her neck to her cheeks. She rushed from the barn, and he followed.

After he'd left, she wondered at the veiled comments of older, married women. What did they find so repugnant about one body yearning for another, the joy of lips touching, skin touching, until aflame with unquenchable desire? After all those nights she'd spent imagining Abe as he worked in the barn, she'd begun to wonder what it would be like to have his arms around her. Now she knew. She'd lain in the rumpled bed, spent, happy, listening to his boots descend the stairs.

After that first night he checked on his father, then went to the barn—which seemed to take less time than it used to—and soon clomped up the stairs, lifting the latch on the unlocked door. He always looked in first, waited for her welcoming smile, before he came to her.

They did not make love every night. Sometimes they sat side by side, silently watching the stars, the moon, through the window, until it was time for him to go. One precious hour, every night, until he said, "I have to go. She'll be wondering where I am." And with a sigh and a kiss, he would leave her.

The old man grew more frail and meaner. She had to watch him, watch that hand, those fingers, all the time. She spent less and less time downstairs. As the days grew longer, she'd sometimes walk out to the wagon road and back, for the exercise. Then she'd wait by the fence, listen to the horses in the pasture again, their hooves sucking mud as they nibbled at fresh shoots of grass. She'd watch the trail. When he turned off the wagon road, she'd go upstairs to wait for the latch to rise, for him to come to her.

"I thought you was a God-fearing woman. A righteous woman," the old man said. He sat at the table, a fork in one hand, a knife in the other, his plate in front of him.

"Oh? And what do you think I am now?"

"I don't think. I *know*. I know ye to be a whore. And with my own son."

She stood still, fearing to turn from the stove to look at him, listening to be sure he wasn't coming toward her. He was too weak to move as fast as he used to. Just those few sentences caused a coughing fit that ended in heavy wheezing and blood smeared onto his sleeve.

He couldn't know. He was asleep. The downstairs was always dark. Abe made sure he was in bed before he went out to the barn . . .

"I ain't sleepin' all the time. I hear him a'climbin' them stairs." He wheezed out a laugh. "I hear them bed springs a'creaking."

She sucked in a breath. Why not? She could hear him coughing. Sound could travel both ways. "You don't know what you're talking about." She carried the pot to the table to ladle out his dinner. "Eat. And stop talking nonsense."

"That be why you don't want me. You want the younger version."

Her hand stopped midair. Broth dripped from the ladle onto the table. "You need to stop talking like that. You need to stop imagining things." She splashed the stew onto his plate and left.

Several days later, in the early afternoon, Abe drove up in his wagon, Mrs. Spaid at his side. Theodosius had just served the old man his midday meal. She pulled back the curtain and fought a growing dread as they pulled closer.

"I told Abe to bring her out here," the old man said. "I've decided to give you a gift. You don't want me, I understand that. But you've taken good care of me and the old woman afore she died. You deserve to be happy."

"What are you talking about?"

"Never you mind. You'll find out soon enough." The corners of his toothless mouth twisted into a smile. "A surprise. For you."

Theodosius held the door open. Abe helped his wife down. She walked directly up the steps onto the porch, brushed past Theodosius, and entered the house.

"What is it, old man?"

"Here, have a seat." Spaid waved his fork at the bench on the other side of the table, dripping food as he did so. "We got things to talk about."

Theodosius felt her pulse speeding. Her hand went to her chest. Abe hung his hat on a peg next to the door and sat next to his wife.

"Well, we're here, Pa. Now tell me why we both had to come out. You know she don't like coming here."

"This is important. Woman!" He waved the dripping fork at Theodosius. "Ain't you got no manners? Give them some food."

Nobody looked at her. Feeling invisible, unable to hear much beyond her heart pounding in her ears, she did as he said. Served the wife, then stood next to Abe a minute too long after she placed the plate before him. The old man looked at her then, his troll smile in place, his eyes merry as he enjoyed every minute of her anguish. She moved away and stood near the stove, awaiting the old man's announcement, awaiting her exposure as a whore who'd been intimate with his son, wondering what Mrs. Spaid's reaction would be. Where would she go once her employment terminated, what would she do? She had some savings now—maybe west to California . . .

"This here is my last will and testament." The old man pulled a sheet of paper from inside his shirt. He unfolded it and placed it on the table, turned it so his son and Mrs. Spaid could read it. "It says everything I own will go to the two of you. Both named, as individuals, bequeathed the house, the acreage, the barn, the livestock. All of it. Worth a pretty penny, I reckon."

What? How was this a surprise for *her*? Although she was indeed surprised. And Theodosius wondered at the amazing transformation of Mrs. Spaid, who picked up the paper. Her body relaxed, her shoulders lowered, her arm seemed supple. She smiled. *Smiled.* "Why, what a lovely turn of events, Father Spaid. We had no idea of your financial circumstances. I mean, back taxes or liens . . . we weren't expecting much."

"There ain't none of that. I own it all free and clear. When I'm dead it'll be all yours."

"Yes, ours." Mrs. Spaid's smile spread. "And half is in my own name?"

Theodosius went upstairs while they finished their meal. The couple lingered for a long time. Amazing how the promise of financial gain loosened that woman up. Why, she might even decide to be nice to her husband. Theodosius would be glad for him, of course. But then he'd probably have no more need to visit with her. And once the old man died, there'd be no need for her at all.

A knock at the door, the latch raised, the door opened. Abe stood awkwardly at the threshold. "I'm sorry. I mean, I won't be able to come here tonight. You know, later on."

"I understand. It's all right."

"It's not all right with me." He stepped inside and his arms went around her. "Maybe it's time."

"Time for what?"

"For me to leave her."

She leaned against the wall, pulling him to her. Words whispered through fervent kisses spoke of their need, their love.

"Abe, stop. What if she comes up here looking for you?"

"She's gone out to the barn to look at the horses. I guess there's a first time for everything. Pa told her one of them was a thoroughbred, worth a lot of money, and that one should be hers, so she had to see. I'd best be—"

"What's that?" Theodosius leaned to see out the door. Flames licking at the front of the barn.

Abe released her and turned to look. "My God, did she knock over the lantern? Stay here!"

By the time he got to the barn, flames had engulfed the door and the front wall. He tried to get in but could not, and ran around to the back. Riveted to the landing, disbelieving her eyes and ears, she sank to the floor, clutching the balusters as if looking through the bars of a jail. The roar of the fire, the wife's screams, the horses and other animals banging and shrieking. He must have gotten the door open in the back because the horses suddenly ran from the barn, their manes and tales flaming as they raced up the trail to the wagon road and beyond. She waited for the other animals to escape. She waited for Abe and his wife to run from behind the barn. The screams stopped.

She ran toward the barn doors. They had burned away, exposing the inferno inside. Heat burned her face even though the barn was still fifty feet away. The wind shifted and smoke, ash, and cinders blew toward her, choking her. She held her apron over her mouth and nose and stumbled to the porch, rushed inside. "The barn is afire!" she cried.

"I know." The old man was smiling, his expression almost gleeful. His coat hung from the peg next to his son's hat. On the floor beneath sat damp galoshes amid fresh clods of mud that left a trail from the doorway.

"You? You set the barn on fire?"

"Oh, she couldn't wait to get out there." He snorted. "Thought she was gettin' some prize horseflesh. All she ever cared about was money. That's how those Lutherans are. Evil. You shoulda seen how she treated me and the old lady while my son thought she was helping out. She was no good. No good for anyone, especially my son."

"What—what have you done?" Her throat felt filled with cinders.

"Why, that's my surprise! You don't want me, you want my son. Now you can have him. He can move back out here and we'll all be one happy—"

Her hands closed around his neck. How surprising that her fingers could go completely around. How fragile his aged spine. She dragged his body onto the bed. He weighed nothing. He was nothing. She threw the door open. In the yard men from town were arriving on horseback and in wagons, running, yelling, hauling buckets of water.

Sobbing, she climbed the stairs one last time, threw some clothing, a hairbrush, a shawl, into her carpetbag before stumbling down to the porch. She untied Abe's wagon, climbed in, and slapped the ribbons on the horse's back. Distracted by the fire, nobody noticed her. The wagon rocked and bumped up the trail, and at the wagon road she turned toward the mountains.

She sits at the top of the porch stairs, glad that she faces the pasture and not the pile of ashes that was once the barn. She is surprised that the dilapidated old house, so ready to fall down all those years ago, still stands. The creak of the old man's rocking chair comes from inside.

The sound of the chair stops. Behind her the door scrapes

open. She stands and turns. "I thought you might still be here."

She can barely see him in the darkness of the night. He's only halfway onto the porch, as if uncertain whether to leave the house. He holds up his Bible. The cover is in tatters, the binding broken. Pages are crumbling as he waves it at her. "Did ye think I'd be burning in hell? No. Ye knew better. Been right here all these years, expectin' ye to return."

She laughs. "I suppose you think I've come to accept your offer? To live with you as your wife?"

"I would like that, yes. 'Twould save your soul from eternal damnation."

"And how has eternal damnation missed snatching your soul? You who killed two innocent people?"

He smiles his troll smile, opens his toothless mouth, and laughs. His nightshirt hangs in dirty tatters. His feet are bare. "Weren't nothing innocent about *her*." He clutches the book to his chest and his smile fades. "I do regret my son. Why would he rush to save her when he could have you?"

Why, indeed.

She reaches into the carpetbag and removes the can of kerosene, begins pouring it onto the steps, flinging it so the liquid sprays across the porch, splashes on the ragged hem of his nightshirt.

He steps fully out of the house, his eyes wide and black in his pallid face. "What are you doing? What—"

She tosses the match and steps back. The blaze crawls across the porch floor, licks up the railing, up the posts. His nightshirt bursts into flame. He thrashes, screams, howls. The Bible flares into cinders. His nightshirt turns to ash. She sees only the outline of him—limned with fire—fall to the floor, writhing. The house catches, flames surging into wood so dry and rotted it explodes into flame. She steps backwards, farther and farther away from the conflagration until she is at the pasture fence. A soft snort behind her, a welcoming nicker, and she turns to stroke the horse's neck, saddened by the shafts of moonlight penetrating the burnt-out places.

Soon the house implodes. The blaze dies down as men on horses and wagons approach from town. Shattered window glass glitters in the pile of ashes. Spirals of smoke rise. The spectral horse's eyes glow in the darkness. She steps through the high weeds and brush, grabs the singed mane, and pulls herself up. The moonlight glows through her own eyes as she turns toward the mountains.

Patricia Grady Cox writes historical novels set in the Arizona Territory. A member of Western Writers of America, Women Writing the West, and the Society of Southwest Authors, she lives in Phoenix with her Australian shepherd, Mustang Sally, and enjoys being able to visit the actual locations used in her writing. Her goal is to transport her readers to another time and involve them emotionally with her characters.

★ ★ ★ ★ ★

Mail-Order Delivery
by Marcia Gaye

★ ★ ★ ★ ★

Despite the weather, the company had made another eight miles today, in mud deep as their ankles, the teams holding the trail. Until now.

The driver of Lucinda's rented Conestoga pulled back hard on the reins. It was not enough to stop the sideways slide toward a drop-off. Rain obscured the view of the wagon just ahead, pouring in a stream from the brim of his hat. The far horse could not gain its footing, flailing half in the air. If not for the yoke and beam, it would be over in a tumble, no telling how far to the bottom of the cliff.

"Mama! Help! Mister Breck, help!"

"Hush, Genie. They're doing all they can."

Spokes from the broken wheel careened downward in a mudslide. Wagon master Thompson and the other men struggled to save the wagon, while Lucinda and her three children huddled together, helpless to do anything but watch. At their feet lay only a satchel Lucinda had managed to toss aside when she and the children scrambled out moments before.

The canvas of the Conestoga caught the wind, adding to the severe tilt. One of their trunks fell from the open back, smashing along the cliff wall, rebounding against outcropping rock, shattering to pieces, bits of their belongings falling heavy with rain to the canyon floor below.

Rocks and dirt scraped the wagon axle, grinding against the iron belt of the wheel. Horses groaned, terror rolling white in their eyes. The sound sickened Lucinda's stomach. She felt as if her stomach would fall from her body and slide over the cliff with all her worldly possessions. She pressed a handkerchief to her mouth though retching produced nothing but stale air. She had had naught to eat since yesterday morning before the rains came.

"Mama?"

"Just pray, Eugenia. Everything will be fine."

Wagon master Thompson gripped the lead horse's bridle with both hands and jerked down. Other men roped two more horses to the axle and pulled them forward. All the shouting accumulated in Lucinda's ears, overwhelming her inner dialogue with the Almighty. The wagon lurched and dragged up onto solid ground.

"Praise be," Lucinda whispered.

It had been too wet to cook, too wet to build a fire. Cold biscuits and apples had stopped the growling in the bellies of her children but the twisting in her own wouldn't allow for food. Rain still fell the next day but weather would not keep Whip Thompson from the task of replacing the busted wheel. When at last the train moved forward, making camp outside Dog Trot, Nevada, the children emerged to stretch their legs.

"Mama, isn't Nevada a desert? That's what the schoolmistress said. Dry and useless, that's what she said."

"Useless? Why, of course not. None of God's creation is useless. There are wonderful things about Nevada we have yet to know for ourselves. I'm certain when the rains stop, we will be quite at home."

Lucinda hoped her own words would be true. No matter where she would dwell, her beloved Matthew would not be with her. So what did it matter where they settled? Her children needed a pa. They needed a home. Nevada would be as good a place as any other.

Duncan Fergus had promised both fatherhood and a warm hearth.

Whip Thompson slogged along and touched the brim of his hat. "Missis Keane, you can stay the night in the wagon if your man don't come before. No need to get a room, you're paid up on the rent of the wagon. The repairs aren't your concern either. Such as this happens on a wagon train. I'm sorry about your trunk. Tomorrow, early, we move on. You'll need to be packed up by then." He kindly lifted Nathan up into the reach of Eugenia who tsk'ed over his muddy feet. Then the whip made his way among the other wagons, settling everyone in.

"Genie, is Susan asleep? I'm going to help fix supper and bring back our portion. Keep the children in out of the rain."

Wet shoes, wet clothes, wet hair. Lucinda hadn't known how they would fare in the dry desert but now she wished to find out sooner rather than later. She was tired of rain, weary to her bones of travel. As she dipped stew into a borrowed kettle her mind pondered when Mr. Fergus would arrive to collect them. She was vexed that he hadn't been waiting. How foolish had she been seeking him out? Had she been that addled by grief?

Back in Kansas City, she'd read notices in *The Star* from men advertising for wives. But she had been the one to place her own notice. *Widow with children seeking father and home in the west.* Shamelessly she begged for a man who would take them in, a man with land and purpose. She hoped for a widower who knew the tensions of marriage.

She did not place her notice in the newspaper, however, but sent it directly to the Nevada postmaster, requesting he pass it to the most respected officer of the law thereabout. Then that officer could post it in a place of discretion, insuring that only men of reliable reputation would reply.

Within weeks Duncan Fergus responded.

A good Scottish name, that.

My Dear Mrs. Keane,

I am writing in reply to your letter of inquiry as to marriage to a man of the frontier. I am a widow man in the territory of Nevada, in a scenic area accessible before the steep climb of the Sierra. I am now without a wife for three years and yearn to be a husband again. I own my home, and in it have one son, four years of age. You have three children and so I expect to give them all the considerations of comfort as my own.

I am of calm temperament, a military man before my settling down, do not cuss nor drink liquor, to which my neighbors can vouch. I read and write well, as this letter is in my own hand.

I will not insult any lady by demanding after her face and figure, but trust you are comely. You stress that you require above all a father for your son, and I agree to that whole-heartedly, yet I also state that a husband is not a name only but a position and a wife knows well the expects of it. A marrying preacher comes through nearly every other month.

Please reply and passage will be provided.

Regards,
Duncan Fergus
of Dog Trot, Nevada Territory

At the fall of evening the rain stopped, and morning dawned clear and bright. A portend of life to come, surely.

Still there showed no sign of Mr. Fergus. Lucinda rose early to dress and put up her hair. Out in the weather as they were, no primping would make an impact. Even a woman plain as she would have liked to make a decent first impression on her intended husband, but she could only manage a rudimentary effort. She had no mirror and silently resigned her bit of vanity to passing foolishness. She washed and brushed the children, as best as possible, and sat them on the porch of the way station.

254

Nathan pulled at her sleeve. "Mama, can I have Whit back now?" he asked.

"Yes, he's in my satchel. Don't spill everything out, now. He's on top."

Nathan grinned as he pulled forth a wooden contraption, which unfolded into the shape of a man, legs and arms strung loosely to a body that hung from a length of twine. The toy dangled, then looked to be dancing as Nathan jiggled his hand.

"Thanks, Mama. Whit can dance for Susan while we wait!"

Mr. Thompson instructed his men to place the one and only trunk up out of the puddles and Lucinda sat on it, waiting.

"The train's got to be movin' along, Missis. You'll be all right here, you and the youngsters." With a tip of his hat he motioned and called out, "Wagons, Ho!" and the caravan turned its back, rolling northward. Only empty ruts marked that it had been there at all.

Twenty minutes may well have been hours, so motionless was her heart. But at last a buckboard rose into view from the open west and soon a team of horses and driver were visible.

"Mama, is that Mr. Fergus?"

"I do reckon so, Nathan. And his boy with him. Genie, hold Susan for me while I greet him." Now her heart was awake, so much so that she feared fainting from its pounding. She stood and waited for the horses to pull up.

A tall man, neither slender nor plump, jumped to the ground. A full black beard covered his features save light blue eyes. He looked her over before speaking. "Missis Keane." He removed his hat and said no more.

"Mr. Fergus. Hello. Yes. Oh, and these are Eugenia, Nathan, and little Susan. And this is your son?" She stepped forward and looked into serious pale blue eyes.

It came into her mind that these two boys would never look like brothers, one being as much like his father as the other like his. Nathan's eyes shone brown and merry, his hair light, like Susan's, while this child was dark except in those striking eyes.

"This is Daniel. Danny, tip your hat to the ladies." He paused. "I do apologize for being so long on the road. The mud slowed us down. Not expecting so much rain all of a sudden like that."

"Our wagon had the same trouble. It nearly went over a cliff. All would have been lost if not for the experienced men who guided it to safety. We lost much of our possessions. But here we are. All of us. How far is it to the house? We missed breakfast and you must be hungry as well."

"Only a couple of hours. Road is dry again now. We et as we rode but there's fried eggs and corn cakes in a poke. It'll stave off hunger till we get home and you can make a proper dinner. There's some jars of cold coffee, and one of milk for the babe."

He hoisted the trunk and satchel onto the buckboard, then held his hand out to Genie to help her aboard. Nathan jumped in next to Danny and the two rifled the sack, Nathan claiming his portion before handing the sack to his sister.

"Hold on, young man. We feed our women before ourselves. Excuse yourself."

Nathan looked downward and mumbled, "Excuse me," as Mr. Fergus nodded.

Out of habit, and with a touch of embarrassment, Lucinda opened her mouth to correct Nathan as well, but thought better of it. It seemed wiser to let the man and boy form their own alliance.

"Now, ma'am, that is, Missis Keane, would you allow baby there to sit with the others so you can eat?"

"Lucinda. You may please call me Lucinda. Yes, of course. Nathan, put Susan between you and the trunk. Give her a cake. And Genie, help her with the milk. Thank you for your thoughtfulness, Duncan. That's all right, is it, to address each other by our given names?" She made an attempt to smile, forcing confidence into it. Her thanks were sincere.

She accepted Duncan's hand of assistance, knowing there was no way to disguise the roughness of her own, as she raised her skirts to take her place on the seat.

Lucinda hadn't imagined much about the house but what rose on the horizon certainly wasn't it. Clay bricks stacked a foundation for notched logs that formed a square not much larger than a summer kitchen back in Kansas. This kitchen-sized cabin had a rock chimney on the north wall but no smoke rose from it. She looked at the house, then looked at the man who had built it.

He nodded and smiled. "See the glass in the windows? Had them special ordered when you wrote that you'd come. That stand of trees there," he dipped his head west, "has a nice spring. I plan to trench it and build a cold spring house for you. And with so many youngsters it may be an idea to dig another outhouse too."

Lucinda shaded her eyes from the hot sun. The land was dry as if there had been no rain at all but patches of green testified to it.

"Mama, where's the garden? And the chicken coop?"

Hoping to answer, she turned a full circle but was none the more informed.

Duncan answered for her. "I see you children have an easterner's idea of homesteading. Don't worry. The garden's behind the house and the coop beyond it. They'll be plenty to keep you busy."

Again he offered his hand to help her step down and she absently said, "Thank you," followed by, "it's a fine place, Duncan, rather small in this view. But fine, I'm sure."

"Boys, hoist that trunk down and tote it inside. The day's burning away."

"I think such a heavy trunk is more than the boys can manage. Eugenia has the baby to handle."

It was true. The two boys grunted, barely inching the luggage toward the edge of the flat buckboard.

"Ah, I see that. Come on, sons, we'll do it together." Duncan hoisted one end, the boys shared the other, and the trunk made it inside.

Lucinda gathered her satchel and her courage. "Come, Genie, let's see what sort of home we're going to make here."

The glass windows allowed afternoon light to flood into the room, a combination sitting room and kitchen, with a fireplace, shelves with dishes, a table flanked with two hard chairs and two benches alongside on a rag rug. To the other side of the room was a rocking chair and a large stuffed leather chair and footstool. A small side table held an oil lamp and a bound book or ledger.

"I'll put this in the bedroom and let you freshen up while I start the fire for supper. I didn't want to let it burn with nobody here, it gets so hot in the afternoons, so banked it over. Won't be a minute." He disappeared into an adjacent room. A room she wanted to avoid but could not.

Behind the curtain, Eugenia reclaimed the day dress and apron she had worn on the way from Kansas. "Mama, where shall I hang my good dress?"

"Just lay it across the bed and we'll arrange later." Lucinda patted her daughter's arm and smoothed Genie's hair, so like her own, limp and dull colored as dry sand. After changing Susan, she also donned her trail-worn dress, covered with a newer apron. It was time to see to dinner.

Nathan and Danny played outside and Duncan Fergus was nowhere to be seen when Lucinda rummaged the cupboards to find what she could make into a meal. The fire smoldered, and a pot of coffee heated on the hearth. A barrel of water stood waiting.

"Well, that's a start," she said to herself. The pantry was well stocked, a nice surprise, and before long the table was laden with turnips, onions, and small slices of dried beef she tenderized with thick gravy. Some rounds of a sort of flat dry bread she warmed and slathered with fat and jam.

"I think we're ready, Genie, don't you? Ring the bell."

Outside she could hear Duncan instructing the boys to wash hands and faces. Then he entered, taking the chair at the head of the table. Lucinda sat at the foot, boys on one bench, girls on the other. Duncan looked square into her eyes.

"Bow your heads, children, and give thanks for this meal and the hands that prepared it." Lucinda waited for him to say the blessing but only a moment of silence followed. Then Duncan filed his plate and passed each dish.

A proper family dinner in our new home, Lucinda thought. *It's a start.*

The heavy desert sun lowered against the horizon. While Genie tidied the dishes, Lucinda gathered little Susan on her lap, the boys at her feet, and read them the storybook she'd toted in her satchel. Susan and Nathan knew it by memory but Daniel craned his neck to follow the drawings on the turning pages.

When all heads began drooping, Lucinda looked at Duncan. He carried one boy then the other up a short staircase and tucked them on a straw-filled pallet. Then he came back for Susan.

"I think until the preacher comes, Susan will sleep downstairs with me and Genie. Where have you made your bed?" she questioned Duncan. "Is there room in the loft?"

"Hmm?" Duncan turned to face the fire. "There's room in the stable for now, I suppose." He scooped Susan up and deposited her on the bed. He opened a large chest and pulled out two blankets, carrying them out the front door. He paused.

"Don't allow the children to venture to the privy alone. Coyotes come right up close at night. Light the torch," he indicated a pole with rags tied tight around one end, "and keep a lookout in all directions. Next we order supplies I'll add in a pair of chamber pots."

He slipped out without saying goodnight.

Mother and daughters sank into a slumber on a real bed for the first time in weeks.

Settling into the cabin took no time at all. The trunk sat against one wall, most of its contents still inside. Space on top of a bureau held Lucinda's few toiletries—a hairbrush and pins, face cream dearly bought when she accepted Duncan's proposal, and tooth powder. She placed a silver framed photograph of herself and Matthew there, then picked it up again.

"Your wedding picture. You and Pa. It should be where you always keep it, where you can see it every day," Genie said.

"Maybe not anymore. It may make Mr. Fergus uncomfortable." She placed it back in the trunk. She smiled, brightening her face. Before Genie could say anything else the front door flew open and Danny's little voice called out.

"Missis, Lady, come out!"

"What is it, Daniel?"

But the boy shied, hugging against the wall and would not say more. Lucinda's heart flipped and she ran out calling for Nathan. With Genie and Susan safe in the cabin, it had to be Nathan who needed her.

She ran to the chicken coop and then to the privy. No Nathan. She called again. "Nathan! Where are you?"

Duncan emerged from the stable. "What's wrong?" he called back.

"I think it's Nathan. I can't find him!"

Rounding the back of the barn she saw her son huddled between two hay bales. Tears streaked his dirty face.

"Whatever is it?" she said as she knelt beside him. She reached to pull him to her and he winced, holding his arm.

"I'm sorry, Mama. We were just playing. I tripped over a rock and my arm hurts."

Lucinda patted the arm, searching for a wound. Duncan picked Nathan up and sat him on the hay while he too ascertained the injury.

"Do you think it's broken?" she asked, concern rising in her voice.

"It seems so. Ornery boy. Playing instead of working. Weren't you boys supposed to be weeding the garden?"

Nathan's chin trembled. "Yes, sir. I'm sorry."

"Well," the man softened, "let's get you fixed up. I'll make a splint."

Duncan went in search of wood and cloth.

"Duncan, his fingers are cold and he can't wiggle them. I think they're turning blue. I fear he needs more than a splint. Where is the doctor?" Lucinda twisted her weary fingers around her handkerchief. "He needs a doctor."

"It'd mean a ride to the way station and then another few miles south. Doctor makes his rounds every few weeks or so. All we can do is go and hope he's there or leave word for him to ride out here, which isn't likely for a broken arm."

Duncan looked up to see the stricken face of Nathan's mother. "Seeing as it's a child, he might come."

The man took the hand that trembled in his. "It's all right."

Arrangements were made with some difficulty. An adult was needed on the homestead to care for the stock and garden. Genie could not be left alone there to do everything. Danny and Susan were too young to be of help and in fact needed someone to look after them. Lucinda insisted she accompany Nathan. But Duncan would not hear of mother and boy traveling alone.

"There's too much chance of danger in the open desert. Indians still prowl this land at times. A wagon wheel can break as the one you yourself witnessed. No, you won't be going. I'll take Nathan myself. You'll do better to manage here."

"Of course, you're right." She prepared a travel bag and kissed Nathan roundly. She tucked him into blankets in the buckboard and waved as man and boy rolled away.

Lucinda turned back to the cabin. Her breath caught at the sight. With the misty gray of the rain gone she could see clearly the bold blue sky with nary a wisp of cloud above. Mountains rose far and away, blocking the horizon. Kansas grass went on forever in a golden waving sea; never had she seen such mountains as this. It seemed that it would take months to reach them yet they loomed so close she felt she heard them breathing.

Slabs of vertical rock gave way to dark green trees, pines she supposed, the pine that made the walls of the cabin. Near the top there were no trees, or if there were, they were covered in snow. Summer snow.

Chores, as numerous as they were, did not interfere with Lucinda's worry over Nathan. All day she tended the garden, such as it was, meager and parched. Danny won her heart with his sweet ways, carrying water, digging weeds, and feeding the chickens. He didn't have much to say to her but she listened as he jabbered to the hens. Snatches of his conversations revealed a tender heart, and a strongly stated sense of right versus wrong. "You have to share," he admonished the fowl when they pecked at each other. "I will do it right, like Pa says," she heard him say under his breath, even though his pa was miles away tending a brother he had just met.

Lucinda prayed thanks for the help of her Eugenia, a dutiful child if there ever was one. When Matthew died, the mother and daughter found solace and strength in each other. Genie's contribution to the family's recovery seemed to give her a single eye of determination remarkable in an eleven year old. A little older and she might have been mistaken for the woman of the house. Lucinda was relieved to see her occasionally playing with Susan and Daniel like a child of her age should.

For her part, Susan was definitely a child of two years. Her normally sweet disposition could melt away in a flash when she was vexed. Her toddling around the cabin caused Lucinda to move some items higher on the shelves and place one of the dining benches on its side as a barrier in front of the fire. Outside was not as dangerous to tiny hands, but someone had to be on constant watch. Daniel could be observed guiding her interests to simple games and away from pitchforks and scythes. The less than three years difference in their ages seemed immense.

Night came with exhaustion but without sleep. The soft breathing of her girls beside her failed to give comfort. Lucinda's mind wandered from Nathan to all that had transpired on the long journey. The loss of their trunk took most of their clothes, the beloved quilt her mother had given as a wedding present when she married Matthew, and the dress she had made to wear for her wedding to Duncan Fergus.

Worst of all, Genie and Susan had lost the mementos of their father. Each child had packed a special item of remembrance. Genie had kept a tourmaline brooch given for her tenth birthday, passed through Matthew from his own mother. For Susan, Lucinda had chosen a small purse made of fox pelt trapped and tanned by Matthew.

Thanks be, the wooden figure Matthew whittled for Nathan

when the boy was just a mite was in her satchel when the wagon slid. She noticed the toy sitting in the corner and sat bolt upright in bed. Nathan would surely be missing *Whit*, as he called the figure. "Want *whit* man," he'd said, holding out chubby baby fingers, trying to say *whittled*.

As she lay in the dark, her concern was immediately turned by spine chilling howling. She hated the sound of coyotes that she knew well enough from the trail from Kansas. This was worse. Louder. More menacing than coyotes. She knew this had to be wolves.

Why her feet moved so slowly she didn't understand. She tried to move faster but felt stiff. Making her way to the embers banked in the fireplace, she stirred, releasing flames that lit the room. Shadows that usually danced lively now hovered with malice, flickering over surroundings that felt unfamiliar. She crept into the bedroom and tucked the blanket snug over the girls. Then she thought to climb the stairs to check on Daniel.

How the children could sleep through the wailing and barking she could not guess. She checked the latch of the door, then peered through a glass window that only reflected her face back to her. She determined that she'd hang curtains as soon as she could buy some cloth.

The din of the wolves carried on for nigh to an hour. At some point it seemed to become melodious, like bells singing.

Light streaming dawn through the windows woke her. Walking to the privy, she scolded herself for giving up sleep to the wolves. The day was to be filled with more chores so she'd have to carry on in spite of tiredness.

The children stumbled about, out of sorts, but she put them to tasks anyway. By the end of the day, she knew the whole homestead as if it had always been hers, though her heart was not so soon attached to it.

Dusk brought the return of Duncan with Nathan beside. Thick plaster-hardened strips of cloth covered her son's forearm, supported by a splint.

"It's to stay on for three weeks. It's not broke in two, just cracked," the boy announced, showing his sisters how it snugged into a sling tied around his shoulder.

Duncan added, "We had to wait for the doctor to come in from his rounds. He said he may make his way here before then to ease your mind, Cindy."

"My friends back home—my friends back east called me Lucy," she corrected him.

After supper, with the young ones asleep, Lucinda told Duncan about the wolves and how she been frightened but then the fear melted and she'd slept to their singing.

"Don't get romantic about wolves. Right now they are content, but when winter comes they grow hungry and bold."

Routine settled in. Routine also revealed what was lacking in living in the cabin. Lucinda's list of goods to buy became long. She needed the curtain cloth, and also cloth enough to replace the clothes they had lost. And more for winter preparation. Even if that was still a ways off it required getting started. Buttons, hooks, thread, and pins—all she had were at the bottom of a cliff. At least one more kettle, maybe two, was needed for proper meal preparation, as well as a stone slab for baking biscuits and bread. A dozen towels. Scissors! An iron. Duncan had but a rudimentary understanding of running a proper home.

She read over the list. *It's a start,* she thought. *All this and more.*

Soap. Tooth powder. The anticipated chamber pots. All manner of pantry items. At some point the children, and herself too, would need shoes even if they did come dear. And books for the children's education! Pencils and paper, or at least chalk and slates.

Lucinda was used to doing for a full family but Duncan was not. It had been just him and Daniel for three years. He never spoke of his wife or her death, and from what the cabin revealed it seemed she had been content with very few comforts. Danny was too young to remember and could say nothing of his mother. In the pages of a Bible in the bedroom, Lucinda found a photograph, dry and cracked, taken on what she supposed was their wedding day. A young girl, with a pretty mouth much like Danny's, stood beside Duncan who was clean-shaven, without the massive beard he now wore.

Feeling furtive as a spy, Lucinda had tucked the photograph back inside the pages.

"The preacher will come to Dog Trot this Sunday. Your young man should be fine as frog's hair to stand up with you." Doc Pritchard smiled as he patted Lucinda's hand. Nathan indeed was healing well, so much so that he barely gave notice of the heavy cast. He did his chores as Duncan expected.

And yet, this news fell on Lucinda like a hailstorm, icy cold pellets scattering gooseflesh up and down her arms in the heat of desert dust. She felt again that sensation of falling, her stomach dropping over a cliff in a windy rain. She gripped the back of the chair Nathan sat on.

She swallowed hard to recover her voice. "I trust we'll see Mrs. Pritchard at the Sunday meeting? It will be so nice to see a woman friend." Her gaze went to the window. "I hope the weather holds," she said absently as she would have back in Kansas.

"Weather's not likely to change by then. Seldom alters course, you know." He packed his doctoring kit into his black bag. "Is there anything you need before the wedding?" he asked with a kindly smile.

"Thank you, no. After a long marriage and three babies, I feel well prepared. Doctor, what is your charge for looking after Nathan?"

"Mr. Fergus is taking care of that. You need not concern yourself. Good day, Lucinda. Nathan, you behave now." The springs of his surrey squeaked under his weight. "Git up," he said to his horse and rolled away.

Hay bales and benches arranged at the front of the way station welcomed the faithful. The groom, counted along with the doctor and the proprietor, numbered thirteen men, some coming more to see what Fergus's mail had delivered than to worship. Four women, including the bride, Mrs. Pritchard, the station keeper's wife, and a hired woman, made up the congregation.

Breaking tradition to marry on the Sabbath seemed oddly appropriate. This wedding did nothing to take into account Lucinda's sense of propriety. Pledging her troth to a man she barely knew, in a place she knew not at all, with her children mere onlookers—it all gave the illusion of an ethereal sight like heat waves rising from hot sand. Visible, but of no substance.

With dancing and merriment unsuitable for the solemnness that fell after a sermon, there was none. No music at all save a hymn in three-part harmony. Due to hot wind blowing over the grounds, folks packed up as soon as the afternoon meal was eaten. Handshakes among the men and gentle pats of reassurance from ladies to the bride were the only signs that a ceremony had taken place.

Lucinda congratulated herself on the practical decision she had made to fashion her wedding dress to be easily altered for everyday wear. The dress that lay at the bottom of that accursed cliff would have been frivolous for the circumstance.

That night Genie and Susie were put to bed in the loft with the boys.

Lucinda could not find sleep, not even that tired slumber of spent exhaustion that newlyweds fall into together.

She was a wife again, not in name only but in body too, and soon, she prayed, in soul as well.

Except for the necessity of having Duncan in her bed, Lucinda's days and nights were much as before.

Duncan stooped at the burning barrel, working the bellows through a hole in the side bottom. The fire would have to burn much hotter to bend the iron needed to forge new hinges. Lucinda insisted that the old ones were not strong enough to stave off marauding wolves. Dread of howling had crept over her spirit, putting her out of sorts. Gone was the notion of wolves singing or sounding like ringing bells.

"When can work begin on a bedroom for the girls?" she broached the subject again. "They don't fit in the loft. You did promise me a proper house before I came and it's what I expected, not a two-room cabin. I'll need a summer kitchen come next year. A keeping room too. You promised me a proper house and I shall have it! With a porch!" She produced his letter as proof.

He took it, ran his eyes over the writing, and dropped it in the barrel.

"That's all I have to say on the matter, Cindy." He grinned, using the name as if telling a joke.

Lucinda turned and marched behind the cabin.

When he'd explained as how it would take months to make enough bricks to fashion a house, Lucinda took to making some bricks every day.

It's a start.

It fell to the boys to keep Duncan supplied with fuel for the burning barrel. Splintered wood and buffalo chips were about all they could find. They had spent the morning stacking both. Then they made themselves scarce.

Lucinda heard Duncan hollering for them.

"Boys, you're lazing off again. You just can't stick to a task, can you? Not to save your lives. Hand it over, I said!"

She wondered for a moment if she should see to what was going on but then bent to her own tasks. Soon, she called for the boys to join her in making bricks.

That night Lucinda thought of a different approach to make her point. "Won't it be nice to have a place for ourselves? Instead of building a room for the girls, we could leave them in this one and build another for us, removed beyond the wall of the new keeping room. Then I wouldn't hear the children and always be running to see what they need."

He rolled over while she got up to check in the loft.

"You all settle down now. You're keeping Susan awake. Nathan, why aren't you asleep?"

"It's all right, ma'am," Danny whispered. "He only misses that Whit toy."

"Well, get him then."

Neither child reached for the shelf where Whit sat in the dark.

Susan sat up. "Whit gone."

"Lay down, Susie. Nathan, get Whit and go to sleep."

Susan patted her mother's face. "Mama, Whit gone."

This time Nathan shushed his sister. "Susan, be quiet. Go to sleep." His voice gave away that he'd been crying.

"Hot. Whit in fire." Susan explained best as she could.

"Fire? What fire? Nathan?" But her son had turned his back.

It was Daniel who spoke quietly. "Pa put Whit in the burning barrel. We wasn't doing our chores. Like he burned up my books

269

a long time ago."

Lucinda hiked up her nightgown and scooted into the loft. Disguising her fury she snuggled the children and gave each a kiss. "You all go to sleep now. It'll be right as rain in the morning."

In the morning when she uncurled herself from the pile of children to climb down from the loft, Duncan was already outside. He was talking to a stranger. A stranger meant one thing. No, two. She would have to make an extra seat at the breakfast table, and she would have to wait to talk to Duncan about what he'd done.

George Harewood introduced himself as a prospector.

"Off to see if they is really gold in Californ'a. Cain't take nobody's word. Gotta go fer myse'f. If it please you, ma'am, I'll take a extry biscuit and ham for the journey."

"Cindy, I'm of a mind to set out with Harewood. A couple gold nuggets and you'll have your house."

Lucinda couldn't believe her ears. Her husband made plans to meet up in two days with this crazy coot of a man, leaving her to fend off wolves and rear children alone in a tiny cabin in the desert.

When she confronted her husband about Whit, and asked about Daniel's books, he only shrugged. "Danny was a bedwetter, never grew out of it until I put a stop to it. You can't coddle youngsters. Too much time in play makes them grow up weak and make nothing of their lives."

"But Duncan, would you really leave the family to go off looking for rumors of gold? You said yourself that children need a pa. You agreed to be my husband and offer a home. What of your word?"

"Cindy, I'm surprised at you. You're a smart woman, not some innocent little gal. You know men well enough to advertise

270

for one. You wrote what you wanted, I responded in kind. Both of us knew well that courtship is a game of *what if* not *what is*. A man promises what he has to to gain a bride. Women know there's nothing to it. You knew full well that the truth of things is not cut and dried. A man does not spend his own larder on some other man's offspring. You tend to the children and provide what you insist is needed. You can't pretend you believed it to be any other way."

He took most of their savings and set off.

She was relieved to see him go.

Without leaves to change color, autumn came without notice. Sunny, dry, and hot, it was the same as summer except the nights grew colder. Her bricks took twice as long to dry thoroughly so she made them longer and more flattened. She spent days canning and preserving what little the garden yielded. Nathan laid snares and she dried all sorts of meats—prairie dog, gopher, jackrabbits—not knowing how they would go down. A drought in Kansas had led to eating frogs when she was a child, but she had not heard of eating gopher. Precisely because she didn't know, she bent her will to find out.

Snakes were another thing altogether. Impossible to trap, they made her squeamish. Yet they tasted good, so she screwed up her face and did what she had to do. One good cut behind the head and the skin peeled right off. She buried the heads so they could never strike. The skins she let dry so they might be used for belts and other things in place of leather.

Discussing this with the way station proprietor one Sunday, she was pleased to find that good money could be had from drying snake skin. Her squeamishness subsided and she went on forays to find the scaly things. She located their dens in the daytime by following the odd tracks in the dust. At dusk, before the wolves set to, she reached into snake holes with a log crook she made, and dragged them out while they were sluggish.

The spring house kept her garden efforts cool and out of the sun. The water rose as the ground cooled, easing evaporation over nights that became longer and darker. Nights more often filled with wolf howling.

Early one morning, Lucinda woke to the sound of a horse calling to the one in her barn. She hurried to dress, sure that Duncan had returned at last. If he had found gold they would be able to outfit for winter.

When she looked through the glass she saw a man and horse and a pack mule. There was something familiar in the man's voice answering the horse, but it was not Duncan.

"Mister Breck! How nice to see you. Are you bringing a wagon train through this way?"

"Well, hello there, Missis Keane. No, no wagons. I've changed course. I'm off to find my fortune, I hope. So you did settle here?"

"Not Keane. It's Missis Fergus now." She swept her arm indicating the homestead. "Yes, this is my home. Let me show you the improvements. There isn't much yet, but it's a start."

She led Josh Breck around the property.

"I've learned a lot of things here. This is my brickyard. I plan on adding to the house. Four children need more space. And over here is the garden. There are still vegetables growing, can you believe it? Harvest in Kansas is over by now."

"Four children?" Breck asked. "You've had another?"

"Oh, no," Lucinda laughed. "I have Daniel, the son of Mister Fergus. He's five years old. Come inside for breakfast. I know the children will be happy to see you again."

The smell of biscuits and coffee brought the children into the kitchen. Nathan greeted their visitor with a handshake. Eugenia smiled shyly and offered him agave jelly that she had made herself. Little Susan padded directly to him and held up her arms so he could place her on his lap. She swiped her finger across his plate, sharing his jelly without invitation, which brought laughter to the table. Even Danny's attention focused on Josh Breck as stories were told of wagon trains and adventures.

After the meal, the children ran to the barn for morning chores. Lucinda poured more coffee and the two sat for conversation. Mister Breck inquired of Nevada and Lucinda asked for news of Kansas.

"And when will Mister Fergus be home?" he asked. "Are you all right on your own?"

Lucinda looked at her hands. "Surely he'll be back before winter proper. Life is different here, not at all like Kansas. They say it doesn't snow this far from the mountains. But I've been told other things about life in Nevada that have proven untrue."

She brightened her face and got up to gather the dishes. "And you, Mister Breck, where are you off to?"

"I'm chasing rumors. There's a chance Nevada has silver, that's what I heard from the Paiute. I'm on my way to find out. You feel that the Territory has been misspoken of, so now I have doubts. The Indians have helped me before and I hope they have no call to lead me astray."

"No! The Paiute? Duncan will not deal with them. Yet you have a common outlook with my husband. It's California gold he's gone to find."

Breck made for his pack and returned with a bundle, which he laid on her kitchen table.

"Missis Keane, that is, Fergus," he began.

"Please do call me Lucy. It's been so long since a friend spoke my name."

"Lucy, I confess I hoped that you could still be found near Dog Trot. Here are some things I owe you."

She unwrapped the bundle to reveal a trove of her belongings, things that had been in the trunk that careened over that cliff during the move here.

"Whatever did you do? How did you . . . ?"

"It weighed heavy on me that I was driving your wagon that day in the rain. When I came back through, I set my mind on retrieving what I could. It was with the help of the Paiute that I found the place. Apologies won't bring back everything, but I hope this helps some."

"Thank you! Oh, thank you, Mister Breck. Just look. Here's Eugenia's brooch! How wonderful. You must present it to her." She skipped to the door and called, "Genie! Come here. Come see!"

Among the treasures were two pieces of her mother's silver tea service. Immediately she made up her mind.

"Silver for silver. Mister Breck, please take these. No, not for coffee on the trail," she laughed at his wonderment. "Please sell them. Then add this," and she produced a golden ring from a chain around her neck. "It is my wedding ring from my Mister Keane, solid gold. The amount won't be a fortune but I wish it to be a stake in partnership in your quest. If you do find silver or gold, then you will bring me a percentage of any profit, yes?"

And so Joshua Breck rode off west to the snowy mountains, taking a piece of Lucy Fergus's hopes with him.

Week after week, Lucinda watched as the snow cap on the mountain spread farther down. Days stayed hot and she fed the garden with the rising spring waters. She also began stacking brick walls to make the extra rooms she laid out. Nights meant cuddling with the children by the fire, reading and making popcorn.

And trying to sleep through the din of howling wolves.

Foxes and coyotes found ways to rebuke her efforts to keep

the chickens safe. To save some she resorted to bringing them inside. How uncivilized would desert living make her? The thought of raising barbarians for children so plagued her she made sure they did school lessons each and every day, including Sunday. The two times the preacher came to Dog Trot she dutifully hitched the horse Duncan had left her and piled the family onto the buckboard for the haul to the way station, making haste to return before dusk.

She began to worry over the tab of credit granted for foodstuffs and dry goods, and prayed that Duncan would bring enough gold to pay it off.

Finally, she received a note. It had not been posted but hand delivered by a passing stranger to the proprietor of the way station.

Dere Cindy,
Returning soon. To busted to continue. Harewood not of best caractere.

Your husband Fergus

So, no gold, then. Yet she offered grateful thanks that she would not face the challenge of winter alone, while imploring the Lord for means to pay the debts.

Duncan arrived to a half-built room attached to the cabin, the walls stacked as high as Lucinda could reach. An opening for a window and another for a doorway gaped on one side. The far wall left a gap for a chimney.

The spring house held jars and sacks of food. The chickens had been returned to the coop.

Lucinda greeted her husband with a smile. His beard showed a streak of gray and his frame felt thinner than she had remembered.

"Come children, greet your father," she instructed when the

youngsters stood in a line outside the cabin door.

"Hello, Pa, welcome home," each said in turn, except Susan, who hid behind Genie's skirt.

Duncan was undeterred. "Well don't just stand there. Come see what your pa has brought from the mountains. Danny, have you been behaving for your ma?" Duncan pulled a poke from his saddlebag, holding it just out of reach from Danny until the boy said, "Yes, Pa."

Spilling the contents on the ground revealed claws and long curved teeth.

"A grizzly bear tried to jump my claim," Duncan teased, "but I made sure he'd not try a second time."

The boys seemed satisfied with the gift and the story. For each girl he produced a piece of glittering quartz.

"Now feed me, wife, I'm about as hungry as that griz was."

Inside the cabin he slipped a small packet from his vest. "Cindy, this is for the household." He poured out small gold nuggets.

"Duncan, I thought the journey was unsuccessful. Your letter . . ."

"No, the letter was a decoy. There was a feller following me and Harewood. I knew he'd try to rob us, so I fooled him. Made myself seem friendly and asked him to take a post for me and mail it ahead. Made it seem that Harewood and me fell out and that I was coming home busted. That put him off our trail. You didn't believe it, did you?"

Lucinda nodded.

"I thought I made it clear enough by all the spelling mistakes. You know I can read and write better than that. My girl, but you are gullible."

That night, with the girls again up in the loft, her husband required marital affection that she would not deny. After he fell heavily asleep, Lucinda lay awake, pondering the life she now lived.

"What is all this?" Duncan's voice boomed as he read the ledger. Lucinda's heart pounded into her ears so that she could barely hear what anyone within a mile certainly could.

She attempted a reply. "Don't you like seeing curtains on the windows? Buttons and needles aren't an extravagance."

"Hairpins! How many hairpins can one woman use?"

He ran his finger down the page. "Books! Tablets and slates. Explain these."

"The children must be educated. The supplies are for their schoolwork."

"We have a Bible. Teach them from that."

"Of course I teach them from it. Ask them to recite chapter and verse. But maps of the Holy Lands won't teach them where they live nor who is the President of their own country. Does a man prefer ignorant children?"

"These are your bills to pay, Lucinda."

Her voice failed her.

"A roof and home, I'll make sure of those provisions. I'll even finish the room at the back for our privacy. But the window will be oilcloth, no more glass. You find a way to pay for those books or they'll be kindling for your new fireplace."

It never did snow that winter, proving that some rumors are fact. Rumors of gold had put food on the table and fire in the hearth. Rumor that Doctor Pritchard had developed gout brought a nice Christmas ham to the Fergus's. A patient had given it to pay his bill and the doctor, in turn, unable to eat rich meat, sold it to Lucinda. Wolves got into the coops at the way station, giving Lucinda the chance to trade chickens and eggs to pay for some of the debts Duncan refused.

She did prevail on him to let her order one gift apiece for the children. Practicality versus frivolity vexed her heart, but compromise won out and they received a set of encyclopedias to share.

From her husband she received an oil lamp for the new bedroom.

Of all the gifts, she remained the most grateful for the old chamber pots, which meant none of her family would have to venture into the deep wild night.

At the first sign that snow on the mountains began to recede, Duncan announced his departure. He was to meet Harewood back at their claim. Rumors of gold had dissipated, or at least not reached Dog Trot, but his hopes stayed strong. He admonished Lucinda to not make mention of any strikes or of his whereabouts.

As he rode away this time she could not lay finger on her feelings. Life was hard without his help on the homestead, yet her spirits felt lighter when he was not there.

She had the comfort of her own bedroom, all snug now under roof, but she found herself often sleeping with the girls. That was where she was when she woke to the sound of horses in the yard.

Mr. Breck!

The children ran to greet him before she could put on a dress and join them.

"Missis Fergus. You are looking well."

"Lucy. You agreed to call me Lucy." She smiled. "Genie, please set a place for Mister Breck and ladle up some rabbit gravy. Boys, you may come inside and listen to tales of Mister Breck's travels if you refrain from peppering him with endless questions."

The children whooped into the house.

Lucinda paused for a moment to ask the question she preferred the children not overhear. "Now, Joshua. What news do you have for me?"

"I'm pleased to report that at least one rumor concerning Nevada can be proved true. We have silver, Lucy. I don't know how rich the vein is yet. But it's enough."

Genie called from the doorway. "Food's getting cold! Come on in."

The boys tried with great difficulty to meet their mother's instruction but their mouths ran as fast as could be. Susan took her place on Josh's lap. At length Lucinda sent them back to their chores, inviting her partner to join her at the spring house.

"I went to buy back your tea cups but they'd been melted down. I'm sorry."

"How can you be sorry for bringing me the answer to my prayers?"

"How do you want your share? In silver or money? There's no bank in the Territory but I could have it sent back east."

The two spoke at length and dusk settled in. They didn't notice until the wolves started.

"You'll not be turned out into the night from my home. I have a proper room for company and you shall have it."

"I will agree to stay in the barn, but not because of wolves. I've spent many nights surrounded by that singing. I'll stay to say a proper goodbye in the morning. To the children, I mean."

"Nonsense and piffle. You'll stay in the house like a decent guest. As you can tell, I have no nosy neighbors to be concerned with."

Over the weeks that followed, Lucinda thought how she would tell Duncan of her strike. There had been no post from him since he left. Her silver kept the family provided for. Then one afternoon another visitor walked onto the homestead.

George Harewood appeared ill at ease, turning his hat in his hands. He stumbled over his own words. "Fergus has went the way of the dearly departed, ma'am. I jist figgered it was on to me to bring you the news. Didn't seem right to put it in a post. A accident, it was. We never did find us more gold. I been totin' this to bring to his boy, a sort of remembrance."

His calloused hand opened to give her a locket. Inside was a photograph of the same young woman she'd seen in another photo, the young woman who had Daniel's smile.

"Well . . ." The prospector wiped his mouth on his sleeve.

Lucinda recognized the hint. "Please let me pack you a meal for your journey. In thanks for this kindness."

Lucinda sat in her rocker while the children did their lessons at the table.

"Nathan, bring me the encyclopedia with the map of Oregon Territory."

The more she read, the higher her spirits grew. Trees. More trees than Kansas and Nevada put together. All the way to the Pacific Ocean. Lumber for a proper house. Dark and fertile land. Game, and streams teeming with fish.

This time she'd outfit and drive her own wagon. It'd be a start.

Marcia Gaye writes frontier fiction and other stories, as well as nonfiction, poetry, and song lyrics. Her western-themed stories have appeared in various publications including *Cactus Country III*, and in the *Contention and Other Frontier Stories* anthology from Five Star Publishing.

★ ★ ★ ★ ★

In the Breaks
by John D. Nesbitt

★ ★ ★ ★ ★

On the first morning in camp, Grandpa had me hold the halter ropes while he saddled the horses. When he pulled the cinch on the first horse, a sorrel named Baldy with a wide, white blaze, the animal reared up and pawed the air, pulling the rope through my hand.

"That cinch is cold," said Grandpa. "The sweat from yesterday froze before it could dry out. He'll be all right, though. We'll let him settle down."

Grandpa went on to saddle the second horse, a larger sorrel with a small patch on his nose, named Snip. The horse did not react to either the front cinch or the rear cinch being tightened.

I continued to hold the horses as Grandpa brought the rifles and scabbards out of the tent and strapped one scabbard onto the saddle of each horse. I watched the whole time, trying to remember all the details. I didn't mind being treated like the sixteen-year-old-girl that I was, standing back and letting the grown-up man do the work that took skill, but it was understood that I was learning in order to do these things myself.

Grandpa told me to mount up first, but Baldy kept running out from under me each time I put my foot in the stirrup. I brought him back to the starting point each time and tried again.

"Look here, Katie," said Grandpa. "Lay your reins on the far side of the saddle horn, and pull your left rein so that his head is a quarter-turn in. He won't run on you because he can't fol-

283

low his head. Now keep hold of both reins as you grab the saddle horn and pull yourself up. Don't grab the back of the saddle. Both hands on the pommel."

I did as I was told, and the next thing I knew, I was sitting in the saddle, and Baldy was standing still.

Grandpa led his horse out a few steps, halted, and got set. He pulled himself up, swung his leg over, and settled in.

The heavyset sorrel began bucking, first in a gentle rocking-horse motion, but when he did not unseat the man on his back, he started bucking higher on both ends. Grandpa hung on as long as he could, but the horse pitched him forward off the right side. Grandpa landed hard on his feet as Snip ran away, bucking and kicking.

"Are you all right?" I asked.

"I think I broke something. I landed crooked on my right foot."

My stomach tightened. "Can you walk?"

"I can move. But I think I broke my ankle." He walked in a circle, half-bent and hobbling, as if he was testing his foot.

"Then I had better go fetch that horse. Do you think I can walk up to him?"

"I think so. He's just standing there. I think he's got it all bucked out of him for the time being. That's just the way it is with some horses on a cold morning."

I slid off of Baldy and handed the reins to Grandpa. With uncertain steps, I walked toward the runaway Snip.

Grandpa was right. The husky sorrel was breathing hard, but he did not have any renegade in him as I laid hold of the rope and led him back to camp.

"What does this do to our hunting?" I asked.

"We still hunt. We don't quit now." He cast a glance at Snip. "I think I can pull myself up into the saddle, and I can ride with you to show you where I had it in mind for us to go. But I don't think I can hunt on foot—least of all in any place that's rough going with downed timber."

I let the realization settle in. "So I'll have to hunt alone? Shoot a deer all by myself?"

"Like I've told you, it's like hunting a rabbit, only bigger."

I felt as if a heavy weight of responsibility was being settled on me all at once. I had left the orphanage in Pennsylvania and had come to live with Grandpa on the ranch just a little more than six months earlier, and I had learned a great many things— how to work around cattle, how to saddle a horse, how to shoot a rifle, and how to clean a rabbit. Now it looked as if I was going to have to take a big step by myself.

Grandpa put all his weight on his left leg, gave a couple of hops, and steadied himself with his right foot. He said, "Don't worry, Katie. We won't starve to death if we don't get a deer, but it'll be nice if we do."

"I know."

"So we'd better get to work, or the morning'll slip away from us. At least Snip here didn't spill the rifle out of the scabbard."

Grandpa was pulling on the front end of the horse to settle him into position when the footfalls of another horse made us turn.

My spirits sank when I recognized Jeff Hayden riding a dull, dark, blocky horse. Jeff had a knack for showing up wherever I was, whether it was on the range, around the ranch yard, or in town. I did not think that his riding up to our camp was a pure coincidence.

He called out in the gray light of morning. "How-de-do, Mr. Cooper. Miss Moran."

Most things about Jeff Hayden galled me, including his constant show of politeness.

"Mornin'," said Grandpa.

I nodded, and Jeff gave me a closed-mouth smile.

"Need any help?" he asked.

Grandpa said, "I don't think so. This boy threw me off, but I need to get back on him, by myself, so he knows I'm still the boss."

"Goin' deer huntin' in the breaks, huh?"

"That's our plan."

"You should do all right. These here blacktail aren't that hard to hunt. Back home, all we've got is whitetail. They'll make you work for it."

I had heard enough of him from before, about coon hunting in Kentucky, and I hoped deep down that I would not have to have anything to do with him in the deer hunt.

"Looks like you're favorin' your foot," he said. "You sure you don't need some help?" Jeff stopped his horse, swung down from the saddle, and strode our way.

As he drew closer, I noted his red hair, blue eyes, pale face, and upturned nose. He did not complicate things by being handsome. I found myself drawing my arms in tight against my sides.

Grandpa did not look straight at him. "We'll be all right on our own. Thanks all the same."

Jeff stopped. "Sure. Just thought I'd offer. I've got the day off, and I thought I might do some huntin' myself. But I can get a deer any time, so if you change your mind, just let me know."

He turned and walked away, leading the dull-colored horse. Ten yards out, he stopped, grabbed the saddle horn with both hands, and swung up into the saddle, stabbing his foot in the stirrup after he left the ground, and swooping with his right leg as he brought it around snug. With a light air he straightened up, tipped his head back, and rode away.

Grandpa went back to pushing his horse into place. I knew Grandpa was stubborn and independent, so I let him strain and pull himself up into the saddle. Snip did not give him any trouble. As Grandpa adjusted his reins, he said, "Go ahead and git mounted."

I had a nervous fluttering in my stomach, but I remembered to hold the left rein snug, and I made it up into the saddle without any incident.

Grandpa let out a long breath. "Well, we got that much done. Let's go see if we can find a deer."

We rode up the slope from our camp, which we had set on a level, grassy area at the edge of the timber on the south side of the Osteen Breaks. The pine and cedar trees grew in some rough, steep places on both sides of the breaks, and trees gave good cover for deer as well as for coyotes, bobcats, porcupines, and an occasional mountain lion. I took Grandpa's word for the mountain lions, but I had seen all the other animals myself. Now I was keeping an eye out for deer.

We followed a trail that I would have thought, when I first came out from the East, was a game trail, but from hoofprints and cow pies I learned that cattle could walk on very narrow and steep paths. This trail angled up the hillside, cut back, and came out on top where it passed between two large rocks. We stopped there.

The breaks consisted of a long pine ridge with countless side canyons and crevices. Up on top, at this place where the trail crossed over, the land spread out, not quite level but not a razorback. This was the spot where Grandpa had decided we would start our hunt.

He took a seat on a large fallen log and held the horses while I made my way into the timber. As Grandpa had explained, the winds blew stronger across the top of the breaks, so I found a great deal of deadfall to crawl over and sometimes under. As the sun began to climb in the morning sky, it sent shafts of light into the standing trees. The hanging pine needles glistened a shiny green, as did the long grass in some of the small, open areas I came to.

From time to time I stopped to let the silence gather as the woods filled in around me. I heard a crow cawing as it flew overhead, and I heard squirrels chattering. I rehearsed what I would do if I saw a deer. I would move to a nearby tree, get a steady rest, and take aim. If the deer had antlers, I would shoot. If it did not, I would decide.

I hunted for more than an hour, moving farther and farther from the place where Grandpa had stayed with the horses. I was not cold at all, though the day had started out frosty. I felt loose and relaxed in my red-and-black-checked hunting jacket. It held in the warmth but did not make me perspire. I liked it for its soft flannel lining, its big pockets, and the pouch in back. It made very little noise when a twig or branch brushed against it.

I stopped near a thick pine tree so that I would not be out in the open. I was hungry already, and I told myself to wait. I reviewed what I had in the pockets of my jacket—two biscuits, a small cloth sack of dried apples, a jackknife with a sharp blade, a folding case of rifle shells, a whistle, matches, a supply of folded newspaper, and a couple of yards of thick string. The whistle was to help someone find me if I got lost. The matches would help me start a fire if I got stranded at night. The newspaper had more than one use. The string would serve to lace up the deer's belly after I took out the innards. That way, I could keep the heart and liver inside and the dirt and leaves and pine needles out. Grandpa had drilled this detail into my head, but it still existed on the hypothetical level for me. The biscuits and dried apples were as real as could be, but I could not let myself eat them when the sun had just climbed to eight o'clock.

Anyway, I guessed it was eight. Grandpa made me leave my dollar watch in the tent. He said a deer could hear it tick, and I should be able to estimate the time anyway. He also told me stories about how easy it was to lose track of time as well as direction when a person was tracking an animal he had shot.

I had plenty of things to think about as I walked and paused, walked and paused, along the ridge of the Osteen Breaks. My thoughts also went back to Grandpa, who I imagined was still waiting with the horses. A year earlier, I would never have thought I would be out here under the wide Wyoming skies, wearing a red-and-black hunting jacket, and carrying a Winchester rifle that went snickety-snick like magic. I had been just one more orphan girl, looked over as a potential chore girl, farm worker, or housekeeper until one day I was told that my grandfather Cooper had traced my whereabouts and was coming to see me.

I could not remember ever being called a pretty girl, or having a pretty dress. The nicest thing I remembered hearing was "She'll be a late bloomer." I felt I was very common, maybe even homely, for people looked me over and then looked over me to the next one. So I must have been a good prospect to go out and be an old man's helper on a homestead of sagebrush, dry grass, and dust.

Still, it was home now, and I could not remember ever having had a home. I was getting used to this way of life, so when Grandpa gave me the old hunting jacket and said, "It's yours now," it all seemed natural.

A tramping sound brought me back to the moment where I was, standing in the pine trees with sunlight slanting in. I heard a few steps, then silence. I could not place where the sound came from. I heard the tramping again, to my right. With the sun at my forehead, I frowned and peered. I saw a patch of color that did not belong to the tree trunks, pine needles, and deadfall—a shadowy dull brown with a tinge of blue. One shape stood in front of another, which in turn stood in front of another. A small file of deer was moving through the timber and had stopped.

I held as still as I could. I needed to wait until the animals gave me a better view, but I needed to be ready if I saw something I wanted to shoot at.

The first deer was a doe. I made out her large, shadowy ears, and I marveled at how motionless these animals could hold themselves. She took one slow step forward. I saw her shoulder muscles ripple. She took another step. The animal behind her was a doe, also. Now the three deer moved together, in a series of hops, which made the tramping sound. They all had large mule ears, but as the third deer disappeared behind a pair of reddish-brown tree trunks, the sunlight glinted on a set of antlers.

My heartbeat jumped. It was like Grandpa said. The buck doesn't lead the parade. He often lets the does go first, maybe even pushes them, and he hangs back to see if it's safe.

I took deliberate breaths to try to keep myself still, but my hands were trembling. I brought my rifle up and steadied myself against the trunk of the tree I stood behind. I eased a shell into the chamber and kept my finger off the trigger. I waited for the animals to appear on the left side of the trees they had gone behind.

A minute later, I saw a dark shape, a doe. It was not where I expected it. It had already moved along the shadowy trail, and I had not seen it. Now that I had them relocated, I lined up my sights and held steady as I waited for the other two to show. The second doe appeared, and I relaxed. I did not want to stay all tensed up. Then the buck poked his head forward. I saw his dark nose and the front part of his antlers, less than a hundred yards away. He took another step, and another. I saw the muscles flex on his front quarters, and I settled the bead into the notch.

I pulled the trigger, and the world seemed to fall apart as the explosion crashed and echoed. The buck lurched forward, first up, then with his head lowered as he plunged into the timber. The two does bounded away, crunching twigs and branches, until all went silent.

My heart was pounding, and my mouth was dry. I couldn't believe I missed him, but I had the greatest fear that he had gotten away.

I hurried toward the spot where he had stood. I was heedless of noise now, as I stepped on branches on the ground and snapped twigs off the logs I crawled over. First, I found a spatter of blood on dry pine needles and dirt, then marks where his hooves had torn up the path as he bolted away. I followed the trail for about fifty yards until I found him lying on his side, still and dead.

I counted three tines on each side of his antlers. His sleek, muscled body had a coat of brownish gray, and bright red blood trickled from a small hole where the bullet had gone in. The realization was settling in that I had just killed a deer. All of my hunting had come to a stop.

Now I had to think of what to do next. I didn't have to worry about following a wounded deer and getting lost, but even at that, I felt alone in a big world all around me. I got hold of myself and reasoned out where I was.

I was in the middle of the woods on the ridge of the Osteen Breaks with a deer I had shot. My grandfather was a long ways in back of me, but I could find him, and he could tell me what to do. I began to walk away, then stopped, turned, and came back. I thought hard. I needed to leave some kind of a signal so I would know how to find my deer again.

Rummaging in my shirt and trouser pockets, I found a white handkerchief that I carried but hardly ever used. I shook it out and tied it to a low-hanging pine branch. Then I set off through the timber, heading toward my grandfather and the horses.

Every once in a while, I turned back to catch sight of the handkerchief.

Grandpa came up with a plan to take the horses along the lower edge of the timber and keep pace with me as I retraced my way to the deer. Once the handkerchief came in sight, I forged ahead with more confidence, and when I arrived at the deer, I called out to Grandpa. He called back. I took off my jacket, laid it on a log, and went to work at dressing the deer as Grandpa had told me.

First, I used my string to tie a leg up to a nearby sapling so that the midsection would be clear to work on. Cutting from the inside out, I opened the pale-colored underbelly from between the hind legs up to the dark chest. Reaching in, I trimmed the connecting tissue wherever the entrails were connected, and I cut away the diaphragm between the intestines and the heart and lungs. After reaching deep down and cutting the windpipe and the gullet, I pulled out the whole set of innards and rolled them in a heap onto the ground. I cut loose the liver and laid it in the cavity. Next, after turning over the purple, splotchy lungs, I slit the sac around the heart, cut it loose, and slipped it into the carcass with the liver.

All of this took about an hour, and much of the work was slippery and made me feel awkward, but I heeded Grandpa's advice and did not hurry on any part of it. When I was done, I wiped my hands on the grass so that at least my palms were clean.

I stood up and rested my back as I waited for the carcass to air out. After a few minutes, I bent to my work again and cut holes along each side of the big cut. I took down the string and used it to lace up the loose sides of the belly as I had been told much earlier.

At this point, the figure of a person appeared to my left, coming from the direction I had come. Within a few seconds, I recognized Jeff Hayden, jumping up on large fallen logs and jumping over the more low-lying ones. He was carrying a rifle, and he had a smile on his face.

"You look like you could use some help," he said as he came within ten yards.

I stood up straight and took a deep breath. I had tied my hair back in the morning, but wisps and strands of it had come loose. My hands and forearms were bloody up to my elbows, and I had gooey blood on the backs of my fingers, so I couldn't brush my hair out of the way. I blew at it as I frowned at Jeff Hayden. "I'll do all right by myself," I said.

He stepped up onto a log and jumped down with both feet together. "Big deer, little girl."

I ignored him as I walked over to my jacket and took a rope out of the back pouch. It was a thirty-foot, half-inch hemp rope that Grandpa had taken from the pack equipment and lent to me for dragging the deer. He told me not to cut it because he wanted to use it later for tying the deer onto the horse. I bent over and began to wrap the rope around the neck of the dressed animal.

Without a word, Jeff moved in close to me, his hip against mine, and laid his hands on the rope. To do so, he stuck his right arm between my left arm and my chest, and he reached his left arm around the other side of mine. In a few seconds, he tied a slip knot and pulled the rope tight under the buck's jaws and ears. I didn't like him taking that liberty with my deer, but it didn't end there. As he backed away and stood up, he rubbed his right arm against my chest.

Dread ran through me. I drew my elbows against my ribs and stepped away from him. "I don't like you touching me," I said.

"I didn't mean nothin' by it."

"I don't care. I don't like it. I don't even like you interfering with my deer."

He wore a half-smile as he stared at me. "You know, I kind of like it when you get mad. Goes with your red hair."

"My hair isn't red. It's auburn."

"Looks red to me." His eyes traveled over me. "I like red-haired girls. We'd make a good pair."

"No, we wouldn't." I looked for as many points of difference as I could find in those few seconds. I noted that his eyes were blue, and mine were green. I despised his pale complexion, his upturned nose, even his superior height. I huffed out a breath. "I wish you would leave. I don't want to have to call my grandpa."

"Huh. You do get mad. But that's all right. I'll leave." He turned away, picked up his rifle where he had left it, skipped over a log, and headed back in the direction he had come.

I could feel that my pressure inside had gone up, and my mouth was dry. The blood on my forearms and the backs of my hands had dried tight, so I moved my hands to loosen them. I leaned over my deer again, untied Jeff Hayden's knot, and re-tied the rope into a bowline like Grandpa had taught me. I didn't care if it took me the rest of the day. I was going to drag this deer by myself.

I held the rope around the back of my waist, leaned into it, and pulled as I stepped backward. The antlered head came up, and the body inched forward. I looked around. Jeff Hayden was long gone, and I was glad of it.

I knew it would be difficult to tell anyone about what had happened. People might say, "It was just a boy getting too close. You know how clumsy they are." Or, "He didn't mean anything by it. It might have been an accident."

But I knew it wasn't. I also knew he didn't do it because I was pretty. He did it because I was a girl and he had the chance to do it. It made me as sick as if I had smelled a snake.

As for boys, I remember thinking that day that I didn't feel one way or another about them. Maybe someday I would meet a fella and want to get to know him better, but I didn't know. I just knew that I didn't like this one boy or anything he had in mind.

In camp that evening, after a supper of deer tenderloin fried in bacon grease, I washed the dishes and wiped out the cast-iron skillet. Grandpa was lying on top of his bed, still dressed, with a gray wool blanket pulled up to his chest. He had his hands folded and resting on the blanket. It had been a long day for him, hobbling around doing everything the hard way.

His eyes were closed, but every once in a while, he would open them. When he saw me looking at him, he smiled.

"You did well, Katie. We've got deer meat to eat, and a pretty set of antlers."

I recalled an image of the deer slung over the saddle, tied snug, with his antlered head lashed to the saddle horn. It was a sight I would remember for a long time. I said, "I wouldn't have known how to do any of it without you, Grandpa."

"Well, we git along all right. Some kids, you take 'em out, and the next thing you know, they're tellin' you how to hunt."

I thought of the deer hanging in the tree near our camp. "We've got a lot of work to do tomorrow, getting packed and loaded up."

"Oh, yeah." Grandpa closed his eyes and fell into a light sleep again.

I looked at him as I sometimes did, and I thought, this is my mother's father. There was a time not long ago when I never knew him, and now it seemed as if I had known him forever. I could not remember a time earlier when someone loved me, but now I knew what it was like to love and be loved. There was nothing else like it, and I was glad to have it for as long as it would last.

John D. Nesbitt lives in the plains country of Wyoming. He writes western, contemporary, mystery, and retro/noir fiction as well as nonfiction, poetry, and song lyrics. John has won many awards for his work, including four Spur awards from Western Writers of America. His most recent books are *Castle Butte* and *Dusk Along the Niobrara,* frontier novels with Five Star.

* * * * *

GOOD WORK FOR A GIRL
BY PAT STOLTEY

* * * * *

Seemed like Mama took the whole of Indiana Territory to do her dying. Every day she coughed harder, slept longer, and lost more strength. After a week on the trail, she stopped eating. A little water kept her alive longer than she wanted, but I couldn't let go.

"Sissy," she whispered. "I'm so sorry. But you're sixteen years old, and strong in mind and body. You can handle whatever comes."

Mama called me Sissy instead of my given name, Cecilia. Named after my father's mother, at his insistence, I felt certain the nickname was the result of an ongoing feud between my mother and her mother-in-law. Grammy didn't like Mama from the beginning and made sure everyone knew how she felt, right up to the day she died.

I guess that's not part of my story, though it does explain why Mama called me Sissy and Pa called me Cecilia.

Those last whispered conversations with Mama were mostly her telling me how to get along with Pa and my brother and me telling her how much I would miss her gentle touch as she brushed my hair or kissed my cheek. I wasn't sure I was as strong in mind and body as she thought I was, but I kept my doubts to myself.

All this time Pa sat next to my brother, Samuel, on the front of the wagon, pushing our two old oxen to stay alive until we made it to the coalfields close to the Big Muddy River, east and north of a growing town called St. Louis I'd read about in school. I'd heard about the Mississippi River too, but the Big Muddy was different. According to Pa, longboats already traveled the Big Muddy, hauling coal on to the Mississippi and downriver.

Pa didn't talk much, except for a geography lesson from time to time and news about the state of the territories in 1811 that Pa had learned from reading old newspapers or listening to folks we met along the way. I could tell he was grieving Mama's death long before she took her last breath. As little as they talked to each other, you wouldn't know they cared much at all. Sometimes I thought Pa did more communicating with our oxen than he did with Mama. It was the little things I saw that told me more about his feelings.

During the day, when Pa stopped to let the animals rest, the first thing he did was peer into the wagon and watch Mama until she opened her eyes and met his gaze. Then he'd duck his head and look away, sometimes failing to hide the tear that edged down his sunburned cheek and disappeared into his whiskers.

As Mama grew weaker and needed cleaning up more often, Pa took a turn at sitting by her side while I got some air and scrubbed her clothes and bedding in the icy water of a nearby creek. Once when I returned, I looked into the wagon without announcing my presence. Pa was down on his knees, his forehead touching Mama's cheek, his shoulders heaving as though he sobbed his heart out. Mama lifted her hand, something I didn't even know she had the strength to do, and stroked his head, her fingers combing his hair.

"You need to have Sissy give you a trim," Mama whispered.

Pa let out a moan that tore at my heart.

After that day, I always made plenty of noise before looking inside the wagon.

The quiet, mostly secret loving I saw that day was one of the reasons my heart ached when I saw Pa barter away our cooking utensils and tools for a crude box for Mama's burying. I knew he couldn't bear the thought of her not having a proper coffin, but I also knew she saw and heard what was happening. The fear in her eyes tore me to pieces.

Mama might have been hot from head to toe, but I near froze to death while doing my daughterly duties. I had to put on so many extra clothes that I could barely move. Late November seemed colder than usual by the time we got close enough to the Mississippi to smell the stench of half-eaten fish littering the riverbanks.

"We've gone too far," Pa said.

"How do you know?" I asked. "You talk to somebody?"

He nodded and gestured toward Mama's pine box that he'd tied to the outside of the wagon. I took that to mean he'd asked the fellow who robbed us blind for a rickety box that might fall apart before we even got Mama buried. Papa had faith in his fellow man, so he would believe anything he heard. Sometimes it worked out. Sometimes not. What could I say? I was in a state of not knowing north from south or east from west, especially on a cloudy day when I couldn't follow the sun's rise and fall.

All this time, while Mama was dying and Pa was grieving and I was doing the motherly and wifely chores of feeding and cleaning and nursing, my older brother, Samuel, sat on that wagon or slept on the ground. He didn't talk. He didn't work. The only time he showed any life at all was eating time. That boy, and I call him a boy even though he was near man-size and should have been hunting and fishing and fixing things on the wagon when it broke down, could eat more at one meal than I could eat in a week.

Pa had told me once that Samuel got kicked by a mule when he was five and that he hadn't been right since. "He can't help being the way he is," Pa told me. "It's my fault. I let him wander around the barn without watching him. Your ma ain't never forgiven me, you know. That's why I can't say nothing and you can't either. That boy's temper will get the best of him someday. You leave him be. I don't want you to get hurt."

So I let Samuel be, but it grated on my mind because it wasn't fair. We could have used his help a hundred times and more as those oxen lumbered on, jostling and bumping poor Mama on her deathbed until I thought her bones would jiggle loose from her scrawny, dried-up body.

Even thinking back about those days makes my eyes water. As Pa would have said, my throat feels like a wad of half-chewed meat got stuck in my craw.

At the time, I couldn't talk to Pa about anything, even to let him know Mama had forgiven him a long time ago for Samuel's accident. I had asked her about that long before she got so sick.

"You can't change the past," she said. "I don't think about it as something your pa did, only something that happened for reasons only God knows."

"Pa thinks you're carrying a grudge," I told her.

"Don't you worry, Sissy. I'll make it right with your pa. He doesn't need to carry that burden the rest of his life."

I don't know if they ever talked about Samuel and the accident after that, but my mind was put at ease about their feelings when I saw them together in the wagon.

The last two days of Mama's life, I sat by her side and held her hand, wet her parched lips, and placed cool compresses on her fevered brow. Her passing was easy for her, but hard for Pa and me, and for Samuel too.

Mama got put in her box and buried somewhere between the Mississippi River and the coalfields we were backtracking eastward to find. Pa had a lot of trouble digging a grave because the ground was frozen partway and full of rocks and prairie grass roots. I tried to help, but I wasn't strong enough in the arms to use the spade. If we'd still had our ax, I might have chopped some ground away, but that ax was one of the things Pa had traded. I left Pa to his labors and built up a fire to make coffee. Samuel came out of the wagon and sat by the fire, pretending there was nothing he could do to help.

When the grave was dug, Pa called me to help lower the box into the ground, shove dirt and rocks back into the hole, and pray. We prayed for a long time before we got to warm up by the fire and drink our coffee. That's when Samuel went to sit by Mama's grave. He was still sitting there in the dark when I finally climbed into the wagon and wrapped myself in blankets. The next morning, when I went out to stir up the fire and wake Pa, Samuel was nowhere to be found. He had taken one of Pa's two muskets, so we hoped he'd just gone hunting.

Pa and I lingered by Mama's grave for a few days, partly to pray and mourn and partly to see if Samuel would come back. He did not. Pa didn't say much, but I knew he had mixed feelings about his only son disappearing into the countryside. One side of his heart would be heavy with sadness and worry. The other side of his heart would feel light and free.

I'm sure he worried about us having only one long gun now. We would be in a heap of trouble if we needed to protect ourselves, because it takes time to get those guns ready to fire. I knew how to prime and load one musket while Pa shot the other, but what can a body do if there's no spare? We'd heard about Indians killing white folks in the territories, but we hadn't seen even one Indian so far. I hoped we'd never see one at all.

I think Pa felt a lot confused about Mama's passing, just the same as he felt about Samuel running away. He'd lost his wife of twenty years, but he was relieved her suffering was over . . . and that his own suffering grew less by the day.

We finally hooked up the oxen, packed the few remaining pans and tools into the wagon, and moved on. It took another week for Pa to find the coalfields and get hired on as a coal picker.

A big snow moved in the first day Pa went to work. With near ten inches covering the coal, work stopped for another week while everyone waited for the sun to come out and the air to warm up. Pa did get credit for that one day, but not until the usual payday two weeks later. We might have starved to death if not for our musket and Pa's true aim. He killed a rabbit, a squirrel, and two pheasants, though all were so full of shot it took hours to clean them. That was my part of the chores. The general store at the camp gave us extra credit to buy a bag of cracked corn for the oxen and a bit of flour for hardtack. It's not the best-tasting biscuit, but it's filling. Hungry enough to eat mud, I didn't complain.

Pa and I weren't the only folks living out of a wagon, although some sported fancier coverings than our torn-up mess. Back when he decided we had to move on from our old farm with its rocks and dried-out dirt, Pa took two of Mama's fine quilts and sewed them together. He split logs into skinny poles and used penny nails to fasten them to the wagon sides. Then he stretched that double-sized quilt over the top and tied the bottoms to the poles to hold the cover on. It only took one big windstorm to rip the quilts apart. Pa sewed them together again and repaired the torn places, using more big stitches to make the cover stronger.

Now that we were settled near the coalfields, the problem wasn't wind as much as the weight of heavy snow and the melting once the sun came out. Our wagon top was soaked clean through and everything on the bottom of the wagon sat in a freezing cold puddle. I don't know how we would have kept Mama warm and dry if she'd lived on.

At least ten wagons, three Conestoga holding up fine but most falling apart, formed a circle around a big firepit that was kept burning night and day with salvaged coal pieces too small for the boss to sell. Every one of the coal pickers had pocketfuls at day's end. The men emptied their bounty onto a blanket set close enough to easily throw the bits into the flames but not so close to catch fire from the heat and sparks. When the pile of coal pieces ran too low, the children joined the women in the woods to look for dead branches. Sometimes it seemed like keeping the fire burning was more important than eating.

Water was easy to come by. A spring in the woods fed a little stream that ran past the camp and into the Big Muddy. Even with the constant flow, its edges froze over in December, but the same pickax used to break up the coal chipped out chunks of ice. The women dragged the pieces back to camp using old feed sacks. Once the ice was tossed in a kettle near the fire, it melted in a hurry.

For Pa and the other coal pickers, staying warm was hard. They'd work like the devil, start sweating, shed their coats, then stop for a rest. Sweat froze on skin and shirt collars faster than a man could turn around and grab his coat. They'd all bundle back up and start all over again. One day Pa came back with blue hands. Two days later, his fingernails started turning dark, then black, then peeled right off his fingers. Samuel had left all his clothes behind, and I figured he wasn't coming back, so I ripped up a pair of his overalls and sewed Pa a pair of mitts so his fingers wouldn't freeze again.

During the day, I worked with the other women and girls to keep the fire going and cook what food we were able to get from the store or trap in the woods. When I got tired of waiting for one of the men to go hunting, I shouldered Pa's musket and went off on my own, mostly scared out of my wits I would run into Indians or wolves. The first time I got back with a mess of rabbits, though, other women joined my hunting posse. Once we started eating more, we also laughed and danced more.

There was no dancing on Sunday, because it was the Sabbath. One of the men preached a sermon in the morning, and even though it was the custom to rest that day, there was no idle time allowed for the coal pickers. They went on to work while the women sat near the fire, praying and talking. By the time darkness fell over the coalfields, the men straggled back to the camp, exhausted and hungry as always. It wasn't long before everyone wrapped up in their blankets and slept as best they could in the cold.

On this particular Sunday, the fifteenth of December, our rest was interrupted sometime during the night.

I jerked awake with no sense of why my heart beat so fast and why the oxen were making noises and stamping their feet. The pots and pans rattled, and the wagon swayed, creaking and groaning as though it might fall apart. I couldn't make sense of the sounds and the wagon's shiver. It stopped all of a sudden. I stayed where I was but heard Pa and some of the men talking.

"Maybe Injuns," said one.

"Might be the wind," said another. "Or a thunderstorm."

"Seems it passed," Pa mumbled. "I'll keep watch. You all go back to sleep."

After a few moments, he leaned into the wagon and asked, "Did that rattling wake you, Cecilia?"

"Yes. What was it?"

"Not sure, but I think you can rest easy now. I'll be out here by the fire if you need me."

I told him I was fine, but it wasn't true. I remembered about earthquakes from my geography studies at school. In my mind, that shaking and rolling was an earthquake for sure. Turned out I was right too. We were awake and eating our first meal of the day when another quake hit. We were nervous right through

Christmas that another one might come and break our wagons apart.

Christmas Day was the first day the workers got to spend every minute with their families instead of picking and carrying coal. The men went hunting early and brought back enough pheasants, ducks, and even a goose to make the celebration special. Pa taught all the children to make rock candy. It was a good day, but it turned out to be the last good day for some time.

Before the joyful feelings had time to fade and for us to welcome the new year, something bad happened at the coalfield overhanging the Big Muddy. I heard later that the shaking had cracked and loosened large chunks of coal, so a few of the men were working to get those pieces free and loaded onto a longboat just beneath. About the time two of them slammed their picks into the wall, the largest chunks of coal broke loose and fell, taking three of the men with them as they fell into the river. A few pieces clipped the barge, knocking one of the boatmen off the side. All four men drowned.

One of those men was Pa.

When the boss came to tell me what happened, I couldn't believe it. My legs turned weak and my breath got caught in my chest. I sat down hard as if the ground had shaken again and knocked me off my feet. Never in a hundred years had I imagined anything would happen to Pa and leave me to fend for myself.

I could take my time grieving, as could the other wives and their children, but there was no time to waste when it came to the burying. The other workers had to get back to the coalfields, so they all pitched in to chip away at the hard ground near the woods. All the dead were buried the same day they died. This time there were no boxes. As soon as the graves were covered, the men went back to work.

Most of the women stayed for a short time to sing and pray with those of us who had lost our loved ones. But it was cold near the woods, and the campfire was warm. We went back to the wagons and our chores.

Pa dying like that left me with big decisions to make and no one to help.

I could sell the oxen and the wagon and pay for passage on the Big Muddy on to the Mississippi and downriver to a town where I might find work.

Or I could stay put and help the other families. I knew how to hunt. Even if I wasn't strong enough to use a pickax on frozen ground or in the coalfield, I could pick and drag or carry as well as any boy my age. At least half a dozen boys already worked alongside the men.

The clothes Samuel left behind came in handy. With the pant legs rolled up and stitched in place, and a length of petticoat run through the belt loops to keep my drawers from falling down, I looked rough and tumble, that's for sure. My hair was too long to pretend I was a boy, but I figured the boss would know who I was anyway. I tied my hair back at the nape of my neck and pulled on my warmest bonnet. Samuel's old boots weren't in great shape, but after stuffing the toes with more torn petticoat strips, I was able to lace them tight enough to stay on my feet. I worked my fingers into Mama's best leather gloves and jumped out of the wagon.

Apparently, I was a great source of amusement for the women and small children. First, they stared, then they outright laughed. As if my strange costume wasn't enough, my way of walking in Samuel's boots made me appear flat-footed and big-footed as well. It didn't matter one way or another. I knew I looked and walked funny, so I laughed along with the others.

It was a fair hike to the big log cabin where the boss spent his days near a warm fireplace. Pa had grumbled about the situation once or twice, thinking a boss ought to be working alongside his freezing crew, especially when his foreman spent most of his time inside the general store where it was warm. Never having met the man myself, or even seeing his cabin, I tried to keep an open mind. It would never do to show resentment toward the very person I hoped would give me work at a decent wage.

The resentment came later, after that boss sat back in his padded chair, looked me up and down, and said, "No!"

"But I need to work," I said.

"No," he repeated, a little softer than the first time. "This is not good work for a girl."

I felt my cheeks grow warm as I turned to go, not wanting this rude man to see my tears. It was not the last time over the years I'd hear the phrase, "not good work for a girl."

As I approached the open coal beds and started around the edge of the field to get back to the wagons, one of the men dropped his pickax and hurried to intercept my path. His coal-dusted clothes and dirty face were no worse than others I'd seen, but his fast pace in my direction felt threatening.

To my immense relief, the man simply asked if I'd found work. He did not speak in the English way, nor did he have the sound of a man who'd lived in the territories an extended time. I stared at him for a moment while I translated his question in my mind.

"No, not yet," I finally replied. "I'm at a loss what to do."

"Whit's fur ye'll no go past ye," he said.

When I stared at him for a long time, unable to decipher his words at all, he smiled. "Whatever is meant to happen will happen," he said, speaking slower and using the English phrasing I was accustomed to hearing. "Perhaps I can be of help. I worked beside your father many times. He told me about your mother and brother and spoke of you as the light of his life."

"He said that?" I was astounded. Pa was not a man to talk of his feelings to anyone, especially a stranger.

"He did indeed. My name is Angus Barrow, and my wife, Margaret, will be bearing our sixth child in the next month. If you would care to bring your wagon alongside ours, sharing what you have with us as we would share with you, perhaps you can be of help to my wife in her difficult days. I understand you know how to fire a long gun?"

"I do and am quite a good hunter. My father taught me well."

"Och. Margaret will take you in and mother you near to death, I ken. I will find you this afternoon when I return to the camp. Now go on with you. Find something to wear that makes you look like the bonnie wain you are."

Did Mr. Barrow tell me to dress like a girl before meeting his wife? I thought so. I hoped so. Once back in my own clothes and boots, bundled against the cold with my heavy coat and the warm bonnet, I fed the oxen their last portion of grain and led them to the stream for a drink of water. Once back at the wagon, I rubbed the animals down to warm their hides, then covered each one with one of Mama's quilts. If the snows came again, the oxen would suffer more than I would. Their fear of fire kept me from leading them closer to its warmth. Where I could sit and warm my hands and toes, the animals would not venture.

Within days of meeting Angus Barrow, I decided perhaps I was not so unlucky after all. Although true that I'd lost all the family I'd ever known, I became part of an even bigger family. The Barrows were warm and friendly and hugged each other at the slightest hint of need. I soon felt mothered as Mr. Barrow had predicted, sometimes even a tiny bit smothered, but I did not complain. The work was dawn to dusk and more, the physical demands far greater than any expected of me before. I hunted and fished, held babies and wiped the noses and rear ends of toddlers, cooked meals and mended clothes. In return, I was well fed from the Barrows' supplies, as were my oxen. They treated me with kindness and taught me skills I'd never even heard of before.

"Ken ye weave a rug?" Mrs. Barrow asked.

"I . . . think not," I replied, not truly certain what the question was. Soon after, I sat near the camp's fire, learning the fine art of weaving on a small makeshift loom constructed of split branches.

"What are you doing?"

I jumped near a foot off the log on which I sat. So engrossed in my weaving I'd put the rest of the world out of my mind, I had not heard the boy approach. Now he leaned over my shoulder, studying the wobbly loom in my lap.

"Mrs. Barrow is teaching me to weave."

"May I sit here and watch?"

I moved my skirt aside to make room on the log, then took a closer look at this fellow. More a young man than a boy, he was tall and thin and far cleaner than the men and boys I saw each day as they returned from the coalfields. He sat down, then folded his hands together across his knees and leaned forward. When he turned his head toward me, his blue eyes met mine and held my gaze longer than I thought proper. I kept on looking at those blue eyes, however, then let my gaze drift to his dark hair, long and tucked behind his ears. My, he was a handsome young man.

My breath caught somewhere in my chest, forcing me to turn away so I could breathe again. I pretended an intense interest in the loom, which had now twisted a bit lopsided in my grasp.

"I haven't seen you in camp before," I said, trying to keep my voice level and a bit aloof. "Have you just arrived?"

"I'm here for a short time before returning to school," he said. "My father owns this land."

"You're the boss's son?"

"I am. My name is Richard."

"Where do you go to school?"

"West Point."

I'd learned about West Point in school and knew of its special purpose. "You'll be a soldier when you graduate."

"Yes, I suppose I will."

I struggled to square the loom, which now appeared to be a weapon of sorts with two pointed ends opposite each other and flattened sides, the webbing made of vines now a tangled mess. Richard took the loom from my hands and quickly bent it to its correct shape. When he returned the loom, he touched my hand. I jerked away as though burned by fire. Then I felt my face flush with embarrassment.

One would think I'd never talked to a boy before.

"I understand your father died in the river accident."

I ducked my head so he wouldn't see the tears that welled up in my eyes.

"My father wouldn't let you work in the coalfield," he said. "Is that why you're helping the Barrow family?"

I nodded, still unwilling to raise my head and let him see the sadness in my face.

"You still own the two oxen and that wagon?"

I nodded again.

Richard didn't say much after that. Out of the corner of my eye I could tell he was surveying the whole camp, his gaze lingering on my wagon and animals for a long time.

I guess Mrs. Barrow had need of my assistance just then. She poked her head out the front of their wagon and then pulled back.

Mr. Barrow, who had come from work to check on his wife, charged out of the wagon and toward the fire as though set on rescuing me from the flames of hell. He tossed a pot full of coal pieces into the fire before marching to my side and demanding an introduction to my young man. My cheeks flamed again. My young man, indeed.

Richard took the interruption well, standing at attention and introducing himself as he offered his hand.

Mr. Barrow seemed startled at first, glancing at me and then toward my wagon, then back at me. Finally, he harrumphed and raised his eyebrows, but took Richard's hand. I noticed that Richard winced just a tiny bit. Had Mr. Barrow chosen a subtle way to warn Richard against sitting too close to me again? I'd never know for sure. Richard smiled and bowed in my direction, said he'd promised his father to be prompt for dinner, and walked away. Mr. Barrow, eyebrows now pinched together in a frown, gave me a nod and hurried back to his wagon.

I wasn't sure what to make of all that attention and decided I'd wait until the next day to ask Mrs. Barrow after her husband had gone to work. As it turned out, her unborn wee bairn decided to raise a ruckus during the night. The next morning, I fetched the camp midwife, assisted with the baby's birth, and took care of the other children.

Too busy to do anything but work, eat, and sleep for the next few days, I forgot all about Mr. Barrow's strange behavior. By the time I had a chance to rest alone and daydream by the fire, I assumed Richard had returned to school. But that's when something bad happened, and I figured out what Richard had really been up to that day he came to the camp.

A tall, skinny man with red hair strolled around the fire, looking at the wagons and livestock as though he was thinking to buy something. When he got to me, he stopped.

"I'm the foreman here. I'm in charge of the workers' pay and the goods the workers get from the store. Your pa was Harry Williams?"

My hopes jumped sky high, thinking there was money owed

my pa that hadn't been paid yet. "Yes," I answered.

"He owed a big debt when he died," the foreman said. "Got way more things from the store than he had earned in work. You have to pay."

My hope turned into the scariest lump I'd ever felt in my throat, making it hard to swallow. A sour taste washed into my mouth and my stomach did a little flip. "I don't have any money," I said.

"But you have your wagon and the oxen."

"That's not right," I whispered. "That's everything I own. My pa died on the job. You should be helping me, not putting me out in the cold."

"You can take your own possessions out of the wagon and keep the cooking pots."

And with that, while Mr. Barrow was off in the coalfield, working hard to earn enough wages to buy and barter at that same general store, the foreman led my dear animals and wagon out of the camp.

This is wrong. Powerful wrong. I looked around the camp and wondered who else knew about this reckoning that would come sooner or later to anyone who didn't work hard enough to keep his earnings ahead of his needs from the store.

Mrs. Barrow was still keeping to her bed in the wagon, so I didn't want to upset her by telling her what had happened. The only thing I could do was keep on helping with the little ones until Mr. Barrow returned from his workday.

As if enough bad things hadn't happened already, another earth shaking started that afternoon, and Mr. Barrow got knocked off his feet. He sprained his ankle and cracked his arm. Being about the strongest and most determined man I'd ever met, he packed snow on his ankle in the evening, then laced up his boot as tight as he could in the morning, tucked his hurt arm into a sling, and went back to work.

I wasn't surprised when the foreman showed up that evening to tell Mr. Barrow he was fired. And that he owed the company store, just like Pa. Mr. Barrow promised to make good as soon as he could work, but the foreman wasn't having any part of that offer.

"Promises might as well be snowflakes," he said. "They melt away in the light of day. I'll just take your pickax and one of those muskets and call it fair."

The musket he took was the one I'd been using to hunt for game. One more thing of Pa's I figured I'd never see again.

That evening, Mr. and Mrs. Barrow sat down with me in their crowded wagon and talked about what we were going to do. Mr. Barrow wanted to set out for St. Louis, thinking he could find a better job where there were more folks doing business. Mrs. Barrow wanted to turn around and go back to Ohio where she had two brothers who might help them out.

I listened to what they were saying, and knew I was to be included in their plans no matter what, but there was just one problem. I didn't want to take that long ride back to Ohio, crammed into a corner of their wagon with all those little ones. Going to St. Louis might be better, and for sure faster, but it wasn't for me to say my thoughts on the matter.

That's when I decided to right the big injustice that had been done to me and to my pa's memory. Telling the Barrows what I wanted to do was most likely a bad idea, so I kept my thoughts to myself while I made a plan.

After a long, sleepless night, I was ready. Once the other men had gone off to work and Mr. Barrow was busy packing snow around his ankle, I said I'd take the other long gun into the woods to go hunting. Before I left the camp, I went to every wagon and told the women what was happening with the men's earnings and the general store, how all my valuable goods had been taken away by the foreman, and how Mr. Barrow got fired and lost some of his things to pay his debt. Then I marched into the woods and followed the tree line all the way around the camp, past the coalfield, and snuck through the woods to the buildings not far from the cabin where the boss had his office.

I figured I'd find my oxen and my wagon in one of those other buildings. I looked around in every direction to see if the boss or foreman or anyone else was watching. It was so quiet, I could hear the chipping noise from the picks hitting the coal even though I couldn't see the coalfield at all.

The trappings for the animals hung on a wall by the stalls where they stood, munching at a kind of dry grass. In the next building, I found my wagon. It still had Pa's tools inside and the musket and the pickax taken from Mr. Barrow as well. I went back to the oxen, got them hooked up to their chains and straps, and led them to the wagon. The next part was harder than I remembered and took longer than I'd planned. Once the animals and the wagon were ready to go, I climbed on the seat and took rightful possession of my belongings that had been stolen from me to pay an unfair debt. No one saw me go.

I couldn't sneak the wagon and two oxen through the trees, so I had to ride out in the open, past the boss's cabin, the store, and the coalfield. A few of the men at work stopped to watch, then went back to work as though they hadn't seen a thing.

When I reached the camp, I stopped next to the Barrows' wagon and told them I was leaving but that I had his pickax to return first. Mr. Barrow grabbed his boot and laced it up, then started throwing stuff into his wagon as he shouted to his wife, "We're leaving this place."

She poked her head out and saw me, looked surprised as all get-out, then said, "Where are we going?"

"We're following Miss Cecilia Williams, wherever she decides to go!"

"Ken you imagine that?" Mrs. Barrow cried.

That day, I couldn't tell you why we didn't see hide nor hair of the boss or the foreman. I thought sure they would be on our trail as soon as they saw we'd disappeared, but nothing happened. We did get followed though. That night we camped near the Big Muddy, just us two wagons. By midmorning the next day, three more wagons from the camp joined us. Five more the next day. The whole camp had abandoned the coalfields and joined our band of travelers.

That's when we learned the boss had gone east with his son, who was returning to school. The foreman was supposed to supervise, but he had disappeared, telling no one where he was going or when he'd be back. We got away free and clear.

We ended up near St. Louis where there were plenty of jobs for the men, although I sometimes thought they spent more time dreaming about heading west than they did performing an honest day's work. I tried to find work in an office, at the sawmill, and even at the stable where the oxen were, but over and over again, I heard those same words: "This is not good work for a girl."

I stayed with the Barrow family for a few months before I found a school that needed a teacher and was eager to hire a girl like me. After selling my wagon and the animals to Mr. Barrow for a fair price, I took a room with a family closer to the school and found their kindness and warmth just as welcoming as that I'd experienced with the Barrows.

The father of my new family was a businessman and was often gone as he oversaw his projects, including a sawmill and the longboats he owned to ship his lumber. His wife was a sweet lady who loved her husband and children and brought laughter to the household every day. Treated as one of the family, I couldn't have been more content.

Teaching school was hard work, but not nearly so difficult as living in a wagon and suffering through cold and misfortune. I counted my blessings every day that I'd found good work and could take care of myself. I missed my old life from time to time, thinking about Mama in her healthy days and Pa working so hard while I just did my chores without knowing what was ahead. Still, my new life suited me just fine.

Later that summer, war broke out with the British. It was not unusual, even as far as St. Louis was from the fighting, to see groups of soldiers passing through. There was even a company of Rangers formed by the folks living around the Big Muddy where the coalfields lay. I might never have known if not for an unexpected visitor standing in the doorway of the schoolhouse one day in May, before the war even started.

To my surprise, the handsome gentleman in uniform was Richard. Still convinced his job back at the camp had been to assess my belongings before his father moved to confiscate them, I did not welcome him in a friendly way.

By the time I returned to the family's home where I lived, however, Richard had already made their acquaintance and enlisted their help in persuading me to listen to his explanation.

Richard's expression was earnest and his manner apologetic as he told his story. "By the time my father returned to the territory after our trip east, it was too late to bring you all back. Father fired his foreman and took over management of the store himself. I didn't learn of your misfortune until I returned from school. Father instructed me to set up a list of goods to be provided to all the workers as part of their earnings and make certain there was an adequate supply on hand. Now, of course, I'm obligated to the Rangers. Father will oversee the store himself."

I believed what Richard told me was true, and that I'd misjudged his intentions that day at the coalfields. Carrying bad feelings toward Richard, his father, and the foreman had been a heavy weight on my shoulders, perhaps heavier than I had realized, for now I felt my spirits lifted. When I met Richard's gaze and held it a little longer than was proper, my cheeks grew warm.

"There is more," he said. Reaching into his pocket, he pulled out an envelope and handed it to me. Inside, I found a deed to ten acres of land north of the coalfields. "The families of each man who died in that accident received a similar payment. You may choose to settle there and build a home, or you may sell the land."

I was astounded. Ten acres. I had no idea what to do with it. "When do I have to decide?" I asked.

"There's no time limit. Now, I must go. The Rangers will move on tonight."

"I won't see you again."

"Not on this trip," he said. "Perhaps one day soon." As Richard reached the door, he turned and took my hand, raising it to his lips in a most gentlemanly gesture. Then he strode out the front door, mounted his horse, and waved before riding away.

The dear lady whose home I shared rushed into the parlor and clasped her hands together, giggling as though she'd just been visited by a handsome soldier herself. "Will he call on you again?" she whispered.

"Perhaps one day soon," I said. "I do hope so."

For now, I would teach my students and think about what to do with my ten acres. I trusted the future to take care of itself.

Northern Colorado resident **Pat Stoltey** is the author of *Wishing Caswell Dead,* a finalist for the 2018 Colorado Book Awards. Learn more about Pat and her books at her website/blog patriciastolteybooks.com, on Facebook www.facebook.com/PatStoltey, and on Twitter twitter.com/PStoltey.

★ ★ ★ ★ ★

LADY OF NEW ORLEANS
BY PAUL COLT

★ ★ ★ ★ ★

It all began with Mr. Madison's ill-advised war. We paid it no mind for two years. The nearest fighting took place three hundred leagues from New Orleans. Then in the fall of 1814, the foul odor of war blew through the city. We heard whispered rumors. Houses such as Chateau Le Belle positively seethe with rumor. Perhaps I should introduce myself. I am Madame Margot B'Olivar, mistress of Chateau Le Belle, the finest, if I may be so bold, bordello in New Orleans. Nichol, one of my girls, first whispered that the Indian fighter, Andrew Jackson, was raising an army for purposes of defending New Orleans. She got the story from one of the gentlemen she entertained. I took it with a pinch of salt. Though a stunningly beautiful high yellow octoroon, Nichol was known to have a vivid fascination with all manner of fanciful tales. I got the news firsthand from a most reliable source, one of my regulars, and may I say favorite, Jean Lafitte.

Monsieur Lafitte visited New Orleans frequently from his enclave on Grand Terre Island in Barataria Bay, owing to his considerable business interests in the city. He offered New Orleans's privileged gentry all manner of fine merchandise for purchase at reasonable prices if one were inclined to overlook the dubious provenance of the goods. Did I mention some regard Jean Lafitte a pirate? Not a swashbuckling, evil-smelling Jolly Roger pirate. Jean Lafitte cut the dashing figure of a lovable gentleman brigand. Still they called him a pirate, though most overlooked the allegation, preferring instead to enjoy the wares he and his band of Baratarians purveyed. I appreciated some of his finer curiosities, though I more enjoyed partaking in the profits of his booty by the sums he lavished on me for my favors. I shouldn't admit it for professional reasons, but as I said, he was a favorite, so favored I might have entertained the devilishly handsome privateer purely on social considerations. Hush now with that. I have my reputation to consider. Fortunately, Monsieur Lafitte was too much the gentleman to gratuitously impose himself upon me.

Lafitte informed me that the British planned to invade New Orleans. Aside from the city's wealth and charm, New Orleans afforded a seaport on the Mississippi, and with it, gateway to waterways north and the whole of the western frontier. The British attempted to recruit Lafitte and his Baratarians to assist them in navigating the bayous for purposes of taking the city. Jean feigned accepting their offer while privately casting his lot with General Jackson in the role of double agent. I hadn't thought of Jean as an American, let alone a patriot. The city's American association came about as a consequence of the American government's purchase of the Louisiana Territory from France. For most of us, annexation by the United States and Mr. Madison's war meant little. We were a port city. A melting pot of races, cultures, and nationalities. We scarcely got along among ourselves, never mind worrying about the whimsy of some upstart nation to our north and east.

It all came to fruition a few weeks later when the general, some call Old Hickory, marched into town with a token force of regulars and a ragtag assemblage of volunteer militiamen from Tennessee. It did little to inspire confidence this force could withstand determined assault by a British command fresh from thrashing Napoleon Bonaparte himself no less. Then there was General Jackson. Tall, gaunt, and gangly, hair gone white, and known to suffer from afflictions of intestinal dyspepsia, hardly the forceful figure of a military leader you'd entrust to defend you against the finest fighting force in the world. As a practical matter, it seemed all the American presence accomplished was to increase the anxiety of those of us who might be subjected to British invasion for having the misfortune to be purchased by our adventuresome neighbor to the north. Here, I confess to being among those fearful of the consequences as might befall our fair city from this folly.

Others soon joined Lafitte at Jackson's standard. If we thought the first lot ragtag, we should better have reserved judgment for the ranks of those who followed. Kentuckians, freed men, Indians and Creoles, a misaligned cadre if ever one were assembled. One offer of assistance escaped my notice as you will undoubtedly understand. The Ursuline Sisters of Our Lady of Consolation Convent offered the general the services of their house and school for the treatment of injured and wounded. Mother Marie de Vizon herself made the offer. As matters would unfold, the Ursuline war effort would not stop at bandaging.

In the weeks that followed into the fall, Jackson reconnoitered terrain surrounding the city with Lafitte as his guide. In this he won Lafitte's admiration. Jean spoke of it one evening as we took cognac à la boudoir, I in a fetching lilac throw, Lafitte in glorious repose. The general's instincts and planning impressed him. The purpose of their journeying sought to anticipate the British advance so as to plan effective defenses. In the course of their reconnaissance, they identified several routes the British might pursue in an assault on the city. They made assessments of the defensibility of each. One plantation-lined approach hemmed in on two sides by river and marsh showed promise. Jean was close-mouthed beyond that. I suspected in due course his British contacts would be given glowing reports designed to lure them into a circumstance favorable to the Americans.

Nevertheless, Lafitte's favorable estimation of the general did little to allay my fears. The British were known to be brutal and ruthless. They'd already sacked Washington City leaving the American capital a smoldering ruin. That victory overcame American regulars. If their best couldn't defend their own capital against British might, what hope had these volunteer backwoodsmen against odds such as these? We didn't linger in war talk over-long, the night called for more gentle pursuits. He left my stipend with the announcement Jackson had him off to Mobile in the morning.

We learned the general did indeed anticipate the British in Mobile. The Redcoats first attempted to land there, hoping to obtain the services of a port and a landward route to New Orleans. Jackson prevailed upon the Spanish governor at Mobile to allow him use of the harbor fort. The general could be most persuasive at bayonet-point. Armed and garrisoned American guns repulsed the British fleet's attempt to enter the becalmed harbor. New Orleans soon buoyed at news of victory. Lafitte admitted it no more than the opening skirmish in a battle yet to be joined. I suspected defeat would serve only to stiffen British resolve.

Jackson returned to the city to a hero's welcome, though he hastily set aside ceremony to deploy his defenses. As December crawled toward Christmas, word came the British had landed on an island just off the coast. From there they ferried troops and munitions to the mainland in barges, preparing to march on the city. *Chalmette Plain* made the whispered rounds of the city. Lafitte merely smiled and affirmed the British assault would follow this plantation-lined lane to the city.

Jackson threw his considerable force of will and the mass of his patchwork army to construct a massive rampart southeast of the city. The fortification rose from the banks of a canal, which served as a moat crossing Chalmette Plain. It blocked passage between an impassable swamp on the east and the Mississippi on the west. All would depend on the general's plan of defense. All, events would reveal, did not rest on the handiwork of men.

The British reached the field in force just after Christmas. They continued ferrying men and munitions to reinforce their camp to its full strength. They made a study of the general's breastworks and by sortie and skirmish probed for weakness. These efforts proved fruitless and costly as Kentucky sharpshooters and Tennessee riflemen took their toll at long range.

Opening salvos thundered in the distance January 7th, 1815. Rolling thunder sent tremors of foreboding through the city. The moment had come. What more could be done? All depended on a white-haired hickory cane and a citizen militia with little or no military training. All depended, it seemed, on no more than frail hope.

Mother Superior led them. The Ursuline Sisters processed down Royal Street, gray ghosts in early evening, bearing a statue of a lady draped in a golden robe, wearing a crown and holding the infant Christ child. Our Lady of Consolation they called her. They carried her to the cathedral in the town square, followed by a growing throng of the city's women. Women filed past Chateau Le Belle in a demonstration of faith. I preferred to think in more pragmatic terms. Asylum in a church might prove the safest place when the British overran the city, as surely they must.

I decided to follow along at the end of the procession. I steeled myself against the icy reception a woman such as I might receive from a congregation such as this, in a cathedral no less. Ladies of my repute are not much given to religious observance. I rifled my memories, trying to recall the last time I entered a church. I gave it up to fiddlesticks and slipped into a back pew in hopes my presence might go unnoticed. It did.

The cathedral presented a massive edifice against the storm clouds of war. Dark stained wood glowed in a chorus of candles, scented of furniture polish and beeswax. Somehow I sensed a feeling of peace despite the persistent rumble of guns. The sisters placed their statue before the candlelit altar and took to their knees. New Orleans's womenfolk filled the pews. I huddled in the shadows of my place hoping no one noticed a jaded woman defiling their noble intention. They took up their prayers. I listened in spite of myself. Simple words. What might these do against the terrors of war? Assuage the fears of the faithful? Slaughter and bloodshed had no part here. Yet here they brought their petitions for what? It remained to be seen.

Hail Mary, full of grace . . .

Grace, surely the Lady be mannered. This grace I guessed something other. Received for goodness perhaps? I felt no grace. Doubted I'd know goodness grace were I to encounter it.

The Lord is with you . . .

With her. Certainly not with the likes of me.

Blessed are you among women . . .

Blessed among these women? No place for one such as me. I fought the urge to flee this place I did not belong, clinging to the presumption of safety I sought. Prayer grated on a lifetime of experience such as mine. Still I listened. As the night wore on, I sensed the words soothe a part of me I hadn't visited in more years than I cared to remember, a place unknown since childhood. What might it be? Innocence? My soul? I laughed. What nonsense. Nonsense and yet I dismissed my own hard-hearted cynicism and listened. Guns accompanied by prayers seemed less threatening somehow. At length I dozed.

I came awake to a light touch in the gray light of predawn. Kind eyes looked on me, hooded by veil.

"Come, join us," she said.

"You can't mean me."

"But I do."

"Do you know who I am? Do you know what I am?"

"It doesn't matter to her. Come."

She held out a hand. Guns rumbled in my ears, war broken out in my heart. Torn, I took her hand. "Who are you?"

"Mother Marie."

I followed. A slight chill prickled the flesh on my arms as she marched me up the broad aisle to the foot of a towering altar overshadowed by some larger presence. Some among the ladies present undoubtedly took umbrage at my intrusion. Mother Marie deposited me in the front pew among her sisters and resumed her prayers.

I sat surrounded by nuns, sheltered from the disdain of polite society. A thistle among lilies, no other way to describe it. At some point in the ebb and flow of emotions battling within my breast, I stopped berating myself over what I was doing there. Seated so close, my eyes were drawn to the Lady. A queen by her crown. I listened.

Day broke over Chalmette Plain. Morning fog rolled a thick carpet off the river and swamp. Lafitte surveyed the field from the vantage of a parapet at Jackson's elbow. The rampart bristled with cannon and sharpshooters. A battery of cannon deployed on the right flank at the river's edge gave a field of fire across the canal and down the face of the rampart should the British reach a point of bridging the canal or scaling the wall. Additional batteries held positions across the river on the west bank. These guns flanked the line of British advance.

Fog lifted over regular Redcoat columns on left and right flanks with its main force drawn up in the center. A fourth assault force was poised to strike across the river in an effort to turn the American cannon there against their own flank.

Holy Mary, mother of God . . .

Mother and son. She knew love, all mothers do. What was it

Mother Marie said? What I am "doesn't matter to her." How could it not? I knew me. It mattered to me. Then it occurred, perhaps that's all that mattered.

The Mississippi current conspired against the river assault force, bogging down barges carrying troops in shallows and driving still others downstream away from their objective, delaying assault on the guns positioned there. With American guns on the west bank of the river still in play, the British launched the main thrust of their assault. The vanguard, charged with bringing forward scaling ladders to bridge the canal and scale the rampart, came under heavy fire. Backwoods sharpshooters devastated their number, forcing abandonment of the ladders.

Pray for us sinners . . .

Yes, pray for us sinners. I certainly came in for that. Who could pray away a lifetime of sin? *The Mother of God,* I heard. At that moment I sensed her looking at me. At me? Couldn't be. Yet I felt it somewhere within. Pray for us sinners.

American gunners poured shot and grape on the British line advancing in force across the broad rampart front. Carnage ensued. British discipline remained staunch in the face of deadly sheets of steel. Holes ripped in red ranks filled by still more fodder for cannon. Officers fell along with their men, the British commanding general among them. The will to advance broke with his mortal wound.

Now and at the hour of our death . . .

The British advance stalled and fell back.

Pray for us sinners, I pondered. *Pray for me?* It seemed possible. Words came to me unbidden from I know not where. *Listen and discern.* The Lady? Could she have spoken to me? How? Still I heard it. *Listen and discern.* Curious word, *discern.* What might it portend?

Late by the sun-stained windows, there arose in the square a celebratory shout. Muffled in the cavernous cathedral we strained to hear.

". . . British . . . withdraw!"

Amen.

Women broke into sobs from relief. Mother Marie held up her arms with her sisters. Eyes lifted to the Lady. Mine drawn, followed.

Hail Mary . . .

We filed out of the cathedral in the blue shadow of early evening. I felt in a daze. What had I seen? What had I heard? What had I witnessed? What did it mean? Where to go? Chateau Le Belle felt surprisingly distant from home. I followed Mother Marie and her sisters. Lost, adrift on some ephemeral tide, propelled by some gentle current. Our Lady of Consolation beckoned. Consolation for us sinners. I was given a room, they called it a cell. I fell asleep listening to echoes. Simple words in my ears.

Days passed. On Chalmette Plain, the British tended their wounded and buried their dead. His Majesty's mighty army battered, blooded, and covered in unspeakable humiliation prepared to withdraw. Our wounded were brought to the convent for treatment. I helped as best I could. I passed evenings in the chapel, considering the meaning of consolation. Mother Marie kindly asked from time to time if she might be of any service. In time, we talked. I told her everything. She seemed not shocked or even surprised the Lady might speak to one such as me. She mentioned a priest I might see should I wish. I listened.

Word arrived the last week in January. A treaty signed at a place called Ghent and since ratified on both sides ended Mr. Madison's war. General Jackson and his troops marched home to New Orleans in glorious victory. At the general's request, we gathered again in the cathedral to celebrate the Holy Sacrifice of the Mass. I sat with the sisters dressed in widow's weeds. I'd not been widowed in any sense, though I felt some kinship with those who had. Mother Marie said it a call to repentance.

General Jackson attended mass in full military dress, his figure having taken on a new estimation by the light of events. Following the service, he visited the convent to convey his thanks to Mother Marie and her sisters for their prayerful vigil. He acknowledged Lady Consolation aided his cause against a formidable force. I must say, by my witness, I believed it.

Days later, Mother Marie summoned me to her office.

"You have a gentleman caller," she informed me.

"No one knows I am here."

"This one does. Do you wish to see him, or should I send him away?"

I thought a moment. "Mother, I have made peace with change in my life, though I do not yet understand the full measure of it. I wonder, perhaps I never shall."

Mother smiled with a nod. She understood.

"I believe I know who this man is. If I look back, I may learn something of why I have come here."

"As you wish, my child. He is in the parlor." She gestured to the door.

Jean Lafitte rose, hat in hand. He looked dashing and elegant as ever in the stark humble surroundings of a convent parlor. A bare room, its walls lined with straight-back wooden chairs, a crucifix only to adorn one wall. Our Lady of Consolation restored to her proper pedestal.

"Margot, I heard you were here. Whatever does this mean? Are you ill?"

I smiled. "Jean, good of you to come. Please have a seat." I took a chair across from him.

Whatever does this mean? His question hung between us.

"No, I'm not ill. I can't say I know the meaning of this. I am learning."

"But this is so . . . sudden. So extreme."

"I suppose it seems so."

"Have you become a nun?"

"No. Not yet. I don't know the sisters would even have me should I think I hear the call."

He shook his head as if to clear it. "Then why are you here?"

"I told you, I am learning. I can't explain it more than that. I can only tell you what happened. When the guns began, I was frightened. The sisters took their statue of Our Lady here to the cathedral to pray. The women of the city followed. I followed too thinking church the safest place when the British came."

"You didn't believe we could win."

"Did you? Perhaps you did. Precious few of us left in the city thought so. The sisters and the women prayed all through the night. I listened. The Lady spoke to me in words I hadn't heard since I was a little girl. In her words, I saw myself as she saw me."

"Spoke to you. A statue spoke to you."

"Not a statue, Jean. The Lady inspired a statue to remind us of her. This much I've learned. The Lady herself spoke to me. I heard her words, *listen and discern.*"

"Discern what?"

"I don't know. Mother Marie says I'll know it when I hear it. I'm still listening. Still learning. This much I know, busy as she was with all the cares of battle, she found time to console a sinner. She found time to wish something more for me than the life I lived."

"And what is that?"

"I do not know."

"What of Chateau Le Belle?"

"What of it?"

"You own it."

"I don't need it anymore. You tell me what's become of it."

"Nichol runs it in your stead."

"Then that is what's become of it."

"You've no more interest than that."

"No more."

"I am but a simple pirate. How am I to understand all this?"

"How am I? Perhaps if you listen."

"Oh, no. Not me. That's where all this started."

"No, Jean. It all began with Mr. Madison's ill-advised war."

In "Lady of New Orleans," **Paul Colt,** critically acclaimed author of award-winning historical fiction, offers an overlooked aspect of Andrew Jackson's improbable victory at the battle of New Orleans. With his victory, Jackson sealed America's claim on the west.

★ ★ ★ ★ ★

The Hope Chest
by Preston Lewis

★ ★ ★ ★ ★

When the hounds took to howling and barking, Mollie smiled with anticipation despite her exhaustion from splitting time between the cotton field and the kitchen where her aging mother grabbed the bucket of table scraps to take to the hogs.

"I'll handle that for you, Momma," Mollie said, wiping her fingers on her apron and taking the pail from her mother's feeble hand as the clump, clatter, and rattle of an approaching team and wagon drew closer, inspiring the hounds to clamor even louder.

"Who might that be?" Fannie Tarver asked her oldest child and only daughter as she patted her gray hair with her gnarled fingers.

Mollie played coy, but knew it was Singe Howell and his sixteen-year-old younger sister, Sarah. "Could be a peddler."

"This late in the evening?" Fannie replied. "Whoever it be, we've finished supper so we won't need to invite them to eat. Things are tight until the cotton's in, and that's six or more weeks away."

Mollie toted the pail past the woodburning stove, which added to the discomfort of the humid Alabama twilight, and around the wooden table with seven worn chairs as she headed for the back door.

"Don't you want to see who's stopping by?" Fannie asked as she patted her hair and pinched her cheeks, trying to add a little color and erase the strain of the day's chores.

"Whoever it is, he won't be interested in me, seeing as how Pa doesn't allow me to have any callers."

"He lets Singe Howell visit you."

"Only because he thinks Singe is too dumb to court me," Mollie answered as she opened the rear door and exited. She toted the pail to the barn, expecting at any moment for her father to summon her back to the wood-frame house to see her visitor.

The dogs still yapped as Mollie hummed "Camptown Races" on the path to the outbuilding, trying to control both the anxiety and exhilaration coursing through her lithe body as she considered what might transpire over the next eighteen hours. Rather than deliver the scraps to the penned hogs, she entered the drafty barn and dumped the leftovers into another bucket she had hung three days ago from a harness peg in the dark back corner. The old pail brimmed with rank waste from meals over the last seventy-two hours. Mollie hoped the bits and pieces of food would be enough as she retraced her steps to the door and latched it on the way out.

The canine ruckus at the house quieted down as Singe drew up to the front porch and halted the team. Mollie's father, Hezekiah, kicked a hound out of his path as he stepped from beneath the overhang to greet the visitors. The squealing dog scurried off as Mollie's four brothers—Jim, Jacob, Bill, and Tilroe, ages eighteen to twelve—trailed in their father's footsteps. Mollie watched her siblings welcome Singe and doff their hats to Sarah, but Mollie didn't catch their salutations. Mollie's mother joined the group and welcomed the pair. After Fannie's brief exchange, everyone turned toward Mollie.

"Mary Ann," Hezekiah called, "you have company."

Her father still addressed her as Mary Ann, though she preferred Mollie, the name bequeathed to her by three-year-old Morgan Camp the first time he saw her as a newborn. Morgan had labeled her his sweetheart that very day and had told both his and Mollie's parents he would marry the baby girl when she grew up. Unable to pronounce Mary Ann, Morgan had called her Mollie, and the nickname had taken with everyone but her sire.

"Mary Ann," Hezekiah yelled again, "company's awaiting."

Not wanting to appear too anxious, Mollie lifted the bucket. "Let me rinse this out first." She walked to the hand pump and cranked the handle, drawing enough water to wash out the residue before hanging the pail on the lever. As she ambled to the front of the house, Mollie vowed to let nothing fluster her. As everyone watched her approach, Mollie detected a glare of suspicion in her father's black eyes. Hezekiah Tarver despised any man that visited Mollie for any reason, but let Singe drop by simply because he thought the young Howell slow and no threat to wed Mollie. Most of all, Hezekiah Tarver loathed Morgan Camp for his long-standing courtship of Mollie. His hatred for Morgan Camp had intensified even after Mollie's suitor left Cleburne County, Alabama, for Texas two years earlier, promising Mollie a grand stone home if only she would follow him to the Lone Star State and marry him there.

"Good evening, Mollie," said Singe, removing his hat and smiling. "I came to pick it up, if you are still agreeable."

As everyone stared at her with questioning eyes, Mollie responded. "Yes, Singe, I am indeed. You can take it for Sarah."

Sarah squealed and clapped her hands, drawing everyone's stares. "Oh, thank you, thank you, thank you, Mollie. I've been dreaming about this ever since Singe told me."

Singe nodded. "Sarah's been excited. Is the price still eighty-nine dollars, Mollie?"

"Yes, Singe," Mollie replied. "It's like we agreed."

Hezekiah elbowed his way past his four sons and stood in front of Mollie, his balled fists on his hips. "What have you got that's worth eighty-nine dollars, Mary Ann? Whatever it is, it's mine."

"No, Pa, it's *not!*"

"Then what is it, Mary Ann?"

"It's my dreams, Pa, my hope chest. Since you won't let me marry the man I love, what's the point in keeping it?"

"That trunk belongs to your momma," he stuttered. "It's what she had when we got married."

"And she gave it to me, Pa. I've been filling it for years for my wedding with Morgan. Since you threatened to kill him if he tried to make me his wife, it can't bring me happiness now. I might as well sell it to a young lady like Sarah. Maybe her pa won't stomp on her dreams."

Atop the wagon seat, Sarah wiped tears from her eyes. "I didn't mean to cause trouble."

Singe put his arm around his little sister. "Easy, Sarah. It'll all work out." He reached below the seat, lifted a jug of liquor, and turned to Mollie's father. "I figured this might make our transaction easier for you to swallow, Hezekiah."

"We don't drink," the patriarch replied.

At least not in public, Mollie thought.

Despite his comment, Hezekiah grabbed the container and shook it. "It feels full. I'll give it to a friend." He looked to his wife. "Fannie, did you know of Mary Ann's intentions for *your* hope chest?"

"*My* hope chest," Mollie corrected.

"Don't sass me in front of others, girl," he spat.

"I'm a woman, Pa. Nineteen years old, I am. Momma had been married to you almost three years by the time she turned nineteen."

"I said don't sass me, girl." He drew back his free hand to slap her.

Defiant, Mollie jutted her chin forward, gritting her teeth and expecting the blow.

As Hezekiah's hand swung toward her cheek, her oldest brother grabbed it. "Don't touch her, Pa," Jim warned, "or I'll whip you."

Hezekiah yanked his wrist from Jim's grasp and scowled at his senior son.

"Thank you, Jim," Mollie said, looking up at the wagon seat. "My apologies, Singe, and especially to you, Sarah. I didn't want this to happen. All I wanted was for this hope chest to bring you the happiness I'll never have."

Sarah cried.

Hezekiah shouted, "Fannie, did you know about her plans for *your* hope chest?"

Fannie shook her head and shrugged. "I gave it to her ten years ago, Hezekiah. It's hers now, not mine. This never would have happened if you had let her marry Morgan Camp."

"Don't you challenge me in front of others, woman." He took a step toward his wife, but Jim grabbed his arm again.

"Don't touch Momma, Pa," Jim snarled.

Hezekiah shook himself free from Jim and backed away from both Mollie and Fannie. "Your ma needs help around here, and Mary Ann was born to help her and her menfolks, not run off with some stranger," Hezekiah explained.

"Morgan Camp was no outsider, Hezekiah," Fannie interjected. "He fancied Mollie from the moment he first saw her cradled in my arms."

"He aimed to steal her from us and leave you with all the woman's work, Fannie."

"You could've helped, Hezekiah. You expect us women to do chores in the fields. Why can't you've pitched in around the house?"

Hezekiah grimaced at his wife. "That's beneath the dignity of a hardworking man."

Jim stepped between his mother and father. "You can discuss this after the Howells leave." He turned to his three brothers. "Boys, fetch Mollie's hope chest and load it in the wagon for Sarah."

Jacob, Bill, and Tilroe hesitated.

"Go on," Jim commanded. "Get it out here. *Now!*"

The trio scurried inside as Sarah's sniffling broke the awkward silence while everyone waited.

As the door opened onto the porch, Mollie watched her youngest brothers grapple with her trunk as they inched it toward the rig. She hated to part with her hope chest like this, but it was the only way she would ever break her father's obstinacy.

The boys slipped past her, struggling with the trunk. "What you got in here, Mollie, rocks?" Tilroe asked.

Jim left his sullen parents to assist his three younger siblings as Singe bounced from the wagon seat and ran to unlatch the tailgate so they could slide in the chest. Sarah's sniffles slowed as the boys loaded the trunk. A smile wormed its way across her lips.

Singe helped the Tarver brothers wrestle the chest into the back, then stepped around to Mollie as Jim and Jacob shut and secured the tailgate.

"Do you want me to pay you now or later?" Singe asked.

"Now," said Mollie simultaneously with her father.

"This deal is between me and Mollie, not you Hezekiah," Singe replied, shoving his hand into his pants pocket and extracting a thin wallet. He slowly counted out eighty-nine dollars and when he finished, his billfold was empty. He handed the money to Mollie.

"Thank you." Turning to Sarah, she said, "I hope you enjoy everything. There's nothing fancy in my trunk, but enough to get you started when you find the right man." She paused and stared at her father. "The right man found me, but it didn't matter to some."

Singe leaned over and hugged Mollie, whispering in her ear, "I'll return for you tonight."

Mollie smiled. "Thank you, Singe, for what you've done."

Singe glared at Hezekiah. "Perhaps one day, Mollie, I'll come a calling to court you."

Hezekiah spat at the nearest wagon wheel. "No fellow's court-ing Mary Ann, not when there's so much woman's work to do around here. You remember that, Singe."

"Sorry you're so disposed, Hezekiah, because she'd make a fine wife."

"Not when I've got chores for her, she won't."

Singe pulled his lanky frame back into the rig, plopped on the seat beside Sarah, and rattled the reins. "Giddyup," he said as the mismatched team of plow horses started forward, making a circle in front of the house before heading up the trail behind the barn toward the Heflin road.

No one spoke until the wagon and hope chest disappeared into the trees with three of the nine hounds chasing and yap-ping at it. Shortly, the dogs returned, strutting back as if they had driven off the intruders.

Hezekiah turned to Mollie. "Gimme that money, Mary Ann."

"No, Pa," she scowled. "It's mine, a pitiful price for my dreams. The whiskey is yours. The money belongs to me."

"Don't be sassing me, girl. I need that cash to get by until the cotton comes in."

"Let Mollie be," her mother interrupted. "She can keep the bills until tomorrow when we'll discuss it."

Hezekiah shook his head, stomped his feet, and yanked the cork from the whiskey vessel. Hoisting the jug to his mouth, he suckled on it, then lowered it and wiped his lips with the sleeve of his work shirt. He strode toward Mollie, but Jim stepped in front of him.

"Listen to Momma," Jim ordered his father. "Let Mollie keep the money overnight."

"Tomorrow it is," Hezekiah said to Mollie, "but I'll expect every penny, all eighty-nine dollars, Mary Ann."

Mollie shrugged, "I'm not giving up what's left of my dreams, Pa."

Hezekiah eyed the bills in Mollie's hand and tried to move closer, but Jim wedged himself between them. The old man shook his head at his oldest son and took another swig of whiskey. Swallowing hard, he loosed a big breath. "How'd Singe come up with that much money? He's too dumb to have gotten it fair and square."

"That's mean, Pa," Mollie said.

"Did I ever tell you how he got his name?"

Mollie nodded, but Hezekiah ignored her and retold the story she had heard dozens of times over the years.

"When he was a boy, he played with matches and set their outhouse on fire and came near doing the same thing to the barn. His ma was at her wit's end to stop him from burning the house down so one day she grabbed him and a match, struck the match, and singed his fingers. He didn't play with fire no more after that."

"You've never liked Singe," Fannie said. "Why do you even let him come around here?"

"Because he wasn't smart enough to want to marry Mary Ann," Hezekiah replied. "He's no threat to us like Morgan Camp. From the day Mary Ann was birthed, he was always trying to take her away from here." He glanced from his wife to his daughter. "I never understood what you found in him, Mary Ann."

Mollie stuck the bills in her apron pocket and raised her chin boldly. "I saw my future. Morgan Camp was a man of many skills, a man that could've supported me in a better style than you ever did for Momma."

"Quit sassing me, girl."

With a sweep of her arm, Mollie pointed at their wooden house. "He promised to build me a fine stone home, not a shack like this. He pledged to give me a home with running water and even a water closet instead of an outhouse."

Hezekiah spat at the porch. "He only said that to get in your drawers."

"Hezekiah," Fannie shouted, "there'll be no gutter talk, not to or about our daughter."

Ignoring his wife, Hezekiah pointed his free hand at Mollie. "He was just sweet-talking you, trying to take advantage of you and steal you from us, your family. That's why I never let him write you no letters."

The defiance drained from Mollie's eyes, and she lowered her head, answering softly, "My dreams died that day because Morgan never sent a letter here. Selling the hope chest removes from this place my last memory of him. Now I can forget him and the stone house he vowed to erect for me."

"You'd've saved us all a lot of trouble if you'd forgotten him a long time ago. Giving me the money tomorrow should rid you of his memory forever." Hezekiah stepped past Mollie to the porch where he sat in his rocking chair. He stared hard at his daughter over the jug, which he tipped to his lips. When he stopped kissing the container, he wagged his finger at everyone. "Now all of you tend your business and leave me be."

Fannie put her arm around Mollie's shoulder. "I'm sorry, dear," she said. "Once I had dreams, but I had to let them go. I got over them. You will, too, one day."

Mollie shrugged, leaned over, and kissed her mother on the forehead. "I love you, Momma, but I'm not abandoning my dreams, no matter what Pa says." She hugged Fannie, then broke from her. "I should retrieve the scrap pail and take it back in the kitchen."

As Mollie stepped away, she watched her three youngest siblings head inside the house while Jim trailed her toward the well. At the hand pump, she reached for the bucket, but Jim grabbed her forearm. She turned and looked at him, uncertain what to expect.

"How will you stop Pa from taking your money, Mollie?"

Mollie smiled. "I'll come up with something, Jim. Thank you for standing up for me."

"He hasn't treated you right, running Morgan off to Texas and keeping him from writing you," Jim said as he released her arm and took the pail from the pump handle.

"What are you going to do, Mollie?"

"I'll think of something."

Jim paused with a queer look on his face, then smiled as if a fog had lifted from his mind. He laughed. "No, you won't think of a single thing, Mollie, because you've already devised a plan. Haven't you?"

Mollie shook her head, trying to hide the fear in her voice as she spoke. "What do you mean?"

Nodding, Jim grinned. "You're leaving tonight, aren't you?"

Mollie's hand flew to her mouth. Jim had figured out her plot. "What are you talking about?" She bluffed.

"The table leftovers." He winked at her. "Now it makes sense."

"You're out of your mind, Jim," she answered with what confidence she could muster.

"I found a bucket of scraps hanging in a corner of the barn. You plan to use them tonight to distract the hounds while you run away. And, Singe is gonna pick you up."

"No, no," Mollie cried, looking to the porch to determine if her father was watching.

"Don't deny it, Mollie."

She sighed, took a deep breath, and tried to calm her nerves. "Please, Jim, please don't tell a soul."

With his free hand, Jim patted Mollie's shoulder. "I won't ruin your dream, Mollie. Going to Texas, are you?"

Mollie bit her lip. Words failed her. Perhaps her mother was right. She wondered if she, too, must give up her dreams. Mollie shrugged. What could she say?

Jim dropped the pail and wrapped his strong arms around her, hugging her and planting a gentle kiss on her cheek. He released her only to grab her shoulders, step back, and look at her.

"Mollie, Mollie, Mollie," he laughed. "You are so clever."

Mollie let her head droop, still uncertain whether Jim stood with her or with their father.

"The whiskey jug was brilliant. You knew Pa would anger and take to drink so you provided him the liquor, hoping he'd get drunk enough not to catch you slipping away tonight. And the hope chest? It was so heavy. You packed all your belongings inside plus your wedding pretties."

Her throat tightening, Mollie swallowed hard. Jim was picking apart her plan as easily as plucking a chicken. She feared two years of work, plans, and dreams had collapsed when they had appeared on the verge of success moments earlier. "But, Jim."

Releasing her arms, he waved away her efforts to explain.

"You couldn't sneak everything out of the house for fear of being caught, so you removed your belongings in front of Pa and Momma and us boys and God and the entire world."

"Actually, Jim, I didn't take them out. Jacob, Bill, and Tilroe did it for me, thanks to you."

"And the money? That's train fare that Morgan sent you. Am I right?"

Mollie shrugged again. "More or less."

347

Jim threw his arms around her again. "I'm so happy for you, Mollie, and for me, too."

Mollie broke from his grasp. "What are you tickled about, Jim?"

"I feared I would have to whip Pa tomorrow if he tried to take your money away. Fighting him would've gone against Momma's teachings from the Good Book."

Mollie felt her eyes moistening. She had promised herself not to cry in front of her father, but this was her brother. A couple tears rolled down her cheeks. "Thank you, Jim. I'm sorry to abandon my brothers, but don't tell the other three until tomorrow night."

"You can count on me," he answered softly.

"Please tell Momma I feel bad for running out on her as I know she needs the help, but my life is mine. Tell her I love her deeply."

"I will. She'll understand. I'm sure she's on your side. I think she felt sorry for you, but couldn't stand up to Pa." He freed himself from her grasp. "You couldn't have done this without Singe, could you?"

"Not at all."

"Pa thought Singe was too stupid to be a threat, so he didn't suspect him visiting us regularly when he was really here to see you."

"Singe is close to Morgan."

Jim rubbed his chin, grinning. "Now I understand. Morgan disgusted me because he lacked the gall to write letters from Texas after Pa threatened him if he did."

"Oh, I got letters."

Jim nodded. "I reckon smarts trump gall. He sent them to Singe to deliver to you."

"Morgan wrote a letter a week. Each time Singe dropped by he tied the envelope to the corner fencepost behind the barn.

While he was visiting my folks, I'd run out to the barn, read it, and tie it back. He took each letter back home with him. I didn't want one of Morgan's letters around the house where Pa might find it."

"You thought of everything, Mollie."

"Everything except you figuring out my plan."

"I'm on your side, Mollie, but I've got to warn you. I've heard Pa has a fellow or two that watches the train station in case Morgan shows up or you try to leave. Be careful in Heflin, but I'll help you tonight."

Jim picked up the pail and started with Mollie to the kitchen door. As they walked, Mollie told Jim that she needed to meet Singe at midnight on the far side of the barn. Jim assured her he would assist. Entering the back door, Mollie pulled from her apron pocket the money that was her ticket to Texas and her dreams. She squeezed the bills tightly, even more so when she saw her mother sitting at the table, sobbing.

Mollie stopped and patted her shoulder, regretting that she must abandon her without a real goodbye. Then she bent down and kissed her momma on the cheek.

Fannie looked up with tearful eyes. "I'm sorry, Mollie, but your pa's a hard man, not given to understanding any needs but his own."

"I know, Momma, but I plan on living my dream in spite of Pa." She peeled five dollars in greenbacks from the stack and handed them to her mother. "Before Pa tries to take it, I want you to have this money. Don't tell him, but buy yourself some pretties at the store."

Fannie smiled. "Thank you, dear. That's a lot of money."

"You know I love you, Momma, no matter what happens?"

"I know, Mollie."

"It's been a long day, Momma, so I'm going to bed. I'm exhausted, and tomorrow will be a trying day."

"That is certain, Mollie. Rest well, if you can."

Mollie stepped away, glancing back over her shoulder, wondering if her gaze would ever again fall upon her mother. She retreated to her cramped room, slid the money into the handbag she planned to carry, then changed into her traveling clothes and waited. She was tired, but too excited to sleep and fearful if she did that she might oversleep. A half hour before midnight, she heard Jim in the adjacent room getting up, putting on his boots, and walking out the front door. He strode around the house to Mollie's open window and helped her climb out into the darkness. After she straightened her dress and checked that the bills were still in her handbag, she walked to the barn with Jim, followed by the hounds. He pointed Mollie up the trail while he retrieved the scraps, emptying the bucket on the ground outside the barn to distract the dogs.

As the dogs wolfed down the food, he trotted along the trail and caught up with Mollie at the farthest corner fencepost in the barnyard pen. As he approached, she patted the post. "This is where Singe left Morgan's letters for me."

They walked along the path to the Heflin road and waited a few minutes before they heard the approach of Singe's wagon. Out of the darkness, he drew nearer, then stopped a dozen paces away. Singe called out, "I don't know who you are, but I've got a pistol and am ready for trouble."

"It's me," cried Mollie, "and Jim. He knows everything and is on our side."

Singe sighed. "I feared it was Hezekiah."

"No," Jim laughed, "he can't walk this far. When I left the house, Pa was passed out drunk in his rocking chair on the porch."

Jim escorted Mollie past the team, paused, and hugged his sister. "I'll miss you," he said, laughing. "So will Pa!"

Mollie kissed him on the cheek. "I wish there was another way, Jim."

He helped her in the wagon and stepped back. "I'm sorry I won't be attending the wedding."

She laughed. "At least I'll be there. At times, I wasn't sure. Tell no one where I went until after supper. By then I should be out of Alabama."

"Okay, Mollie, you be careful and write us now and then."

Singe said, "Thanks, Jim, for your help." He doffed his hat to him, then turned to Mollie, offering her two small twine-wrapped bundles. "It's your letters from Morgan. They'll be something you can read on the train." Singe shook the reins and started the wagon toward Heflin. Mollie twisted in her seat, waving at Jim until he disappeared in the darkness, and then slipped the letters into her handbag.

"You got Sarah home safely, Singe?"

"She's asleep in bed."

"She did a great job pretending the hope chest was to be hers."

Singe laughed. "I actually believed her, and I knew better."

After that they rode wordlessly to Heflin, stopping on the outskirts of town. Mollie slept on quilts from her hope chest on the wagon floorboard while Singe threw a blanket on the ground. By eight o'clock, they were at the depot where Mollie bought a one-way ticket and checked her trunk through to Abilene, Texas, where her betrothed planned to meet her. Singe purchased a round-trip passage to and from Anniston, thirty miles away. If they made it that far without a hitch, Singe had promised to telegraph Morgan Camp of their success and Mollie's arrival time. Afterward Singe would catch the next eastbound train back to Heflin.

Three other passengers bought tickets and took seats in the depot. Mollie was glad that others had entered the station so she and Singe blended in with the crowd, but then another man came inside. Wearing a bowler atop his head and eyeglasses that gave his eyes a beady look, the man kept fidgeting, making Mollie more nervous, as his suspicious gaze fell on her.

"Let's move outside," Mollie suggested to Singe.

"More folks might see us there," he replied.

"Maybe so, but the fellow in the bowler keeps staring at me."

Singe helped Mollie to her feet, and they strolled out onto the platform.

"Jim told me that Pa had people watching the railroad depot for Morgan or me. I fear this man is spying for Pa."

Singe accompanied Mollie to the end of the planked platform as the suspicious fellow stepped out the station door and looked their way.

"See, Singe, he followed us."

With that, Singe slipped his hand in his pants pocket and pulled out a small revolver, which he lowered to his thigh. He marched over to the stranger and began asking questions. Though Mollie could not hear what they said, Singe remained calm while the other man wrung his hands. Singe put the pistol back in his trousers and returned to Mollie smiling with each step.

"It's a reporter for the Heflin paper and he's out early looking for a story. He says you intrigued him and wanted to know what you were doing."

"What did you tell him, Singe?"

"I told him you were eloping. I also let him know I couldn't stop him from writing a story, but if he mentioned you by name, I'd come looking for him with my pistol again. He wants to talk to you."

"I suppose I could, as long as nothing appears in the paper for the next two days."

Singe motioned the reporter over and explained the conditions of the interview. After agreeing to the terms, the fellow visited with Mollie about her elopement, her betrothed, and Texas until the whistle of the approaching locomotive signaled the nearness of the train that would carry Mollie to the Lone Star State.

The interviewer wished both Mollie and Singe well as they climbed the steps into the passenger car. Travelers filled only half the coach so Mollie and Singe chose empty seats facing each other. As the train inched away from the station, Mollie smiled for the first time since dawn. She could not believe her dream might come true. After an uneventful ride to Anniston, Singe arose and congratulated Mollie on her escape and her upcoming wedding. She stood and threw her arms around him, giving him a long kiss on the cheek.

Singe grinned, "Save that for Morgan."

"It's from both of us."

"We'll miss you in these parts, Mollie."

"How can Morgan and I ever repay you?"

Singe laughed. "It's reward enough knowing I outsmarted your pa. He's always thought I was dumber than an empty barrel. Looks like his barrel isn't full either." He shook her hand, then departed as the conductor yelled a final time for passengers to board. As the locomotive finally pulled away from the Anniston depot, Mollie glimpsed Singe through the telegraph office window, dictating a message for the agent to send to Morgan.

Once the train picked up speed and put more distance between her and home, Mollie felt free, like she was truly herself for the first time in over two years. She occupied herself rereading Morgan's letters, brushing from her clothes and hair the ash and tiny cinders that had blown in through the open windows, and watching the landscape as she crossed from Alabama to Mississippi to Louisiana and finally into east Texas where the terrain was much the same as in the previous states. On the trip of more than 900 miles, she changed trains four times, the final occasion in Fort Worth. After the Texas & Pacific train departed Fort Worth for the last 150 miles to Abilene, Mollie watched the countryside pass. It was unlike any she had ever seen. Long gone were the tall pines, the lush green grass, and the moist skies of home. Here the sky dominated the horizon, overwhelming the scattered trees and plants that paid homage to the vast heavens above. She wondered if she would ever adapt to the harsh land of West Texas.

Mollie prayed that Morgan Camp would be waiting for her on the station platform. As she neared Abilene, she pulled a small square of mirrored glass from her handbag and looked at herself, grimacing at the soot and specks of cinders smudging her face from the open windows. It would be better if he was late to the depot, she decided, so she could at least wash her cheeks and forehead and look more presentable, but when the train reached the depot, she spotted him standing proudly in work clothes, his arms folded across his chest. He was even more handsome than she remembered, tall and lean, a coal-black mustache beneath innocent blue eyes. Her heart fluttered. She stuck her hand out the window and signaled. Morgan recognized her, removed his hat, and waved it her way as he stepped to the edge of the platform to greet her.

Grabbing her handbag, she jumped up from her seat and ran down the aisle as the train stopped. Morgan awaited her at the steps. As she moved toward him, he reached up and grabbed her with his strong arms, taking her from the passenger car steps and kissing her, holding her, and looking into her green eyes.

"Two years I've waited for this, Mollie," he said. "Welcome to Texas and your new home."

"Oh, Morgan, I look such a mess after the train ride."

"You look beautiful, Mollie," he said as he released her. "I've got a Baptist minister waiting in the depot to marry us."

"Oh, no, Morgan. I need time to freshen up and get my wedding dress from my hope chest. I want to look my prettiest for you."

"You look wonderful as you are, and I didn't bring dress clothes, Mollie. Besides, we need to get home this evening because I have too many chores to attend."

This was not how Mollie imagined her wedding day and her dream. For a moment, she questioned if she had made the correct decision. Maybe her mother had been right—that women had to let go of their dreams. But Morgan offered her his arm. His gesture overcame her doubts, and she strode with him to the freight car as the railway agents unloaded the baggage.

Mollie spotted her hope chest. "There it is," she told her betrothed, pointing to the trunk that appeared to have managed the trip well.

Morgan waved a porter over and gave him a dollar. "See that chest?" The fellow nodded. Morgan pointed to a tarp-covered freight wagon on the street at the end of the depot. "Put it in that rig."

"It's heavy," Mollie added, puzzled that she would be riding a freight wagon, rather than a buggy, to her new place.

Morgan took Mollie's arm and led her into the depot and introduced her to the minister who would marry them. He greeted Mollie, then asked a pair of arriving passengers to serve as witnesses. It was happening so fast that Mollie could not believe she was saying "I do" just moments after she had arrived in Abilene. Morgan placed a ring on Mollie's finger, but Mollie blushed because she had no ring to offer her new husband. She never thought she would wed right off the train.

"I now pronounce you man and wife," the minister intoned, and it was over, nothing like she had dreamed.

Mollie took her first breath as Mrs. Morgan Camp.

The reverend told them he would file the marriage certificate with the Taylor County clerk's office the next day. "It's official with God," he said, "but paperwork will make it official with the State of Texas. I wish you both all the happiness in the world."

Morgan leaned over and kissed Mollie. "Welcome to Texas, Mrs. Camp. Now, I want to take you to our place. It's two sections a dozen miles north of town along the Clear Fork of the Brazos."

Mollie anticipated with joy riding beside Morgan on the way to her new home. He helped her get seated on the wagon bench and climbed in beside her. As he took the reins, she slid her arm inside his and leaned on his shoulder. He shook the lines. As the wagon lurched ahead, she nestled closer to her husband.

"Don't get too comfortable, Mollie, because I've got to stop by the livery stable and get another wagon," Morgan informed her. "I'll need you to drive it home behind me."

Mollie sat up and pulled her arm from Morgan's. None of this was happening like she had imagined for her wedding day. She would guide a freight wagon to her unseen home on the night of her honeymoon! Her mother had been right.

At the livery stable, Morgan helped her climb out of the wagon and pointed to another covered with a tarp. "That'll be your ride."

Mollie sighed.

"I know it's not what you expected, Mollie, but let me show you something." He pulled a piece of paper from his shirt pocket and unfolded it. "I tore this from the Montgomery Ward Catalog."

Morgan offered his new bride the page from the mail-order directory. The sheet, labeled "Modern Home No. 52," showed the designs for a two-story stone home. Confused, Mollie looked at the floor plans with a front room, dining room, kitchen, and bedroom downstairs and four bedrooms upstairs. "Is this my home?"

"No," Morgan replied, slapping the side of the nearest wagon. "This is your home, inside the wagons."

Perplexed, Mollie shook her head.

"I bought the No. 52 kit. These wagons'll carry the materials we need to get started on your rock house. Stone was too expensive, but I've got the forms to make concrete blocks that will work even better as they'll be uniform in size and shape."

Mollie stared at the plans, then at her husband. "Morgan, you bought this for me?"

He nodded. "I promised you a stone house, and I'll build it for you. It may take a year, but I hope to complete it by our first anniversary when you can wear your wedding dress for our house warming. We'll have to live in a shack for a spell, but when I'm done, you'll have the best house in the community."

Mollie didn't know what to say. She folded up the catalog page and slipped it in her handbag, then flung her arms around her husband, hugging him. "Let's head home," she managed.

Morgan helped her atop the wagon seat, assisted her with the reins, and released the brake. "You follow me to our place." He bounded to his rig, jumped aboard, took his seat, and rattled the lines, beginning their first journey together as man and wife.

Mollie directed her wagon behind Morgan's and started for the meager home she had yet to see with the materials for the dream home that was yet to be. She smiled, knowing for once that her mother had been wrong. Mollie would not have to sacrifice her dreams after all.

Preston Lewis is the recipient of two Spur Awards and a Will Rogers Medallion Award for written western humor. He is a past president of Western Writers of America and the West Texas

Historical Association, which has awarded him three Elmer Kelton Awards for best creative work on West Texas. The most recent of his thirty novels are *Bluster's Last Stand,* the fourth book in *The Memoirs of H.H. Lomax* series of comic westerns, and *The Fleecing of Fort Griffin,* a western caper. Lewis and his wife, Harriet, reside in San Angelo, Texas.

ABOUT THE EDITOR

Hazel Rumney has lived most of her life in Maine, although she also spent a number of years in Spain and California while her husband was in the military. She has worked in the publishing business for almost thirty years. Retiring in 2011, she and her husband traveled throughout the United States visiting many famous and not-so-famous western sites before returning to Thorndike, Maine, where they now live. In 2012, Hazel reentered the publishing world as an editor for Five Star Publishing, a part of Cengage Learning. During her tenure with Five Star, she has developed and delivered titles that have won Western Fictioneers Peacemaker Awards, Will Rogers Medallion Awards, and Western Writers of America Spur Awards, including the double Spur Award-winning novel *Wild Ran the Rivers* by James D. Crownover. She is also the editor for the highly acclaimed Five Star Western anthologies of original stories including *The Trading Post* (2018), and *Hobnail* (2019). Western fiction is Hazel's favorite genre to enjoy. She has been reading the genre for more than five decades.

The employees of Five Star Publishing hope you have enjoyed this book.

Our Five Star novels explore little-known chapters from America's history, stories told from unique perspectives that will entertain a broad range of readers.

Other Five Star books are available at your local library, bookstore, all major book distributors, and directly from Five Star/Gale.

Connect with Five Star Publishing

Visit us on Facebook:
   https://www.facebook.com/FiveStarCengage

Email:
   FiveStar@cengage.com

For information about titles and placing orders:
   (800) 223-1244
   gale.orders@cengage.com

To share your comments, write to us:
   Five Star Publishing
   Attn: Publisher
   10 Water St., Suite 310
   Waterville, ME 04901